Received On:

DEC 13 2017

Ballard Branch

The House
by the River

D0047270

NO LONGER PROPERTY OF
SEATTLE PUBLIC LIBRARY

The House by the River

LENA MANTA

TRANSLATED BY GAIL HOLST-WARHAFT

This is a work of fiction. Names, characters, organizations, places, events, and incidents are either products of the author's imagination or are used fictitiously. Any resemblance to actual persons, living or dead, or actual events is purely coincidental.

Text copyright © 2007 Lena Manta
Translation copyright © 2017 Gail Holst-Warhaft
All rights reserved.

No part of this book may be reproduced, or stored in a retrieval system, or transmitted in any form or by any means, electronic, mechanical, photocopying, recording, or otherwise, without express written permission of the publisher.

Previously published as Το σπίτι δίπλα στο ποτάμι by Psichogios Publications in Greece in 2007. Translated from Greek by Gail Holst-Warhaft. First published in English by AmazonCrossing in 2017.

Published by AmazonCrossing, Seattle

www.apub.com

Amazon, the Amazon logo, and AmazonCrossing are trademarks of Amazon.com, Inc., or its affiliates.

ISBN-13: 9781542045896
ISBN-10: 1542045894

Cover design by Shasti O'Leary Soudant

Printed in the United States of America

The House by the River

INTRODUCTION

Silence. After the lightning lit up the landscape, nature waited for the thunder to shake it, to make its wildness felt. The thunder lagged, and the silence grew menacing. The moon remained hidden behind clouds. In the darkness, they had lost their fluffiness and looked like heavy, leaden curtains. The thunder finally clapped, straight from Mount Olympus, which ruled threateningly over the plain as if Zeus himself had sent it, just as he had once done.

The house by the river shook lightly. The big chestnut trees framing it seemed to be trying to protect the house from a mysterious danger. Their branches caressed the roof gently, almost embracing it. The large garden with its beds full of vegetables spread out numbly, hoping that after such tension, it would finally start to rain. The rain still hadn't come. The river was the only thing that had nothing to fear. It flowed lazily along, knowing that soon it would welcome not only the water the winter rains brought, but also the snow. Then it would come alive again and grow fierce, and it would travel eagerly to meet the sea and lose itself in its vastness. It had done this for centuries now. It knew its fate and wasn't anxious about the future.

A misty light from a kerosene lamp trembled at one of the windows. The man on the bed was bathed in sweat. He accepted the doctor's ministrations, while beside his pillow stood his wife, lamp in hand, her face buried in her handkerchief. The whole room stank of unbearable rot. The doctor lowered a handkerchief from his own face.

"Open the window, Kyria Theodora," he whispered. "We'll die in here!"

The woman hurried to obey his order. She set the lamp on the bedside table, ran to the window, and flung it open. Cool air rushed into the room and she breathed it greedily. She peered outside, but it was completely dark. A flash of lightning lit up the landscape, and then everything plunged into darkness again. She knew every hill from where she stood, every stone, every tree. Although she knew that the thunder would come, when the ground shook, she was shocked and took a step back, as if her own body had been struck. She returned to her place beside her husband and the doctor. Despite the atmosphere inside, she had been revived by the night air; the smell of the nearly rotten leg seemed to cling to the furniture, even to the walls.

"Gerasimos, I have to cut it off," said the doctor in a harsh tone, looking at the bedridden man. "And tonight! I have everything I need."

"No!" groaned the man.

"But it's madness what you're doing. You'll die, do you understand? The infection has progressed rapidly; soon, it'll be too late. As a doctor, I can't let you delay any further."

The sick man reached up and grasped the other man by the lapel. For a man wasted with fever and illness, the strength of his grip seemed unnatural.

"You have no rights over me," he announced with effort. "I won't live as a cripple."

"You prefer to die?"

"A thousand times!"

"And what about your children? Have you thought about them? About your wife? They need you, Gerasimos. And you . . . although you could be saved and offer them something, you prefer to die?"

Gerasimos let go of the doctor's lapel and fell back exhausted on his pillow. Believing that he'd come to his senses, the doctor bent over him.

"You're a reasonable man, Gerasimos. We'll give you a wooden leg; you won't stay a cripple. You'll live a normal life beside your wife and children," he explained calmly.

"What sort of life is that, as half a man?"

"Gerasimos, you don't become half a man because you lose a leg. Let me go and get my instruments and we'll get that leg taken care of right away."

"I told you no!"

The doctor stood up, shaking his head helplessly, and turned to the woman.

"Speak to him, Kyria Theodora. Or he'll die!"

"I know. But in all the years you've known us, have you ever seen my husband change his mind? Have you ever seen him take notice of any opinion except his own?"

The woman bent her head submissively, and the doctor turned back to his patient.

"Gerasimos, you must understand. It's a matter of days. If I don't cut it off tonight, you won't live, do you hear me? I've been telling you for so long, I've begged you for so long, but tonight you have to make a decision! After this, there's no going back!"

"There was no going back from the time I stepped on that cursed nail and paid no attention to it. Go, Doctor! There's nothing more for you to do here. I won't change my mind! The leg will stay where it is and I'll reach the next world with all my limbs in place. I won't live as a half person."

"Come to your senses, Gerasimos! How important is a rotten leg? Your soul . . ."

"My soul will be crippled if I lose this leg. Leave!"

The doctor turned to Theodora, who signaled to him not to insist anymore, and he understood it was pointless. He fixed his gaze on Gerasimos, who looked at him, eyes burning with fever, full of stubbornness.

"I've never known anyone like you, Gerasimos."

"That means you'll remember me all your life. I'll see you in the afterlife, Doctor! And if your travels bring you this way, come by and see how my wife and children are doing."

Gerasimos died a week later, leaving his wife behind alone and unprotected with five daughters to raise. He had just turned forty-six.

THE FIRST YEARS

Gerasimos met Theodora one summer in Pieria when she was just twelve years old and he was twenty-seven. Like all the girls her age in that era, Theodora picked cotton. Her family was poor and they needed every extra bit of income she could bring home to their small cottage with its seven mouths to feed.

Gerasimos came from a good family. When he was born, no one would have imagined that he would be an only child, but his mother died giving birth to him and his father never remarried.

Fortunately for the baby, an aunt was found to raise him, because his father, a hard man by nature, became even more severe after his wife died. The boy grew up quickly and became the handsomest, tallest fellow in the neighborhood. Many a young girl's heart beat for him, but all he did was break their hearts. By the age of twenty-five his reputation with women had grown so terrible that mothers ushered their daughters indoors when he passed by. The stories of his reckless, womanizing nature were legendary. One girl in a neighboring village was even rumored to have thrown herself off a cliff because of him.

Tall, fair skinned, with broad shoulders and a body as straight as a cypress and eyes as green as the leaves on the trees, he could take his pick of whatever women caught his eye. He had grown used to hearing long, drawn-out sighs as he passed by, sighs that spoke of unfulfilled yearning, but he hadn't yet chosen the one who would be the mistress of his life. So for as long as he remained single, the hopes of the girls rose, while the mothers' hearts beat faster in case this "Satan" took a fancy to one of them.

When she first met him, Theodora was an unattractive girl with two tight braids that hung on either side of her head. He made no impression on her. Gerasimos, on the other hand, seemed magnetized by the child's glance and was surprised at himself when he found he couldn't get her out of his head. He saw her a month later at a village festival with her brothers and her parents. This time her braids weren't hanging down but wound in a crown around her head. Again his gaze was fixed on her.

His friend Lefteris noticed and dug an elbow into his ribs. "Are you OK? Are we so short of girls that you've turned your attention to the youngsters?" he teased.

Embarrassed, Gerasimos turned his head in another direction while out of the corner of his eye he continued to watch Theodora, who was absentmindedly staring at the people dancing. This girl had something that made her stand out. She held her head proudly, and her eyes had a dignity and seriousness that didn't match her age. Gerasimos had made cautious inquiries about her family. They weren't from these parts, but had come to the mainland from Syros three years earlier, hungry and in rags, to try to find a better life. The youngest of the children had been born a few months earlier, but everyone said that he was sickly and wouldn't survive.

Theodora's baby brother confirmed the rumors. He died just a month after the festival and for the first time, Gerasimos set foot in a funeral service. His elderly aunt wondered why her nephew had wanted to come with her, but she didn't say anything. Gerasimos was moved by the sight of the young, black-clad Theodora, her lips pressed tight to stop herself from crying as she accompanied her brother with dignity to his last resting place. That night, Gerasimos didn't sleep at all. Theodora's image tormented him, and at the same time he wondered what was wrong with him. What devil had cursed him with this obsession with this little kid?

The next day he left for Katerini. He needed to escape. He drank, he partied, he stayed out all night, but the tiny figure in black continued to dominate his thoughts. He returned to the village to face another tragedy. This time, the girl's family would bury two children together. Theodora's two brothers had been playing and hadn't noticed how far from home they'd gone. By the time they were ready to come back, night had fallen. They fell into a ravine and were found the next morning following an all-night search by the men of the village. No one was unmoved by the great tragedy that had hit the bereaved family.

Gerasimos went to this funeral too. For the first time in his life, he felt his eyes well up with tears. Theodora walked beside her parents as if hypnotized and hugged the only sister she had left. Her eyes cried out a great *why?* but nobody appeared to pay her any special attention. Only Gerasimos—only he dared to approach her after the funeral. He stood beside her without speaking, not knowing what to say. Theodora raised her head and looked at him.

"Are you all right?" he asked her in an unsteady voice.

"No," she answered simply.

"How can I help you?"

"Nobody can. Only God could, but He didn't want to." She looked at him again and half closed her eyes. "I remember you. You have a big, beautiful horse."

"Yes," answered Gerasimos and smiled. "Have you ever ridden a horse?"

"No."

"Do you want to ride mine?"

Without saying anything, she took his hand. Gerasimos felt a lump in his throat. At that moment he knew that the little girl in black was his destiny.

◆ ◆ ◆

It impressed everyone that Gerasimos and little Theodora had become inseparable, but no one was suspicious. Because of the difference in their ages, everyone naturally assumed that his preoccupation with the young girl sprung from sympathy for her losses. After all, he had persuaded his father to take her father on permanently in his work. But Theodora didn't remain a child. She grew up rapidly, and at fifteen, she was tall and beautiful, with blond hair and black eyes. That's when the villagers began to gossip, and Julia decided to speak to her daughter.

She found her sitting in the backyard, gazing at the moon.

"You can't have what you're looking at!" she told her ambiguously.

But Theodora understood immediately where her mother was going.

"Maybe not the moon, but Gerasimos isn't the moon," she answered calmly.

"You're right. He's not the moon, he's even worse. He's the sun and he'll burn you!"

"If I'm going to be burned, I'd rather it be by the glorious sun rather than simple fire, Mother."

"So, tell me how you completely lost your mind, my girl. Do you even know what you're saying?"

"I love him, Mother."

Julia looked carefully at her daughter. "Has he laid a hand on you? I want to know."

"Never. He hasn't even kissed me. He's waiting till I'm grown up."

"I'm afraid you don't know what's happening to you, daughter. I'm afraid this story won't end well."

◆ ◆ ◆

Three years passed and nothing changed except Gerasimos's love for Theodora, which only grew stronger. Every day she left her house to meet him in some deserted place. They had decided not to give the villagers an excuse to talk, so they made their public meetings less frequent. This calmed everyone down, and many people said that Gerasimos had finally tired of his game with the young girl and gone back to his old habits. Certainly, he often left for Katerini, and they all imagined there was some woman business going on.

The day Theodora turned eighteen, Gerasimos was away from the village. Two days later, though, he came back and they met secretly near the river that ran beside his house. The time had come. Their plan was simple: They'd meet at the little chapel beyond the village. There, the priest, who Gerasimos had spoken to, would be waiting for them. Gerasimos's friend Lefteris, who had a dual role to play in the wedding ceremony, would be there too. In keeping with tradition, he would exchange the crowns the couple would wear on their heads—placing Gerasimos's crown on Theodora's head, and vice versa—and he'd explain to their parents what had happened. Right after the ceremony, the couple would leave until the situation calmed down.

At first Lefteris nearly went crazy when he heard what his friend had to say. "What's that you're saying? Are you mad? The girl's too young."

"No she's not. She's a woman of eighteen."

"Yes, but you're thirty-three already. The whole village will be on your tail!"

"It doesn't bother me. I've loved Theodora since she was a kid."

"You're not making sense! Seriously, do you understand what you're about to do?"

"How can you ask me that? You, who were the first to understand what was happening to me?"

"Damned if I understood you. I thought it was something innocent!"

"Are you going to preach to me forever before you do what I asked you?"

"Gerasimos, wait and think about it a little longer! It's crazy what you're planning to do. Stones and curses will follow you."

"Why, Lefteris? Is it a crime I'm committing? I'm marrying the girl I love, just like hundreds of others have done before me. And in the end none of it bothers me. Let them say what they like."

Lefteris didn't manage to stop him. In any case, he didn't have any other arguments.

News of the wedding fell like fire from heaven on the village and like a lightning bolt on their families. Julia fell down in a dead faint, and Theodora's father hit his head against the wall until he cut it open and they had to call the doctor to bind it up. Gerasimos's father was furious and, for better or for worse, he fired Theodora's father on the spot. He even reached the point of saying he would disinherit his son. It was then that his sister, Gerasimos's aunt Tasso, quietly stepped in. Only Gerasimos would know of her interference, but even if anyone else ever heard about it, they wouldn't have believed it.

This quiet woman had sacrificed her whole life to help raise her nephew and had never let anyone harm him, including his father. That evening, she waited until her brother was asleep and tiptoed into his room with their father's knife in her hand. She rested the blade on her brother's neck, so that when he startled up, it lightly grazed his throat.

"Who is it?" he shouted, terrified. A second later he recognized his sister and looked at her in amazement.

"Tasso, what are you doing here in the middle of the night?" he asked, and tried to sit up fully, but she pressed the knife harder against his throat and he kept still.

"Don't move or you'll be in trouble!" she hissed wildly.

"But—have you gone crazy? Do you want to kill me in cold blood?"

"A father who never cared about his son except to disinherit him because he married a girl he loves doesn't deserve to live!"

"He's my business. Why are you interfering?"

"Me? How could I not? Who was it who raised Gerasimos and turned him into a fine young man? Who cried and who feels the most for him, if

10

not me? I won't let you harm him. Swear a solemn oath this instant that you won't disinherit him. Otherwise I'll slaughter you like a goat and he'll inherit from you tomorrow. Speak!"

She knew she'd won before she heard her brother's reply, and she left his room as calmly as she had entered it.

◆ ◆ ◆

Far from all this, the two lovers were now free to enjoy a love that had been bottled up for so many years. They didn't have time to concern themselves with the trouble they had left behind. Greedily they breathed each other in and dove into the sanctuary of the body and soul. A love stronger than all their past Platonic dreams had been awakened. Their happiness was boundless, their desire unquenchable, and their bodies tireless. They returned to the village three months later with their first child in Theodora's belly. They had won and they knew it. Everyone opened their arms to them, and if Gerasimos's father's were really only half-open, it wasn't important. The knife was always tucked in Tasso's belt and her brother knew it. The two young people could begin their life.

Their first child was a girl. She was born on a hot May day, and she was as beautiful as the spring that brought her into the world and the love that engendered her. Even though Theodora had an easy birth, Gerasimos was very anxious throughout it, as he couldn't forget that his own birth had cost his mother her life. When his wife's pains came, he began acting so crazily that his aunt turned him out of the room. The midwife, who'd been sent for very quickly, knew her work well, and the woman in labor was by far the calmest person of all. Her mother, who was also there, told her later that she had never seen a person or an animal give birth like that.

"All women let out a cry or two!" she told her, as Theodora held her daughter in her arms. "But you didn't even let out a groan!"

The only one who didn't involve himself with the arrival of this new life was Gerasimos's father, who came home that evening and didn't even ask about his daughter-in-law. Aunt Tasso gave him his dinner with tight lips. Only when she threw him the bread instead of putting it down beside him did he raise his eyes.

"Do you take me for a dog, throwing me a dry piece of bread?" he asked her angrily.

"You're worse! A dog would be concerned about something other than himself," she replied.

"What's your problem with me this time?" he asked.

"Your daughter-in-law's pains started today."

"So? Did she give birth already?"

"No, she's waiting for you!" Aunt Tasso replied sarcastically.

"My late wife had contractions for two whole days!"

"And that's why she died straight after. Theodora had the baby earlier this afternoon."

"And how do you expect me to know?"

"You could have asked me!"

"OK then. I'm asking you now."

"Your daughter-in-law had a little girl. May your grandchild have a long life!"

"A girl?"

"Yes, does that bother you?"

"Girls get married and leave."

"Yes. And they turn into the daughters-in-law who look after their fathers-in-law as Theodora has looked after you. Ungrateful man! What's your problem, and why are you angry with the girl?"

"Why are you lecturing me?"

"Because as soon as you've eaten, you'll wash up and give your blessing to the new mother. A proper blessing, like she deserves, damn you! And furthermore . . ."

"OK. I'll do it. Leave me in peace now!"

When he went to see the newborn, he even managed to smile at his daughter-in-law under the watchful eye of Tasso. He only seemed bothered when his son told him that the baby would be named after her grandmother, Melissanthi.

Little Melissanthi filled the house by the river with life. From the beginning, she was drawn to the water that snaked its way past the hedge. Her mother often took her on walks to the riverbank and the little girl watched with intense interest. But when she got older, she never went into the water unless someone else was with her. As much as she loved it, she also seemed afraid of it.

Two years later Theodora brought their second child into the world. It too was a daughter, but very small, and at first Theodora was afraid. She remembered her infant brother who had died: he had also been very small. However, it soon became apparent to her that her daughter might be tiny, but she was sturdy, strong, and lively. Perhaps more than they wished and more than they could bear. They baptized her Julia, giving her the name of her other grandmother, who was proud of the little one's liveliness, if not her irritability and her shouting, which no one could bear. These, combined with her muscular strength, enabled the little girl to boss everyone around, including her grandfather.

Gerasimos's father, whom everyone was scared of and no one crossed, was a plaything to Julia. As she grew up, she managed to do whatever she wanted with him. She practically gave him orders, and he actually obeyed them—which was something nobody could understand. She was only five when she decided that she wanted a dog, and what's more, it had to be black. She waited until her grandfather came home in the evening to ask him. Naturally, she couldn't know that the permanently grumpy old man couldn't stand dogs, ever since he had been a child and a dog bit him badly on the leg.

As soon as he'd eaten and seated himself beside the fire to smoke a cigarette, the child climbed determinedly up on his knees and settled herself down. Her grandfather looked at her irritably.

"Don't you have anywhere else to sit?" he asked sharply.

But Julia answered him without a trace of fear in her eyes. "I want to ask you something," she said. "I want you to bring me a black dog tomorrow!" Tasso, standing behind her, had trouble suppressing a laugh.

"What's that?" the old man shouted, then scowled. "I don't like dogs."

"But it'll be mine. I'll look after it. What does it matter to you?"

"It'll be a nuisance, always underfoot. And maybe it'll bite."

"Grandpa, are you afraid of dogs?"

The old man rolled his eyes and Theodora hastened to pull her daughter away, but Julia held on to her grandfather with all her strength.

"Leave me alone!" she shouted to her mother. "I'm not getting down until Grandpa promises to bring me a dog."

Theodora gave up and turned toward Gerasimos, who was smiling. "Why are you just sitting there?" she scolded. "Why aren't you trying to put some sense in your daughter's head?"

"My daughter has a lot of sense," he replied.

"But she's stubborn," his wife answered.

"And everyone knows where she got that from," added Gerasimos as he looked pointedly at his father. "That's right, isn't it, Father? Isn't pigheadedness inherited?"

The old man looked at his son and then turned to his grandchild. "Why do you ask me and not your father?" he said to her curtly.

"Because you're my grandpa. Diamando's grandfather is going to buy her a horse! She told me so today. Why can't you buy something for me too? I want to tell Diamando, 'My grandfather bought me a dog!'"

A silence followed the little girl's words.

"I'll bring you the dog tomorrow," the old man answered after a few moments, and Theodora was stunned. "But if it gets near me or if it bites me, I'll kill it on the spot!" he declared angrily.

Having gotten her way, Julia just smiled broadly, then wrapped her arms around her grandfather's neck and gave him a loud kiss. Silence fell upon the room once again, and the old man looked at his granddaughter with a severe expression that masked the surprise her impulsive gesture evoked in him.

"Now that you've got what you wanted, will you finally get off me so I can roll this cigarette?" he asked Julia, who smiled at him again and calmly got down from his lap.

The dog was indeed all black, and it came the next day in a box. It was a small puppy, and as soon as she saw it, Julia cried out with joy.

"Thank you!" she shouted. "You're the most wonderful grandfather in the world," she added, then took the dog in her arms, and, still jumping up and down with excitement, went to look for a place to put him.

"Eh, you hear that?" Tasso said to her brother. "It looks as if you've found your boss, brother, and that was something God was saving for you."

The third child born to Gerasimos and Theodora was yet another girl, and they called her Aspasia. Theodora felt bad that she hadn't managed to give her husband a son, but it didn't seem to bother him. When she produced a fourth girl and revealed her sadness, Gerasimos scolded her.

"Have you gone crazy, woman? What difference does it make that we don't have a son? We have four children and they're all healthy and very beautiful."

"Yes, I'm grateful for all that, but a father needs a son. And what's more, daughters need dowries to get married. Don't look at me like that—our situation was different."

"So? I'm sure we've got something or other to give our daughters. And besides, they're all so beautiful that when we give them away, their intended husbands will certainly give me something extra." He enjoyed this joke and told it often. He was proud of his girls, each one more beautiful than the one before her.

After their fourth daughter, Polyxeni, was born, a fifth one, Magdalini, followed. This last birth was difficult for Theodora and the doctor advised her not to have another child. But Theodora just looked at him and said,

"Until I have a son, I won't quit having babies, Doctor, so don't waste your breath any further."

When Gerasimos announced Magdalini's birth, his father became quite annoyed and burst out, "This wife of yours certainly knows how to arrange things, doesn't she?"

Gerasimos frowned. "What's that you're saying now?" he asked, matching his father's angry tone.

"She has saddled us with a bunch of females, and we haven't seen a son yet!"

"So?"

"Girls marry out. They marry and leave! Who's going to work the fields?"

"I want children, not servants to work for me."

"And our name? Who'll keep that going?"

"Stop worrying about our family name and think about more important things! God decides what He'll send us, and it seems He likes sending us girls. So let's be thankful they are healthy—and that we are too and can enjoy them! There are worse things that could happen, Father. My mother had a boy, but died before she could even know me. She never got to enjoy watching me grow up! And what about you? You had a son—but did you enjoy me? Were you ever proud of me? Leave me be, Father."

But his father didn't calm down—and neither did Theodora. A few months after Magdalini's birth, she announced to her husband that she was expecting again. Gerasimos was only worried by the news and cursed himself for not taking precautions. A sense of foreboding nagged at him throughout the pregnancy. When Theodora's pains began, weeks before her due date, he was overwhelmed with fear. With great difficulty, his aunt managed to persuade him to take the children for a walk by the river while Theodora labored. As it turned out, the child was a boy. But as soon as Theodora saw him, the image of her dead brother came before her eyes and they filled with tears. She knew her son would not live. The doctor diagnosed a serious problem with his heart. Nothing could be done. The baby was condemned. Two weeks after his birth, he died in his sleep, leaving Theodora inconsolable and Gerasimos struggling to bring her back to herself. Even his father didn't dare say anything.

◆ ◆ ◆

A few months later, life in the house by the river found its rhythm again, but Gerasimos made it clear to his wife that they wouldn't have any more children. However much she remonstrated, he was adamant.

Thanks to their mother, who had spoken very calmly to reassure them, the girls had recovered from the death of their brother.

"Death isn't as bad as we human beings think it is," she'd explained. "Whoever dies, especially a baby, goes directly to God and becomes an angel with pure white wings. There, beside the Almighty, the baby is happy and laughs all the time. So it's a sin for us to cry for our little boy who is happy."

The girls looked at their mother's eyes and her peaceful gaze calmed them down. Since she wasn't crying, that's how it must be. Little did they know that Theodora held on to all her tears until she was alone.

When the youngest daughter, Magdalini, turned one, her grandfather became seriously ill and took to his bed for the first time in his life. The doctor said that his lungs had been attacked by a disease, and they shouldn't expect him to recover. The old man wouldn't allow anyone to care for him except his daughter-in-law. Only she was allowed to sit up all night at his bedside. When he asked her to send for a priest to hear his confession, she began to cry. As soon as the priest left, the old man asked to speak with her alone. She approached the bed and sat beside him.

"You asked for me, Father?" Theodora asked him calmly.

"Yes," he answered, breathing with difficulty. "There's not much time, and I don't want to leave with this burden inside me."

"You shouldn't tire yourself," she said, trying to stop him.

But the old man made a gesture with his hand. "I'll have plenty of time to rest where I'm going. But I haven't much time left here. So be quiet and listen to me. I owe you an apology."

"But Father . . ."

"Be quiet, daughter-in-law!" he ordered her. "I know my sins. When I found out about you and my son, I wasn't pleased. I behaved badly and I turned your father out of his job. When you came back as a bride, I didn't welcome you as I should have, and if my sister hadn't stopped me, I would have turned my son out too. I was stupid and cowardly."

"Cowardly? You?"

"Yes. Because when I saw I'd made a mistake, and that you loved Gerasimos with all your heart—and not for his fortune—I never said I was sorry. I'm saying it now, though. I lost my wife very young— maybe that was the reason I was so wrongheaded and stubborn. Don't be fooled because we don't admit it, but we men are stupid and unbending. Without a woman beside us to show us what's right—"

At that moment, a fit of coughing interrupted him, and Theodora took his hand. "Enough, Father," she said. "You don't need to say any more. I've never held anything against you. Every parent imagines their child's wedding, and we deprived you of that."

"That's my own fault too. Now that I'm leaving this earth to join my Melissanthi in heaven, I hope she won't fly at me for the way I behaved to our only son—she was quite a shouter."

Theodora smiled, as did the old man.

"You women shout a lot," he observed. "And you complain."

"Can you keep a secret?" his daughter-in-law asked, smiling slyly. "They're our weapons against your pigheadedness."

Both of them were quiet now, and the old man squeezed her hand.

"You're a good girl," Theodora's father-in-law finally said, breaking the silence. "Decent and strong. You'll need that strength. My son is like all of them. Stubborn and egotistical."

"And I'm stubborn too, Father . . . and a complainer!"

"I know. And that's the only way you'll manage with him. I know I'm doing this very late, but at this moment, I give you my blessing. May you live long, my daughter . . . and always be strong with your husband and children!"

Theodora bent her head and kissed his hand. The old man stroked her hair.

"Call Gerasimos for me now," he said. "I need to speak to my son before I leave."

The funeral took place two days later, with the whole village following the sad procession. They buried him beside his wife, and Theodora prayed with all her heart that he was finally reunited with his Melissanthi.

Gerasimos accepted the death of his father calmly. "I lost something I never had," he told Theodora that same night when they were lying exhausted on their bed. "My father was always a dark figure beside the fireplace. A strange man. Often I asked myself whether it was because of my mother—if she loved him, or if she quarreled with him . . ."

"Before he died, your father told me she shouted a lot." Theodora smiled at the memory, and Gerasimos looked at her.

"You got on well with each other before he died, didn't you?"

"Yes. He wanted me to forgive him. What a shame! If that had happened years earlier, we would have been better off. Everyone in the house would have been happier. Do you know something, Gerasimos? There's nothing stupider than holding words inside you that should have been spoken at the time. Except hiding feelings that should have been expressed as soon as you felt them."

"My wise wife," Gerasimos teased her.

"Don't make fun of me!" Theodora said, glaring at him. "When someone dies, what can you say to them then? Who will you say it to? To his grave? Take my sister Anna and me, for example."

"Why are you remembering her now?"

"Every day I think of her and I curse myself for not learning to read and write so I could send her a letter in America. I wonder if I'll ever see her again."

"Don't be upset—what's the ungrateful girl ever done for you? As soon as he asked for her . . . what's the husband's name?"

"Peter. Anna was very fortunate to marry him. They say people live differently in America. Maybe she has a better life because of him."

"Yes, but she left without knowing the place or the people or even the language. It couldn't have been easy for her. Doesn't your mother keep in touch with her?"

"Anna wrote to Mother once or twice, and Mother went to the schoolteacher to have him read it to her. He wrote an answer for her too."

"I could write to her for you if you like."

"I know you could, but I can't really speak to her that way. She wouldn't open her heart to me, because she'd know someone else would read the letter and learn her secrets. And I don't even know who writes her letters. Anna didn't go to school either. Is that really how a civilized society is made? Only men get to know how to read and write? Why don't all people learn to read and write? You know it's different in the cities. It's only in the villages that we girls don't learn. But that's not right! Gerasimos, I want our girls to go to school."

"Why are you thinking of that now?"

"I shouldn't have kept Melissanthi and Julia at home," she answered as she sat up in bed. "I was wrong to listen to you. I want you to go and enroll them in the school."

Gerasimos sat up and looked at his wife in surprise. "What's got into you tonight, woman? And how am I going to enroll them now in school? Melissanthi is nine already, and Julia's seven."

"It doesn't matter, let them be older. It's better than being stunted all their lives."

"But there aren't any other girls at the school."

"All the better! Maybe the others will follow our example and send their girls to learn how to read and write. The world's changing, Gerasimos. What our parents did is one thing, and what we do is another. You've never done what other people do. Why start now?"

"But what will the village say?"

"Since when have you cared about what the village says? Aren't you the least bit ashamed to act concerned about their opinion now? I never expected that of you."

"We really stirred up a mess in our heads tonight! We started with my father and look where we ended up. Anyway, school started two months ago. Leave it. We'll start them next year."

"They'll go this year. And you'll go tomorrow to talk to the teacher. Unless you'd rather I went instead."

"Have some sense, woman!"

"Am I crazy because I want my children to be educated? For them to become human beings?"

"And all the women who didn't go to school before now, what are they?"

"Stunted, like me. We can't even read a newspaper or write a letter! It's a wonderful thing to know how to do these things. But I know why you don't want us educated. You're afraid of us."

"I know I'll regret that I asked this, but what do we men have to be afraid of, woman, from you females?"

"That once we're educated we'll be equal to you, and that you can't bear. They told you wrong, husband, we're not stupid. We're more intelligent than you are, but you want to keep us down so that you'll look better!"

"Enough of this. Your head's just spinning in circles tonight. Where did you hear all this nonsense you're babbling about?"

"Why must I have heard it somewhere else? Can't these be my own thoughts? And if you don't do what I said, and do it tomorrow, you and I are going to have a problem."

"I say we talk about it tomorrow. I'm half-dead. Can't you see that and have some pity for me?"

"You don't need my pity."

"For God's sake, woman, I buried my father today. Let me recover and we'll see."

"There's no need for us to see anything, and don't put on that air of the bereaved son with me, because I know you. Nor does your father's death have anything to do with what we've been discussing."

"Are we going to talk about this much longer? My eyes are closing."

"Until you promise me you'll go to see the teacher tomorrow, there'll be no sleep for you or me tonight."

"How did I get myself into this trouble?"

"Promise me what I asked and the trouble will disappear this very moment. It's in your hands."

"OK, fine."

"You promise?"

"I swear to you! Can I go to sleep now?"

"Sleep, my dear! Who's stopping you?"

Gerasimos threw her an angry glance, but Theodora just smiled innocently at him. She kissed him on his forehead and lay back down. Gerasimos went to say something but immediately stopped himself. He too lay down, blowing out the lamp.

◆ ◆ ◆

The next day Gerasimos went to see the schoolteacher. As soon as it was discovered that their daughters were going to school, a lot of the villagers came to the house to find out how it had happened. Theodora credited her husband, "who was always ahead of his time with new ideas." Aunt Tasso smiled. She'd never married—but she understood men. "They never change their minds!" she'd always said. "But they're easily turned around by any woman who has a mind of her own."

In the end it turned out that Theodora was right: a lot of the village women followed Gerasimos and Theodora's example and sent their daughters to school. When Aspasia turned six, she followed Melissanthi and Julia, but from the beginning it appeared that, unlike her older sisters who were excellent students, she had no aptitude for learning. But she had other talents. Aspasia loved to sing and her clear voice could often be heard in the house. At school they always chose her to sing some suitable song for the festivals.

◆　◆　◆

Black clouds thickened dangerously over Greece, and rumors of a coming war with the Italians were spreading the summer that the ship *Elli* was torpedoed. Gerasimos brought newspapers to the house, frowning more deeply every day. In front of their children, Theodora and her husband didn't speak about it. But as soon as they were alone in bed, she sat beside him and waited for him to tell her the news. Along with her children, Theodora had learned to read a little; she could make out the headlines in newspapers, but she found it tiring, trying to sound out, word by word, the articles about impending war, so she gave up. Instead, she relied on her husband to tell her what it said in the papers and all the news that the men heard on the radio in the local coffee house.

Aunt Tasso, on the other hand, sat silently in her chair, her eyes fixed on the fire. She was getting old now, but she could see well enough to knit. She could hear her nephew and his wife talking on the other side of the door to their room and tears trickled down her cheeks. She had lived through another war and she had prayed it would be the last, but as things appeared, it wouldn't be.

The mobilization for war, when it came, took all the young men away from their homes. So the reins they'd held passed to the hands of the women, who now had their own work to do as well as the men's. Like all the other women, Theodora said good-bye to her husband with tears in her eyes. Every time one of his letters reached her hands, she made Melissanthi read it aloud to everyone and then she took it with her to bed. In the lamplight, she read it syllable by syllable, again and again until she'd learned it by heart and then she slept with it under her pillow. In the morning Gerasimos's letter would be placed among the household icons so that the Virgin would keep him in her mind. Once a week she had Melissanthi, whose handwriting was beautiful, write him the family news and at the end, in the uneven letters she had learned to form, she wrote, "I love you. Be careful!" Then she kissed the letter and put it in an envelope.

She didn't dare tell him that since he'd left home, Aunt Tasso had died peacefully in her sleep and that they had found her the next morning with a smile on her face. It wasn't the sort of news to tell a man who was fighting on the front amidst the snow, cold, and hunger. Let him come home safely first; then there would be time to weep for the woman who had raised him with so much love and tenderness.

News of the Greek army's victories reached even the distant villages at the foot of Mount Olympus, and everyone celebrated. Theodora wondered to herself if any of those who were rejoicing ever thought about the cost of each one of those victories, what a toll of blood the country had paid. She wondered at everyone's optimism and kept her fears to herself. Hitler would never leave an ally to be destroyed. How long would it be, then, before he sent his own army in, and how long would the Greeks last when they were attacked by two enemies who outnumbered them and were better armed?

Although Gerasimos was careful about what he wrote to his family so as not to upset them, the news from the front didn't remain hidden. Young men fought with all their strength, but the hospitals filled with more and more wounded and hundreds of men whose limbs were lost to frostbite. Hunger cost more lives. Even if the Italians were an enemy they could face, Theodora doubted the same would be true of the Germans.

As it turned out, she was right. However much the spirit of the country remained eager to fight and win, the nation's body—its sons—lay mutilated and wounded in the hospitals. The occupation began, and everyone knew it wouldn't be easy. The successes of the occupiers were more or less known; other countries had already fallen and experienced firsthand this "civilized" German rule.

Gerasimos came home a shadow of himself, but at least he was still healthy. When the occupying German troops entered their village, everyone clenched their teeth and lowered their eyes. It wasn't only to hide their intense fury from the strutting victors, but because all the villagers, some more than others, were ashamed that they hadn't managed to cast the occupiers all into the sea. But they knew this wasn't the end, that the game would be lost or won in faraway Egypt. If they hadn't, perhaps they would have committed suicide en masse. But they knew. They found out, with some delay, that not everything was lost, however much the German propaganda tried to persuade them of the opposite.

The occupation showed its hard face at once, but as expected, the cities had the worst of it. The news from Athens was tragic. The losses were terrible, and starvation took its toll. Adults, but more often children, died in the streets, and to add to it, reports of the torture carried out by the Gestapo in their prisons made even the most composed Greeks turn pale. The Resistance may have been proud of whatever blows they inflicted on the occupier, but they were punished with mass executions of innocent people. History would have to expend a lot of ink writing about heroism, but in the end it didn't need to. Blood and gold came to take its place, in quantities appropriate to so much self-sacrifice, so much strength, so much pride.

A year had passed since the flag with the swastika on it was first raised above their village. Spring advanced and colored the fields bright green. In Gerasimos's house by the river, Theodora had hidden a few vegetables that would save the family from hunger. They planted vegetables in the garden as they'd always done, but it wasn't certain that they would be able to put them in their mouths. Like birds of prey, men of the occupying army passed through, collecting what they needed to sustain them, indifferent to the hunger of the occupied. "Looting raids" Gerasimos called them, and Theodora agreed, clenching her teeth each time. But she couldn't do anything except think up a thousand and one ways of securing some food for her children. She blessed her father-in-law, who had built a secret cellar, completely invisible to the unobservant eye. The house appeared to be built on a flat rock beside the river, but the old man, for some unknown reason, had used dynamite to open a big hole underneath the spot where the house would stand, capable of holding three people below the kitchen.

There, Theodora also hid a goat and two hens that she managed, with a thousand torments, to save one day when Germans arrived suddenly at the house. She was digging in the garden, with her two younger daughters playing nearby, when Julia came running, with Arapis the dog behind her, and warned her.

"Mama!" the child howled. "Germans are coming! I was playing with Arapis farther down there and I saw them."

"Oh dear! There go the goat and the chickens!"

At that moment she remembered the secret cellar. It was dangerous, but she didn't have any other choice. She took the animals down through the hole with Julia, telling her she could do whatever she thought was necessary to keep them from making any noise that would give them away. Then she snatched little Magdalini in her arms and went back to her garden and waited, while six-year-old Polyxeni clung to her dress.

Four men got down from the jeep and approached Theodora, who pretended to be watering the vegetables. She looked at them with confidence.

"What do you want?" she asked abruptly, and was taken aback when she heard the German answer in Greek.

"Madam, we want a little food for our army, which is suffering."

Theodora smiled ironically before she answered him. "I'm sorry, my people are suffering too, but you should have realized we are a poor country. Anyway, there's nothing for you to take—you took it all the last time."

"So what are you watering?"

"Tomatoes. But as you see they're not ripe yet. Do you want to eat them green?"

"And in the house?"

"I have nothing in the house."

"Please allow me to verify that personally."

He passed her and went ahead, but Theodora ran and reached the kitchen before him. She silently asked the Virgin to forgive her for what she did next. Still holding Magdalini, she pinched her hard and trod with all her strength on Arapis's tail. The child and the dog protested with all their strength. Magdalini was famous in the family for her deafening cries, and Theodora relied on this to cover any sound coming from the hiding place. Frightened and prompted by sisterly solidarity, Polyxeni started to cry as well, further masking any noise.

Pandemonium now reigned in the kitchen, with the two children wailing pitifully and the dog howling for its ill-treated tail. The Germans wore uncomfortable grimaces and their chief, having glanced hastily around the kitchen, went on to the other rooms. Theodora had nothing to fear there. Still, she could hardly breathe until they left, the dust trailing behind their vehicles. She kissed Magdalini, who had finally calmed down, and lifted her dress to see that she had a big bruise on her leg where she'd been pinched.

"What did I do? I'm like a crazy person." she said to herself, and stroked the tearstained face of her daughter.

Then she remembered Julia, who was waiting, shut in the dark hole, and she ran to pull her out. Julia had tied the goat's mouth shut with one of her ribbons while she held the chickens' beaks together with her hands. Mother and daughter began to laugh.

That night passed in general high spirits for Gerasimos's family as Theodora described to her husband how their animals were saved. Not even little Magdalini cried, despite remembering the unjust pinch she'd experienced. Even Arapis forgot the injustice he had sustained but, like the intelligent dog he was, he avoided his mistress and her shoes from then on.

When the children were asleep, Theodora took her usual place beside her husband in front of the fire. He looked at her sadly.

"What's the matter, Gerasimos?" she asked.

"I saw Ilias yesterday. We fought together in Albania."

"I know. How is he?"

"I don't know, wife, but if I were in his place, I don't think I could bear it. Once he was a six-foot-tall, strapping fellow. And now he's stuck in a chair with the legs of his pants empty, an amputee."

"The important thing is that he survived and returned to his wife and children."

"Is that the only important thing? That this woman loved him when he stood up and now she'll live with him, nursing him like a child? She'll lie down in bed with half a man—doesn't that mean anything? How will she see him as her husband again?"

"Gerasimos, do you hear what you're saying? That the wives of all those who were crippled by the war love their husbands less now? When I met you, I loved you because you were like the sun. You were a daring lad, but later . . . Look, no matter what life brings us, I love you. I'd love you if you had a hand missing or a leg or both of them at once."

"No, Theodora. I don't know about you, but I wouldn't want to live with missing pieces. I'd prefer death a thousand times!"

◆ ◆ ◆

The nail Gerasimos trod on a few months later was from the fence surrounding their house. It had been destroyed by a sudden storm, and he decided to mend it the very next day. He began removing the broken pieces, but out of carelessness, he stepped on one that had a rusty nail sticking out of it, which pierced the sole of his foot. He cursed from the pain, but he paid no attention to the wound until, instead of closing, it began to turn black and his leg began to swell. He didn't say a word to anyone and tried to treat his painful limb by himself. He began to limp, but simply told his wife that his old, worn-out shoes didn't protect his feet from stones, so they were hurting.

It was the fever that finally confined him to his bed, and when Theodora saw the state of his foot, she panicked and called the doctor. When she saw the doctor's frown, she understood that things were very serious. When all of his efforts to counteract the infection failed and he told them he would have to cut off the leg, Theodora knew that she'd lost her husband. Gerasimos would never allow the leg to be amputated. Whatever she said to him, she couldn't persuade him. However much she pleaded, he didn't accept it.

"This time, wife, your nagging won't have any result," he said, smiling.

"You think this is a time for jokes? The doctor made it clear. You'll die if they don't cut it off!"

"I understood. But you know that I'll die even if they do cut it off. Do you remember that conversation we had a few months ago, when I saw Ilias with his legs gone?"

"But it's not the same. You won't be a cripple. You'll have a wooden leg and you'll walk with a cane like so many other people."

"Stop it, Theodora! Even when I just think about it I go crazy!"

"Gerasimos, I beg you! Think about me. Think about our children. We need you."

"I can't, wife. I don't want to live as a cripple. Don't pester me when I've already made my decision."

"But it's mad! You can be saved and you choose death."

"I choose for my body to die but not my soul. If I live as a cripple, my soul's finished. I'll never be the same. I'll never be the man you loved!"

Theodora bent her head and let the tears flow. Gerasimos stroked her hair and looked at her with eyes that burned with fever.

"You once said to me—just to see if you remember all the things you said—that it was foolish to keep words inside you that should be expressed at that moment, remember?"

Theodora nodded her head in agreement and he continued.

"But we've said them all, haven't we? You know how much I've loved you, how happy I've been living beside you, that I've never regretted for a moment going against everyone and marrying you. There are no secrets between us, and no hidden feelings. So I don't want you to cry. You're a strong woman; make our daughters strong like you!"

◆ ◆ ◆

As the dirt, little by little, covered Gerasimos's wooden casket, Theodora thought she was living a nightmare. As she stood beside the hole that gaped in the earth like a hungry mouth, with her five daughters crying pitifully beside her and the rain falling like a heavy veil, she let her life pass before her. A bright sun illuminated all the previous years. But now it seemed that there was only fog in front of her.

Standing beside her, twelve-year-old Melissanthi reminded her of herself when she first met Gerasimos. Her second daughter, Julia, stood on the other side of Melissanthi, looking even smaller than usual, as if she'd been worn down by grief. Theodora felt her youngest daughter, Magdalini, squeezing her frozen hand and looked in her direction. She saw then that her other daughters, Polyxeni and Aspasia, were waiting to take courage from her. What would she do? How would she manage?

That evening she put the children to bed, then turned away all the relatives who had decided not to leave her alone. She would have to get used to being on her own. She sat near the fireplace in the spot where Gerasimos always sat and fixed her eyes on the fire. The rain had stopped but the wind was strong. From time to time the windows creaked annoyingly. But in some ways, their grating noise was a relief—a little sound from the window, a crackling of the fire that broke the lonesome silence.

The next morning Theodora was still in the same place. Melissanthi, who woke first, threw two logs on the dying fire. Moving as quietly as she could so as not to wake her mother, she covered her with a jacket and then sat at her feet, watching the flames revive. The flames danced drunkenly as they devoured the wood, and the girl turned her gaze first to her sleeping mother, and then to the house. This house had suffocated her for as long as she could remember. Once, when she'd climbed high up the mountain with her father, he had shown her the vast plain spreading out at their feet. "You see, Melissanthi," he'd said, "how endless the plain is? How could you imagine anything other than this?"

"What's beyond the plain, Father?" she'd asked him.

"The whole world," Gerasimos answered.

"So why do people live in one place instead of going to see the world?"

"Because however far you go, my child, there's always something farther away. However high the mountain, as soon as you reach the top, you'll see that there is a taller one. But a person has to put down roots somewhere."

"Only the trees and the plants have roots. People have legs to go forward."

"And a brain to know when to stop," continued her father. He kissed her, adding with pride, "You're a very clever girl, Melissanthi!"

She missed her father very much but she still didn't agree with him. She wanted to go ahead, she wanted to fly. The house by the river stifled her and there were times when that river, the one she'd loved so much since she was little, seemed like a rope tied around her neck that wouldn't let her breathe.

Theodora woke and found Melissanthi curled up at her feet. "Couldn't you sleep, child?" she asked, stretching to counteract the stiffness of her body from sleeping in the chair.

"Yes. I woke up not long ago. Why did you sleep here?"

"I was sitting here last night and fell asleep."

"You miss Father a lot, don't you?"

"A lot."

"What will you do now, Mother? Will you marry again?"

Theodora looked at her in surprise. "What are you saying, Melissanthi? Who told you such a thing?"

"I heard two old women saying it yesterday. They said that because you're still so young and so beautiful, and because you have an inheritance, you'll find someone who'll take you, even with five children."

"I've never heard such nonsense, and when my husband's not yet cold in his grave! Listen to me carefully, Melissanthi. No one will replace the husband I've lost, because no one is worthy of him. And because you're a woman too, I'll give you a piece of advice: if the man who asks for your hand is not the one and only, don't take him!"

"Even if he's rich, Mother?"

"What does being rich mean? Don't confuse money and happiness; those things don't always go together."

"And what if the man who asks for my hand takes me far away from here?"

"Is that what you want? To leave?"

"Yes, Mother. For me this village is . . . how can I say it? That mountain over our heads presses down on me; it cuts my breath off."

"In the old days they used to say that the gods lived there."

"I know. But the gods were clever. They took the summit and left the ruined mortals down below, unable to see faraway lands and dream about what lies beyond them. I see the sea over there, and I long to get on a boat and travel all over the world."

"I hope you can achieve that, but remember that it's this corner of the earth, stuck on the rocks below Olympus, that will always be your home. You'll always find a harbor here. Only here will you find the truth of your life, because your roots are here, Melissanthi, and nothing changes that."

Melissanthi rested her head on her mother's knees. Theodora tenderly stroked her hair and the two of them stayed there for a long time, just staring at the fire.

◆ ◆ ◆

They passed a very difficult winter. Snow and frost had destroyed everything, and hunger surrounded their village. Theodora tried desperately to secure the basic necessities for the children and herself. If it hadn't been for the goat and the chickens, they would certainly have died of hunger. She'd spend an entire day with her feet sinking into the cold mud just to collect a single sack of wild greens. The next day she'd go to Katerini to sell them. She'd usually manage to make a little money doing this, but each time, until she got back home, she'd be stiff with fear; if she ran into a German patrol, they'd steal what little she'd managed to make.

That afternoon she came home happy. She'd managed to sell not only the sack of greens, but a few eggs she'd saved from her hens. A wad of notes, mostly of little value because of the inflation, was well hidden in her stocking. Stuffed into her pocket was an onion. Anyone who took it for a wad of money would be disappointed and, hopefully, move on without looking further.

The three Germans who'd stopped her a few meters outside the village immediately looked as if they didn't have good intentions. As soon as Theodora saw them, she straightened her back and glared at them with contempt.

"What do you want?" she asked abruptly.

"Where were you going at this hour?" one of them asked in terrible Greek.

Theodora wondered again, *What the devil? Did all the Germans speak Greek now?* "I'm going home," she answered.

"And that thing filling up your pocket? What's that?"

"It's an onion," she said, pulling it out. "So that I can eat! Maybe you want that too? In any case, you haven't left us anything! And now, if you want to kill me, go ahead! If not, let me go home. My five children are waiting for me to come back."

For a moment the Germans stood still with uncertainty. Then they moved away. Without a second glance at them, Theodora went on her way, praying that the beating of her heart, which was knocking at her chest from fear, wouldn't be heard. She reached her house and only when she closed the door did she let the tears of tension and agony flow freely down her cheeks.

Three days later her village was very severely tested. A group of resistance fighters trapped and blew up a German convoy of ten trucks carrying munitions that had passed through their district. Unwillingly, Theodora was a witness to the scene as she splashed through the mud to gather greens, and her blood froze when she saw from a distance the blinding flash and heard the deafening noise. For a few moments she stood frozen to the spot, trying to recover from the shock, and then her brain sent her a single word to help her recover: *Reprisals!* She knew the Germans would pay back their loss of men and weapons to the absolute limit. Her clouded brain began to work, and her instinct warned her, *The children! The children are at school right now. That's where the bastards will strike!*

The next moment she began to run toward the school as if a thousand demons were pursuing her. She slipped in the mud, her legs were cut as she fell and got up, her clothes were torn and ripped by branches, but nothing bothered her. She had to get there, otherwise the blow would be terrible. Like a madwoman, her hair disheveled, cut and bruised, with torn clothes and out of breath, she reached the school and nearly broke down the door as she fell on it. The teacher jumped up in fear and turned pale the minute he saw what a state she was in. He ran toward her, along with her daughters, who were also disturbed at the sight of their mother.

"What happened, Kyria Theodora?" the teacher asked.

"The children," she said, breathless. "We must hide them! They blew up some German trucks . . . Reprisals!" She realized she was speaking incoherently, but her breath couldn't find its proper rhythm.

The teacher didn't need to hear any more. "Quickly, children! Go! Climb the trees, hide among the leaves, and don't move from there until tomorrow morning, whatever happens. God preserve you, Kyria Theodora. You go too!"

She was running again, this time with her children behind her. She arrived at the house just as she thought her soul would leave altogether—her heart was beating so furiously in her chest. She took the children down through the hidden trapdoor in the kitchen, gave them a little water and bread, and with the last of her strength dragged the heavy table over the entrance to the hideaway. Covered in sweat, she collapsed on the floor, her chin trembling uncontrollably. The sound of her teeth chattering was the only thing that disturbed the complete quiet of the house. She must have spent some time like that because when she managed to stand up it was already dark. Her legs trembling, she approached the window. The house was some way from the village. There was no way she could find anything out, nor did she have any intention of leaving her children. She closed the shutters and lit a single candle in the room before she opened the cellar to take the children out and hug them in her arms. The girls, deathly pale, clung to her and she could hear her every heartbeat.

They spent an agonizing night. With the trapdoor open for any emergency, Theodora and her five daughters prayed to the Virgin to save their village from disaster. In the morning they were afraid to even go outside. Theodora was scared to go to the village too; she didn't want to know how many had paid for yesterday's explosion, and in what way.

A creaking on the verandah made her whole body shiver with fear. Somebody was there. In a flash she pushed the children through the trapdoor and pulled the table back over it. She threw wood on the fire, then stirred the ashes, keeping hold of the heavy iron poker when she was finished.

Someone knocked. It seemed impossible that it could be Germans knocking so considerately. She listened.

"Kyria Theodora? Are you in there?"

She sighed with relief and opened the door wide for the doctor, who was standing on the doorstep.

"It's you, is it, Doctor? You made my blood freeze! Come in!" she said.

As he entered the room, he looked curiously around him. "The teacher told me what happened yesterday," he whispered. "May God keep you, lady, for the good you've done! You saved the children!"

"What happened, Doctor? Did you find out?"

"I don't know if it was divine intervention that made you think of the children, but immediately after the attack, the Germans made for the school. They dashed in, but naturally they didn't find anyone."

"Serves them right!"

"Afterward, though, they went berserk! You can't imagine what happened in the village . . ."

"Did they take a lot?" Theodora's voice had cracked.

"Fifty people, madam!"

"Christ and the Virgin!"

"They kept them in the square for an hour with the whole village around them and they asked us if we knew anything about the 'traitors' who blew up the trucks. And because nobody said a word, they began killing them in front of our eyes, one by one!"

"All fifty of them?" she spat.

"A bullet in the head for each one, before the eyes of their mothers and wives!"

"Curses on them! And then?"

"Afterward they calmed down and let us quietly bury our dead."

"The children? What happened to the children?"

"Thanks to you, everyone was fine. We got them down from the trees. Most of them have bad colds, but they're all fine."

"Blessed be His name!"

After the disaster that had struck so many homes, the village was plunged into mourning. The rage was silent and impotent for now. But a people whom history had condemned to be tested again and again could only be patient.

◆　◆　◆

When the village bells sounded announcing the liberation, pandemonium reigned. At first, they didn't know why the bells were ringing, and they were afraid. What else was waiting for them? Later, though, they all realized, almost simultaneously, that the sound was joyful, liberating . . . and then they understood. The rumors that had multiplied recently, about the war going from bad to worse for the Germans, weren't baseless. Their faces lit up. The sound of the bells could mean only one thing: liberation! Everyone came out into the streets; everyone hugged each other; everyone laughed and cried at once. Theodora opened the trapdoor in her kitchen, took out the Greek flag she'd hidden there, and wrapped it around her shoulders before she rushed out with her children to meet the rest of the smiling faces in the square. Dancing and singing had begun and a large fire was burning in the middle. The celebrations would last until the morning.

No one was expecting the civil war that immediately followed. Certainly not the village, which found itself experiencing even worse hunger than it had during the occupation. The battles were brought to their doorsteps, to the courtyards of their houses, and Theodora had the impression that a nightmare had begun again—but this one was worse than the last, because, on both sides, the weapons were in Greek hands, and the blood spilled was also Greek—only Greek. History took out her pen again to write this tragedy in black letters—black as the times themselves. The nation had stood up to its occupiers and vigorously fought against their tyranny—and now its children were slaughtering one another.

Greece did something she hadn't done before: she lowered her head in shame, like a mother who can't control her family. She removed her crown of laurels. Then she turned her eyes to God and begged Him to help her in this difficult hour. Every sacrifice had to be made to end the schism. Now was the time to gather up the pieces and go forward, to stand up with the help of her children. Those who were still alive.

◆ ◆ ◆

Theodora stared wide eyed at her mother when she'd finished telling her what she had to say.

"What on earth are you saying, Mother?" she shouted and got up from her chair.

"Why, child? What did I say to you? I told you to get married! You're still young and your children need a father."

"My children are fine and for just that reason, you should have thought before saying such a thing to me!"

"But you need to have a man in the house."

"We needed a man in the house when the war was on. But seeing that I managed even then, what would I do with one now? I'm just fine the way I am. My fields are producing well, my children are growing up and becoming beautiful and good, my house is in order, and I don't miss having a man. Leave me be, Mother!"

"Yes, my girl, but the children will leave one day and you'll be alone. Look at me. You married and left home, and my Anna too, and I don't know if I'll see her before I die. Who do I have? Only your father. You'll be left all alone."

"I prefer that."

When her mother left, Theodora looked around her house. A chill spread inside her even though the sun outside was hot enough to crack rocks. Her daughters were in the village with some other girls, decorating the church for the Feast of the Virgin. She opened the door and went out into the yard and looked at the garden beds, nicely in order. She glanced at the river, sparkling in the sunlight, as if molten gold flowed on its bed.

Then, as though drawn by a magnet, she headed toward it, took off her shoes, and waded in up to her knees. She took a handful of water and splashed it on her burning face. A small branch drawn by the current was traveling carelessly on the surface and she followed it until it was out of sight. Her daughters found her like that and were astonished.

"Mother! What are you doing there?" Polyxeni asked.

Theodora turned and looked at them. They really were very beautiful. They had taken the best features of herself and Gerasimos. A moment later she got out of the water and sat on the bank.

"I was hot and I went into the water to cool down," she answered. "Is that a bad thing?"

"But you never go into the river!" Aspasia insisted, and they all sat down near her and looked at her anxiously.

"There are moments when a person does things they don't usually do. That isn't bad."

"What's the matter, Mama?" Melissanthi asked in a soft voice.

Theodora looked at her firstborn. She was fifteen. At that age Theodora was already in love with a man fifteen years older. "Nothing's the matter with me, Melissanthi, it's just that your grandmother was here and she was doing some matchmaking for me."

Exclamations could be heard from her daughters' mouths.

"What does matchmaking mean, Mother?" asked Magdalini. She was just seven years old and had some gaps in her vocabulary.

"Matchmaking," Julia undertook to explain, "is when they tell you to marry someone!"

Magdalini looked at her mother in surprise.

"Are you going to marry someone else?" she asked. "Will we have a new father?"

"Your father is the only father you'll ever have, and no one will take his place," Theodora answered in a tone so firm it startled the little girl.

"Did you ever think about us leaving?" asked Melissanthi.

Theodora looked at her oldest daughter in surprise. "Leaving? To go where?"

"To another place! What's keeping us here?"

"Everything! Whatever we have is here, Melissanthi: the fields, the house, the river."

"There are fields everywhere, and houses all over the world!" she insisted. "And if there's no river beside them, what does it matter?"

"No, child, that won't happen. If I go, I'll feel like I've been uprooted and I couldn't bear that."

"Yes, but then you'll be keeping us here too."

"What are you saying, Melissanthi? How am I keeping you here? You were born here. This is your place, your land."

"Wherever the land is, is a homeland. That's what I say!"

Theodora was silent and turned her gaze again to the river. If all her girls had the same mentality, then her mother was completely right: a great loneliness awaited her. "I don't know what the future has in store for us," she said to her daughters. "But I'll tell you something to remember this hour by: life is like the river that flows in front of us. It carries you easily with it and pulls you wherever it's going. And a river doesn't come back. If it takes you away, you can't come back. Always be careful of the river . . . make sure it doesn't carry you away."

She was silent again as she continued thinking. The girls contemplated their mother's advice, except for the youngest, who didn't understand a word of what she was saying. But she saw that all her sisters were paying attention, and so she began to throw pebbles into the water to keep herself from getting bored. She was surprised when she heard her mother call attention to her idle game.

"Watch what Magdalini's doing," said Theodora. "She's throwing stones in the water. But none of them move from the place where they fell. The river doesn't carry them because of their weight. Wherever they fall, that's where they stay."

"Is that what you want for us too?" asked Melissanthi again. "To become stones so we're not dragged away?"

"Yes."

"Then didn't it occur to you that stones sink just because they're stones, Mother? They reach the bottom and they stay there; they don't go anywhere! I'd rather be a little branch and travel than a stone and drown at the bottom of the river."

Theodora looked at her daughter and then at the others. It was obvious that they agreed with their sister, even if they didn't understand the full meaning of her words.

"You're a very clever girl, my daughter," she observed tenderly.

"Father used to say the same thing," the girl said with a laugh.

"Every one of you will do whatever is in store for you, and what that is, only God knows. I hope I won't lose you, but if it's for your good, let that be! Just remember that as long as I live here this house will exist, and the door will be open to all of you."

◆ ◆ ◆

A week after Melissanthi finished middle school, the matchmaker came to the house with her first suitor. He was a young lad from the village, twenty-six years old, and from a good family, but Melissanthi rejected him without a second thought.

"If I'm to marry someone who'll offer me the same life I've led since I was born, I can do without him!" she declared disdainfully, and Theodora gave her a worried look.

It was quite clear that Melissanthi wouldn't accept anyone from the village. Tactfully, Theodora told the matchmaker she might want to consider bringing someone from Katerini. But three months later, Melissanthi also rejected a businessman from there, and Theodora became even more concerned.

The following year, a public works project brought new residents to Katerini, people who took the opportunity to get to know the broader region. Fokas Karapanos was a civil engineer from Thessaloniki who became enchanted by the village in the shadow of Mount Olympus with its stone-paved streets, tall chestnut trees, and magnificent view of the sea. He was also enchanted by the beautiful eyes of Julia.

He met her one day when he was drinking coffee in the village café, when Julia dropped by on her way home from school. Julia's grandfather was also in the café, and Julia and her sisters came in to talk to him. Fokas couldn't take his eyes off the beautiful girl. At first, Julia noticed him only in the way she noticed any unknown face. But his gaze—the way he looked back at her with interest—made an impression on her. Their second meeting took place one afternoon when Julia was coming back from her grandmother's house and Fokas was taking a walk, admiring the nature and the view. He could hardly believe his eyes when he ran into the girl. She stood still as he approached and he smiled at her.

"Look, here we are meeting again!" he said confidently to her.

Julia feigned ignorance. "Do you know me?" she asked.

"We haven't been introduced, I realize, but I saw you a few days ago at the café," Fokas explained, looking a little embarrassed. "You came in to talk to some gentleman and you were with some other girls."

"Oh . . . yes!" said Julia slyly as if she'd just remembered. "It was my grandfather; my sisters and I went in to talk to him. What are you doing in our neighborhood?"

"I've recently come to Katerini with a group of engineers in connection with a road that's being built. But I love your village and I often come here when I have some free time."

"What do you like about the village? It doesn't have anything special."

"Except for you?" he asked and the girl blushed. "Your village, Miss . . ."

"My name's Julia."

"And I'm Fokas. So, Miss Julia, since you live here you may not realize it, but this area has something special, something wild and at the same time peaceful and calming. The air here is quite special. It smells of pines and earth. I don't know how else to explain it."

Fokas also couldn't explain anything else that happened after that. Julia haunted his days and nights. She became an obsession, and he did everything he could to turn up in her village and see her.

Theodora noticed that her daughter had suddenly lost her appetite and was always ready to run errands outside the house and take the goats to pasture—duties that she, like her sisters, had always tried to avoid, even to the point of quarreling. It didn't take much for her to understand what was going on. It may have been many years since she'd fallen in love with Gerasimos and invented all sorts of excuses to leave the house and meet him, but the memories were still fresh. Who, she wondered, was the lucky man?

The roof nearly fell in when she saw Fokas standing in front of her, asking for Julia's hand. Fokas told her sincerely how he loved her daughter, how he wanted to marry her, how he did not expect a dowry, nothing else mattered to him. But Theodora would have to accept that he would take her away with him as soon as the wedding was over because he lived in Thessaloniki. For the first time since her husband's death, Theodora understood how alone she was, and how much need she had of a second opinion. Her daughter had made it clear that she loved Fokas and wanted to marry him. She also contrived to make it understood that even if Theodora didn't give her consent, she would follow him.

Her own mother and father accepted the news calmly, which surprised Theodora.

"Aren't you going to say anything?" she asked them, irritated by their attitude. "I tell you that my child is going to marry a foreigner, a man I know nothing about, and on top of that, he'll take her away to Thessaloniki!"

"What do you want us to say?" her mother answered. "Julia is not a little girl anymore."

"And he's about to turn thirty! So he's younger than Gerasimos when he ran off with you," her father chimed in. "And anyway, from what you've told us, he's educated, handsome, and the main thing—he loves your daughter! What more do you want?"

"It's not so simple, Father. Julia . . . how can I put this?"

"Julia is the first of your birds to fly the nest, and that's always painful," her mother told her with understanding. "That's what I felt like when poor Lefteris told me you'd secretly married Gerasimos. So let the little bird you've hatched fly, because whatever you do, you won't achieve anything if you try to stop it."

Theodora knew how much truth lay in her mother's words. She gave Julia and Fokas her blessing, the wedding took place a few months later, and the couple left for their new life. Just before they got into the car to drive off, Theodora found her daughter standing beside the river, staring sadly at the water.

"What's going on, Mrs. Karapanos?" she asked her cheerfully. "Maybe now that you're leaving, you're regretting it?"

"No, Mother. Fokas loves me and I love him. I'll be happy wherever I go with him. But I never expected to leave here. This house by the river was my whole world."

"That's what happens when a girl marries."

"And to think that Melissanthi was always the one in a hurry to leave."

"Her time will come. You make sure that you are happy. And if something goes wrong, if it's not all you dreamed it would be, the river won't take this house—it'll always be here." Mother and daughter hugged each other, tears wetting their cheeks.

And a little cloud of dust from Fokas's car was the last memory Theodora had of her second daughter.

❖ ❖ ❖

Apostolos Fatouras was a major tobacco merchant in Athens. At thirty-nine, he was already a widow. His wife had died in an accident two years earlier, leaving him a huge fortune. Her wealth was, in fact, the reason he'd married her; he was honest enough with himself to admit that and he certainly didn't intend to remarry. He led a happy life and was never lacking in female company because first, he was a very handsome man, and second, his money was a significant advantage. The fact that he didn't have children didn't bother him at all.

He found himself in Katerini for a tobacco deal and he was rather irritable, especially since at the last moment, his companion announced that she couldn't come with him. He hated traveling alone and so he had invited a friend along for company. But the choice of friend was a mistake. Christos was a nature worshipper, and the area bewitched him. He wanted to explore it willy-nilly. Apostolos, not once but many times, cursed the moment that he'd asked him to come along. Christos dragged him into ravines; they visited water mills and scrambled up rocky crags to admire the view. The worst thing was that Christos, an aficionado of ancient Greek history, especially mythology, insisted on conveying everything he knew or didn't know to Apostolos, who was bored to death.

It was evening and they had just finished another guided tour. Christos had literally dragged him to see the Baths of Aphrodite, thinking that his friend couldn't possibly have any other interest but to see it. The beauty of the landscape left Apostolos unmoved; the three linked basins among the pure white rocks had nothing to say to him, nor, of course, did the deep blue of their depths. The unearthly beauty that they emitted was not to his taste, and so he smoked one cigarette after another until his friend had taken as many photographs as he deemed necessary, which were a lot. The sun had started to set and Apostolos had no desire to be in the mountains after dark.

"Shouldn't we get going?" he said gently to his friend. "It's getting dark and we don't know the area well."

Christos's answer filled him with relief—he'd already prepared to do battle if his friend declared a desire to linger. "Yes, unfortunately we have to leave," Christos agreed. "You're right, we mustn't be caught in the dark in this wilderness. But how I wish we'd had more time! Isn't it magnificent, Apostolos? The gods knew where to choose to live! I almost envy them!"

"If I, on the other hand, had to live in such desolation, I would die of boredom!" Apostolos retorted cynically, drawing an admonishing glance from his friend.

"Poor Apostolos. It seems to me that all those years spent with your tobacco business have managed to dull your brain and your eyes. Look around you! Imagine the most beautiful goddess, Aphrodite, taking off her cloak, letting her blond hair fall freely over her white shoulders, and then lowering her body into these pools! Imagine the water flowing over her alabaster skin and watching her sigh with pleasure at the joy of the refreshing water. Imagine her diving and wetting her hair and later the drops caressing her divine body. Imagine . . ."

"Stop! This isn't imagination anymore, my friend. You've become a true hedonist."

"Apostolos, you're so prosaic. Don't you have anything inside you?"

"Of course I have. A desire for *tsipouro* and some little snacks to warm up. Come on, Christos, let's go! Otherwise, we'll be caught in the dark."

They ended up in the village at the café, drinking *tsipouro* and enjoying the delicious snacks the café owner, Kyrios Pandelis, had prepared for their enjoyment.

"This is a reality that I prefer to all your fantasies, my friend," Apostolos declared cheerfully, as he held up the transparent liquor. "And if the gods you admire so much drank nectar, who can tell me that it wasn't like the *tsipouro* we're drinking tonight in this village forgotten by gods and men?"

Christos didn't answer. He looked around him as if he couldn't get enough of his surroundings. This village, "forgotten by gods and men," as Apostolos had put it, had an incomparable charm. It was only September, so the inhabitants hadn't yet gathered in their houses, secure beside the fire, nor was it too late for people to be out. Children were running up and down shouting happily, grandfathers were drinking their little glasses of *tsipouro* at various other tables, and some girls were sitting on a stone bench nearby, casually chatting.

"I visualize Aphrodite something like that," Christos suddenly observed, pointing to Melissanthi, who was sitting a few yards away from them, laughing at something the girl next to her said.

As he raised his glass toward his lips, Apostolos looked in the direction his friend was pointing, and his hand just stopped in midair. "Her, certainly. For the first time I agree with your taste. Look at that body! Look at the hair! Molten gold. Heavens above!"

As if something were drawing her gaze, Melissanthi turned to the two men and fixed her eyes on Apostolos. He looked at her with obvious admiration, and she seemed to smile at him. Then she turned her head back before anyone watching might notice.

Apostolos went to stand up, but Christos stopped him.

"What do you think you're doing?" he asked, holding his friend by the arm.

"But—didn't you see? She smiled at me!"

"So? Where do you think you are? In Athens, in one of the cafés you frequent? Or in some sophisticated salon waiting for someone to introduce you to the prettiest girl in the room? We're in a village, Apostolos. Pull yourself together! Some of these peaceful men sitting at the tables next to us could be her father and brothers, and I have no desire to find myself with a black eye—and that may be the best-case scenario."

"Oh—maybe you're right but I'm bewitched!"

"I'll help you recover. The girl is twenty at most."

"What's that got to do with it?"

"Nothing. Except the fact that you're forty. Now that has a lot to do with it! This tender morsel is not for your teeth to chew on."

"Christos, you're talking silly nonsense."

"I'm trying to keep you from *doing* something silly. Now pay up and let's go before we find ourselves in trouble."

It was all Christos could do to persuade Apostolos to leave. And the next day, when he'd finished his work, Apostolos showed no desire to return to Athens. On the contrary, in the afternoon he got dressed, smartened himself up, and put on cologne. As soon as Christos saw him, he scowled.

"Where are you off to all dressed up like that?" he asked.

"Well, what do you think? Are we going to stay in the hotel? Aren't we going for a walk?"

"Actually we should be setting out for Athens, since you've finished your work here."

"But I didn't really finish . . . all my work in the area," Apostolos replied suggestively.

Christos anxiously approached his friend. "Apostolos, I don't like the look of you. If you've got anything on your mind concerning the girl we saw yesterday, get rid of it! The girl is young. She's not like the ones you're used to going around with."

"That's exactly why I like her, my friend."

"Forget about her, Apostolos. Let's get away from here."

"I'm not going anywhere until I meet her. If you want to leave, leave."

"And leave you behind to turn things upside down? Forget it! I'm staying. I want to see how far you get with this."

Not even Apostolos knew how far he'd get. And the experienced Mr. Fatouras certainly didn't expect to be caught up in the trap of love; after all, he'd cleverly avoided it for so many years. And to fall for such an unworldly little girl? He never saw that coming.

After their first meeting in the square, Melissanthi confessed to herself that this man was something different. He was more amusing than any other man she'd ever known, sure of himself and more smartly dressed than even the doctor, and he looked as if he must be rich and lived a good life. Coming back home that night, she unconsciously sighed. The unknown man was only passing through the village, so she certainly wouldn't see him again. And yet, a man like that would suit her. Maybe he was from Athens. By the time she reached the house she was irritated that destiny had landed her in such a desert, where the only men around were shepherds or farmers. She was jealous of her sister. She got to live in Thessaloniki, a big city, whereas Melissanthi herself was rotting in the countryside. It wasn't fair!

As soon as Theodora saw Melissanthi, she knew that some storm had disturbed her mind. When her daughter had that look, it would be hard to get words out of her.

The next afternoon, Melissanthi set out again for the village. She was bored to death there, but it was worse at home, with her mother and her younger sisters driving her crazy with questions. She was irritable again, and took it out on the bushes around her, furiously tearing off their leaves. When she came upon Apostolos, smiling at her, she nearly stumbled and suddenly turned pale. Instinctively she cast her eyes around her to make sure no one was watching them but the road was deserted.

"Good afternoon," she said, smiling, and was annoyed with herself for not having worn the other dress that suited her better.

"Good afternoon," he greeted her in turn, while he couldn't help thinking how she looked even more beautiful close up.

Her eyes weren't exactly brown; they had something of the color of honey in them mixed with wine, and the brows that crowned them were fine drawn and delicate. Her lips were moist and her cheeks red. Apostolos's gaze dared to travel farther down. Her body was slim and desirable, even when covered by the unattractive dress she wore.

Melissanthi was not at all bothered by Apostolos's examining gaze, because it gave her the opportunity to observe him herself. He was a head taller than her, and she wasn't short. He was slim, very dark, with a few white hairs adorning his temples. His eyes were also dark, almost black, and his glance indicated to her quite clearly that he liked what he saw. His clothes cried out from a distance that they were very expensive and his shirt must have been made of silk. She'd never seen such a well-dressed man. Even his shoes had gold monograms on them. He must be really rich to have his initials on his shoes! Their eyes met again.

"What's your name?" Apostolos asked.

"Melissanthi," she answered.

"You have a very beautiful name. As beautiful as you are!"

"Thank you. And you? What's your name?"

"I'm sorry, I didn't introduce myself . . . Apostolos Fatouras."

"Pleased to meet you."

Melissanthi only just managed to stop her eyes from widening. She'd heard of this man! Her grandfather said that he was a big tobacco merchant and everyone on the plain gave their tobacco to him because he was honest and very reliable with his payments. So, aside from being handsome and well dressed, he didn't realize what else he had. Her interest was aroused even more. But she'd have to find out if he was married. A man like that couldn't be single.

"What are you doing in our part of the country?" Melissanthi asked, feigning ignorance.

"I had some work in Katerini, but I took the opportunity to explore the surrounding countryside. Your village is really beautiful."

"I suppose that depends on your perspective. If you lived here all the time like I do, you might not like it so much."

"Don't you like it?"

"I do and I don't. I don't have any other choice, though. Will you stay long, Mr. Fatouras?" she asked politely.

"I'd prefer it if you didn't speak to me as if I were a respectable old man. I told you, my name's Apostolos—unless you see me as an old man."

"Of course not!"

"It wouldn't be strange. To a young girl of your age, maybe I look old."

"I think that you . . . you're fishing for compliments!"

They both laughed, and unconsciously they took a step closer to one another. They looked deeply into each other's eyes. Apostolos realized that he had fallen suddenly and unexpectedly in love. This girl must be his at any cost. On her part, Melissanthi understood that the man standing in front of her was her ticket out of the village. The fact that he was handsome, that was an added bonus.

The tension of the moment was broken by Melissanthi, who had to find out, before she dared to hope. "Tell me, Apostolos, is your wife with you?" she asked.

"I have no wife, Melissanthi," he answered with a smile. "I'm alone in life. I came here with a friend who had the kindness to accompany me. And you?"

"What do you mean, 'you'?"

"Now that you've learned I'm single, I imagine I have the right to find out if you are free?"

"Of course I am! Otherwise I wouldn't have been standing and chatting so long with you."

They looked at each other again. Apostolos swallowed a lump that was blocking his throat and took a deep breath. It wouldn't have taken much for him to take her in his arms and kiss her until her knees gave way, but even for a man like him, there were limits.

"Tell me about yourself, Melissanthi. I want to find out about your life."

"My life is of no interest," she answered sadly.

"Whatever concerns you is interesting to me," Apostolos replied.

They began to walk and without being aware of it, they headed away from the village. They were alone, and all around them the trees and bushes hid them from prying eyes. Melissanthi told him everything about herself, and with her every word, her every movement, he knew that he wanted her and he would have her. It was the first time in his life he'd felt like this, and he was still young enough to be able to get what he wanted.

Melissanthi had finished her tale and was looking at him. "That's all there is," she said simply. "Have I disappointed you?"

"Why do you say that?"

"What interest can a village girl like me have for a man like you?"

"That's exactly why you interest me! Because you're not like any of the women I've met until now. Since I met you yesterday in the square, you've been going round and round in my brain. I would say that you are in my heart, but I don't want to frighten you."

"You don't scare me, but I do think you're in a hurry."

"Melissanthi, I'm nearly forty, and my experience allows me to know for certain what's happening to me. I'm not some young greenhorn."

"No, you're not. And if you were, we wouldn't be here together now—if that tells you something."

Apostolos came a little closer and Melissanthi made no move to distance herself from him. She kept looking into his eyes until he took her in his arms and fixed his lips to hers.

Only for a moment did Melissanthi feel strange, as if she were a little ashamed, but the next minute she abandoned herself to his embrace with no more hesitation. No one had ever kissed her before and the experience moved her. If Apostolos had let her, she would have continued to delight in the experience of this first kiss. Released from his embrace, she became aware of what had happened and lowered her head, blushing scarlet. She covered her face with her hands but Apostolos raised her chin and looked at her tenderly.

"It's been years since I kissed a girl who turned red as a poppy. Don't be ashamed, Melissanthi. A kiss is not something bad or cheap."

"Yes, but we've only just met one another. Apart from your name, I don't know anything else about you. How did I do this?"

"It was probably my fault. But since you want to find out about me, I'll tell you."

The story Apostolos told was not exactly the truth, but it was the only thing he was able to tell her without feeling ashamed. He told her how he'd met his wife but he neglected to add that he'd married her for her money. He explained to her that he'd lived alone since he'd been widowed but he neglected to clarify how much he'd gallivanted around, drinking and dancing and throwing himself into ephemeral erotic relationships. When he finished his story, Melissanthi knew that Apostolos Fatouras was her man and that she would follow him to the ends of the earth. For the moment, though, she must return home because the hour was late and she would get a severe scolding from her mother. She said a hurried good-bye to him after they'd agreed to meet at the same place the next afternoon.

Neither of them closed an eye that night. Apostolos felt as if he were twenty years old again, and refused to listen to the voice of reason, represented worthily by his friend. He was crazy about Melissanthi, and the memory of that kiss unhinged him. He was dying to take her in his arms again and he counted the hours until the next afternoon. Whatever Christos told him fell on deaf ears. Melissanthi, on the other hand, felt ashamed of that kiss and when she came home she felt that her sisters, and even more her mother, would know what she'd done. Nevertheless her female nature had awoken and demanded to be fulfilled, despite the fact that Melissanthi herself knew nothing about it. The only thing she knew was that she couldn't wait for her meeting with Apostolos the next day.

She arrived, almost running, at their meeting place and although she was a quarter of an hour early, Apostolos was already waiting for her. Without a second thought, she rushed into his arms and waited, hungrily, for his kiss. Apostolos didn't disappoint her since he'd been waiting for the same thing and hadn't been able to put it out of his head since the morning. Afterward, they sat, out of breath, under a tree and looked at each other.

"Melissanthi, I'm in love with you," he confessed to her passionately. "It doesn't bother me that I met you only two days ago. I feel as if I've been waiting for you all my life!"

"Apostolos, I don't know what to say . . ."

"Just one thing. Will you marry me?"

She wanted to sing, to dance, to shout. She felt as if she were living the only dream she'd had for so many years. She looked him carefully in the eyes. "Are you sure this is what you want?" she asked.

"Naturally I'm sure! I want to marry you. I want to take you away to Athens and buy you whatever your heart desires. They'll probably all die of jealousy down there because I'll have the most beautiful wife in the world!"

"Apostolos, you're acting like a little child," Melissanthi scolded him while the bells of her vanity were ringing merrily inside her. Her eyes shone with pleasure at what she'd heard. It was everything she'd ever dreamed of: clothes, jewelry, fancy things . . .

"You've made me feel like a child again," he answered, and folded her again in his arms. "So? Will you be my wife?"

"I want to be your wife, but I don't want to hear what my mother will say. I think we'll have problems."

"Leave it to me," he reassured her.

◆ ◆ ◆

Theodora smiled broadly at her mother, who was seated opposite her on the verandah, drinking coffee.

"So, Mother, I think the older you get, the more you're losing it!" she observed cheerily.

"You've gotten older too! You think you've got your head screwed on," her mother shot back, annoyed. "I tell you that man doesn't know what's the matter with him!"

"And what should I be doing about it?"

"Make a move! Every day he's in the village pretending to be a tourist. Get dressed, do yourself up, and see if you can find out where he's going!"

"And what if I did all that? What would happen? As soon as he saw me, would he fall down or run and get a marriage license?"

"Don't make fun of me, Theodora. You're young and beautiful. And your father knows him: he's almost in his forties, a widower with no children and lots of money. And besides all that, they say he's good looking! Fatouras is just right for you."

"If it's as you say, what makes you believe that he'll turn to look at a woman my age with five children? The man came to our neighborhood for work, not to find a bride. If he wanted to marry he would have done it in Athens where he lives and where he must be surrounded by young and beautiful women from the capital. And the fact that you're thinking all this is ridiculous. You must accept the fact that love and love affairs are over for me."

"Who's talking about such things? I'm talking about a lot of money. It would be to your advantage and your children's!"

"Mother, you never know when to just stop talking. And one of these days, it's going to come back and hit you in the head."

◆　◆　◆

The well-dressed man on the doorstep was smiling happily at her, but Theodora just stood there for a few moments as if she'd been turned to stone.

"Excuse me, what can I do for you?" she finally asked, certain that he'd lost his way in the countryside and was looking for directions.

"You're Kyria Theodora, aren't you?"

"Yes, I am. And who are you?"

"My name is Apostolos Fatouras, and I wanted to speak to you."

Hearing his name, Theodora was overwhelmed and stood aside for him to enter. Only the previous day her mother had spoken to her about him and today here he was in her house, tall, certainly good looking, and smiling. Her brain tried to start working, to understand what business Fatouras had here. She rejected the crazy notion that her mother had interfered in some way to bring about the conclusion she wanted. Suddenly she realized that she had been silently staring at the man all this time, as if in a trance, as he waited patiently in the middle of the room.

"Excuse me," she mumbled in embarrassment. "Please sit down."

"Thank you."

Apostolos looked around and chose an armchair to sit in. Theodora sat opposite him.

"I'm a little confused, sir."

"Fatouras is my name. I'm a tobacco merchant from Athens."

"Certainly, but I don't understand what you want. I don't have any tobacco to sell you."

"I didn't come to buy anything from you, madam," Fatouras explained. "I came to ask you for something."

"What do you want from me?"

"Melissanthi. For my wife!"

◆ ◆ ◆

To the river! Theodora ran there to be alone and catch her breath after all she'd heard. Apostolos had left smiling, as sure of himself as he'd come, and had managed to extract a promise from her that he'd have her answer within two days. But Theodora knew that the question was merely a formality. No consent was necessary on her part. She stood on the bank, watching the water flow in front of her feet. In a moment of madness, she nearly threw herself into its green brilliance and allowed it to carry her away.

The soft sound behind her warned her she was not alone. She turned and saw Melissanthi watching her, arms crossed on her chest. Her whole stance cried out that she was ready for a fight.

"I have no intention of quarreling with you, my child," Theodora said.

"Whether you quarrel with me or not depends on what you say to me!" Melissanthi answered.

"Do you love him?" Theodora looked her daughter in the eyes.

Melissanthi lowered her eyes before she replied. "I want him," she declared.

"It's not the same. I asked you if you love him."

"What does it matter? And if I don't love him now, I like him. So I will love him."

"Melissanthi, I must know the truth. Do you like Fatouras or his money? If he was poor, would you want him?"

"What does it matter? I like Apostolos the way he is. If I'd seen him in rags, or in a farmer's clothes covered in dirt, no, he wouldn't have been the same to me. But that's not who he is."

"In other words, you were dazzled. You don't want him; you want the life he can offer you. Wealth, fancy clothes, and a sophisticated life in Athens."

"And what's wrong with that? I don't want to grow old in this village or marry a farmer, have a child every year, and work in the fields! I want to leave, and Apostolos will take me away from here. That's what matters to me."

"Yes, but even if he were to take you to Paradise, when the door of your house closes, there'll be the two of you. If you don't love him, it won't be easy."

"It'll be harder to stay here!"

"Aren't you worried that he's so much older?"

"On the contrary, it reassures me. He fell in love with me. I'm younger and beautiful, so he'll always want me and I won't ever have to chase after him. Anyway, you are one to talk. Father was fifteen years older than you!"

"I worshipped your father! It's not the same."

"I didn't say that I'm not interested in Apostolos or that he repels me. And besides, what more could a village girl with no education hope for?"

"Oh, you're not in your right mind! You're young."

"Take a look at me, Mother. Look at my village clothes. In Athens the girls wear beautiful clothes. They have earrings hanging from their ears and their fingers are decorated with rings that have stones in them. In Athens the women have their hair beautifully done and they smell of perfume, and they paint their faces with makeup. In the evenings they go to clubs where there's music and they dance and enjoy themselves. That's what he'll offer me, and I'll love him out of gratitude because he will have saved me from a miserable life in the village. I'll marry him, Mother, and you can't stop me! I'd like to have your blessing . . . but I don't really need it."

A little later Theodora went to her mother's house with an inscrutable expression on her face. She sat and rested her head in her hands. It felt as heavy as cement.

"What are you doing here? Why the long face?" her mother asked straightaway.

"Remember all the things you told me the other day about Fatouras?"

"Don't tell me you decided to do something."

"I didn't have the chance. He decided to do something first."

"You don't say! Isn't that a stroke of fate. What did he do?"

"He came to my house and asked for Melissanthi's hand!"

Theodora's mother was struck dumb. She sat down in a heap with her mouth open and her eyes popping.

"That's exactly how I looked when he told me he loved her and wanted her for his wife."

"Hmph! The old rake! Did our girl take a fancy to him? She's a baby compared to him. He could be her father!" Julia burst out.

"Don't even start with that, Mother, because from what . . . the groom tells me, your granddaughter isn't so innocent."

"Christ and the Virgin!"

"And if all the saints were to fall down from heaven, it wouldn't change anything. My daughter declared that she wants him and she'll have him with or without my permission."

"Does she love him?"

"Melissanthi only loves two things: Athens and money. You can't imagine what I had to listen to from her. She's so calculating . . . so cold . . . I've seen a lot in almost forty years, but I never thought like that!"

"That shows she's clever, Theodora."

"You call that cleverness?"

"She knows what she wants, and she's found a way to get it. If she wants more than you or I do from this life, that's her own business. And if he can give her what she wants, that's good enough for me. So happy wedding!"

◆ ◆ ◆

Melissanthi and Apostolos married right away. The wedding was held in the village, and none of Apostolos's friends or associates from Athens were invited. Christos, naturally, served as best man, and before anyone could quite comprehend it, Melissanthi had her little suitcase in hand and was ready to leave. Apostolos would take her first to Thessaloniki to shop, then to Athens.

Standing in the middle of the kitchen, the newlywed said good-bye to her sisters and mother.

"So," she began uncomfortably. "The time has come . . ."

"Will you ever come back?" asked the youngest, Magdalini, with tears in her eyes.

"Look, it's not like I'm going to America," Melissanthi said, trying to smile, but she was visibly moved. "I may even come back at Easter."

"Don't be so sure," Polyxeni rejoined, and her tone was sharp. "You were crazy about leaving the village. Why would you want to come back? Who knows? You may go on a trip abroad at Easter."

An embarrassing pause followed, but Theodora broke the silence.

"Stop all this silly talk and kiss your sister," she said. "Wish her happiness in her new life!"

The girls hurried to do as their mother told them, and Melissanthi coolly accepted their kisses and wishes. Then the sisters left, and mother and daughter were alone.

The girl turned to her mother. "They made me angry," she whispered.

"They'll miss you, that's all it is."

"Polyxeni seemed to be angry with me."

"She's like you. She wants to leave, too—maybe even more than you do. Anyway . . . it's not the time to talk about that. Good-bye, Melissanthi, and good luck!"

"Do you hold it against me, Mother?"

"No mother holds anything against her child. You wanted to leave and you managed it. I'll tell you what I told your sister when she left: this house will always be here, waiting for you. If you suffer wounds in your new life, only this house can heal you. Right now you want to run away and never want to look back. But that might change someday. And if it does, your home will always be here."

Theodora embraced her daughter and kissed her, and as she watched her get into the car with her new husband, she silently made the sign of the cross. Just as it had been when Julia left, Theodora's last image of her daughter was a cloud of dust trailing behind the car that took her away.

◆ ◆ ◆

Life returned to its usual routine, and Theodora busied herself with work. She only felt the absence of her two daughters at mealtimes, when she saw their empty seats at the table. She'd wonder what they were doing in their new lives. Neither of them seemed inclined to make regular contact, although now and then a card or a short letter would arrive. But the promises they contained, of imminent visits, remained just that—promises and nothing more. Theodora looked at her three remaining daughters and asked herself what lay ahead for them. Each one was different from the others; the only thing they had in common was their desire to live far from their village.

No one knew where Aspasia—who was as beautiful as her mother—had inherited her love and talent for singing. When her daughter was little, Theodora admired her voice, but now she worried. Clearly, the girl had a passion for performing and was dying to try her luck at it professionally. Theodora knew an artist's life could be difficult, and she feared Aspasia would struggle to survive.

Polyxeni, on the other hand, seemed only obsessed with herself. Her beauty was more refined than that of the others, her features more delicate, and she was so full of herself that it irritated her mother and elicited comments in the village. A lot of people called Polyxeni stuck up, and Theodora didn't think they were wrong. She'd repeatedly caught her daughter staring in the mirror, reciting poetry affectedly. She'd scold her for this, but Polyxeni simply ignored her mother's disapproval. Instead, she looked at her almost with an air of superiority and left the room with her head held high.

As for Theodora's youngest daughter, she seemed calmer than the other two, but was quite studious. In fact, her mother was afraid to ever take a book from her hand. At school, Magdalini's grades were excellent, and her teachers said that she must continue her education. Yet Theodora rejected the idea, because she knew that to continue her studies, her daughter would have to move by herself to some large town, and she just couldn't accept that.

More and more often, Theodora escaped to the river, where she allowed her thoughts to flow freely. Every now and then she climbed up high on some slope and looked out toward the sea spreading endlessly in front of her. She wondered what must be on the other side of the horizon. Apart from the time when she married Gerasimos, she'd never left her village hidden in the trees below Mount Olympus, where black clouds rolled in low each winter and deafening thunder rattled your insides.

When Theodora was very small, whenever the thunder struck, she'd turn her gaze to the wild summit of the mountain, in anticipation of something more to come. She never exactly knew what she was waiting for. It was the same now—something was coming, but she didn't know what.

◆ ◆ ◆

Stavros Mantekas cursed under his breath again. He had to admit that he was lost. As the heavy truck groaned, he wondered whether its old tired motor would abandon him in the wilderness. He stopped on a flat stretch and turned the engine off. He must find someone to give him directions, but what sort of crazy person would be wandering about in this wilderness? He lit a cigarette and sat down on a rock. It occurred to him that he must be very tired. Otherwise, how could he explain the voice he heard singing as clearly and beautifully as if it had come from the sky? He looked around him. The voice was coming from somewhere nearby and seemed to be getting closer.

When Aspasia saw the young man sitting on a rock, she abruptly stopped singing. He was looking at her as if he was in a daze. She gave him an annoyed glance for intruding on her private moment. This little flat place was hers; it's where she'd come to sing in peace whenever she could get away. What did this young man want? Why had he turned up in front of her?

Stavros stood up, and before he could say a word, he silently noted that this girl with the heavenly voice was very beautiful.

"Excuse me," he said. "I must have frightened you."

"Yes," Aspasia replied. "I didn't expect to find anyone in this deserted place."

"So I wasn't wrong to think I was lost."

"You're lost?"

"Yes, I have to deliver an order to some store, and I've never been in this area."

"Which store is your order for?"

"The owner's name is Pandelis Karavassilis."

"Ah! He has a grocery store in our village."

"And where is that village?"

"As soon as you make a turn, you're there!"

"Really? From a distance, it doesn't look like anyone lives in this area."

"All the villages here were built like that. It was probably for safety from the Turks. Just when you think there's not a soul around, a whole village leaps out before your eyes."

"And do you live there?"

"Since I was born, Mr. . . . ?"

"Excuse me. My name is Stavros Mantekas."

"My name is Aspasia."

"A lovely name, and a lovely voice you have, miss."

"Thank you. Will you stay in our village?"

"I'll have to. It'll be dark very soon. I got lost here in the daylight. There's no way I could find my way at night."

"And where will you stay?"

"I'll sleep in my truck. I often do that."

"It gets really cold at night around here."

"Unfortunately, I don't have any choice. It's night, it'll pass."

Theodora's mouth fell open when she saw her daughter enter the house with a young man. Aspasia quickly explained Stavros's story and announced to her mother that they'd feed him and let him stay until the morning. Then he'd take his truck back to Larissa.

Stavros turned out to be very good company. He was a pleasant man with a polite manner and very talkative. Originally from Edessa, he lived with his family in Larissa. He had finished school, but not without some trouble because he didn't like learning. He'd become a professional driver to help support his mother, whose husband had died when Stavros was only ten. Now that he was twenty-eight, he managed to make enough from his work to get by easily and not have any debts.

As Stavros spoke, Theodora watched her daughters. As usual, Magdalini was distracted. She just wanted to finish dinner and lose herself again in some book. Polyxeni was also uninterested in their guest's stories. She clearly looked down at this young man for his humble origins and his even humbler work. Sometimes Theodora wondered where her daughter's attitude came from. She always sat at the table with her back quite straight, ate with small bites, and spread her napkin on her knees. At first they'd all laughed at this last gesture, but Polyxeni shot back that only ignorant people tied their napkins around their necks.

When Theodora turned her gaze toward Aspasia, she saw her looking at Stavros with interest. The girl laughed at his stories about his work, and her eyes were shining. If she hadn't already lost her heart, it was only a matter of time.

Theodora made up a bed for Stavros in the kitchen and he thanked her a thousand times for saving him from spending the night in his dilapidated truck. She herself wouldn't sleep tonight—not with an unknown man in her house. She made her daughters lock the doors to their rooms and did the same herself, but she couldn't stop listening for any suspicious noise. At midnight, she tiptoed into the kitchen, where she found Stavros sound asleep. She went back to her room and stood in front of the window. The sky was clear and the moon cast its full light on the earth. In spite of herself, Theodora sighed. If Stavros were to come back to the village, it would be bad news for her. She looked at the moon again and asked why fate demanded that she live alone. Why couldn't her daughters choose to marry village lads?

The moon had no answer for her. It wasn't responsible for people's fate. All it could do was look at them from high above and witness their most secret moments, to hear their sighs and see their tears. It didn't even make its own light, so how could it help?

Stavros got up before dawn. Theodora found him in the courtyard checking the engine of his enormous truck and brought some coffee to him. She sat beside him while he lit a cigarette.

"Are you leaving right away?" she asked.

"I have to," he answered. "My boss will probably shout at me because I didn't come back last night. I want to thank you, Kyria Theodora, for your hospitality. I don't know if anyone else would have done that in your position. You fed me and let me sleep in your house even though I'm a stranger."

"We're all people, Stavros. We must help each other when we can."

Stavros looked around him. "I like it here. It's so quiet."

"Tell that to my daughters, who all want to leave."

"Nobody appreciates what they have. Here, the air is different than it is in Larissa. It's more pleasant."

"That air is swelling my daughters' brains!"

Stavros laughed heartily and stood up. "However much I'd like to stay, I must leave. I have a long road ahead of me."

"If your travels bring you to our village again, you know you'll be welcome at my house!" Theodora said, then wondered to herself why she'd blurted out the invitation.

"Thank you. Next time, if I come, I'll try to leave enough time to fix the stair to the verandah. The wood has rotted and I nearly killed myself this morning when I was coming down!" he answered, smiling, then extended his hand. "Please tell the girls good-bye for me when they wake up."

Theodora watched him leave, knowing deep inside that very soon Stavros Mantekas would return to their village and her house.

◆ ◆ ◆

The step was fixed, the roof was mended, and the old kitchen table was sanded and painted again thanks to Stavros. Theodora wondered exactly how he managed to arrange a route through their village nearly every ten days. But she knew that when someone really wants something, everything is possible. In the end, Stavros became a virtual member of the household; everyone got used to him and if he was occasionally late in arriving, their faces clouded over, especially Aspasia's. Theodora knew her daughter was in love, although she couldn't tell if the feeling was reciprocated. Stavros was polite to Aspasia, as he was to everyone in the family, but he never indicated any desire to be alone with Aspasia.

Soon after Christmas that year Stavros came to visit again. This time, he got caught in a snowstorm that prevented him from leaving. So he went on foot to Mr. Karavassilis's grocery store, where he telephoned his boss, who, however much he yelled, couldn't argue with the weather. Stavros settled himself in the house by the river, and Theodora remembered what it was like to have a man around to help her. He brought in the wood and fed and watered the animals so none of them had to go out in the cold. In the evenings they'd all gather around the fire and Magdalini would read aloud from one of her books. Or they'd listen to Stavros's stories, which were very entertaining.

After ten days, the roads reopened and Stavros was ready to leave again. The previous evening he'd gone to feed the animals as usual. But this time, Aspasia secretly followed him. For some time now she'd felt her heart beating for him. She longed to catch his eye, and every time he left without showing the slightest hint of interest, she was all the more disappointed. That evening, though, she'd made up her mind to clarify the situation.

When Stavros felt the freezing air rush into the barn behind him, he turned to see who was there. He froze in surprise when he saw Aspasia.

"Aspasia! What on earth are you doing here at this hour and in this cold?" he asked.

Aspasia approached him before she answered. "I came to see if you needed help," she whispered, as she looked at him with unmistakable longing in her eyes. Stavros stepped back, placing a pile of hay between them.

"As you see, I'm managing well," he answered, his voice betraying his sudden discomfort. "Go inside, you'll catch a cold."

Aspasia walked around the hay and looked him in the eyes. Stavros took a deep breath and moved away. Even the animals could sense his anxiety. Aspasia approached him again and grasped the pitchfork in his hand to stop him from moving away.

Stavros pulled the fork from her and threw it to the other end of the barn, leaving Aspasia stunned by his violence.

"What's the matter with you?" she asked him. "What did I do to make you angry?"

Stavros grasped her hard by the arm and shook her roughly. "Why did you come, Aspasia? What business do you have alone with me? Don't you understand anything yet?"

"What is it I should understand?" The girl was completely at a loss. "I just wanted to be alone with you for a little while—for us to talk."

"To talk?" Stavros seemed beside himself. "Do you realize how hard it's been for me to be around you? How do you expect me to keep ahold of myself while we're alone? What do you think I am? I'm a man and . . ."

He didn't continue. He had trouble breathing. Finally, he pressed his lips to hers in total surrender. As a sweet sense of dizziness flooded her, Aspasia finally understood that Stavros hadn't been avoiding her because he was uninterested. Rather, he'd been trying all this time to control his feelings. Happily, she curled her arms around his neck and returned his kiss with the same intensity.

As Stavros's caresses became more daring, Aspasia clung more tightly to him. When her legs wouldn't support her anymore, they found themselves rolling in the hay while he covered her with his body. As his hands traveled all over her, she felt herself vibrate like a musical instrument and groaned with delight. Then, suddenly, she found herself alone on the hay. Stavros had leapt up and was now punching a wooden beam with his fists. Aspasia sat up and looked at him in surprise.

"Stavros, what's the matter?" she asked.

He turned angrily toward her again. "You ask what's the matter after what just happened?" he shouted. "Your mother welcomed me into her house and I betrayed her! Any longer and we would have . . . in her own home! That's why we shouldn't have been alone together. That's why I've struggled for so long against this."

Aspasia understood and calmed down. The next moment she got up and came close to him.

Stavros looked her in the eyes. "I love you," he said.

A smile lit up the girl's face. "Now I know. And I love you. That's why I came here tonight, to tell you and find out how you felt. I've been asking myself for so long and you never . . ."

"I respected you and your mother, and now I feel very bad. How can I look her in the eye?"

"You're going to have to find a way. Because she would never give me to someone who's afraid to look another person in the eye, even his mother-in-law!"

"Mother-in-law?"

"She'll be your mother-in-law when we marry."

"Do you mean—you'll marry me?"

"If you ask me to!"

Stavros held her tightly and Aspasia pressed her lips to his again, but then he stopped her. "No more! Resistance has its limits and I went beyond them today. I'll speak to your mother tonight."

"Tonight?"

"I don't want to deceive her for another moment. I respect her tremendously. Go back to the house now, and after dinner I'll ask her if the two of us can talk privately."

Aspasia went back to the house with her heart beating loudly and her body humming from her first acquaintance with sexual delight. That night they ate in silence, as everyone was immersed in their thoughts. After the girls got up from the table and said good night, Stavros stayed behind to smoke. Theodora looked at him angrily.

"I thought you were an honorable man!" she said sharply.

He looked at her with guilt written all over his face but surprise in his eyes. "Me?" he whispered.

"Don't make me angrier by taking me for a fool! My daughter followed you to the barn tonight, and when she came back, anyone could tell from a mile away that she'd been kissed. What right did you have to lay a hand on her? I gave you my trust!"

"Whatever you say, you're right. But I swear to you that I tried. I love your daughter, I loved her from the first moment I saw her, and that's why I tried for so long never to be alone with her. But today . . ."

"Today when she followed you, you didn't pass up the opportunity!"

"Please don't say that! You know I'm a decent man. If you must criticize me for something, let it be that I was a coward and I didn't confess my feelings before tonight. But I want to marry Aspasia. I love her."

"And from what I understand, she loves you."

"That's what she said. I'm not rich, certainly—I'm not like your other sons-in-law, but I'll try to make a good life for her and make sure she doesn't want for anything."

"The wealth of my sons-in-law never mattered to me. The only thing I wanted was to have my children near me. But from what I understand not even Aspasia will stay."

"I won't lie to you—we'll be leaving. We may even leave Larissa. My boss, Kyrios Alekos, wants to open another branch of his business in Kalamata and he's asked me to run it. The money will be better."

Silence fell upon the room.

Stavros knelt down in front of Theodora. "Will you give me your permission to marry your daughter?" he asked with deep soulfulness in his eyes. Theodora could not ignore his plea.

"I'll allow it," she answered, but she knew that once again the decision had already been made without her.

Theodora was much more certain of the wisdom of this match than she'd been with her other daughters. She had lived with Stavros. She knew him, and she knew how much he loved Aspasia. She had only one concern, which she revealed to her mother when she told her the news.

"Who have you come about this time?" Julia wanted to know as soon as she saw her daughter approach.

"And how do you know I'm coming about a wedding?" Theodora asked.

"I've learned to tell from your face! Who are you marrying off this time?"

"Aspasia."

"Well, it was high time! And who's the lucky man?"

Theodora sat and told her mother everything. Julia already knew about Stavros, more or less, having heard about his stays with them now and then.

"I figured he had his eye on someone, but I didn't know who," Julia said, then looked directly at her daughter. "Come on, tell me the rest now!"

"What rest? I told you everything. Aspasia is marrying Stavros."

"So why do you look so worried? From what I understand, the young man may not be as rich as Apostolos or as educated as Fokas, but he's a good fellow, a hard worker and respectable."

"I'm not worried about the bridegroom. It's the bride that worries me."

"But you told me she's absolutely crazy about him?"

"Now, yes. But for how long? I know my daughter. I'm afraid of her love of singing—it could get in the way."

"You're worrying about ridiculous things. Now that she's fallen in love, Aspasia won't be the same. Anyway, when she has children, she'll stop thinking about singing. She'll have other things on her mind.

"I hope you're right."

♦ ♦ ♦

Mother and daughter stood facing one another while Stavros waited in the car. The wedding was over and they were ready to leave. By now, Theodora knew the scene by heart. She was living it for a third time. Once again, she'd watch her daughter leave a trail of dust behind her.

Theodora looked at her Aspasia. "So, that was it. You're leaving now," she said.

"Yes, it's time to say good-bye," whispered Aspasia sadly. "It seems hard to me."

"I've gotten used to it by now," her mother answered.

"It seems like a dream to me that I'm leaving. I'll miss you."

"You won't miss us, Aspasia. We'll miss you, yes. But you're starting a new life with the man you love, and you'll have other things to think about. Just don't forget your home."

"The house by the river," Aspasia said, as if she were speaking to herself.

"Yes. Remember all you've learned in this house and make sure you bring it to your new home. Stavros is a good boy, so respect your marriage!"

"Why would you say that to me? You know how much I love him!"

"I know. But I also know your restless spirit, your sharp mind, and your passion for singing. You have to calm all those things, my daughter, and be satisfied with what your husband's love offers you. And if the trials are very strong, remember that here, in this corner of the earth, is the river. Dive into it to purify yourself again!"

"Like the swimmer of Siloam we learned about in religious classes?" Aspasia tried to joke about it, but her mother's look made her serious again.

"I want you to remember what I said, my child. And I'll ask the Virgin to give you light and strength."

They hugged each other tightly.

A few minutes later the familiar dust filled Theodora's eyes and tears blurred her vision. She turned around and looked at the river. Anger suddenly overcame her as she felt it was making fun of her. She ran at full speed to the bank and furiously began throwing stones into the water. Every stone raised a little jet, and a thousand circles disturbed the calm surface. Panting, Theodora continued until she was quite out of breath. Tears poured from her eyes. For once, the peace and quiet drove her crazy. She wanted to scream but stopped herself. What did she want? Her children tied to her apron strings? They fell in love, they found what suited them, and they left. Had God signed a contract with her that they would always be beside her? She dried her eyes, stood up, and began walking toward her house. As she got closer, it seemed to her that even the house looked sad, in spite of the two chestnut trees that embraced it with their comforting branches. She, on the other hand, was growing old with no one at her side.

Theodora turned her gaze toward the sky. "Where are you, I wonder, Gerasimos?" she said. "Do you see me from up there? Do you understand what a mistake you made when you chose to leave? Do you think that it would matter, at this moment, if you had a missing leg? I need you beside me; I need your laughter to make me smile. You were wrong, Gerasimos. Wrong and selfish."

As soon as she'd uttered these words she felt ashamed. A little while later she began digging furiously in the already well-turned soil of her garden.

Theodora's mind couldn't comprehend that her father didn't exist anymore. Her heart froze just as her body did when she saw him motionless in his bed. He'd just left suddenly, without warning.

She wondered at herself when she realized that despite the numbness in her brain, her body continued to function normally. She helped her mother dress her father's body; she prepared the house for however many would come to sit through the night. A tiny glimmer of thought reminded her to send a telegram to Anna with the news. She wanted to send the same message to her daughters but her mother forbade it.

"But he was their grandfather!" Theodora protested.

"So let them remember him alive. First of all, our Aspasia is a newly-wed. Do you want to bring her here for a funeral? Melissanthi is probably away on some trip and Julia wrote to you last week that she's sick. Do you want her to get worse? Leave your girls in peace. As for your sister, I doubt if she'll come. She left us behind years ago—do you think she really cares about us now?"

But for once her mother was wrong. Shortly before the funeral Anna turned up and everyone was amazed. However, her appearance had nothing to do with her father's death—the telegram hadn't reached her. It was all a coincidence, the sort that fate loves to arrange.

After so many years, Anna had decided to surprise her family with a visit. Little did she know that her father had already arranged his own surprise, and a macabre one at that. The shock was tremendous for everyone. Theodora and her mother were traumatized when they saw Anna in her expensive fur coat, her face carefully made up and her hair dyed blond. Anna greeted them with a smile that quickly faded when she saw the house full of weeping mourners. Everyone froze for a few moments, then resumed their crying, although now they were crying both tears of joy and tears of mourning.

Theodora watched her sister all evening and couldn't believe that this mature, well-dressed woman was the same sister she'd played with, cried with, and followed into a dozen scrapes that had driven their parents to the limits of despair. Anna herself cried inconsolably because she hadn't arrived in time to see her father alive. She wondered how fate could be so cunning and cruel. The trip she had dreamed of making for years, the surprise she had planned for months, had ended in a fiasco.

Polyxeni and Magdalini were the ones most affected by their aunt's arrival. They only recognized her from photographs and the stories that their grandmother Julia had told them about her. Polyxeni stroked the fur coat that Anna had left on a chair. She'd never touched anything so soft and beautiful. She looked around to make sure no one was watching her, then rested her cheek on the fur, breathing in her aunt's faint perfume. When she caught her mother looking angrily toward her, she quickly moved away and went to sit where she could privately observe her aunt at leisure.

"She's a *lady*," Polyxeni said to herself, and she didn't let the new arrival out of her sight. She tried to commit to memory her aunt's every movement, even her posture.

Magdalini hadn't paid so much attention to her aunt's arrival, but she also admired her. She tried to connect the lady she saw with the girl she'd seen in pictures, with her tight braids and knees scratched from running.

◆ ◆ ◆

It was an hour before dawn when Theodora went out into the yard to get some air. She sat on the bottom step and looked at the sky, which had lost a little of the wildness of night. Here and there the blackness above her was turning gray, a sign that in a little while the sun would perform its daily miracle and paint the dome of the sky blue. She sensed that she wasn't alone and turned to see her sister sitting beside her.

"If I remember right, this is where our mother made us sit to have a snack," Anna said nostalgically.

"Yes, you're right," Theodora answered flatly. She hadn't forgiven her sister for staying away so long.

"Do you hold it against me for not coming back all these years?" Anna asked, as if she had understood.

"I can't say I resent you, but there were times when I was angry with you. Why, Anna? Why didn't you come to see us before now?"

"It wasn't easy, Theodora. Sometimes I missed you so much that I'd say, 'Tomorrow I'll get on an airplane and go see them. I can't bear it anymore.' But the next day, I'd get pulled back into my usual routine, and the next airplane would leave without me."

"I understand. There are rivers and tides everywhere, I suppose, real and otherwise. Their business is to carry along anyone who's too weak to resist them . . ."

"I always found out what was going on in your lives," Anna said.

"We didn't know what was happening with you, though. What were you doing all those years? How is your husband?"

"He's fine. We wear ourselves out managing our lives, Theodora. From a distance, America may seem like the land of opportunity and wealth, but to earn that wealth you have to work hard, to suffer, to sacrifice your life."

"Why didn't you have children?"

"At first it was because we both had to work and I had no one to help me. Later, when we tried, it just didn't happen. But you more than made up for what I couldn't do. Five daughters!"

"I still have two of them with me. The others married and left, just like you!"

They stopped speaking. The sky took on the colors of dawn, and the day looked as if it would be a cheerful one for everyone except them. Later, they accompanied their father to his last resting place, along with their mother, who sobbed with grief for the man who'd been beside her most of her life. Theodora insisted that Anna and their mother stay at her house, which was bigger and more comfortable.

Anna was enchanted by the beauty of the landscape. She was fascinated by the river, and the absence of creature comforts didn't bother her at all. She adapted easily to the rhythms of the village as if she'd never left. This almost disappointed Polyxeni, but what really hurt her was the fondness her aunt showed for Magdalini. The two of them would disappear for hours while Anna rediscovered the place she grew up in and saw all the changes that the passage of time had brought.

Magdalini would listen with fascination as Anna described her life in America. She never tired of hearing about the big roads, the cities, and the way of life that seemed surreal compared to life in the village. When she heard about the universities, and the women who studied without any obstacles and worked in beautiful offices or shops, she nearly lost her mind. The girl became almost depressed until Anna had an idea.

"If that's a joke, it's in bad taste!" Theodora said angrily to her sister.

"But why? If you really think about it, it's perfectly logical."

"What are you saying, Anna? That I should give you my child for you to take the devil knows where and for me not to see her again? And for what reason? To study? What's Magdalini going to do at a university?"

"The girl wants to get an education!"

"She's educated enough! What's she going to do with more education? Where will she need it?"

"Now you're not making sense and you know it. Magdalini has a good mind. Why shouldn't she use it?"

"Because I don't want her to leave."

"Now you're being selfish. Are you going to think about what's good for the child or for yourself?"

"Who told you that one precludes the other? My daughter can be happy here too."

"How? If she marries a farmer or a shepherd?"

"What's wrong with a farmer or a shepherd?"

"Nothing if that's what she wants. But Magdalini wants to leave."

"You've stirred up her mind!"

"Theodora, I understand how you feel, but you're not thinking clearly. No one can persuade anyone else to leave unless they really want to. And you've always known that your daughters had that desire! Look at the older ones. As soon as they found someone who'd take them far away, they married and left. But Magdalini doesn't want to marry. She wants to study. You have no right to stop her."

"And you don't have the right to steal my child away from me! You're taking her because God didn't give you children of your own."

"You shouldn't have said that."

"Well, I did. And I won't take it back. Magdalini is my child and I won't let her follow you!"

Theodora found herself by the river again, having slammed the door behind her as she left her sister alone in the house. She sat on the bank, thinking. Why had she been cursed with losing her daughters one by one? Why had fate decided to leave her all alone in her old age, without the sweet presence of her children and grandchildren? As she began to cry, the image of the river became distorted to the point where its waters and her tears became one.

The sound of footsteps made her spring to her feet. She expected to see her sister standing there, prepared to confront her. Instead, she saw the black-clad figure of her mother, and judging from her expression, she knew.

"Be careful what you say," Theodora warned her.

Julia looked at her daughter intently, then sat down on a nearby rock. She signaled for her to sit beside her, and Theodora obeyed.

"You know your sister is right," she began calmly. "This will be good for the child. It's what she's meant to do."

"Anna shouldn't have interfered," Theodora cut in, still angry.

"Anna did you no harm. Inside, you know it. But you're angry that your children are leaving, so you won't admit it."

"Yes, but if Anna . . ."

"If Anna hadn't come back, if she hadn't spoken to the child about America, Magdalini would have found another way to leave. Don't fool yourself. Anyway, we parents must never think about ourselves, but about what's good for our children."

"And what's good for my Magdalini?"

"For her to study like she wants to, and . . ."

"And . . . ? Why did you stop, Mother?"

"Because you never did want to hear the voice of reason. I told you ages ago to remarry so you wouldn't be alone. I brought you the wealthiest doctors, but you—"

"We're not talking about me right now. We're talking about my child. What good will come of her going to America? What does she have to gain other than the chance to study?"

"Are you serious? Your sister and brother-in-law have no children, but they have a fortune! Who are they going to leave it to? Your Magdalini."

"Really, I don't believe you! Where is your brain? What are you thinking?"

"I'm thinking rationally. And you should too."

"That's not rational, it's cold calculation!"

"Call it what you like, the truth doesn't change."

"So, you're telling me I have to turn my heart into stone because Anna has money? My daughter's not for sale."

Julia stroked her daughter's hair, which had begun to turn gray. "Listen to me, my daughter," she continued in a voice that had become tender. "Magdalini isn't a little girl anymore, so you can't stop her. All you can do is to pray that she'll be strong and happy. Give her your blessing so she won't leave with a heavy heart and prepare to comfort the other one."

"Who? Are you talking about Polyxeni?"

"With that one you're really in trouble! She's worse than the others. She's crazy for fame and fortune. When she finds out that Anna is taking Magdalini to America, while she has to stay in the village, you're in for some storms! Big storms! Mark my words."

◆ ◆ ◆

Theodora's mother was right again. The announcement of Magdalini's departure drove Polyxeni to hysteria. She cried, she howled, she beat her head so violently that Theodora had to give her a slap to stop her. Polyxeni managed to resume some composure, but was still very upset.

"Why can't I go with them?" she asked through her tears.

"Do you want to study? Maybe I missed something?" her mother said sarcastically.

"Yes, I want to be an actress!" Polyxeni answered.

"Ah, yes, of course! An actress!"

"Yes!" shouted Polyxeni. "And you can't stop me. Not you or anyone else. I'm leaving!"

"Where are you going? Are you leaving alone?"

"I'm not silly like the others. I'll do whatever I do alone. I don't need a man or an aunt who doesn't have children and takes in strangers!"

If she hadn't been so distraught at losing Magdalini, Theodora might have realized how serious her daughter was at that moment. But she didn't, and afterward, she never forgave herself for it.

The days leading up to Magdalini's departure flowed like the river outside their house, with its occasional surges and eddies. The girl's mood changed from one moment to the next. She'd smiled happily at the thought of her new life, then cry because she'd soon have to leave her mother and face so many unfamiliar things. The atmosphere in the house was tense. With tight lips, Theodora forced herself to speak to Anna, while Polyxeni spent most of the day sulking in her room. When the time came for her younger sister's departure, she kissed her coldly, said a stiff good-bye to their aunt, and returned to her self-imposed exile. Theodora said good-bye to her sister with the same stiffness. Then she embraced her daughter, who was crying.

"Don't cry, my child!" she said, although she only just managed to hold herself together. "The best things are ahead of you. And if something doesn't go as you want, don't be ashamed to come home. I'll buy the ticket for you; you only need to send a message. Your home will always be here."

"And the river?" Magdalini smiled through her tears.

"And the river," her mother answered. "Make sure you become what you dreamed of, but always remember this corner of the earth!"

Once again, Theodora watched the familiar dust as it rose up behind the car that took her daughter away.

She turned to her mother, who was standing beside her, crying. "Do you know something?" she murmured. "I'm tired of saying good-bye to my children. I'm tired of seeing that same dust cloud behind them. I wonder when it'll be the last one's turn."

"I'm afraid you won't have the opportunity to say good-bye to the last one, or see that dust again," her mother answered.

"What do you mean?"

"Look at her. She's like a wild animal, that Polyxeni. Ready to run away. She's just waiting for the chance, and she won't bother to say good-bye to us."

"Don't frighten me. I've had all the sadness I can take. I don't need any more. Your words scare me, Mother—they always turn out to be true."

"I only want to warn you."

Despite the warning, when Polyxeni left, the thunder came straight down on Theodora's head. Everyone was shocked when the girl ran off one night with a troupe of traveling players, just six months after Magdalini left. After her sister's departure, the girl had retreated more and more into herself.

Every time the occasional photograph arrived from one of her sisters, Polyxeni only got worse. She looked at her siblings, well-dressed and smiling, almost with enmity and then disappeared into her room. Theodora worried a lot. She could hear her daughter through the bedroom door, reciting poems or telling fantastic stories or impersonating some heroine born from her imagination.

When the traveling players came to the village, everyone gathered to see them. Some laughed, some made fun of them, but only Polyxeni seemed enchanted by their mediocre interpretations and their ragged costumes. No one suspected what the girl had in her mind, and nobody noticed when she hopped into their truck, not even the players themselves.

She left a note for her mother. When Theodora found it and managed to make out what it said, she let out a small cry, then fainted. Julia, who'd been living with them since her husband's death, found her daughter a short time afterward on the kitchen floor. She bent over her, trying like a madwoman to make her come around. When Theodora finally did, she immediately started to cry and explained between sobs that Polyxeni was gone.

The old woman put her head in her hands. "My God, what shame!" she whispered and began crying too.

"You were right, Mother!" said Theodora, wiping her eyes. "We didn't even see her dust. My daughter, the last daughter I had at home, didn't even want to say good-bye."

"What are we going to do now?" asked Julia.

Theodora looked at her mother calmly. She dried her eyes and came close to her. "We won't do anything, Mother, because there's nothing we can do. Polyxeni is a big girl now. Let her follow the road she chose. We'll just pray that God looks after her and helps her do what she dreamed of."

"And us?"

"We'll stay here . . . in the house by the river. We'll watch it flow and we'll wait."

"Wait for what?"

"For the children to return or for death to take us, whatever comes first."

MELISSANTHI

Although she was exhausted from trials of the journey, Melissanthi, now Mrs. Fatouras, looked in wonder at the entrance to the hotel where she and her husband would stay for the next few days. Never in her life had she seen anything like it. The white marble floors shone; chandeliers, enormous and bright, hung from the ceilings. Although she was wearing a dress that Apostolos had bought her, Melissanthi felt very ugly, very provincial, compared to the elegantly dressed people around her. She was certain that everyone was looking at her disdainfully.

To make matters worse, her husband leaned toward her and said sharply, "Melissanthi, stop staring around you like a fool!"

The girl hung her head, blushing deeply, then followed him to the reception area, where Apostolos gave his name in a curt voice. Everyone behind the counter fell all over themselves to serve him, a sure sign that he was a regular customer. Her fear and insecurity grew. What did she know, in fact, about this man after such a brief engagement?

As soon as he'd received Theodora's permission to marry her daughter, Apostolos had left the village to prepare all the necessary paperwork for the marriage. Fifteen days later he returned, laden with gifts for her and her sisters. Melissanthi was impressed by the beauty of the simple white wedding dress he'd bought for her, by the silk stockings, and most of all by the ring with the flashing stone that she'd wear alongside her wedding band. For her sisters, he'd bought blouses and stockings unlike anything they'd ever seen and delicate pieces of jewelry that they were crazy about. For her mother, he'd bought a thick woolen jacket that she seemed very pleased with. He'd even remembered her grandmother and grandfather and brought them gifts as well.

In the few days leading up to the wedding, Melissanthi and Apostolos went for short walks, usually with his friend, Christos. Only once or twice were they left alone. During those moments, they didn't really talk. Rather, Apostolos would take her in his arms. Swept away with passion, Melissanthi never got the chance to ask him all that she wanted to learn about her future life.

So what did she know? Nothing. Everything seemed strange to her and a little frightening. Nobody had told her what to expect, especially on that first night. What would happen now, when they went upstairs to their room and for the first time she lay down on the bed with him? Her mother had tactfully tried to explain a few things about the "duties" of a wife, but she'd been vague in her advice, too embarrassed to discuss such things in detail with her daughter.

As they went up to the room, Melissanthi continued to keep her eyes low, so as not to suffer another scolding from her husband. A porter carried their luggage, and as soon as he put the cases down, Apostolos gave him some money. When the door finally closed, her husband approached her and raised her chin.

"What's the matter?" he asked. "Why are you keeping your head down all the time?"

"If I raised it, I'd only look around like a fool and make you angry," she answered sheepishly.

At that moment he smiled at her. "My poor little one! I really insulted you. I should have anticipated that you'd react like that and explained some things before we came in. I'm sorry."

"I should say sorry to you because I made you ashamed."

"You made me ashamed? Never! I just didn't want you to provoke any sarcastic remarks that would have upset you. Do you like it here?"

"I've never seen a more beautiful place. But this is the first time I've left my village, and . . ."

"And it frightens you?"

"A little. My biggest fear is that I might disappoint you."

"There's nothing to fear. You're tired. Do you want us to go out to dinner, or should I arrange for them to bring it to us here?"

"Whatever you want."

"All right. Since it's our first night, I'll go down to the bar and have a drink while you relax and have a bath. I'll order dinner. Then we'll eat quietly on our balcony with the wonderful view of the Thermaic Gulf. What do you say?"

"I think that's best. I don't think I'm ready to meet the world."

Apostolos blew her a kiss and disappeared. Melissanthi felt relieved to be alone. She locked the door behind him, then finally looked around her. The suite was enormous; it even had a sitting room with velvet sofas and armchairs. Delightedly she touched the beautiful furniture, sinking her feet into the deep carpet. She avoided looking directly at the huge double bed, but did notice that it was impressive. Heavy curtains hid a door that led to a very large balcony. She drew them aside and stepped out into the clean air that smelled of the sea. She breathed its freshness in deeply and looked around her at the lights of the city. She felt she was living a dream and she didn't want to wake up. Now that she'd married Apostolos, she'd never have to live in the poor, miserable village again.

She sighed with pleasure and turned back to the interior of the room. A door at the far end attracted her attention. Surely it must be a bathroom. When she crossed the room and opened it, she couldn't suppress a cry of delight. White marble everywhere and a flood of light. A huge mirror dominated the room and there were big towels so white that Melissanthi was almost afraid to touch them. There were soaps too, and little sachets with multicolored contents that were totally foreign to her. She opened one and a wonderful smell overwhelmed her.

She turned on the tap and immediately hot water flowed out, steaming up the large room. She undressed and got into the water. She used the best-smelling soap and felt intoxicated by its scent. When she got out of the tub a little while later, the feel of the huge bath towels on her body was like paradise.

Having finished her bath, she faced the problem of what to wear. She looked with distaste at the little cloth suitcase she'd packed. She realized that the cotton nightdress her mother had given her, the one with the handmade lace, wasn't going to do. Two robes were hanging in the bathroom, so she put one on and sat comfortably on one of the velvet armchairs, enjoying the luxury of the room.

When Apostolos returned and saw her sitting there, with her damp hair and the bathrobe emphasizing her nakedness underneath, he felt a lump in his throat. He turned his attention to the porter who was following him, pushing their dinner on a cart. As soon as Melissanthi saw the strange man behind Apostolos, she blushed and drew her robe tightly around her. But the porter didn't even raise his eyes. He passed straight to the balcony and with rapid movements, began setting the table out there. When the door closed behind him, Apostolos, avoiding her gaze, said: "I'm going to take a bath too. We'll eat in a few minutes." Then he disappeared into the bathroom.

Apostolos let the cool water calm him down. He was conscious of the fact that his wife was young and inexperienced, so he mustn't frighten her. On the contrary, he must hold himself back.

They ate, talking very little and enjoying the view, the good food, and the fragrant wine. Apostolos made sure to keep his wife's glass full and watched her carefully, waiting to see on her face some sign of relaxation from the alcohol. When Melissanthi laughed playfully at something he said, he knew that the spirits had performed their miracle.

Nothing and nobody had prepared her for the experience that followed. Apostolos had mustered all his patience as well as all his technique to make sure that this first time would be a happy and unforgettable one for the young girl. For all her inexperience, Melissanthi was demonstrative in her movements. Despite the alcohol, though, when Apostolos undressed her, he could see her eyes fill with shame, and his caresses and kisses at first provoked embarrassment rather than delight. But his patience prevailed and Melissanthi soon found herself sighing in his arms until the climax came for them both. The pain she felt, as this was her first time, didn't lessen the intensity of her pleasure. Afterward, she slept, satisfied, while her husband lay awake, moved by the experience of watching this young girl become a woman in his arms. He wasn't tired; rather, he was ready to go again.

A short time later Melissanthi woke up and looked at him. "Aren't you sleeping?" she asked.

"No, I can't. You go back to sleep," he whispered, his voice a little hoarse.

"If my man can't sleep, how can I?"

She stretched out her hand to stroke his cheek—and it was as if she had lit the fuse of a bomb. Apostolos's thrusting surge of desire inevitably consumed them both; its fire lit their bodies and souls.

The trip to the shops the next day was yet another new and intoxicating experience for Melissanthi. Apostolos kept his promise to her completely. He bought her everything but the town itself. Even she finally complained that she didn't have forty feet to wear so many pairs of shoes, nor a hundred hands to hold so many handbags. They bought only the necessary clothes, though, because Apostolos wanted them to visit the best fashion houses when they returned to Athens, where everything would be custom made. They also didn't visit a hairdresser, in spite of Melissanthi's wishes. Apostolos was adamant about this: he adored his wife's hair and didn't want it cut. He loved touching it and it drove him crazy when he saw it spread out on her pillow or when it fell freely on his chest.

At the end of the day, they returned to their room exhausted, but not too tired to find themselves embracing again in their large bed. Melissanthi's body drove Apostolos crazy; he couldn't remember how long it had been since he'd felt like this about a woman. It was impossible for him not to touch her, not to kiss her; he wanted to lock himself in this room with her and keep her in this bed for the rest of his life. What's more, her reaction to his touch only made him lose his head even more. She seemed as insatiable as he and had proved herself to be a good pupil with an exceptional talent for lovemaking. She quickly learned how to make him lose his self-control and she laughed happily at her achievements.

Melissanthi turned out to be a surprise to Apostolos in every way. After just a month in Thessaloniki, she'd acquired excellent style; nobody would have known that she'd spent all her life in a remote mountain village. She loved to read and bought a lot of books about the arts. One morning when they were eating breakfast, she announced, "Apostolos, I want to learn a foreign language."

"Which one?" he asked.

"French, I think—don't all the ladies in Athens know French?"

"Yes, but what made you think of it?"

"I want to educate myself. Is that bad?"

"No, my darling, but I didn't expect it."

"As soon as we get back you'll find me a teacher and I'll begin lessons straightaway. I don't want your circle of friends to say you married a villager."

"You are my circle and only you interest me."

"Yes, but from what you said, you have a very busy social life in Athens, and I don't want to be behind those other women in anything."

"By virtue of your beauty alone, you are already the most impressive woman they'll have ever seen!"

"Beauty isn't everything, Apostolos," retorted Melissanthi. "I don't want them to say something to me in French and not understand."

"All right, all right! When we go back I'll have to see to my work, anyway, so you'll have plenty of free time at your disposal."

"You haven't told me anything about Athens. What's it like? Is it much bigger than Thessaloniki?"

"When we go there you'll see. Compared to Athens, Thessaloniki is like a big village."

"Impossible."

"And yet . . ."

"And your house?"

"You mean *our* house," Apostolos said. "It's a big house in a neighborhood called Kypseli. The bedrooms are on the upper floor."

"It has two stories? Why?"

"Because that's the way they build houses. So, upstairs are the bedrooms and bathrooms, downstairs are the kitchen, my office, and the living rooms."

"Living rooms? As in more than one? How will I manage all that?"

"What do you mean?"

"How will I clean it? How will I look after it?"

"Sweetheart, you won't even make a bed. We have a household staff to do all those things."

Melissanthi's eyes opened wide when she heard this.

"What did you imagine?" Apostolos asked. "That I'd married you so you could spend your time in the kitchen? We'll have two girls living with us to help maintain the house. We'll also have a cook, and Maria comes once a week to do the washing."

"That's a whole army. So what will I do?"

"You'll tell them what to do, you'll relax, you'll go out shopping, you'll make love to me—is that not enough?"

"For all day, every day? No. Apostolos, I won't manage to become a lady."

"You're a lady in any case . . . except, I have to say, in bed. There I don't want a lady! I want you as you are now—insatiable and demanding."

The slightest mention of the bed made both their eyes shine. And the flame became a conflagration.

◆ ◆ ◆

Apostolos was right about Athens, and Melissanthi was crazy about it. She never tired of looking at all the cars, the people hurrying by, the shop windows with their shining lights, and the dozens of things for sale.

When they returned home from their honeymoon, their staff was waiting for them by the front door. Melissanthi was careful to hide from them the excitement she felt at living in such a large house. She didn't want to appear like the ignorant girl who'd been dazzled by the luxury of the hotel on that first night in Thessaloniki. She knew she'd have all the time in the world to admire all the beautiful marble, expensive furniture, silver, and crystal when no one was watching.

"So, how does your new house seem to you?" Apostolos asked when the staff had gone away.

Melissanthi looked around her before she answered. This place was nothing like her village home with its wooden floors and old furniture, its smoky hearth and faded ottoman. "It's magnificent, Apostolos," she answered with a laugh. "I feel as if I'm in a dream!"

"And so do I when I hold you in my arms."

"Don't you dare!" she said with a smile as she recognized the expression on his face. "We're not alone here."

"They won't come back anytime soon; they have work to do. Besides, I want you now, and I can't see why I should be deprived."

The next moment he locked the door and soon afterward they were rolling passionately on the thick carpet of the living room.

The staff quickly learned not to disturb the master and madam when they were alone together, even if the house were falling down. The girls sighed whenever they heard the couple's noisy lovemaking, which was often. The newlyweds seemed unable to keep their hands off each other.

The hours that the couple spent apart while Apostolos worked seemed endless to both of them. When he'd return, his body would once again become the epicenter of Melissanthi's life. His hands, in particular, drove her crazy with their caresses. Often, in the morning, she didn't want him to leave her without giving him something to remember her by, something he'd have to hurry back for in the evening. And Apostolos was always ready to satisfy and to be satisfied.

While he was busy showering attention on his new wife, Apostolos was notably absent from all his former hangouts. Friends and acquaintances wondered where he was. His honeymoon had ended—why hadn't he turned up? Fed up with this neglect, Christos went to Apostolos's office one day, angry and ready to scold him.

"Welcome!" Apostolos greeted his friend warmly.

But Christos looked at him severely. "I'm impressed that you recognize me; it's been such a long time since you've seen me," he shot back. "It looks like you're not even ashamed."

"Why should I be ashamed? What did I do?" Apostolos wondered.

"Do you have to ask? You were gone for a month in Thessaloniki. That's fine—we knew you were on your honeymoon, but it's been months since you came back, you son of a bitch, and you haven't even given us a sign of life."

"But I'm still on my honeymoon, my friend," Apostolos answered smiling. "Or at least I'm stuck in honey up to my neck!"

"Ah, it's as good as that?" Christos said mockingly.

"You don't have any idea what a creature I married, my friend! Melissanthi is the answer to every man's dream, believe me. She's the perfect woman!"

"And when you say 'perfect woman,' I'm guessing you don't mean at running a household."

"Melissanthi was born to offer pleasure above all things. That's all I'll tell you. I count the hours until I can go home and be with her. Now do you understand why I haven't been around?"

"All right, I understand, but you've become an issue in our circle."

"Why?"

"Because everyone wants to meet the young girl who tied you up at the drop of a hat. They want to find out what you saw in a village girl from Mount Olympus. For three months, you've been in Athens, and they haven't seen you anywhere, not at a restaurant, a club, at the theater. The rumors are running wild. Thekla Papaioannou says you're hiding your new wife, that she's probably not fit to be seen."

"Really? Is the lady jealous? Doesn't she see what a mess *she* is?"

"You didn't think she was a mess when you shared her bed last year."

"There it is! That's exactly why I don't want to introduce Melissanthi to the jackals in our circle. I don't want her to learn anything about . . . the past."

"But you can't hide her forever. Besides, your wife must realize that a forty-year-old is bound to have past lovers."

"Yes, but I have no desire for her to hear about my adventures, and those hyenas wouldn't hesitate to tell her chapter and verse."

"Especially the ones you dumped."

"Exactly."

"I don't think any of them would dare to say anything," Christos said. "They all know your temper. And I don't have to remind you that each one of those 'hyenas' is married, so it's not in their interest to tell anyone about their performances in bed with you."

"You're probably right about that," Apostolos agreed. "So what do you suggest?"

"Next Saturday, Karabatis is giving a reception."

"I know. He sent me an invitation."

"So make an appearance with your new bride," Christos went on. "And put an end to the gossip. Some of the gentlemen, I have to tell you, are glad that you got married."

"How nice of them."

"Not nice at all. They're just glad now that you'll leave their wives in peace."

The two friends laughed together. Christos stayed awhile longer, but he couldn't help noticing how often Apostolos looked at his watch. Clearly, he was willing time to pass so he could return to his wife. If Christos wanted to be honest with himself, perhaps he was a little jealous of his friend.

◆ ◆ ◆

"A reception?" Melissanthi shouted. "What do you mean when you say reception?"

Apostolos had announced his desire for them to go to Karabatis's party, and now his wife was looking at him in a panic.

"Why are you like this, my darling?" he said, trying to calm her down. "Don't you know what a reception is? A hundred or so social gadabouts will be walking around with glasses in their hands, and we'll exchange social pleasantries until the time passes and we can go home. If we're lucky they might have a good band and we can dance. That's all it is."

"For you, maybe. But I've never been to something like that. What will I wear?"

"One of the dozens of new outfits that are hanging in your closet. To be honest, we've hidden ourselves inside all this time and nobody in our circle has met you. And everyone wants to see the beautiful woman I've married."

"That's what I'm nervous about. They'll all look at me like some curiosity. And what if they don't like me?"

"That's the last thing I'm worried about, and it shouldn't worry you either. I'm happy with you and nothing else matters. What concerns me is that they might give you the evil eye out of jealousy!"

That night, if Apostolos's friends were jealous, no one could blame them: Melissanthi had never looked more beautiful. She encountered a number of smiles, some artificial, some friendly. She shook a lot of hands and accepted dozens of blown kisses, which were something totally new to her. Apostolos introduced her to so many people, it was impossible for her to remember all their names. She smiled when she recognized one familiar friend, Christos, among the others waiting their turn to greet her. When his turn came, he embraced her warmly and kissed her on the cheek.

"Finally!" he cried. "You and Apostolos stayed away for too long!" he scolded them both. But now that he saw her again, he understood why his friend had kept her to himself. The little village girl didn't exist anymore; a young lady had banished her, a woman of astonishing beauty and grace.

With Christos now there to keep his wife company, Apostolos went to get drinks.

"I'm glad to see you again, Christos," Melissanthi began shyly.

"Don't worry, honey," Christos soothed her. "You're doing fine."

"Really? I feel as if they're all talking about me."

"And you're probably right, but don't blame them. Apostolos's marriage was a surprise to everyone. And then you two hid away for three months. Everyone was curious, and rumors started circulating. Now that they've finally seen you, they can't help but to talk."

"You say that as if it was the most natural thing in the world."

"It is. If your husband doesn't keep you locked up in the house all day, you'll get used to the . . . comments."

"Gossip, they call it in my village," Melissanthi pronounced with a grin.

"In our circle, it's called 'social criticism,' and you'll soon indulge in it yourself. It's inherent in men and women."

At that moment Apostolos returned with their drinks and found them laughing conspiratorially.

◆ ◆ ◆

The first year of their marriage passed before they knew it. On their first Easter, Apostolos asked his wife if she wanted to go back to her village, but the horror on her face was enough to assure him that she definitely did not, not even for a few days. Inwardly he was relieved; he realized that he too had no desire to be squeezed into his mother-in-law's house. He knew he wouldn't be able to rein in his passion for his wife, which was bound to shock Theodora and the girls. So they sent a card and extravagant gifts instead, salving their conscience and giving them a sense of having done their duty.

They spent the holiday at home, together with Christos and his wife, and soon after, Apostolos gave Melissanthi his gift. She almost fainted from happiness when she opened the package and saw the two airplane tickets for Paris. Another dream was beginning.

In Paris it was as if love was floating in the air. There, nobody was surprised when a couple stopped in the middle of the road to exchange passionate kisses; on the contrary, everyone smiled understandingly. Influenced by this heated erotic atmosphere, Apostolos and Melissanthi's lust exceeded that of their honeymoon. For the first time, the girl's sexual ardor and inexhaustibility made Apostolos anxious, as he realized that he was no longer twenty years old.

Every morning, Melissanthi woke at dawn, determined not to miss a minute of the trip. She delighted in waking her husband up too, using her body as an alarm clock. They walked all over Paris, as she wanted to discover every corner she could. Sometimes she dragged him to some deserted spot and they made love in the bushes, in danger of being seen by some passerby. In the evenings they loved to dance at various clubs, and when they returned to their hotel the next morning, she was ready to start their erotic games all over again.

When they returned to Greece, Melissanthi looked more beautiful than ever. Apostolos, on the other hand, looked exhausted. Christos noticed his friend's fatigue when he visited him in his office a few days later.

"What's up, old friend?" he asked in surprise. "You look tired. Are you sick?"

"No, but I might be soon!"

"Why? Was the trip so tiring?"

"Absolutely exhausting."

"Well you didn't have to explore the whole of Paris. You could have left some for next time."

"It wasn't the tourist activities that exhausted me," Apostolos clarified, and the embarrassment in his voice let Christos know what he meant.

"Don't tell me," his friend blurted out. "That girl is like dynamite!"

"And she spent me!"

"You don't say! I never expected to hear you say that, my friend. You, who had them two at a time, and sometimes three. I don't believe it."

"You'd better believe it. Melissanthi is completely into sex now that she's discovered it. She wants it as often as she wants to eat! Until now, that hasn't been a problem, but it will be soon. I'm not twenty years old anymore."

"But she's still very young."

"Exactly! I went to a doctor and he gave me vitamins."

At this point, Christos began to laugh loudly, which made Apostolos mad.

"A great friend you are!" he shouted irritably at him.

"I'm sorry, but if you really think about it, it's funny."

"Not to me, it isn't."

"Come on, things aren't so tragic. Melissanthi is a young girl and it's natural for her to dive right into . . . sport with the passion of the newly enlightened. She won't be like that forever. Wait until she has children. Then you'll miss the time when she always wanted you!"

"You think so? It's already been nearly two years since we got married, and with such . . . performances, without any protection, and she hasn't got pregnant. In my first marriage, I knew that my wife was sterile, but now—do you think I have a problem that I don't know about?"

"Nonsense! It just hasn't happened."

"I hope you're right. Melissanthi is young. She'll certainly want a child."

"Have you talked about it?"

"She hasn't said anything to me about it. But every girl who gets married wants a child, right?"

"Just as she's . . . unusual in everything else, maybe she is in this too. Anyway, don't think about it. If it's to come, it'll come! As for the other issue, take your vitamins and stay away from the house a little. I bet the atmosphere of Paris influenced her. Even if you're not in love, you fall in love there. And how much more so when you're newlyweds. Chin up, my friend, and know that you have my undivided sympathy in your misfortune."

Christos laughed again while his friend just glared at him. Then, in spite of himself, Apostolos starting laughing too.

◆ ◆ ◆

Some time passed before Melissanthi finally realized she was bored to death. She'd been married for three years, and life had ceased to offer her any new excitement. Apostolos was gone all day, every day. When he came home late each evening, he didn't even kiss her good night— their love life had been drastically reduced. Suddenly she realized that she didn't have a single friend. It was true that she'd never had close friends in the village, but now she lived in almost complete isolation, shut up at home much of the time with nothing to do. She still went out regularly with Apostolos, usually to the theater, but when they got home, he simply fell asleep. She longed for the days when they used to come back and make love until morning. Now, she tried everything to arouse him. Sometimes her efforts worked, and she felt as if the magic of those first days had come back—Apostolos would once again be full of desire. But her successes were few and far between.

One night they went out to a club and drank so much that Melissanthi had to drag Apostolos to the car. There, she gave herself to him, and he responded with such intensity that she thought their troubles had passed. When they got home, Melissanthi got undressed and approached her husband again. With quick movements, she freed him of his clothes and climbed on top of him, a position she knew he liked. Apostolos was once again aroused, although he came with difficulty, something she was experienced enough to understand.

Later, when Apostolos had fallen asleep, Melissanthi carefully observed him. Her husband looked tired. There were dark circles and wrinkles under his eyes. In fact, there were a lot of wrinkles that she hadn't seen before. The skin of his neck looked soft, and his body seemed a little flabby. Suddenly, she felt as if she was committing some sacrilege, so she turned out the light and lay down. This was all in her mind, she thought. Apostolos was still very young, otherwise he wouldn't have responded to her seductions like he had, especially in the car. He'd practically ruined her clothes as he'd torn them from her body. Fortunately, she'd been able to hide her disastrous state with her coat when they'd come home. Any thought that her husband was losing his youth and vigor, she decided, was ridiculous.

Card playing came into Melissanthi's life completely by chance. A lot of the parties they attended those days had a card room filled with eager players. She asked her husband to teach her to play, mostly out of curiosity rather than any real interest in playing. She preferred dancing at parties, as it gave her the chance to be held by Apostolos. Lately, Melissanthi felt like her husband satisfied her sexually in measured doses, like prescriptions from a pharmacy.

When Apostolos taught his wife to play cards, he wasn't surprised to learn that she had a mathematical mind. After all, he was accustomed to discovering Melissanthi's many capabilities. He was relieved when she took to playing, devoting herself to games late into the night, as this seemed to distract her from her sexual appetite. His doctor had stressed that his heart was tired and he mustn't overdo it. He of course didn't dare to mention this to his wife, since it would underline the fact that he wasn't so young anymore.

On Christmas Eve, they attended a party where, for the first time, Melissanthi played cards in a group without her husband. Initially the women welcomed her into their foursome, but they soon realized that Fatouras's beautiful wife was a difficult opponent. She had an amazing memory, and nothing drew her attention away from the game, the result being that when it was over, they had to pay her a lot of money. They could have all stopped there, but the determination to beat her drove them to invite her to another game two days later, and Melissanthi happily accepted. Why not? she thought. Apostolos would be late again, and the house suffocated her. Perhaps if she had a child . . .

This thought had been tormenting her more and more lately. Each time her mother wrote, she asked her if she was pregnant or why they were putting it off. Melissanthi never answered, because she honestly didn't know what to say. She'd never taken precautions with Apostolos, so shouldn't she expect to have at least one child or two by now?

Still, she'd never mentioned it to Apostolos, just as he had never brought it up to her. Even when she overheard unkind remarks on the topic from friends in their circle, she kept silent. In her heart she really wanted a child. But she'd concluded that Apostolos must have some problem and that discussing it would only embarrass him. Perhaps it was his age. Lately she'd been thinking a lot about her husband's age. She'd begun to notice the differences between him and other, younger men, but she knew she didn't have any right to complain. She was grateful that cards provided her with an especially happy distraction.

As Melissanthi continued to indulge her new hobby, she was gone from the house quite a few evenings each week. For Apostolos, this made life simpler. He'd come home early from the factory, eat something light, and sit in front of the fire with an interesting book. He no longer found himself permanently on the alert to avoid his wife. Lately he'd managed to restrict their sexual intercourse to once every ten days, and he was completely happy with this routine, since it didn't tire him out and improved his performance. In between, he enjoyed some respite and took handfuls of pills, always in secret, as Melissanthi had no idea as to the state of his health.

Eventually, what every card player is afraid of began: bad luck. Melissanthi started to lose—a lot. The more money she lost, the angrier she became, and the more nervously—and dangerously—she played. But the result was always the same: she came home without a penny in her pocket. She kept drawing money from her account until the bank manager informed Apostolos, who became furious. Melissanthi had overdone it. By this point she'd lost large sums, and Apostolos began to suspect that she'd turned to playing in the clubs, where they were certainly systematically cheating her. So he decided to intervene. That night he waited up for her.

When Melissanthi came home at dawn and found her husband sitting in the living room, she went to pieces.

"What are you doing up at this hour? Why aren't you asleep?" she asked him in surprise.

"I was waiting for you," he said calmly. "How did the game go?"

"I'm still waiting for my luck to turn," Melissanthi explained, but something inside warned her that her husband was angry.

"It's useless waiting for your luck to turn. Where you go, they're making a fool of you!" Apostolos had raised his voice.

"What do you mean?" Melissanthi shot back angrily.

"While you were playing with women of our circle, you still had some hope of changing your luck. But at the club you've started frequenting, they're robbing you."

"Do you really think I'm so stupid? That they could actually fool me?"

"Those vultures could steal from anyone. It's not a question of cleverness, but it's certainly ridiculous to lose your money just like that. You're losing a lot, Melissanthi. You're always at some club, you've forgotten your mathematics, and the situation is getting worse by the day. You know that you've spent all the money I put in the bank for you? It was a lot of money, Melissanthi. Other people work all their lives and still they can't make one-tenth of what you've wasted at the tables."

"So what do you want me to do? I understand everything you're saying, but try to understand that I had bad luck."

"That's the classic argument of the card player. Melissanthi, listen to what I'm telling you. You won't ever win. They all think like that and they all end up deeper and deeper in debt! I've seen people destroyed by their passion for cards."

"None of this would have happened if you hadn't disregarded and destroyed my passion for you!" Melissanthi shouted furiously.

Apostolos was thunderstruck. "What did you say?" he asked in a voice that came out like a whisper.

"What you heard!" Melissanthi went on. "Or do you think I don't understand what's going on? Don't underestimate my intelligence, Apostolos. In the beginning it suited you that I learned to play cards. We played for hours instead of spending our time in bed like we did before. Later, when I started playing with the others and I was out until late, it was even better for you. Isn't that true? At least, when I played,

I didn't ask you to make love! Why, Apostolos? Why didn't we stay the way we started out? What changed?" The girl's eyes filled with tears.

"You can't understand, Melissanthi . . . You can't . . ." he muttered flatly.

"Nor can you! And now that I've found something that gives me a little happiness again, you want to deprive me of that too!"

Apostolos stood up. "I'm sorry that you see it like that," he murmured. "I do whatever I can to make you happy. Since the beginning of our marriage, that's what I've done. If you can't understand that life isn't only about sex and can't be lived in bed, you're more immature than I thought. Regardless, I can't allow you to leave us penniless. So from now on, you'll find in your account only as much as I think is necessary for you not to harm me financially. If you choose to spend it at the card table, you'll have to do without the luxuries you've grown accustomed to."

Apostolos gave this entire speech without taking a breath. Then he said good night and went up to their room, leaving Melissanthi alone, shaken by waves of impotent rage. She grabbed a vase and hurled it at the wall.

The very next day, Melissanthi realized that her husband wasn't joking. In her bank account she found only enough to cover three or, with care, four evenings of cards. She had to find more money, however she could. Apostolos had already taken all of her jewelry and locked it in a safe, purportedly because he was afraid of a robbery. In reality he had no desire to see so much gold and so many precious stones being sold off to bet on the cards. Melissanthi was furious but she didn't dare say a word. She would have to find another way to get cash.

It never occurred to her that she was stealing from her husband. The way she saw it, it was his fault that she was penniless, just as it was his fault that she'd been so lonely and never had a child. Melissanthi would unstitch the seams in his pockets, just enough for a gold coin to fall through. Then she'd take one or two, or sometimes three. He'd notice that they were missing, but seeing the torn pocket, he blamed himself for not taking better care of his clothes. On the other hand, he congratulated himself when he saw that his wife's bank account wasn't depleting so quickly now.

He proudly announced his success to Christos the next time he saw him, but his friend only shook his head as if he wasn't persuaded.

"What? Do you doubt that I've managed to rein my wife in and stop her from running to the clubs?" Apostolos asked.

"You may have managed it, but in my experience, card players aren't easily stopped by that sort of thing. But there's something else that bothers me. I really wonder why it didn't cross your mind."

"What's that?"

"Melissanthi threw it in your face that the cards are a substitute for the sex she's been deprived of."

"But what can I do? The doctor . . ."

"The doctor was right to tell you to slow down. The problem is that you're not being honest with your wife! If Melissanthi knew that you had a heart problem, she wouldn't think of pressuring you. And she'd feel neglectful whenever she turns to the cards."

"Yes, but she'll see me as an old man."

"She knows she didn't marry a young man. You're forty-something and that's middle aged. She's aware of that."

"The next thing I know, you'll be calling me an old geezer!" Apostolos protested.

"My friend, you're not an old geezer but either your age or your heart problem will eventually make you unsuitable for a girl as young as Melissanthi."

"Where exactly are you going with this?"

"I'm trying to make you understand that if it's not the cards, it'll be something else that Melissanthi turns to to fill her life, and that something might hurt you even more than the card playing."

"You mean she'll cheat on me. No, she won't. It's not like I neglect her. We go out often, I take her to the theater, to the movies. Last year we went to London and . . . on the other subject, it may not be every day, but when it happens, I put all I have into it."

"That 'when it happens' is the problem. True, once a day may not have been a rhythm anyone could have kept up forever, but to go from every day to once every two weeks, if that . . . it's a big step down."

❖ ❖ ❖

Melissanthi secretly continued her visits to the club, always careful of the hours she spent playing. When Apostolos returned home each night, she was usually already there. As for the money, she limited her bets. That, combined with her changing luck and the gold coins she took from her husband's unstitched pockets, helped her mitigate withdrawals from her bank account. For good measure, she also joined the ladies' card game from time to time, but they didn't satisfy her anymore, even though she always won.

That Sunday morning, Apostolos knew he'd had thirty gold lira in his pockets. He had counted them the previous night, before he'd hung his jacket on a chair in their bedroom and gone to bed. Melissanthi had gone to the club that night while Apostolos was at a business dinner and was now down to her last penny again. Without thinking, and with her mind caught up in her need for money, she took four whole lira from her husband's previously unstitched pockets.

When her husband woke up, he put on his bathrobe to go downstairs to drink coffee, but then remembered the liras and took them out of his jacket. He counted them, mostly out of habit, and realized that four were missing. He saw the small hole in the seam of his pocket, but couldn't find the missing coins anywhere on the bedroom carpet. Since he'd gone nowhere before bed the night before, it didn't take him long to realize that he'd fallen victim not only to his wife's stealing, but to her broader deception. The whole time he had thought Melissanthi was confining her card playing to her afternoon games with the women. Now he understood why her bank account balance hadn't fallen to zero that very first week. The lady had discovered another bank, a more secure one.

The blood that rushed to his head made him breathe faster. He was furious. He would have liked to go downstairs and give her a beating for deceiving him for so long, but he knew that wouldn't do any good. Nor, of course, could he go on playing the fool.

"What plans do you have for the afternoon?" he casually asked her a little later as they were drinking their coffee.

"Nothing special," she answered, leafing through a magazine. "Since you're leaving, I thought I'd go and see Mrs. Stathopoulos."

"Cards?"

"Just a little game to pass the time. Maybe you don't want me to go?" she asked innocently. Apostolos ground his teeth with anger but managed to smile.

"Why don't you go? Bela is an old friend—I sometimes play golf with her husband. It's a nice house and you'll have fun. Don't overdo it."

"Of course I won't. You see how well I'm doing now?" Melissanthi said, unaware that she'd been discovered. "I don't go to the club anymore, only to people's houses, and not every day."

"I see that, and I see you don't withdraw a lot of money from the bank. I'm very happy about it. Bravo!"

Without any shame, Melissanthi smiled sweetly as she accepted her husband's congratulations, then looked down at her magazine again. She was sure that tonight she'd hit a winning streak. The four lira she had in her pocket gave her more confidence. Tonight she'd win back everything she'd lost in the last months.

Later that day, Melissanthi stepped through the door of the club and almost ran up the stairs. She dashed into the card room, but as soon as she reached her table, the smile froze on her face. In her usual seat was Apostolos, grinning back at her. As soon as she saw him she realized she'd been caught. The smile disappeared from his lips and his eyes shot daggers at her. When he stood up to approach her, Melissanthi was afraid for the first time in her life. She almost stepped backward, but her husband stretched out his hand, took hers, kissed it with gallant politeness, and then made her sit beside him while he continued his game uninterrupted.

Melissanthi thought she would faint. Surely everyone could hear her heart beating so hard it was about to break. Very quickly she realized that something wasn't going right in the game. Apostolos had an inscrutable expression on his face. He was playing as she'd never seen him play before, with intense concentration, and opposite him her usual opponent, who always won, whatever she did, looked as if he were sitting on hot coals.

She was confused when she heard her husband speak to the man in that calm tone she knew so well, and which didn't herald anything good: "You have three choices, sir. Either we continue, regardless of the fact that I recognize your marks on the cards; we change packs and play honestly; or we give up the game. Choose!"

The other man threw down his cards irritably and jumped up. Apostolos collected the chips in front of him quite calmly, took his wife gently but firmly by the hand, and headed for the cashier. Melissanthi was still on the verge of fainting and her state got worse when she heard Apostolos speak again.

"I'm sure all of you understand that I could have called the police, but I'm not a do-gooder who wants to save the rest of you. It's enough for me that you will not accept my wife here again. I imagine I make myself understood."

"Certainly, Mr. Fatouras," his erstwhile opponent managed to whisper, and Apostolos smiled sarcastically.

They went out silently into the street. More roughly than she'd ever known him to, Apostolos pushed her into the car and drove them home.

Inside she was boiling with anger, but she didn't dare say anything so long as her husband was at the wheel driving madly like the wind. When they went into the living room, she burst out uncontrollably.

"I'll never forgive you for what you did tonight!" she shouted. "You humiliated me! How dare you?"

"You dare to say that to me after you've been stealing from me for months? I trusted you, and right under my nose you stole lira from my pockets that supposedly had holes in them."

Realizing that Apostolos had found out her game, Melissanthi froze in her place.

"You don't have anything to say?" he went on. "Did you think you could go on making a fool of me indefinitely without being caught? How could you have told me so many lies all this time? How could you steal from your own husband?"

Melissanthi couldn't get a word out. For the first time she understood what she'd done and she was overwhelmed with shame. Her actions rose up in front of her in their true dimensions, and they didn't warrant any excuse.

"And to think I'd warned you that they'd cheat you in there," Apostolos added. "Did you pay any attention? Did you think that after a few months in a club they'd turned you into an expert? Do you realize how much you've been made a fool of?"

As long as Melissanthi stayed silent, he grew angrier and angrier. He approached her and grabbed her by the arm.

"Have you nothing to say?" he shouted and shook her roughly.

Her hair, loose as he always liked, hung over her face. Her breasts protruded provocatively from the evening dress she wore, and her lips were half-open. Her breath, which came out short and fast, scorched his face. He threw her to the carpet and fell on her furiously. For a second Melissanthi was shocked, then she responded. Her body hungrily accepted his rough caresses and hard kisses and reciprocated with the same intensity. She tore at his clothes and couldn't restrain her cries of joy as she welcomed her man, the man she had met so long ago, not the old man whose kisses and embrace had been reduced to a lukewarm drizzle, incapable of quenching her body that burned with desire.

Their climax left them breathless. Melissanthi looked at him and realized how much she'd missed this side of Apostolos. She was ready to begin again, but the endless months that had passed with sex in installments frightened her. Naked as she was, she got up and walked to the bedroom, then got straight into the bath. She was startled when she realized Apostolos intended to join her, and she could hardly believe her luck when he grabbed her again under the hot water.

If this whole episode had managed to awaken her husband's former sexual appetite, Melissanthi was content. After that evening, Apostolos became the lover that she'd once worshipped. For his part, he was surprised himself that his body was responding again to the charms of his wife, while his heart didn't demonstrate any disturbing symptoms. Even the doctor admitted that he didn't understand what was going on. Apostolos let himself go back to living the sex life he'd previously had with his eager wife. He cut his work hours, coming home early each day, and they spent their evenings together like they used to. On the weekends the two of them went on trips to the country. On one of these they even decided to buy a country house in Lagonisi.

Melissanthi was so crazy about the little villa that Apostolos bought it for her without a second thought. It was in a deserted spot, a long way from the sea, but with a wonderful view of the water, and it had big verandahs so that even from far away, they could admire the endless blue. Apostolos was impatient for it to be ready, dreaming of the weekends they would spend there, protected by the isolation of the house, making love all day. The bad days behind them seemed almost unreal.

As suddenly as they'd begun, however, so they returned. Apostolos's months-long burst of sexual enthusiasm turned out to be his swan song. His heart condition got worse and his doctor told him unequivocally that he'd have to be very careful if he wanted to live. Melissanthi, still completely ignorant of her husband's condition, didn't know what to think when he began making ridiculous excuses to avoid her, even changing rooms to leave her all alone in their enormous bed. Whatever efforts she made to attract him were in vain.

The house in Lagonisi was abandoned until Melissanthi began to go there alone and spend endless hours walking by the sea or reading on the big verandah. She learned to drive and acquired a car for her trips. During her time alone, she racked her brains trying to understand what had made her relationship with her husband turn colder than ever before. Certainly he was polite to her, but he rarely visited the room that had become only hers, and when he did, it was as if he did so out of duty, without any intensity. Finally, she began to find excuses to avoid him herself. One time it was a headache, one time her period. She was hurt when she realized that Apostolos seemed relieved that he wasn't obliged to come near her, but eventually she was indifferent. It was as if her body, which had longed for love as if it were oxygen, had frozen. All her desires froze with it.

Melissanthi closed herself off from everything, and only when she found her husband offering her a pretty bracelet for her birthday did she realize she was thirty years old. Panicked, she asked herself how the years had tricked her, passing by without her being aware of them. She felt her loneliness weighing her down more than ever. For the first time, after so long, images from the past came into her mind, and she wondered how her family was.

She had regular news from her mother. She had learned about her sisters' marriages and Polyxeni's shocking decision to secretly leave the village. But she avoided regular communication. Her letters were almost telegraphic and she was careful only to refer to the good things in her life, emphasizing how happy she was. As she looked at the sea, her memory cast her back to her village, and her old self was awakened. She became the young girl again with the heavy braid down her back who climbed like the family goats on the mountainside and looked out over the sea, just like she did now. Except that then she longed to leave for a life she thought was ideal. Now, after all these years had passed, she realized that in the end it wasn't.

A light wind was blowing, lifting her hair, and she breathed deeply the smell that came straight from her past. The sea faded before her eyes and the river appeared with its green reflections. Her house: the house by the river. There was no point asking why her life had gone so badly. What had her mother said? "Life is like the river that flows in front of us. It carries you easily with it and pulls you wherever it's going. And a river doesn't come back. If it takes you away, you can't come back . . ."

That's what had happened. The river had pulled her away. She was a little ashamed of herself. She had married a man who'd offered her everything and now couldn't offer her anything more. She'd behaved like a spoiled child. Perhaps if they'd had a child. At least then there'd be something to fill her life. But after so many years, she must give up the idea. And yet, she rebelled against this. *Every woman has the right to motherhood,* she thought. Her own childhood home, always full of her and her sisters' voices and teasing, came back into her mind. How happy her mother seemed when she looked at them, even when they quarreled about some chore they were trying to avoid or for some other silly reason. How sweetly she smiled when she held one of her children in her arms. But Melissanthi herself had never felt like that. Apostolos had given her everything, but he had deprived her of the most important thing. He'd bought a beautiful doll for himself and showered it with gifts and jewelry; he'd used it for as long as he could, then left it all alone.

For the first time Melissanthi felt as if old age was like an illness you could catch, and she was afraid that she would soon look like an old woman, faded and full of bitterness because of the empty life ahead of her. She was thirty years old and living alone in a huge house with a man who grew older every day and was incapable of giving her what her body and soul longed for: sex and a child. What if she were to leave?

She quickly banished the thought. Where would she go? Certainly not back to the village. Whatever her mother had said, Melissanthi knew she wouldn't be able to bear even a week there, not after the life she'd got used to. So there was no way out.

◆ ◆ ◆

Angelos Flerianos was what his name suggested: an angel. At thirty-two he'd become very much in demand in the smart circles of Athens, not just for his immaculate good looks, but for his impressive manners. His courtesies were carefully expressed so that they didn't seem like simple flattery. All in all he was the perfect candidate for a husband for many young ladies, and as a lover for many of their mothers. He had just returned from abroad where he'd completed his studies, and everyone was saying that in addition to his good looks, he was very clever. He had studied civil engineering and had worked for some years in Italy. His love for his country and for his parents, who had insisted on his returning home, were the two basic reasons why he'd arrived in the salons of Athens.

The ship owner Seremetis's party celebrating Greece's Carnival season was the social event of the year, especially since he invited half of Athens. That night Melissanthi decided to dress up as the queen of Egypt. Attired in a suitable costume that outlined her slim silhouette, with her hair hidden under a dark wig and with striking makeup like Cleopatra, she was unrecognizable and dazzling. Apostolos hardly seemed like her companion, even standing beside her, dressed as Mark Antony.

"They used to be a striking couple," one of the partygoers observed. "But Apostolos looks like her father now!"

"It's a pity, the way he ended up," said another.

"I've heard he has a problem with his heart," said a third person.

"Ah, that explains why he's gone downhill so fast!" added her companion.

Similar comments were repeated in various clusters of people that night, although the couple had no idea. Melissanthi chatted with Christos's wife, Nitsa, a tired forty-five-year-old who'd had the unfortunate idea of dressing as a revolutionary, while Apostolos chatted with Christos, who was dressed as a priest, a costume that really suited him. Melissanthi smiled politely at the woman, who was making her dizzy talking about a problem she'd had with her kidney, while she silently cursed the fact that they'd accepted Seremetis's invitation. Lately she was more and more bored at parties, where they mixed only with people of Apostolos's age. The young couples avoided them, and she didn't blame them—the young men had very little to say to her husband, and what's more they liked to dance for hours and have a good time. Apostolos avoided even dancing now. He complained that his feet hurt, that he didn't like the modern dances, that the loud music irritated him, and that he preferred to sit chatting in one of the drawing rooms. Beside him, Melissanthi usually kept time with her feet and looked on nostalgically at the other couples as they spun around the floor.

Angelos was bored with Seremetis's party, as well, although he was too polite to show it. He had accepted this invitation, like the previous ones, only after his mother had insisted. He had to admit that she was right to push him: he'd already begun to get work building villas for many of the people whom he'd met at these tedious affairs. Now he found himself dressed as a Roman centurion in a robe that suffocated him, beside an elderly woman, the wife of some industrialist who had entrusted him with the plans for a single-story house in Kifissia. Angelos would have loved to escape from the woman's endless chatter but he couldn't see a way out, so he just smiled politely, answering her questions with feigned interest, while his gaze wandered freely around the room.

His eyes opened wide in surprise when they fell on perhaps the most beautiful woman in the crowd, and from that moment he couldn't stop staring at her. She was sitting next to a woman dressed as a revolutionary and appeared to be following everything she said. But, precisely because he was in the same situation, he could see that the beautiful woman was bored. She was slowly sipping her drink and Angelos shivered at the sight of her lips resting on the glass. His heart raced as he felt uncontrollable desire to approach her, to hear her voice, to meet her eyes. He noticed the two older men who made up the group. One of them must surely be her father.

"Excuse me, Mrs. Davaris," he said, interrupting the flow of the old woman's conversation. "Do you know who that woman is dressed as Cleopatra? I feel as if I know her, but right now I don't remember where from."

Mrs. Davaris looked where Angelos was pointing and her face lit up. "But of course! Certainly I know. It's Melissanthi Fatouras, the wife of Apostolos Fatouras, the tobacco merchant. He's sitting next to her, dressed as Antony. But where do you know them from, Angelos, my boy?"

"I don't know her. I made a mistake. I took her for a girl I studied with in Italy. With these costumes, you know, it's easy to get mixed up."

"I said the same myself," murmured Mrs. Davaris, and she continued her chatter where she had left off, leaving Angelos to his thoughts.

So, she's the wife of the man I took to be her father. Now Angelos looked at her with renewed interest. This creature was unbelievably beautiful. It was as if unseen strings were pulling him toward her.

Melissanthi felt as if it wouldn't take much for her to start crying from hopelessness. If she had to listen for another moment to the mishaps of Nitsa's kidneys, she would become hysterical. She desperately looked around her like someone drowning in the middle of the ocean, but there was no help in sight.

"Excuse me . . ."

A polite voice was addressing her husband. A Roman centurion—or perhaps it was an ancient god. Someone sculpted with so much beauty couldn't be earthly. Apostolos turned to the young man who now saluted him in Roman fashion and smiled.

"Hail Caesar!" he said to Apostolos and Apostolos returned his greeting.

"Hail, valiant fellow!" he answered.

The young man introduced himself. "I'm Angelos Flerianos."

"Flerianos?" Apostolos repeated. "Are you related to Kostas Flerianos, the lawyer?"

"He's my father, Mr. . . ."

"Fatouras, Apostolos Fatouras."

Introductions followed all around. Only for a moment did Angelos seem to lose his composure, when he held Melissanthi's hand in his. Her white fingers seemed to him like precious porcelain and when he placed a formal kiss on the back of her hand, he felt as if he was paying homage to something ethereal. Her perfume enveloped him like a silk cloak, and he breathed it in deeply. Her eyes, which were looking at him with interest, seemed to him like shining stones that had the power to stop his heart but at the same time to give him life. He forced himself to take part in some formal and meaningless conversation before he dared to ask the question that had been burning on his lips.

"Mark Antony, could I dare to take your Cleopatra for just one dance?" he asked Apostolos.

Melissanthi held her breath and was surprised when she heard her husband reply cheerfully: "Young man, I give you permission, on the condition that you protect her, if necessary, with your life!"

"I swear to you," Angelos answered in the same tone, and offered his arm to Melissanthi, who felt her legs trembling.

She followed him onto the floor. The orchestra played a splendid tango and Angelos took her in his arms with such formality that no one could have imagined that his whole body had caught fire from her touch. They whirled to the sounds of the musicians but Melissanthi didn't dare raise her eyes to look at him. She was afraid of herself and of the shiver that ran down her back. Angelos held his body at the prescribed distance from hers, but the hand that rested on her back seemed to be made of molten iron. It scorched her, making her burn all over. Her cheeks, she realized, were bright red, but inside herself she begged the music not to end.

And Angelos didn't feel anything less. Her perfume clung to him, driving him crazy; it made him feel as he'd never felt before. He wanted to squeeze her in his arms and take her somewhere where he could have her to himself, where he could find out everything about her, every secret thought, every hidden desire. He wanted them to be far away in a paradise made especially for them, where her body would grant him eternal life and at the same time torment him.

As soon as the dance was finished, he blew her a formal kiss and led her back to her husband. He politely said good night to them both, although he couldn't fully conceal the love that burned in his eyes for this woman who had come so unexpectedly into his life. He got into his car, unsure of where he was going, and drove almost blindly, as he kept seeing her image in front of him and the small space around him had filled with her perfume. When he got home a short time later, he lay down on his bed, fixed his eyes on the ceiling, and let himself relive, minute by minute, their dance. Without a second thought he decided that she would be his—otherwise he would literally go mad.

Melissanthi couldn't wait to leave the party, and blessed her husband when he announced he was tired and took her home. She lay down naked on the bed, her body burning all over, and replayed in her mind, minute by minute, the dance. She felt as if, without exchanging even one word, she and Angelos had said everything. She knew that it was one of those rare instances when two people meet their other half and no words are needed to explain it. She'd spent so many months trying to persuade herself that love was in the past for her, but it had taken only a moment to turn everything upside down. A single dance had shown her that she'd fallen into a state of numbness incompatible with her age and her sexual desires. She had no inhibitions; no inner alarm sounded, because her whole being had been shaken by the appearance of Angelos and the feelings he aroused in her. She would face the consequences of this desire, whatever they cost. She knew from the first moment that it wouldn't be forever and that it would have to happen with the utmost secrecy and discretion. She owed her husband that much—and more. She knew that she shouldn't abandon him or deceive him like this, but her body and heart didn't recognize any obligation. Angelos would be hers; otherwise she'd go mad.

Neither of them had said anything about their next meeting. They hadn't planned it, but, as if they had, Angelos and Melissanthi set out on the same day, at the same moment, for the same destination: Lagonisi. The day after the dance, Melissanthi told Apostolos that she needed to get away for a little while and would spend two or three days at their country house. Her husband wasn't surprised. He knew that his wife especially loved that house and he smiled when he saw her loading books from his library into her luggage.

"Apart from all those books," he said, "take some warm clothes with you. It's very cold."

"I don't expect to go out of the house much," Melissanthi answered.

"Why don't you take Daphne with you to look after you?" he suggested.

"I can do without her," Melissanthi was quick to answer. "I'm going there to relax. If I've got Daphne asking me every hour what I want to eat or polishing the silverware, it'll get on my nerves."

It was true that she didn't want anyone with her, and she rarely brought along one of the girls who worked in the house. She preferred to look after everything herself. She could be a housewife for a few days, even though she'd almost forgotten what that entails, just as she'd forgotten what it was like to be a woman.

The day after the dance Angelos got into his car without knowing where he wanted to go. He didn't understand how he'd ended up in Lagonisi. He'd never visited the area. But he found himself walking on the shore, throwing stones in the sea, with the leaden sky above his head and a frozen wind in his face.

As soon as Melissanthi arrived at the house, she dropped off everything, then got back in her car and drove toward the beach, despite the fact that it looked like rain. When she saw Angelos coming toward her on the sand, throwing stones into the sea, she froze on the spot, certain that he hadn't yet sensed her presence.

Angelos stopped suddenly in front of the vision that played out before him. It had to be a vision, because it couldn't possibly be her. He stood there, gazing. Without the heavy makeup she wore as Cleopatra, and with her long hair blowing in the wind like silk ribbons around her lovely face, she looked even more magical.

As their eyes met—his as blue as the sea and hers the color of wine and honey—the young couple felt drunk with enchantment. A hazy smile lit up her ethereal face, a smile only for him, and he felt his heart stop at the sight. His hands, sure and firm, grabbed ahold hers, which had automatically reached out to meet him.

"If this is a dream, I'd rather not wake up," he told her simply and Melissanthi smiled.

"Two people can't see the same dream at the same time!" she answered. "What are you doing here?"

"I was suffocating in my house," he said. "I went out to get some air and I don't know how, but I found myself here. You?"

"I have a house here. I came for a few days," she answered, shivering at the coincidence. All the fates were on their side.

"And Mr. Fatouras? Didn't he come with you?"

"He couldn't leave his work."

She stopped speaking and they looked at each other as they both silently asked themselves why they were wasting time talking

116

pleasantries. Then, like kindred spirits, they began walking side by side on the deserted beach.

"I want to know everything about you," Angelos declared.

In a low voice, Melissanthi began telling him about her life. She didn't hide anything from him or deny any responsibility for mistakes she'd made. She was honest about the motives that had led her to marry Apostolos, and didn't cast any more blame on him for the state of their marriage than was appropriate.

"Do you love him?" Angelos asked, as soon as she'd finished.

Before answering, Melissanthi stopped and looked at him. "If you're asking me if I'd leave him, I have to tell you that I'm grateful to Apostolos for all that he's given me, and I'll never abandon him, whatever happens, whatever the cost is to me," she answered.

"I understand, even if that wasn't the purpose of my question."

"I don't love him anymore—at least not in the way that a woman should love the man she married. I feel for him, though, and I will never hurt him."

"You're an honorable person, Melissanthi, and I admire that."

"I wouldn't say that what I'm doing now is honorable, nor what I've been feeling about you since I met you yesterday. You and I know where it will lead."

"Yes . . ."

They stood looking at one another. It began to rain but it meant nothing to them. The heavy drops were what they needed to quell the fire that was burning their whole beings. Without speaking, they returned to their cars and Angelos followed Melissanthi to her house.

They crossed the front step, dripping.

"I'm really afraid we'll catch a bad cold," she called cheerfully and hurried to change her clothes.

A few minutes later they were both sitting in front of a roaring fire, wearing bathrobes and sipping brandy. The wood crackled with a tender sound as it burned, while the rain lashed the windows. Although the storm felt somewhat like an annoying and unwelcome visitor, at the same time its song caressed the ears of the two lovers, like musical accompaniment to their conversation. Angelos listened delightedly as Melissanthi told him stories about her childhood by Mount Olympus. He was enchanted by her description of the tall chestnuts and plane trees that shaded the place and never tired of hearing about her childhood scandals and the house by the river. They laughed a lot at the adventures of Angelos while he was studying abroad. He didn't hide from her his romantic entanglements. He also told her about his childhood, about his parents, whatever there was to tell about himself. They didn't talk about the two of them, or their future, nor did they touch each other. Morning found them still sitting by the fire that they'd fed all night and which was still filling the house with a sweet warmth.

The sun refused to emerge that day, which may be why they failed to realize that dawn had broken, shut up as they were in the warm house with the curtains drawn. They only understood that the night had passed when Melissanthi's eye fell on the clock above the fireplace.

"Do you know what time it is?" she asked.

"No! And I'm content not to."

"It's six o'clock in the morning, Angelos!"

"And . . . you want me to leave and you're telling me tactfully?"

"Certainly not! But I do want some coffee," she answered smiling. "And to be honest, I'm hungry!"

They ate their breakfast and then went back to the fireplace with two cups of coffee. Angelos threw more wood on the fire, sat down on the woolen rug, and stared for a while at the graceful dance of the flames. He turned and looked at her face and the calm that had spread over her features, then leaned over and planted a kiss beside her lips. Melissanthi turned toward him, and their lips met. They both knew that from here on there was no turning back. Hungry for one another, they quickly shed their clothes. Their passion burned with such intensity, it was as if their bodies envied the fire beside them. It was the beginning, and contrary to every law, they knew that what they felt right now would never end. It would inevitably overwhelm them, their souls and bodies defenseless to its demanding power.

They stayed for three days and three nights in that house stamped by their love. For three days and three nights, they gave and took the nectar of their souls and bodies. They tasted its sweetness, they immersed themselves in its sacred perfume, and they were born again from it. Whatever fate had in store for their future, nothing would rob them of these days they had shared. Nothing and nobody could come between them except for God. Only He, the Ultimate Judge.

Melissanthi returned home to Apostolos with a heavy heart. She allowed him to kiss her on the cheek and wondered at herself that she could still look him in the eye after everything she'd done in the last three days. That evening, when they were eating, she watched her husband carefully and observed that he looked older than ever. The few white hairs he had when she met him had taken over his whole head. There were bags under his dull eyes and his face had lost its former brightness. Even his posture had changed. Apostolos, who had always looked so proud and erect, had begun to stoop and shrink. She almost felt sorry for him, but wondered at the same time why he had changed so much. She remembered her grandfather who, when he was the same age, looked so much younger and more vigorous. Even a short time before she married, she remembered him walking quickly, his body straight as a candle, climbing the mountain like a teenager and running here and there all day without getting tired. Why couldn't Apostolos's legs carry him like that now?

"Are you feeling all right?" she suddenly asked her husband.

He looked at her in surprise. "What put that into your head?" he said.

"I don't know, you look tired . . ." Melissanthi murmured, already regretting her question.

"There's been a lot of work to do at the factory lately. Maybe that's why."

"Apostolos, you must take more care of yourself! You're not—" She cut herself off, conscious of what she was about to say.

"Why did you stop? Because you would have said that I'm not young anymore? It's the truth, my dear, and I know it better than you do," Apostolos answered calmly.

"I didn't want to make you feel bad," Melissanthi whispered regretfully. It wasn't enough that she had deceived him; she had to hurt him on top of it.

"You didn't make me feel bad. The only thing that makes me feel bad is that I deprive you of some pleasures that other young women like you have," he reassured her tenderly.

At that moment Melissanthi jumped up from her chair, her eyes full of tears, and embraced him. "Don't ever say that again!" she shouted. "I'm perfectly fine. You haven't deprived me of anything; you've never deprived me of anything."

"I deprived you of . . . a child."

Melissanthi looked at him intently. Never, in all the years of their marriage, had Apostolos touched on that subject. "What are you saying?" she responded in a voice that trembled.

"We've never discussed it, but . . ."

"And it was a good thing that we never discussed it. There wasn't anything that we could do about it," she said quickly, wanting to end the conversation there.

The night, in the quiet of her room, Melissanthi thought about her husband's remarks. She couldn't understand what had provoked Apostolos to bring up the subject of children, especially now. Before long, though, the conversation faded from her mind and her thoughts flew unhindered to Angelos and the wonderful days they'd spent together. They'd agreed they would avoid their social circle, so they wouldn't find themselves together at parties. They would be completely discreet, completely careful. Melissanthi was absolutely firm on that subject. Angelos respected her wishes and only accepted an invitation when Melissanthi informed him that she had declined it.

The house in Lagonisi, hidden in the wilderness, far from inquisitive eyes, was the ideal place for them to meet. Apostolos hadn't set foot in the place in years and showed no desire to go there now. The little villa had become Melissanthi's regular refuge. More and more often she left Apostolos and set out in her car for Lagonisi. In summer, the region was a delight, but they had to be even more discreet. There were more people about, and although the villa was isolated, it was more likely that someone would observe that there were two cars parked there, so Angelos left his car some distance away and walked to the house. There, with the curtains drawn, they indulged completely in one another.

Whenever they planned a trip to the villa, Melissanthi couldn't wait to abandon herself to Angelos's arms. If their departure was delayed by his work, she thought she'd go mad with desire. Every fiber of her body wanted him; his absence pained her and she paced around the house in Kypseli like a lion in its cage, full of irritability. But all that passed as soon as Angelos telephoned her to say they could leave. She would drive as if she were being pursued, and the miles seemed endless until she finally arrived and could surrender herself to their unquenchable passion.

◆ ◆ ◆

Christos looked around him in surprise. Apostolos had invited him to dinner and he'd assumed they'd be joined by his friend's wife.

"Isn't Melissanthi here?" he asked.

"Melissanthi's in Lagonisi."

"Again?"

"What do you mean by 'again,' old friend?"

"During the last month she must not have spent even three days with you. Whenever I ask you how she is, you tell me she's in Lagonisi."

"And where would you like her to be in August? All of Athens is away."

"Yes, but you're here. I'm sorry, it's not for me to say, I know, but why don't the two of you go somewhere together?"

"You know why. The state of my health won't allow me to go on long trips. As for Lagonisi, Melissanthi may like it, but I get unbearably bored there. Still, I can't stop her from going. When it comes down to it, I can't offer her anything better. Leave it, my friend. I didn't expect to end up like this, but . . . just leave Melissanthi alone. Under the present circumstances she's trying to enjoy herself. With dignity. She's a young girl shut up in a cage for life with an old man!"

"Hey! Not so old."

"Not in years, but my physical situation gets worse and worse."

"Meaning?"

"Meaning . . . nothing. That's just why it's better for her to leave."

◆ ◆ ◆

Meanwhile, in Lagonisi, Melissanthi and Angelos were having their first argument.

"What are you saying?" she shouted at him irritably. "We made it clear at the beginning! I'm never going to abandon Apostolos! Why are you putting me in such a difficult position now?"

"I love you, Melissanthi. I can't manage without you."

"You don't have to live without me. You have me."

"Yes, but how often?"

"Whenever we can. You're the one who has a job, you're the one who's always delaying our coming here. Why are you complaining?"

"Because I want to have you with me every day, every hour, every minute. I want us to get married, to have a family."

"That's not happening."

"Melissanthi, my parents are putting pressure on me to marry, and I don't blame them. I have a job, I earn plenty of money—they're right to want to see me with a woman at my side."

"And what do you think would happen? Do you think your parents will jump for joy when you present them with someone else's wife?"

"It wouldn't bother them."

"If you think that, you're naive! If I divorce Apostolos to marry you, everyone will curse us. Don't you understand?"

"No, I don't want to understand it. In the end, they'll talk; they'll talk, and they'll get over it and leave us in peace!"

"Angelos, try to understand. Apostolos is my husband. I don't want to hurt him when he's been nothing but good to me, always. He offered me everything."

"But I can offer you everything too. In fact, I can offer a lot more than an old, tired husband can. And money—if that's the issue, I promise you won't do without anything."

"You shouldn't have said that! What do you think I am? A calculating woman whose only interest is a man's wealth?"

The shock on her face brought him to his senses. The next moment he was kneeling in front of her, begging for forgiveness.

"I don't know what I'm saying anymore," he said. "I'm sorry, my love! I'm terribly sorry. I love you, Melissanthi. I'm like a madman when you're not beside me!"

"If you ever speak to me like that again," she warned him coldly, "it's over. From the first day I made it clear to you that Apostolos has given me everything. I feel for him, and I'll never abandon him. It's bad that I'm with you but that's because . . . you're something I can't control. Don't make me regret that too."

"No! Never regret what we feel for each other. You're my life, Melissanthi. Don't blame me for struggling like this!"

"I'm sorry I can't offer you more," she whispered. "I love you too, you know that, but I can't become yours in the way you want. I am yours in the only way I can be: with my body and soul."

She demonstrated this to him soon after. They made love with the urgency of two people who can only possess one another during stolen moments. But Melissanthi knew that the preceding quarrel would be their last. For some time, she'd been able to see the end of the alley they were walking along. Angelos was just thirty-three years old and both handsome and successful. It was only a matter of time before the pressure from his parents to marry would be too great. There was also his own need to consider, to have a woman beside him on a permanent basis, a woman for good and bad times, a woman to give him children. She had been with Angelos for a year and she didn't see how it could continue much longer.

And then came the remorse—tormenting, fierce, and merciless. It hadn't bothered her throughout their entire affair, but now she felt it in full force. It was wrong, what she'd done to all those around her. First of all, she had deceived her husband in a shameful way. He slept peacefully, ignorant of the fact that the house he'd bought to please her had been transformed into her love nest. She'd left him alone for end-less days, when perhaps he needed her but never told her out of guilt for imposing such a restricted life on her. Next in the chain of remorse was Angelos. There the fates dug their sharp nails into the depths of her soul. What right did she have to keep him in a relationship that didn't lead anywhere? What right did she have to deny him the life he deserved? His parents were completely right. He should have a family, and as long as she imprisoned him in her embrace, he wouldn't have one. She had no illusions. Angelos loved her and was ready to make any sacrifice for her, but if she really adored him, shouldn't she set him free? Perhaps he would suffer in the beginning, but afterward he'd find his way.

In an effort to put an end to her story with Angelos, Melissanthi asked Apostolos to take her on a long trip. She would leave Angelos a letter explaining to him that it was all over and asking him to respect her decision. It would be easier that way, because if she had to face him, she might not be able to go through with it. It was Apostolos, however, who ruined the plan.

"What you're asking me can't happen, Melissanthi!" he shouted.

"Why? It's been years since we've been abroad," she complained. "Anyway, I'm not asking you to go somewhere you don't like. I thought we'd spend a month in Paris, and right after that, if we're in the mood, we could go to London! And then we've never been to Spain, and there's always Italy."

"First of all, it's impossible for me to be away from my work for so long. You're talking about at least a three-month trip."

"OK, if not three months, then what about at least two?"

"It's not happening, Melissanthi. I can't leave."

"But why? You used to go on trips all the time and you enjoyed them."

"It was different then. However much I want to please you I can't do it . . . unless . . ." Apostolos broke off.

Melissanthi looked at him in surprise. "Unless what? If you can only go for a shorter time, that doesn't bother me. Just tell me yes. I really need to get away for a little while. Please, Apostolos."

"Why don't you go by yourself?" he asked.

"By myself?" Melissanthi was nearly speechless.

"Yes, go to Paris—you enjoy it—and stay as long as you like. You speak French, you know how to get around by yourself from the times we've gone there together. Where's the problem?"

"But . . . alone?"

"Why not? When you disappear for weeks in Lagonisi, do you have friends there? I don't go with you."

"But Lagonisi is one thing, Paris is another."

"That's silly! Just because I can't come with you, I see no reason why you have to sit like a prisoner with me. You'll go, you'll have a change of view, you'll shop, and I hope by Christmas you'll have come back."

"Have you gone crazy, Apostolos? It's only October."

"I know what I'm saying. Paris is like that. You won't even notice the time pass. And if you do, well, you mentioned wanting to go to London as well."

"Oh no. Since you won't come with me, I'll only go to Paris. In a month, at the most, I'll be back."

The letter she would leave for Angelos troubled her a lot. Hand and mind didn't work together, and she wrote versions and threw them away until there was a heap of crumpled paper on the floor beside her. She'd run out of time. The next day she was leaving. Everything was ready; her suitcases were even by the door. She had to figure out how to say good-bye to him, in a way that would make him understand that their separation was final.

On the way to the airport, she had the taxi stop by Angelos's office, where she slid the white envelope under the door. He would find her letter in a few hours, but he wouldn't be able to do anything about it. By then, she would have taken off for the City of Light, where she'd find a way to face the darkness that would envelop her from now on. As the airplane took off, Melissanthi felt her heart ache, knowing that when she returned, loneliness would be waiting for her again. The dull house in Kypseli and her empty life. She had already decided that as soon as she got home, she would sell the house in Lagonisi. It would be impossible to go back there, where every corner held the memory of a love that had the misfortune to be born in the wrong place at the wrong time.

Paris greeted her with rain and a dull atmosphere that weighed down her spirits even more. She hailed a taxi and gave the driver the name of a hotel that wasn't as large as the one she and Apostolos used to stay in, but had a better view of the Seine. Her first order of business when she got to her room, despite the rain, was to open the door onto the balcony and rest her gaze on the great river. Once again, she'd sought refuge beside a river, just like when she was a child. Back then, she would let its green currents carry all her cares far away. Then she would go back home feeling lighter. If only this moment were so simple. It had been a month since she'd sent even a card to her mother. Theodora was capable of figuring out that something wasn't going well in her daughter's life, even from a conventional letter. Besides, Melissanthi didn't want to write lies, and naturally she couldn't tell the truth.

Just then, Angelos came into Melissanthi's mind, and she wondered how he'd reacted to her letter. In her imagination she could see his blue eyes darkening, just like the sky as soon as a shower broke. She didn't doubt for a moment the pain he would be feeling by now. She had chosen her words very carefully so as not to leave him any hope. She avoided saying where she was going, only that she'd be gone for quite a long time to allow him to get over his initial grief.

The tension of the past few days and the sleepless night she'd spent before her trip began, together with the hot bath she'd taken, helped her to sleep deeply until morning. Still, when she woke up she felt that her long sleep had offered neither rest nor a sense of well-being. She pulled the curtains and looked at the landscape. It was still raining; everything was dull and gray.

"Better," she said to herself. "The weather matches my mood."

She dressed warmly, put on a raincoat, and went out for a walk. She couldn't stand to stay shut up in her room. The absence of Angelos was already so painful she almost regretted leaving him. She thought of taking the first plane back, of running to find him and leaping into his arms, but her last dregs of logic held her back. She kept walking until she felt her legs wouldn't carry her anymore, then hurried into a little bistro that smelled wonderfully of fresh coffee and croissants.

She sat near the window to watch the rain that had grown much heavier, like a thick curtain, lashing the streets. People under umbrellas were walking hurriedly while the cars threw up jets of water as they passed. At the next table a couple sat holding hands, their eyes shining with the love they felt. The girl was leaning against the man and he was speaking tenderly to her, now and then planting a kiss on her lips.

At that moment Melissanthi wondered just who she was kidding. Why had she thought that, in a city where love ruled completely and uniquely, she would be able to forget her own love? What did it matter that she was doing the right thing? Since when did the heart admit its mistakes and eagerly withdraw? Melissanthi suddenly stood up, paid her bill, and, careless of the heavy rain, went out again into the street. At least under such a downpour she wouldn't see others living what she had abandoned.

She almost smiled when she nearly bumped into a couple kissing in front of her, completely absorbed in one another. Without intending to, she stopped and stared at them. The couple separated themselves, then ran away, laughing under the rain. Melissanthi felt the rain on her own face, but to her it wasn't rain; it was the blood of her wounded spirit. She returned exhausted to her hotel and ordered a meal brought to her room. Then she called Apostolos to tell him lies about the good time she was having.

Three days in Paris had wrecked her. Even though the weather had improved a little, the sun, dull and murky, came out rarely. It didn't have the strength to revive her or the city. Melissanthi had walked more than ever and looked in dozens of shop windows without remembering anything. She spent hours in the Louvre, incapable of appreciating its beauties. She drank and ate without tasting anything, asking herself constantly what she was doing here, and yet she didn't leave.

Five days later a strange day dawned over Paris—something like a duel between the sun and the clouds. Although at first it gave every appearance of being a sunny day, in the end heavy clouds defeated the sun, which hid behind them despite its efforts to rule. When it found some unseen opening, it sent its rays down—just enough to announce its presence, but immediately afterward a leaden wall imprisoned it.

Sitting at an outdoor café despite the cold, Melissanthi absent-mindedly watched the contest, certain that the waiter she'd asked to serve her outside must think she was crazy, at the very least. But it was impossible for her to go back into the small, warm café full of the voices of people who were living, who had feelings and could express them, whereas she felt empty of everything. It was as if her pain had turned her to stone.

The first drops of rain that fell on her were quite heavy, a sign that a storm was coming. Melissanthi looked at the black sky and hurried to get up. Her hotel was close, but the way it was beginning to rain, she'd be soaked in a few seconds. Walking quickly, she took the road back. It was obvious that the raincoat she was wearing couldn't protect her. She went into her room dripping and cursing. What had happened to Paris? Maybe, given the way her mind was scattered, she had arrived in London and didn't know it? She undressed and got into the bath, where she let the boiling water suck all the freezing rain out of her, then got out and wrapped herself in a warm robe. She didn't have many choices. She would spend the afternoon shut up in her room, happy that she had enough magazines to pass the time.

The knock at the door surprised her. She hadn't ordered anything and she wasn't expecting anyone. Certain that somebody had made a mistake, she opened the door with a conventional expression on her face, ready to answer the stranger politely. Her mind refused to accept what she saw. Her logic rejected the sight, and she began to think she'd gone completely mad. In front of her stood Angelos, his features distorted with tension, his eyes red, and his hands deep in the pockets of his overcoat. Melissanthi took two steps backward, giving him the opportunity to come into the room and slam the door loudly. He grabbed her by the arms and shook her hard. Melissanthi's hair escaped from the towel that held it and crowned her face.

"Don't do that to me again!" Angelos groaned.

He indicated he had more to say but he couldn't speak. He pressed his lips to hers with a force that showed how deeply he was hurt. He pushed her roughly onto the floor and fell on her just as he was, with his clothes soaking wet from the rain. Despite the pain his every movement caused her, Melissanthi, for the first time in days, felt alive. She helped him remove his clothes, and gave herself to him completely, her heart singing hymns and her body opening like a rose petal that accepts the sun's beneficent invasion into its velvet recesses. His quiet weeping frightened her and woke her numbed brain. She turned and saw the tears flowing down his face, fed by two blue lakes that couldn't bear the storm of his soul.

She sat up, shaken. "You're crying? Why?" she asked, reaching out her hand to stroke him.

Angelos shot up. He wrapped a towel around himself and lit a cigarette. His gaze, impossible to read, was directed out the window toward the rain. "Why did you do that, Melissanthi?" he asked. "Why did you go away and leave me that letter? Didn't you realize you were driving a knife straight into my heart? Didn't it cross your mind that every word would open another wound?"

"I thought I was doing the right thing," she whispered as she put on her robe and clung to him helplessly, wanting his protection.

"What cuts us in two can't be right!"

"When I was growing up, my father died because he refused to let them amputate his leg to save him from the infection. He'd stepped on a rusty nail."

"And what does our love mean to you? Is it an infection that made you try to cut us in two? Why? So that we can have a crippled life?"

When Melissanthi didn't answer, Angelos tried again. He took her by the arm, gently this time. He looked at her tenderly and his voice emerged as a whisper.

"I can't live without you, my darling. If you force me to do without you, then I'd rather die. I can't breathe without you, and the sun doesn't come out when I'm far from you. What can I do with a life in the darkness? When I read your letter, the ground slipped from under my feet. Don't do that again to me, Melissanthi . . . please!" he said and held her tightly in his arms, with the urgency of a man who had nearly lost his life in a shipwreck.

When he released her, Melissanthi sat overwhelmed on the bed. "How did you know that I was here?" she asked.

"I was lucky—but also cunning."

"Meaning?"

"I went to a club that I know your husband goes to. I pretended I had run into him by chance and started a conversation with him. I asked him, out of politeness, how you were, and it didn't require a great effort for him to tell me everything, even the name of the hotel where you were staying. Fortunately I had a passport ready."

Melissanthi lowered her head thoughtfully and Angelos took her face in both of his hands.

"Listen to me, Melissanthi. Your husband is a good man who once rescued you from poverty. You generously gave him so many years of your youth and beauty and stood beside him with dignity and love. Right now he can't offer you anything you want, and you can't give him anything he can bear—so what harm are we doing?"

"Maybe it's too convenient, this position of yours?"

"Melissanthi, it's not right for you to feel sorry for your husband at a time when without you I'm lost. And I know you feel the same. You can't persuade me it's not so."

"I never said I'd stopped loving you."

"So never leave my side!"

"But it's wrong for you to be tied to a woman who can't ever be completely yours."

"Yes, but with her I'm happy, whereas with another woman I'd only have a bad copy of life. I swear to you that I'll never ask you to marry me again. I'll be beside you on your terms; it's enough not to lose you."

She looked at him, her eyes filled with tears that spilled down her cheeks. Angelos collected their salt before his lips traveled to her neck, before his hands pressed her hopelessly in his embrace.

Paris was suddenly flooded with light, and life was filled with color, now that Angelos held her hand on endless walks in the lovely city. The store windows suddenly acquired interest. Melissanthi found a thousand things to buy. She admired everything she saw and pretended not to hear his complaints that she was tiring him out in the cold. At night in the hotel, though, she was all his. She drove him crazy with the smell of her body, and his heart beat fast when he saw her eyes shining just before her pleasure was complete. They abandoned themselves to lovemaking all night, to the point where they didn't have the will to leave their room, even for breakfast.

They both knew that they couldn't postpone their departure any longer. The month had passed, and they could no longer extend their stay in their earthly paradise. Angelos's parents had already begun to be anxious every time he communicated with them, and on her side, Melissanthi understood from Apostolos's voice that he wished his wife to come home.

They booked their tickets for their return a day apart, for fear of meeting anyone they knew en route. Melissanthi left first. As soon as she arrived at the house, it seemed to her more depressing than when she left, and her husband seemed older. She felt guilty. In an effort to throw off the melancholy that the house provoked, she immersed herself in renovating it, overlooking the complaints of Apostolos as his wife decorated every room in the latest fashion. The 1960s had introduced a trend toward lighter furniture and brighter colors, and Melissanthi felt much better when she'd gotten rid of the huge sideboards and heavy suites. Only Apostolos's study—which she'd been strictly forbidden to enter—remained untouched.

On New Year's Eve, Melissanthi organized a big party, in spite of her husband's resistance to the idea. He had no desire to fill the house with various irrelevant and lazy people, as he characterized them. She, on the other hand, wanted to have a good time. They were always shut up by themselves in the house, their only visitors being Christos and Nitsa, who made Melissanthi dizzy with her thousands of imaginary health problems. Melissanthi invited everyone they knew, even Angelos's family, since his father was an acquaintance of Apostolos. She didn't want to find herself far from her lover when the New Year was beginning and Angelos was wild with joy. Of course they both knew that in front of so many people they would be confined to meaningless conversation, but at least they could exchange whatever expressions of love they wished with their eyes.

The evening was a complete success and everyone congratulated the hostess on her splendid organization. Apostolos, however, seemed to be in an especially bad mood, and, a little after the arrival of the New Year, he withdrew to his room with the pretext of a headache. The festivities were at their height but none of his wife's pleas could persuade him to extend his presence as the host.

No one noticed Melissanthi go out into the garden to breathe a little of the freezing air of the first day of the New Year. She wrapped her fur coat around her and fixed her gaze on the stars shining on that sweet evening. When she sensed someone behind her, she didn't need to turn around to know who it was. Angelos wrapped his arms around her, with his lips resting on her hair.

"Happy New Year, my love," he whispered.

She turned and embraced him, then rested her head on his chest. "Happy New Year, Angelos!" she said.

The young man lifted her chin, then covered her lips with his.

"They say that lovers who begin the New Year together will stay together," he said when they'd finished their kiss.

"I'm happy, Angelos," she said softly and clung tightly to him, making him lose control.

Their breathing grew heavier as they cast their clothes aside and lay down on her fur coat, hidden from view by the thick bushes around them. They returned to the party some time later, although Melissanthi had to enter by the back door and change her crumpled dress and fix her makeup before anyone saw her. She simply explained her new attire as the result of spilled champagne. When the last guest left at dawn, she fell exhausted into her bed and smiled when she noticed the discarded dress still spread across a chair in her room. Her thoughts returned to the garden and the erotic interlude that had played out there in the first few minutes of the New Year.

◆　◆　◆

Melissanthi knew that nothing good would come out of the meeting. On the contrary, she saw Hell open its doors, waiting for her to step over the threshold. Mrs. Flerianos had asked to visit her, and had suggested that they should be alone, even requesting that she give the servants a day off. Now she was sitting opposite Angelos's mother. Her appearance was hard while she looked carefully at Melissanthi in a way that made her blood freeze in her veins.

"I suppose that we are alone . . ." Mrs. Flerianos began drily.

"Just as you asked," Melissanthi said.

"Good. I don't imagine either of us would want any witnesses to what we're about to discuss."

"I don't understand, Mrs. Flerianos."

"I think you understand completely, Mrs. Fatouras, except that I don't think the term 'Mrs.' suits you!"

"Did you come to my house to insult me?" Melissanthi shot back.

"I came to your house to talk about my son. And don't tell me again that you don't understand, because I don't know what I'll do."

"Very well. I'm listening to you."

"I know you've been having a relationship with him for some time."

"How do you know about it?" Melissanthi replied quietly, knowing there was no point in denying it.

"I saw you with my own eyes, taking your clothes off!" the woman shouted, her face red with anger. "Of course I'd rather have been blinded than come across that sight. But on New Year's Eve, when I stepped outside from your party to get some fresh air, I didn't imagine that I'd find the two of you."

"Please—you don't understand," whispered Melissanthi, ready to burst into tears.

"What don't I understand? You are a married woman. What business do you have with my son?"

"We love each other," Melissanthi answered steadily, but her calm tone made Angelos's mother even more furious.

"How dare you even say the word *love* when you're referring to a man who isn't your husband?"

"Mrs. Flerianos, let me explain."

"I don't want to know more details. I asked around and found out all about you. Fatouras picked you up from your goat village and turned you into a lady—and you repaid him with such disgusting behavior! You should be ashamed, but women like you don't have any shame; they're not even aware of their own immorality."

"Mrs. Flerianos, please!"

"Not a word. You'll leave my son alone, now!" Mrs. Flerianos's voice sounded like a gunshot.

"I tried, I tried to break things off . . ." Melissanthi murmured. "Try to put yourself in my place."

"In your place? And how do you imagine that I could fall so low? And if you think that you can persuade me of the purity of your feelings, don't bother! You married a man more than twenty years older than you for his money. Now that he's getting old, you've gotten involved with my son who's young and can give you all the fun you want!"

"Now you're being disgusting," Melissanthi protested.

That same moment, Mrs. Flerianos shot up like a spring, raised her hand, and gave Melissanthi a hard slap. "A luxury whore like you can't call me disgusting! Bitch!"

Melissanthi's body felt as heavy as lead. Incapable of responding to the woman's aggression, she looked at her without any expression. "What do you want from me?" she asked.

"To leave my son in peace!" Mrs. Flerianos shouted.

"But it's not only in my hands. If you had let me speak, I'd have told you that I tried to get away from him for his own good, precisely because I recognize that this has no future. But he didn't let me. I went abroad and he came to find me. I wanted us to separate, but he told me he couldn't bear to be away from me."

"Who knows what tricks you used to seduce him!"

"Don't you see that such simple-minded exchanges don't belong in this conversation, Mrs. Flerianos? I love Angelos, but for his own good, I'm prepared to cooperate. And however strange it may seem to you, I agree with you. At some point, Angelos must have his own family, and if I were a mother, I'd want the same thing for my own child."

Mrs. Flerianos looked at Melissanthi through half-closed eyes, as if she were trying to enter her soul and read the truth therein.

"I'm telling you the truth," Melissanthi said firmly.

"I don't know if you're telling me the truth or what I want to hear. But I'm warning you, and you'd better take my words seriously. If you don't do something to disentangle from my son, I won't hesitate to tell your husband everything, and I won't stop there. I'll tell it to everyone in our circle, to the whole of Athens! You won't have a friend in this town! In the end I'll even make you go back to where you came from! Do you understand what I'll telling you?"

"I understand—except that I don't know how to do it."

"In a way that takes away all hope. I want a complete end to this relationship."

"Angelos loves me and he knows how much I love him. He's told me a thousand times that he doesn't want to live without me. To drive him away, I'll first have to persuade him that I've either stopped loving him, or that I've been deceiving him all this time. Which of the two do you prefer?"

"What I prefer is for you to disappear and for him not to care about you. He's young; the women line up for him. In a month from now he'll have found someone else and will have forgotten about you, you can be sure of that."

◆　◆　◆

Melissanthi remembered every word of her conversation with Mrs. Flerianos. And she wondered if his mother would ever forgive herself for so readily having condemned her son to death. Angelos Flerianos didn't exist anymore. Melissanthi had immediately honored the woman's wishes and broken up with him. Exactly one month later, he ended his life with a bullet to the head. He had wept, he had begged Melissanthi on his knees, he had cursed her, he had hit her, and he had almost raped her. But Melissanthi was adamant. She didn't love him anymore, she told him. Everything was over. She repeated it to him again and again like a recording, until Angelos couldn't bear it any longer and put an end to his hopelessness in the only way he could.

He left a short note saying that his death was a suicide, and a letter to his mother explaining that his life had lost any meaning because he couldn't be with the only woman he had ever loved. He begged her to carry his secret love for Melissanthi to the grave and not to bother his former lover at all, not even to approach her. In any case his secret would remain just that. His mother would take it with her as madness wrapped itself around her brain. She was the only one responsible. She had placed the gun in her son's hand by asking Melissanthi to drive him to despair. At the funeral of her only beloved son, Mrs. Flerianos laughed constantly and asked her husband why they weren't playing music for Angelos to dance.

Melissanthi learned of Angelos's death the evening it happened. She was playing cards with Apostolos when Nitsa telephoned. As soon as she heard who it was, Melissanthi was irritated, and made up her mind to firmly tell her friend that these health issues she enumerated every time they spoke required the help of a psychiatrist, not a doctor. But that wasn't why Nitsa had called. In tears, she told Melissanthi the terrible news about Angelos. A few moments later, Apostolos saw his wife collapse on the carpet, the telephone left swinging like a pendulum. He also heard Nitsa repeating the awful thing that had happened. He knelt down and whispered some comforting phrase to Melissanthi, who'd turned deathly pale, and tried to bring her around. As soon as his wife was conscious she burst out in a loud wailing. Without saying a word, Apostolos embraced her tenderly and let her express her pain. With sure movements he accompanied her to her room, gave her a tranquilizer, and waited until she slept. For the first time in a long while he didn't sleep in his room but lay beside her to take care of her. In the morning he persuaded her to drink a cup of tea in which he'd dissolved another tranquilizer. With his care, Melissanthi spent those first difficult hours in a soft haze. He never left her side except to attend the funeral, confessing that leaving her was the most difficult thing he'd had to do in his life.

That same afternoon, Melissanthi refused to drink Apostolos's tea.

"No, Apostolos," she said decisively. "I know you put a tranquilizer in that cup, but sleep isn't a solution. Besides, I think I owe you an explanation."

"I don't want to hear anything, Melissanthi, and I mean it!"

"But I—"

She tried to object, but Apostolos stopped her. "You're a very sensitive soul, and it's understandable for you not to be able to bear the unjust death of a young man who was so good-looking and capable of many creative things. I understand you, my dear and . . . since you've recovered, I'll leave you in peace."

"No!" shouted Melissanthi in despair. "Don't leave me alone, Apostolos! I'll go mad! Please stay with me tonight."

Apostolos had already risen to his feet. He looked at his wife's pleading eyes, sat down again beside her on the bed, and put his arm around her shoulders. Melissanthi leaned her head on his chest and let her tears flow freely while her husband tenderly stroked her hair and gently wiped her wet cheek. She hugged him tightly and went to sleep curled up like a baby, letting out small groans of pain, while beside her, he counted her breaths all night long.

The next day, before it was quite light, Melissanthi got up without waking her husband, dressed, and left. A little while later she stood in front of Angelos's grave and stared as if hypnotized at the freshly turned earth with hundreds of wreaths on it. Her mind couldn't contain the unjust loss. She felt as if she were living a nightmare that would soon end and she would find herself again in his arms. They'd laugh as they used to; they'd watch the sunset at Lagonisi together.

She went back home, destroyed. Apostolos was drinking his coffee and she wondered why he was still at home.

"Didn't you go to your office?" she asked dully.

"I didn't want to leave you alone yet," he answered. "What do you think of the two of us going for a drive?"

"Where will we go?"

"Maybe we can go to the sea and walk for a little, and then, if you feel like it, we can eat at some restaurant. What do you say? Would it cheer you up to do something like that?"

She didn't answer him, but he took the initiative and got them both settled in the car. He didn't ask her where she had gone before dawn or make any indiscreet allusion. As they sped along the highway, Melissanthi stole a look at her husband and wondered how much he knew about her relationship with Angelos. Her instinct told her that he must know a lot, if not everything, but her conscious mind rejected it. What husband would accept the infidelity of his wife and stand like a real friend beside her in such a situation? On the other hand, Apostolos had never been stupid or naive in his life; it was impossible for him not to have understood what was going on. Melissanthi looked at him again and Apostolos, as if he sensed it, turned to meet her gaze. He smiled tenderly and squeezed her hand, then returned his attention to the road.

At the beach, Melissanthi showed no desire to talk, so Apostolos walked silently beside her and just held her hand tightly. Later, they sat at a restaurant, where he persuaded her to eat. It was the only thing he insisted on, and he watched her take every bite until he was satisfied by the amount she had eaten. His behavior brought tears to her eyes. She wanted to speak to him, wanted to ask him to forgive her for everything that had taken place behind his back, but when she tried, Apostolos cut her off tenderly but firmly. Again, he attributed her melancholy to her sensitive spirit. Melissanthi was at a complete loss. Her husband was acting like an ostrich that buries its head in the sand, and this behavior didn't suit him at all. She didn't know what to think anymore.

◆ ◆ ◆

A month after Angelos's death, Melissanthi realized that something was wrong with her body. So she went to see the doctor. The smile on his face when he announced that she was expecting a baby seemed to her to be in poor taste. The woman had no doubt that it was Angelos's baby. But the doctor, who knew the family well, believed that Apostolos Fatouras was finally going to have an heir.

Melissanthi returned to the house in a daze, while unbearable thoughts whirled in her head. She lay down on her bed, her gaze fixed on the ceiling in an effort to go beyond it, to reach higher, to touch God and ask him what sort of joke this was. She didn't expect an answer, naturally, but her guilt gave her a probable one: all this was her punishment, and now she had to find a solution right away. To get rid of the child was something she didn't even want to think about. It was Angelos's child, the fruit of a great love, and since he was gone, it was the only thing of his she had left. But then there was Apostolos to consider. After so many years of marriage without having conceived by him, how could she burden him with another man's child?

For the first time in a long while, she felt the desire to leave. Her village, which had once suffocated her, now seemed like the perfect refuge for her and her baby. Its forests and steep slopes seemed like a harbor in the storm of her soul, the house by the river a shelter for her ruined life, and her mother's embrace her protection from harm.

Her thoughts were interrupted when Apostolos hurried into the room, his face distorted by tension. She immediately jumped out of bed.

"Are you all right?" he asked in a choked voice.

"I'm fine. Why?" Melissanthi wondered.

Apostolos allowed his body to fall heavily on the edge of the bed, and Melissanthi sat down beside him.

"What's the matter with you? Why are you like this?" she asked him anxiously.

"I ran into Kostas—your doctor. He mentioned that you'd been to see him but he didn't tell me what happened! Are you all right?"

She was trapped. Her husband was looking at her anxiously, and there was no way out. The truth demanded to come to the surface, like a giant iceberg that had somehow been pushed to the bottom of a dark sea. Obedient to its own dynamic, it was determined to rise.

"Melissanthi, why won't you speak to me?" Apostolos asked. "Is something going on with your health?"

"I'd like to say no," Melissanthi began, taking a deep breath. "But it would be a lie. For some time I've had some abnormalities, and Kostas told me . . ." She stopped again. She had never felt she was strong, and telling the truth at this moment demanded a tremendous effort from her.

"Melissanthi, don't torture me! Whatever is happening, I want to know. Basically, if it's something serious, we're leaving tomorrow for abroad."

"It's not necessary for us to leave. At least not together. If you decide that you don't want me near you, I'm prepared to leave and you won't ever have to see me again."

"What nonsense are you telling me now?"

"Apostolos, I'm pregnant," she whispered, her gaze was fixed on the floor. It was impossible to look him in the eye.

A heavy, threatening silence fell on the room, so complete you could have heard the flight of a butterfly. Melissanthi was holding her breath, and she knew Apostolos was probably doing the same. A second later he exhaled loudly, and Melissanthi shivered. She didn't expect to feel his arms embrace her. And the happy tone of his voice was completely unexpected.

"My darling," Apostolos said, smiling now. "Why didn't you come running to tell me right away, instead of shutting yourself up in the house? Why did you frighten me like that, naughty girl?"

Unable to believe what she was hearing, Melissanthi dared to look at him. His lips were smiling and his eyes were shining. She looked deep into them for some sign, something that would reveal that Apostolos was passing judgment, something that would show his real feelings, perhaps his anger, but she only found joy, true joy.

"Apostolos, did you understand what I just said to you?" She wanted to be sure. "I'm pregnant!"

"Of course I understood it! Why do you act as if this is something bad? And what nonsense were you telling me before, that I wouldn't want you near me, that you'll leave? Why wouldn't I want you? For so many years we didn't have a child and now that God has decided to give us one, you behave as if some disaster has struck."

"Apostolos, things aren't so simple . . ."

"A child is never simple, I understand that, but it's also a great joy."

Melissanthi looked at him again. This was not her husband. He suddenly seemed naive.

"Apostolos, I don't understand why you're choosing to be blind, even though I'm grateful to you for your attitude all this time. You've behaved so tactfully, with enormous understanding, even if I didn't deserve it. But you know that the child . . ."

He cut her off quickly. "The child is what we've waited for all these years," he said. The tone of his voice made it clear he had made up his mind and would allow no going back. "It's your child and mine!"

The way he stressed this last phrase confirmed for Melissanthi that her husband in fact knew: the child was not his. It also plunged her into a deeper sense of amazement, that he could accept another man's child as his own.

"Apostolos, listen to me," she said.

But his look stopped her. "Melissanthi," he said, raising his voice. "This is the last time I'll say this to you. Don't make me repeat it. Nothing has changed in our marriage since the day we first wed. You're pregnant and the child will have my name. Have I made myself understood?" He waited for her to nod her head in agreement before he continued. "I want you to take good care of yourself, leave the past there where it belongs—that is, behind you—and behave like a happy expectant mother! Tomorrow I want you to choose a gynecologist who'll take care of you, and start preparing a room for the child. Spend a fortune!"

Tears were streaming down her cheeks. Apostolos reached out his hand and tenderly wiped them away with the tips of his fingers. "Those are the last tears I'll permit you," he said softly. "Our child deserves the best, and the best is two parents to look after him with love. He'll bring so much joy into this house. Let's express ourselves with smiles and not with tears . . . OK?"

Melissanthi hid herself in his arms, sobbing loudly. That moment, deep inside her, a strange fear was born. With the help of Apostolos, she had cheated her fate. So what punishment awaited her now? She had deceived innocent people. So now was she deceiving herself too by accepting a protection she didn't deserve?

◆　◆　◆

Melissanthi's son was born on time. Apostolos spent agonizing moments before they announced the happy news to him, and he was grateful to his friend Christos who stayed at his side. Sitting together in the waiting room, Apostolos clenched and unclenched his hands.

"Calm down!" Christos scolded him. "Melissanthi is young and strong; everything will be over before you know it."

"I hope so! I'm so worried about her . . ."

"It's because it's your first. I was like that with my first child and I'm ashamed to say it, but when Nitsa announced her second pregnancy, the only thing I thought about, coward that I am, was the nightmarish hours of waiting."

"I'm too old for this!" Apostolos said to himself.

"Come on now. It's true you took a while. You told me that because of your health problems you avoided . . . you know. And then, Apostolos, I have to confess, I was a little bit afraid . . ."

"Afraid of what?"

"Ah, well, Melissanthi's a young woman and she disappeared for a while at Lagonisi. You know how people are, and I don't leave out myself."

"Did you imagine that Melissanthi had found someone else?" Apostolos asked, smiling bitterly.

"Hey, what can I say? It crossed my mind. Do you remember that poor Angelos? Something was said about him and your wife. Don't worry! Just nasty talk."

"Nothing nasty, Christos . . ."

"What do you mean?" Christos's eyes opened wide in surprise.

"That it was true. Angelos and Melissanthi were a couple for a long time—from when they first met at that Carnival dance. They fell in love—they were both young and beautiful."

"Apostolos, you're talking nonsense. The waiting has upset you more than I realized!"

"I know very well what I'm saying, my friend. I was never stupid. I knew my wife—I knew her very well. I understood from the very beginning what was going on."

"And you didn't say anything?"

"As a husband, I was practically washed up. I couldn't offer her anything except money and that wasn't enough."

"It was enough when she married you!"

Christos's judgmental tone made Apostolos turn sharply toward him. "You forget that when I married her, I was all fire and strength! I have no illusions, Christos. Melissanthi married me for my money and because I could offer her a life far away from her village, but later I offered her other things that were extremely important for her. Angelos came into her life suddenly, and their attraction was too strong for me to push him away and for her to pass him up. I also know that since Melissanthi is not unethical, she never thought of leaving me and making me look like a fool to my circle of friends. She behaved tactfully. It's true they separated for a while, at her initiative, in an effort to put things in their place. She left for Paris, miserable, and Angelos, in an even worse condition, followed her. In fact he came to find me. He ran into me, supposedly by chance, but his purpose was to find out where Melissanthi was."

"And you told him?'

"Actually I sent him straight to her, but in such a way that he didn't realize that I knew, and neither did my wife."

"What can I say?"

"Whatever you say, it doesn't matter anymore. I love her, I wanted her to be happy, and I did everything because of that. Unfortunately Angelos's mother found out; I don't know how."

"How did you find all this out?"

"His father, as you know, was a former legal advisor of mine. After the disaster struck them, his wife went mad."

"I heard that. She wasn't herself at the funeral."

"Flerianos told me that his wife couldn't tolerate a relationship her son was having and begged the girl to break it off . . . Angelos couldn't bear it and killed himself."

"And he told you all this without knowing that he was talking about your wife?"

"Of course! Even though, from what people say, Angelos left some letter for his mother. The important thing is that Mrs. Flerianos found Melissanthi, and Melissanthi did what was asked of her . . . she was probably forced to. Of course nobody expected such an outcome."

"That must be why his mother was unhinged. And Melissanthi?"

"Melissanthi was devastated, naturally."

"But you were there to comfort her."

"And I'll accept Angelos's child as my own."

The last sentence found Christos unprepared. His eyelids began to tremble while the blood rushed to his head and dyed his whole face red. He jumped up as if he'd had an electric shock. "Apostolos!" he shouted.

"You're the only one who will ever know all of this. I have complete trust in you, which is why I've revealed it to you. The child who'll be born tonight is Angelos's, but it will grow up with my name."

"Are you crazy? Things like that don't happen!"

"The fact that I'm here, beside my wife who's giving birth, shows quite obviously that everything can happen. I couldn't offer the joy of motherhood to the only woman I've loved in my life; the least I can do is to embrace the child as my own."

Christos suddenly sat down beside Apostolos, exhausted. "It's a great burden you've placed on me tonight, my friend," he said softly.

"I know, but I know you can bear it, otherwise I'd never have told you. I needed to talk to someone and you are the only one, for decades, who has stood beside me through good times and bad."

"I imagine that Melissanthi is aware that you know everything."

"She wanted to tell me the truth right after Angelos's suicide, but I didn't let her, just as I didn't let her tell me the truth about the child."

"Why?"

"Because it would be easier to go on if I pretended I didn't know. If we'd reached the point of talking about all this, afterward she wouldn't have been able to stay with me, and I didn't want to lose her. Of course she wanted to leave when she found out she was pregnant, but I didn't let her."

"You are a man to be admired."

"I'm to be pitied, Christos, but I don't regret any of it. Melissanthi is my whole life. If I had let her leave, it would have been like committing suicide."

"In the end this woman leaves her mark on whoever she passes."

"Yes," Apostolos agreed. "I completely understand why Angelos blew his brains out when he lost her. I believe I'd do the same."

"So what happens now?"

"Now? I told you: the child is mine, it will have my name and be my legal heir. So I will have made my Melissanthi secure."

At that moment the nurse came out smiling and announced to them that Mrs. Fatouras had given birth to a very healthy little boy.

The child's arrival was like a brilliantly shining sun that lit up Melissanthi and Apostolos's life. The infant held his father's heart in his microscopic hands. Indeed Apostolos seemed to have lost interest in everything else. His entire world was transported to the baby's room. He sat beside him for hours on end, watching him as he slept. When Melissanthi nursed him, Apostolos watched in ecstasy; when she bathed him, he was always there and insisted on drying the tiny body with reverence.

Apostolos's circle of friends greeted the news that old Fatouras had acquired an heir with a slightly skeptical attitude. But they put their cynicism aside when they saw how much the child had changed him, how much it had given him new life. Full of pride, Apostolos showed off the baby, taking him for walks in his stroller, and later he took him to the factory, despite Melissanthi's protests that a place where they made cigarettes wasn't the best place for a small child. Her husband had truly changed—Melissanthi saw it herself. His stooped shoulders had straightened, his face had regained some of its former brightness, his disposition seemed younger, and his laughter, loud and clear, was heard much more frequently in the house, almost always provoked by some accomplishment of the child.

The couple baptized their son before he was a year old. Apostolos wanted to give him a neutral name or perhaps name him after Melissanthi's father. But Melissanthi was insistent: the child would take the name of the man who had embraced him and vowed to bring him up with love.

Whenever little Apostolos smiled at her, Melissanthi was almost in pain. She saw Angelos come to life in front of her eyes. The child's blue eyes and some of his expressions were exactly those of his father. Fortunately everything else was just like his mother and so they'd avoided certain comments that Melissanthi trembled to think of. Every day she thanked God for what He had given her and begged Him to forgive the sins she'd committed. Every day she was more afraid, as if she was waiting for lightning to strike from above and burn her. She blamed herself not only for Angelos's suicide, but for Apostolos's attitude, as if it were she who had obliged him to do what he did, as if she had suggested that he accept her actions and the result.

Little Apostolos grew up surrounded by love. The only thing that concerned his parents were his frequent colds, which were usually accompanied by a dry cough that no doctor could diagnose. In the end, they concluded that the boy had some allergy. At school it was apparent that he'd inherited his father's mathematical brain, capable and very clever. When he announced that he wanted to be an architect when he grew up, Melissanthi put her hand to her mouth to stop herself crying out, and Apostolos shivered, but being the cooler headed of the two, he praised the child for his lofty ambitions and assured him that he'd have every help in his studies.

That afternoon the three of them had gone for a drive to Kifissia to eat ice cream. Little Apostolos was playing with some children a little way off. When Melissanthi saw her son fall, she imagined he'd tripped and waited for him to get up by himself. It was a rule with her not to go running in a panic at every small accident the child had, as she saw other mothers doing. He was a boy; she must learn to contain herself for his own good. She wanted him to be a true, strong man. But her heart stopped when she saw the child lying motionless on the ground, and the other children gathered around him shouting in fear. Without breathing, she ran to where he was and knelt beside him. She lifted his head and shouted his name loudly, but his pale face remained motionless, his eyes closed. Melissanthi howled his name again with all her strength, but the person who answered her was her husband.

"Get up, Melissanthi, and leave him to me. We must take him to a hospital."

Afterward she remembered very little of that trip, which seemed the longest of her life. Apostolos drove like a madman, his hand pressed on the horn of the car so most of the other cars pulled over, their drivers staring curiously at the woman crying loudly with a child in her arms. At the hospital she had the feeling that everything was happening very slowly. Voices were distorted when they reached her ears. She saw people around her as if in a warped mirror and felt as if her legs were made of rubber. She leaned against the wall to support herself. Beside her was Apostolos, and she could hear him breathing heavily. The minutes that passed from the moment the doors closed behind her son until she saw a doctor approaching seemed like hours.

"Mrs. Fatouras, I'm sorry . . ." he said, and his voice was calm.

Melissanthi looked at him, unable to understand. Why was the doctor sorry? When would she see the child? She heard Apostolos beside her take a deep breath.

"What happened, Doctor?" he asked.

"We don't know yet. His heart just stopped . . ."

Speechless, Melissanthi shook her head as if it was a way to refute what she'd just heard.

"What do you mean when you say his heart stopped?" she finally said. "But he'll get better, won't he?" she asked, her voice pleading, even for a lie, and making the doctor uneasy.

"Mrs. Fatouras," he said, "you must be strong. Your son . . . didn't make it. He was already dead when you brought him in. I don't know what to say . . . I'm truly sorry. When a child dies, we feel powerless too."

Melissanthi finally understood. She let herself slide to the floor, as her soul slid into an abyss of despair. She was taken to the doctor's office to recover. There, she saw the doctor standing above her and remembered everything. Even in her bewilderment, she noticed that her husband's face looked unnaturally dark.

The following days passed without her living them. The autopsy showed that the child had a genetic weakness of the aorta, which had resulted in an aneurism. No doctor could have diagnosed it. The news of the boy's death exploded like a bomb. Apostolos and Melissanthi's house filled with people. Everyone gathered there to share their condolences with the tragic parents, and all were shocked by the sight of the two of them. Dry eyed, Melissanthi sat in an armchair as if she didn't understand what was going on around her, and it was quite clear that Apostolos had to make an enormous effort to stand up.

At the funeral everyone cried except Melissanthi. With her body completely rigid, she didn't accept the support of anyone's arm. She followed her child to his final resting place all alone while directly behind her walked Apostolos, supported by Christos and Nitsa. They came back home with heavy rain pounding the streets mercilessly, as if nature itself was venting its anger. The house filled with people again, but nobody spoke. Rather, a strange silence prevailed. The only thing that could be heard was the sound of coffee cups carefully set down on their saucers, and just as often, the sound of a cigarette lighter being lit. No one had any desire to speak at such a moment.

"Melissanthi is not well," Apostolos whispered to Christos after the other guests had tactfully left.

"Are *you* well?" his friend asked him, his face full of anxiety. "Why don't you go and lie down for a little while, and I'll send the doctor to you?"

"I'm all right," Apostolos replied, although his appearance belied him. "But Melissanthi . . . she hasn't shed a tear since the first moment."

A little later, with great effort, Apostolos went and sat beside his wife. "Melissanthi . . ." he began, not knowing how to go on.

His wife looked at him, her face empty of any emotion. Her voice came out strangely, colorlessly, and she began to speak as if she was delirious. "I shouldn't have kept the child, Apostolos—it didn't belong to me, that's why God took him. You never allowed me to speak about it and I respected that, but it was my mistake. I married you knowing you were my opportunity to leave the village, and I was stupid. What had my village done to me that I never wanted to see it again? I never said I didn't love you, but now I know that I didn't love you in the way every woman should love her husband. Angelos was my real love, but I didn't have the right—you knew it. Don't deny it! I shouldn't have listened to his mother. I should have been strong, I should have told you the truth, I should have left with him, but again I hid myself behind

151

you. I justified myself by saying I didn't want to harm you, but I was lying. I did worse because I deceived you behind your back. I accepted your self-sacrifice in accepting his child. Again, I didn't have the courage to take the child and leave, to go back to the village I should never have left. It suited me that you didn't want to discuss it. I took your generosity and made it into a shield to hide behind—in the end I was a coward all my life. I couldn't bear the village life and I became a hostage. I couldn't bear a great love and I hid. I took the man who loved me and drove him to suicide . . . and for all this, my child paid with his life."

She wanted to say more and would have, had she not been interrupted by the heavy thud Apostolos's body made as he fell to the carpet. Christos and Nitsa ran to him, but Melissanthi knew it was too late.

"He's gone too," she said dully.

While Christos was loosening her husband's tie and trying to bring him around, Melissanthi quite coolly called an ambulance.

Two days later, no one could believe it as they gathered at the same cemetery to bid farewell to Apostolos Fatouras, just as they had to his son. They all asked how this woman, who had buried both her husband and her son within two days, could bear to stand up. They didn't know how to offer her sympathy. No comforting words rose to their lips; they didn't even dare to approach her. Only Christos and his wife walked beside her, weeping, while she, once again, remained dry eyed and erect. After the ceremony ended she asked to be left alone by the graves, where the two, the younger and the elder Apostolos, each rested side by side.

They all respected her wishes, although Christos withdrew to a discreet distance so as to keep an eye on her.

"I lost both of you," Melissanthi whispered.

Christos couldn't hear what she said, but he saw her lips opening and closing. Then she collapsed on the two graves and began weeping loudly, rolling on the ground and howling like a wounded animal. He was almost happy to see her finally burst out. He'd begun to fear for the state of her mind. Thunder struck and heavy rain began to fall, but even then he didn't move from his place. Melissanthi seemed oblivious to what was happening around her. Her weeping became a dirge and the dirge, a lament. He left her alone to vent her grief a little while longer, then approached her, knelt down, and took her in his arms.

"That's enough, Melissanthi," he said softly. "Let's go . . . they're together now."

As if she'd suddenly lost all her strength, Melissanthi allowed him to pick her up and carry her away. They had gone some distance when she managed to free herself from his arms and started running in the opposite direction. Christos started running after her, his heart in his mouth. When he caught up with her, he understood. Melissanthi was standing next to Angelos's tomb, staring at his photograph.

"Why?" she shouted, her voice breaking. "Why did you take him? Why did you envy me and my happiness and take my child? He was mine! He was the only thing I had from you! Why?"

Fresh sobs racked her body, then she fell in a heap on the marble. With her fists she kept hitting the tombstone repeating *why?* like a needle stuck on a record. Christos approached her again and put his arms around her shoulders.

"Melissanthi, this isn't necessary!" he said. "Our little one will have his two fathers to protect him in Paradise. Come, my girl. Let's go!"

She let him lift her up. Soaked and muddy, the two of them reached the car where Nitsa was waiting. She looked in surprise at the awful state they were in, but one glance from her husband, and she knew not to ask any questions. At Melissanthi's house they changed her clothes and persuaded her to take a tranquilizer and lie down. The two of them stayed near her all night, stroking her hair as she wept and moaned, even in her sleep.

The next morning, the sun showed no intention of shining, so the lights were switched on early. Melissanthi woke to find Nitsa sleeping beside her and Christos in an armchair nearby. She despised herself again. She could never manage to judge people or situations correctly. She had never valued these two as she should have, and they had been her only support in the last few days. She had seen Christos as aged and heavy and found Nitsa boring and stupid. As she lay on her bed, her whole life began to pass in front of her eyes. Her mistakes and her superficiality rose up in front of her like giants with hard, merciless faces. She had always only been interested in the obvious. She had never sought the deep, fundamental things. She got up as quietly as she could, but Christos opened his eyes as soon as she moved. She signaled to him not to disturb Nitsa and they managed to leave the room without making any noise. In the living room she ordered some coffee from one of the servants.

"How do you feel?" Christos asked once she'd had her first sip.

"Empty. Christos, I want to thank you for all you've done. I don't know what I'd have done without you."

"That's what friends are for, Melissanthi."

"I imagine you heard a lot of things from me, words that must have shocked you."

"I didn't hear anything I didn't already know."

Melissanthi looked at him in surprise and Christos smiled at her.

"The evening you were giving birth, while we were waiting, Apostolos told me everything about you and Angelos."

"I still don't fully understand why he didn't just send me away."

"Because he loved you. He thought that because he didn't offer you everything you wanted from a husband . . ."

"Christos, I'm sure that you know a lot more. Tell me about Apostolos. Why did he change so much after the first years of our marriage? Why did he stop even sleeping in the same bed with me?"

"Because he had a problem with his heart."

"His heart?"

"Yes. The doctor who was treating him had told him to be careful . . . you know what I mean. You were a young woman full of desires and accustomed to something else."

"So why didn't he tell me? Why didn't he explain it to me, instead of making me feel so much rejection without knowing the cause of it?

"I told him it was a mistake to keep it from you."

"And I . . . my God! We made so many mistakes! Instead of trying to figure out why my husband had changed, I turned to the first man who—"

"Melissanthi, I know you loved Angelos. Apostolos knew it too. He knew it wasn't just a question of flesh but of the heart. That's why he behaved as he did. He loved you very much."

Melissanthi hid her face in her hands.

"Apostolos told me the day before your son's funeral that if something happened to him, he had left a letter for you in his office."

Christos's words made her jump like a spring from her chair. She ran to her husband's office and came back a minute later holding an envelope. She gave it to Christos.

"You read it to me," she urged him and sat down.

Christos looked at her hesitantly.

"I don't have any secrets from you, Christos," she reassured him. "Read it for me, please."

With unsteady hands, Christos opened the envelope, and in a voice that trembled slightly, he read what his friend had written.

Melissanthi, my dear . . . if you are holding this letter, it means that I am no longer alive. Since our child died, I've felt that my end is very near, but I'm not afraid. I'm only sad that you will be alone. You know how much I love you just as I know that you love me in your way. You were very young when we married, and I never wanted you to grow up. Perhaps that's why I never told you that the strong lover you married couldn't be beside you in the same way anymore; that he would have to transform himself into just a companion . . . into the father you lost when you were very young. When I understood what was happening with Angelos, I felt that divine justice had knocked on my door.

You see, I never told you this, but I married my first wife for her money. I lived my life the way I wanted to, as discreetly as I could, and I kept enjoying life after she died. If you really think about it, you and I had a lot in common, even though I was very cynical. I was governed by logic and calculation, while you were controlled by your impulses. I don't regret our marriage for a moment. You made me feel completely happy. Even the child, for as long as God allowed us to have him near us, was an addition to my happiness. Financially, you will be taken care of for the rest of your life. If you're wondering what you'll do from now on, look inside yourself and you'll find the answer.

Apostolos

Christos stopped reading, his eyes full of tears. He looked at Melissanthi and saw that a strange calm had spread across her face.

"Melissanthi?" he asked her nervously.

"I'm all right," she answered.

"What will you do now, Melissanthi? Do you know?"

"I know."

Apostolos was right once again. The answer was inside her and she didn't have to search long to find it. There was nothing for her in this city, nothing that she would miss. This time her choice was a positive and conscious one—she wasn't escaping and no sudden impulse was directing her steps. She would never become a small branch again, vulnerable to the drag of the currents. The time had come for her heart, heavy as a stone, to pull her to the depths, to help her settle at the bottom and to return where nothing more could wound her. She needed peace, she needed her house . . .

The house by the river.

JULIA

Julia watched the figure of her mother growing smaller and smaller in front of the house and the river. It seemed to her as if the chestnut trees moved their branches to say good-bye, and she felt her eyes grow moist. She looked at the road that opened onto the unknown and then turned to face her husband. She knew very little about him, she had to admit that. The few months of their engagement hadn't taught her much, but the fact that her in-laws hadn't turned up at the wedding didn't seem favorable. Fokas had tried to excuse them: a bad cold had confined his mother to her bed; his father couldn't leave her alone. Only Fokas's uncle attended to represent the family, and it didn't take much for Julia to understand what was hidden behind the hemming and hawing of the otherwise very likeable man. Her in-laws didn't approve of their son's marriage. Julia didn't want to think about what sort of reception lay in store for her. Fokas told her that as soon as they arrived in Thessaloniki, they would stay in a hotel for a few days to be alone, but then they would go to stay with his parents until they made a home for themselves.

Julia asked herself how long that would take, and how she'd manage to live with people who had no doubt taken a dislike to her even before they'd met her. It must have come like a bolt out of the blue when they found out that their only son had gotten mixed up with a village girl whom they knew nothing about and who certainly didn't have the same qualifications as a civil engineer. Kyriakos and Evanthia Karapanos might seem like a threat, but Julia had made up her mind to defeat them.

"You've been looking at me for an hour, but I can't make out what's on your mind." Fokas's voice startled her, making her jump.

"It would be better if you had your attention on the road," she said firmly.

"Don't worry, I know where I'm going. What I don't know is what you've been thinking about for so long as you sit there in silence," Fokas answered cheerfully. "I'm suspicious that your mind is taking strange turns; it would be good for me to know what path it's on."

"If you really want to know . . . I was realizing how little we know about each other."

"It's true that we've hardly been alone together in all these months, so we haven't had the opportunity to say much to one another. But we have the whole of our lives in front of us for that. What you should be thinking about, Julia, is that I love you very much. Do you love me?"

"If I didn't love you, would I have followed you into the unknown all by myself, without any idea of what was waiting for me? But the truth is I don't know anything at all: I don't know what you like, what annoys you and what irritates you. Nothing."

"Oh, that's easy. I like everything, lies annoy me, hypocrisy irritates me, and I love my wife—even if she's not my wife yet in the full sense of the word!"

Julia blushed bright red and looked out the window in embarrassment. She remembered the moments when she and Fokas were alone and he took her in his arms. His kisses and caresses drove her crazy—so much so that she had to admit there were many times when she asked herself what would have happened if Fokas himself, panting, hadn't pulled himself away from her. What would have followed? Only once, in his car, did his caresses become very daring. He had touched a place on her body that she herself avoided touching, and Julia remembered how loudly she had groaned, unable to suppress all the excitement he had provoked in her. Fokas too seemed to have lost control. He had positioned his body above hers and she felt an abyss swallowing her. It was as if she couldn't breathe, but at the same time she knew she had never felt so alive.

Every time Julia asked her mother to explain how relations between a man and a woman worked, she would change the subject and seemed more embarrassed than Julia herself. As for that "first time" that all the older women spoke about in low voices—what made it different from all the other times? Why was there such awe and secrecy about something that was supposed to give pleasure and satisfaction? Suddenly Julia felt as if she'd taken on a lot more than she could bear. His parents, her new life, and above all the night to come—all of it was swimming around in her head, which felt so heavy that she let it fall back on the headrest of her seat.

A sweet sleep overtook her. Beside her, Fokas smiled and wondered how he'd stand the wait until they reached the hotel. Julia, abandoned to sleep, was even more beautiful and desirable than ever, and the preceding months had nearly exhausted his self-control. He stepped on the gas a little more urgently.

He had a lot to think about, but tried to push it all to the back of his mind. His parents, particularly his mother, were among the big problems. She had almost frightened him when he told her that he'd fallen in love and planned to marry. At first Evanthia had simply stared straight ahead, as if she'd turned to stone. After that Fokas saw her face cloud over; her brows lowered threateningly and her lips tightened, and for a moment he became a child again. He remembered that this particular expression on his mother's face never foretold anything good. Usually it was followed by a beating. A moment later, though, time returned to its correct dimension and he became a thirty-year-old man again.

"What did you just say?" his mother asked in a low voice.

That voice was another sign of danger but Fokas looked at her confidently. "I think you heard me very well," he said in a calm voice. "I love a girl and I'm going to marry her."

"That much I heard! Who she is I didn't understand."

"You understood that too, but since you want me to, I'll say it quite happily again. Her name's Julia and she's from a village below Mount Olympus. I met her when I was working there and I love her. She's the most beautiful girl I've ever seen. What more do you want?"

"To tell me you're joking!"

"Mother, you know I've never joked about something so serious. I love her and before you say something you might regret, I tell you that everything is decided. I asked her mother's permission already and the wedding will take place in three months. We'll come straight back here after the wedding and we'll stay for a short time until we make our own home. Did you understand everything, or did I tell you everything at once and confuse you?"

He wasn't expecting what followed. In front of his eyes his mother was transformed into a wild animal. She howled and screamed; she smashed whatever she found in front of her. If his father hadn't come in to stop her hysteria, Fokas didn't know what she might have done. His mind couldn't take in what his mother had said. He had never seen her in such a state, and never imagined she would object so violently. Even when he was young, he had understood that she wanted him to always be hers, and he was aware that his father almost always gave way to her wishes, which were expressed almost like orders. As he grew up, he noticed that his mother was becoming more and more overprotective, but he pushed back and they often quarreled. Evanthia did everything she could to interfere with his life. She had an opinion about his group of friends, she didn't hesitate to express her feelings about every one of his girlfriends, and in a mysterious way she managed to be aware of everything, to the point where Fokas began to believe she was following him. Three years earlier she had begun a campaign to find him a suitable wife but always according to her prescriptions, which were diametrically opposed to his. All the candidates she had presented to him were girls who were scared of Evanthia and would have been completely obedient to her wishes. Naturally, all of them, without exception, had huge dowries that would, in her opinion, ensure her son's fortune. Fokas stubbornly refused every such suggestion and declared that it was his affair and his choice who he would marry. The announcement of his marriage with Julia was the proof that he meant what he had said to her for so many years. Still, he hadn't expected such opposition. In the end, Evanthia categorically refused to attend his wedding, although she accepted that the couple could stay for a while in her house. This news surprised Fokas, but he regarded it as an indirect retreat on her part and calmed down a little.

The traffic was heavier now. They had entered Thessaloniki and he had to pay attention. The hotel he had chosen for them to spend a few days in was outside the city in a quiet suburb, with few people but a lovely view of the Thermaic Gulf. It wasn't especially luxurious but it had the basic comforts.

Julia woke up shortly before they reached the entrance. She looked around her and then turned sadly to Fokas. "I don't believe it! I slept the whole way! It's unforgivable."

"I forgive you, though," he said tenderly to her. "You were exhausted; you needed it. Why do you apologize?"

"I should have kept you company. So many hours of driving—you're the one who must be tired."

"I'm fine. I'm used to driving long hours. See, we're here! How does it look to you?"

Julia looked at the big building, enchanted. They got out of the car and at the same moment a young man appeared to take their luggage.

The room seemed enormous to her and the view from the balcony took her breath away. Fokas came close and took her in his arms. She leaned against him to smell the fresh air and a little of his cologne. His breath burned her neck. Each breath set off small electric shocks along her spine. She was almost disappointed when he drew away and went into the room. She followed him.

"I think I'll have a quick bath," he said, opening his suitcase. Julia was surprised when she detected embarrassment in his voice. "I won't be long," he continued and she saw him disappear immediately behind a door.

The girl stayed there looking around the room. Their bed was waiting, made up with clean white sheets, and she sat on the edge of it. In her suitcase was an embroidered nightgown and she didn't know whether to put it on or to keep her clothes on. She hadn't brought much with her. Fokas had told her they would buy new clothes in Thessaloniki, more suitable for city life, and she understood that he was telling her tactfully that her clothes weren't appropriate for the wife of a civil engineer.

In complete confusion she watched him emerge from the bathroom with wet hair, wearing a robe. He seemed so distant to her, so strange, that she was tempted to open the door and run back home to her village.

"Your turn now!" Fokas said cheerfully. "There's another robe in there for you."

"Yes—I'm going . . ."

She slipped into the steamy bathroom and hurried to draw a bath. Once she was submerged in the hot water, she felt more relaxed, but was aware that she was trembling slightly. When she got out of the tub, she wrapped herself in the robe and pulled it tightly around her, as if she could protect herself from all the fears that suddenly threatened to overwhelm her. Her feet refused to lead her back into the room. Julia sat for a few moments on the edge of the bathtub and her breath came sharply. Finally she berated herself—cowardice never suited her. She stood up decisively, raised her head, took a deep breath, and came out into the room.

Sometime later, lying beside him with his arms wrapped tightly around her, she remembered the awe in the voices of the women when they spoke about the "first time." Now she understood. Something so strong, so beautiful and at the same time painful, was rare. Nobody had prepared her for everything she would feel. However ignorant she was, she realized that Fokas had been considerate of her inexperience; he had aroused her emotions and made her a woman in a unique and imaginative way. She closed her eyes, calm and happy, knowing that this marriage was the only right thing she had ever done. She remembered her mother forever saying that her father was her sun. Now she too had found the sun that would illuminate the rest of her life.

Julia watched the days pass and wished that she could stop time so that the two of them could stay there forever. For his part, Fokas did everything to make her happy. He bought her all the clothes he thought were necessary. And Julia never tired of touching the beautiful fabrics that covered her body. She basked in the adoration of her husband, who, each time they made love, led her further into the forest of delight, where she discovered, amid its soft foliage, that the rainbow with all its colors was always there waiting for her.

The day had arrived. His parents would be expecting them for the midday meal and Fokas was urgently needed back at work. Their stay at the hotel would have to end. As Julia collected her clothes, she wanted to cry at the thought of ending their honeymoon and plunging into the cold sea of duty. She had asked Fokas to describe his parents in detail and what she heard didn't reassure her at all. She could also tell that her husband was trying to hide some things. It was apparent that Evanthia would not be very welcoming toward her daughter-in-law, who would be stuck with her alone all day while Fokas was away at work. Julia didn't know how she would confront the battles ahead but she was sure about one thing: she loved her husband and she wouldn't let anyone come between them, not even his mother.

However well prepared she was to meet her mother-in-law, Julia hadn't expected the shiver she felt when Evanthia's frozen glance fell on her. When the couple arrived at the Karapanoses' lovely apartment in the center of Thessaloniki, Evanthia opened the door herself to greet them. Julia had never seen an apartment block, so she stood back in awe to admire the enormous building. It seemed incomprehensible to her that so many people were living one above the other. When she had recovered, she found her mother-in-law looking at her with dislike; it was obvious from her expression that she held Julia largely responsible for her son's "mistake." In light of the cold stare, Julia was shocked when Evanthia embraced the two of them and kissed them, although the young bride couldn't help thinking that even Judas's kiss was more genuine. Kyriakos, the father-in-law, was an easier case. He didn't seem to have any hard feelings toward his son and showed genuine admiration for the beauty of his daughter-in-law.

"Now I know why my son insisted on marrying you," he observed warmly, but his smile faded as soon as he saw his wife's expression, and he nervously coughed.

"The truth is that the news came as a surprise," Evanthia said in a dry voice. "I always thought my son would marry someone from our circle . . . perhaps an architect."

"Mother," said Fokas, cutting her off.

"All right," she answered. "I didn't say anything wrong. Your wife must understand that it's natural for every mother to have dreams for her son."

"But of course I understand," Julia chimed in. "All parents make plans for their children," she added. "But my grandmother always says, 'When people make plans, God laughs!'"

Silence reigned after that while the two rivals sized one another up. To break the tension, Fokas led his wife away to their room. It was a big, light bedroom that, in addition to the double bed, held two big armchairs under one window and a large closet. Julia liked it very much and smiled. She had to admit that her mother-in-law wasn't lacking in taste; in fact, Julia intended to reproduce many of the things she saw in the house she would make with Fokas. Certainly, under the present conditions, they would have to set up house as quickly as possible. Still, she kept these thoughts to herself as they sat down to eat, and to officially accept, with the accompaniment of wine, the good wishes of Kyriakos and Evanthia for their wedding.

The first evening in her in-laws' house passed quite peacefully. After the meal, Kyriakos asked his daughter-in-law questions about her and her family, and Julia answered willingly, all the while feeling Evanthia's heavy gaze resting on her. She described her house by the river in detail, and as she spoke, Fokas noticed the nostalgia in her voice.

Later, in their room, Fokas brought up what he had heard. "Julia," he began tenderly, "earlier, when you were speaking to my father about your house, it sounded like you miss your village and your family.

"But . . ." she said.

Fokas, however, put his hand to her lips. "Don't try to excuse yourself," he said, pretending to be severe. "Something like that is completely natural. But I want you to know that nobody is holding you a prisoner here. If you ever feel really homesick for your family, I want you to tell me and I'll take you to see them. We don't live at the end of the world."

"Oh, how I love you, Fokas!" she whispered and looked deep into his eyes. "As long as I have you beside me, I won't miss anybody, because you're my whole world now. Just don't leave me."

"Never!" Fokas said emphatically and bent to kiss her.

The door opened wide and made the two of them jump up. Evanthia had come into the room with two glasses of water in her hands.

"What's going on, Mother?" Fokas said in a harsh tone.

"I brought you some water in case you're thirsty in the night," she answered.

"First of all, if we're thirsty, we know where the kitchen is! And secondly, what's happened to your manners, Mother? Did you forget them outside the door, like you forgot to knock before you came in?"

Evanthia blinked rapidly as if she'd received a bullet in the chest. Surprise, pain, and finally anger passed over her face. "I'm sorry, I didn't think," she hurried to say.

"We thank you for thinking of us," Fokas continued now in a softer tone. "But I'd ask you in the future to knock on the door before you come in."

Evanthia cast a look of contempt at her daughter-in-law, left the two glasses on the bedside table, and went out, closing the door behind her.

Julia turned to Fokas. "I think she's angry."

"It's a good thing for rules to be established from the beginning," he stressed.

"In any case, your mother doesn't like me," Julia dared to say.

"Don't pay any attention to my mother, love. She wouldn't like any woman I loved or married. Don't take it personally. When she sees that we love each other and that I'm happy, she'll calm down."

"I hope so. But Fokas, I beg you to find us a home of our own quickly. Don't be upset with me, but . . ."

"I understand. Be patient for a while. A little way down from here there's an apartment block that's nearly finished—I did the design. The owner is a friend of mine, and I'll tell him to hold on to an apartment for us."

"It doesn't have to be something big, not for now at least. Two rooms are enough for us. I just want us to be by ourselves. We've never spoken about finances. I don't know how much money you earn, and how much money we need to live on each month. My father always gave the money to my mother and she decided how it was spent. With you, though, I don't know. I want to say . . ." Julia suddenly felt overwhelmed, as if she might burst into tears.

At that moment Fokas took her in his arms. "I don't want you to be sad, my darling. When we leave and move into our own house, I'll do the same as your father; I'll give you so much for the household for the month and something for yourself, for your personal things. Are you happy?"

"I think I am . . . yes. It's all so new to me."

Fokas held her tightly and she felt herself grow calm in his strong embrace. And indeed when her husband opened her blouse and planted a kiss on her neck, Julia completely forgot her insecurities and her mother-in-law.

◆　◆　◆

Evanthia went into her room and realized she was trembling.

Kyriakos, who was lying on their bed reading a book, looked at her in surprise. "Whatever's the matter with you?" he asked.

"That lazy good-for-nothing won't be around for long!" she declared.

"Are you calling Julia a good-for-nothing? Evanthia! The girl is just fine, and what's more, she worships our son just as he worships her."

"What are you talking about?"

"I'm telling you the truth, Evanthia."

"You call that love? Our son was her ticket out of her goat village. She smelled money and a fancy life and she snared him."

"And our son is a fool!" Kyriakos said sarcastically.

"Our son is still a man. Two pretty eyes and an eager embrace are enough for him to fall into a trap."

"Evanthia, you're raving. And not only are you raving, but you underestimate Fokas. He's a clever man. He saw what suited him in Julia, and that's why he married her."

"And she's leading him by the nose. Do you know that a little while ago he turned me out of his room and demanded that I knock on their door before I go in?"

"He's right. How dare you go into the room of a married couple without knocking?"

"I took them some water in case they were thirsty."

"Ah, woman! You don't seem to remember. When you're in love you don't quench your thirst with water."

"Now you're being vulgar!"

"Evanthia, come to your senses. It was you Fokas was trying to protect when he told you to knock before you came in."

"What was he protecting me from?"

"From a spectacle unsuitable for mothers. The young people are in love. Be reasonable! You shouldn't go into their room for any reason. You might find them in bed—and not because they're sleeping—and then you'll all be in an embarrassing position."

"Stop it! You're making me angry!"

"Woman, however much you don't like it, your son is married."

"That's easily fixed."

"Ah! Tell me you've gone crazy!"

"I'm fine, and I'm just telling you so you know: this marriage won't last long—I'll see to it. I didn't educate him so he could marry the first village girl who came along."

"First of all, we raised him together and gave him an education together. Secondly, if he loved this girl, he had every right to marry her. For God's sake, he's thirty years old! Did we need anyone's permission or approval when we fell in love and got married?"

"What does that have to do with it? We were introduced by mutual friends. We were from the same social class and so we married. If I remember rightly, my poor father gave us an impressive dowry. Have you seen your daughter-in-law? Fokas even paid for her clothes. That's why he didn't bring her to us right away—so he could smarten her up first!"

"Evanthia, I'll tell you one more time: leave them alone. Approach your daughter-in-law honestly, embrace her like every good mother-in-law does, and you'll see that everything will be fine."

Evanthia threw him a disdainful glance and turned her back on him. She had a lot to think about.

From the very next day, Julia understood that it would require tremendous reserves of patience to cope with her everyday life. Fokas and her father-in-law left very early in the morning for work, leaving her alone with nothing to do. She got dressed and began to tidy their room. She made the bed, put her and Fokas's clothes in order, and then looked around, not knowing what to do next. She decided that she couldn't spend all day shut up in her room, so she took a deep breath and went downstairs. Evanthia was in the kitchen.

"Good morning, Mother," she said politely.

Instead of answering her, her mother-in-law gave her a cold look. She thought of turning around and retreating to the safety of her room, but cowardice never suited her. So she ignored the other woman and made herself some coffee. She sat at the table and watched Evanthia cooking. She paid no attention to Julia, as if she didn't exist, so when she'd finished her coffee, Julia washed her cup and left the kitchen. There was no sense in her staying here. Before she left, though, she saw her mother-in-law taking the cup she had just washed and washing it again. Hot lava flowed in her veins. The anger that swelled inside her clouded her mind and she became once again the Julia of the village, famous for her outbursts. She approached her mother-in-law who was just putting the rewashed cup into the dish drain.

"Didn't I wash it well, Mother?" she asked and her voice trembled. "Have you washed it properly now? Or maybe, because I drank out of it, it will never be clean again? Perhaps it's better if we make it disappear!" Taking the cup with a sudden movement, she threw it on the floor, where it smashed into pieces.

Evanthia rolled her eyes, unable to speak.

"Anyway, unlike the cup, you won't make me disappear—nor will you break me!" Julia said, and left the kitchen with her head held high.

There was no point in staying any longer in the house. Her husband would be home for lunch and she was suffocating in the inhospitable atmosphere. She took her handbag and went out to explore Thessaloniki. Perhaps she'd find a suitable apartment. She didn't need to wait for Fokas.

At lunchtime the family gathered around the table in a silence more unpleasant than an uproar. Evanthia sat stiffly, her lips tight. Julia fixed her attention on her food and the two men exchanged confused glances.

"So," Fokas began, trying to start a conversation. "What did the two ladies of the house do this morning?"

Instead of answering, his mother got up and went into the kitchen. When she returned she was holding the broken cup in her hands. "This is all that your wife did today!" she said drily. "She drank her coffee, broke the cup, and then took to the streets! She's only been home for half an hour!"

Fokas was stunned. He turned to Julia, who, as if she'd heard nothing, continued eating her meal. "Julia?" he asked her, completely at a loss.

The girl put the last bite in her mouth and then stood up. "Your mother and I," she began assuredly, "have agreed that I'm not only undesirable, but incurably sick. You know, like people with tuberculosis. So whatever I touch, it's not enough for it to be washed. It's better to destroy it. Isn't that right, Mother?"

Julia calmly took her plate and her glass and smashed them. Then, with a light nod, she said good-bye to Fokas and her in-laws and returned to her room. Only there did she let the tears flow freely down her cheeks. Fokas followed her almost immediately and found her standing beside the window, looking at the road. He closed the door softly behind him, then sat down in an armchair and lit a cigarette.

"When you're ready, I'd like to find out what happened," he said. "It's impossible that you've suddenly gone crazy and started to smash things. What's going on, Julia?"

In a completely colorless tone, Julia told him in detail the episode of the controversial cup. She nearly lost it when, as soon as she'd finished, she saw Fokas starting to laugh.

"I never expected you to laugh at this moment," she flung at him crossly.

Fokas put out his cigarette and came to her. He put his arms around her and kissed her tenderly. "Before we married, on one of my visits to the house, I was alone with your mother one evening. She was in a nostalgic mood and she told me lots of stories about your childhood. Indeed she warned me that beneath your miniature appearance lurked a fiery temperament, and God help anyone who bothered you or the people you love. She also told me that you were famous in the neighborhood for your nerve, and whatever you had in mind you always managed to achieve. So I'm very pleased that my mother met her match, just like your grandfather did once upon a time."

"She told you about my grandfather?"

"Naturally! You were the only one who wasn't afraid of him, and the only one he did everything to please. He even gave you the dog, Arapis, despite the fact that he didn't like dogs. As you can see, my love, I'm aware of all your sinful past."

"So you're not angry with me that I behaved like that with your mother?"

"I'm angrier with my mother because she behaved like that toward you. I know that things will be a little difficult until we find our house, but after today I'm a little more at ease. You can manage very well with the Cerberus called Evanthia. Just don't carry it too far!"

"I never bother anyone unless they bother me."

Fokas laughed hard and hugged her. His laughter reached the sitting room and Evanthia turned pale. Kyriakos shook his head in disappointment, then got up from the table, and, taking his newspaper, disappeared into their room.

◆ ◆ ◆

Four months passed before the right apartment turned up. Julia wore her legs out tramping all over Thessaloniki. The apartment that Fokas was waiting for in the new block hadn't worked out; the owner wanted to sell it rather than rent it. And despite all the new construction in the city, it wasn't easy to find the sort of place they wanted. One had no view, and Julia was adamant about that. Another was expensive, and the next had a kitchen that looked like a prison. Staying at Evanthia's became more difficult every day, as she took care to ensure, but Julia displayed a stubbornness and an honesty that caused all the carefully warped schemes of her mother-in-law to stumble and fail. In fact the house was almost becoming a battleground with everything that went on. The two men tried to keep the peace but after four months they threw up their hands. They accepted their defeat one Thursday when Evanthia left the house early in the morning to attend a funeral.

Her mother-in-law went out rarely, if at all, so Julia felt as if someone had given her an unexpected gift. With no one around to object, she cooked all morning and put all her art into making the food. It was the first time in four months of marriage that she had cooked for her husband, so she decided to make a red stew with pasta, a dish she knew he liked. She was almost disappointed when she heard the key in the lock, indicating that her mother-in-law had returned. They greeted one another coldly as Julia set the table.

The men returned for lunch on time and sat down to eat. Fokas was the first to dig in, followed by his father. Immediately both men made faces of disgust and spat out their bites against all the laws of good manners. Julia looked on, the smile fading from her face. She had tried it earlier and knew that the stew was a complete success. The moment she put a forkful in her mouth to see what had happened, she saw the satisfied look on her mother-in-law's face. She must have emptied a whole packet of salt into the meal.

The dining room fell silent, and Julia looked at her mother-in-law. "I imagine that you're proud of what you've done," she said.

"Me?" Evanthia looked surprised. "What did I do? I've been out all morning. If you don't know how to cook, don't blame me for it."

"Until you returned the food was fine. I imagine you emptied the salt into the saucepan while I was setting the table."

"You're crazy!" yelled Evanthia.

"Enough!" Fokas had jumped up in a fury. "Mother, this is too much, even for you!"

"You're blaming me? This girl has bewitched you and you believe everything she says!"

Evanthia was beside herself. She wept and shouted out completely incoherent phrases.

Kyriakos stood up calmly, took his wife by the shoulders, and pulled her into their room.

Fokas turned to Julia. "I'm really sorry. It was completely childish what she did. I don't know what to say."

"Don't say anything. Take me out somewhere to eat; I'm dying of hunger."

Fokas looked at her with gratitude for not wanting to discuss the situation any further.

The next day, Fokas's father went to see him in his office.

"Father, what are you doing here at this hour?" Fokas asked in astonishment. "Why aren't you at work? Has something happened?"

"One at a time with the questions, son," Kyriakos replied smiling. "First of all I'm not at my work because the store is mine and I can leave whenever I like. And right now, I want to drink a coffee with my son.

As to whether something has happened—what more has to happen for us to find a solution and stop things from getting worse?"

"You're speaking about yesterday . . ."

"You and Julia have been living with us for four months, and every day reminds me of the Albanian front in 1940. Snow everywhere, freezing, and bombs falling. And fine, I was fighting then. But now I'm a noncombatant, a civilian. And my house is a war zone!"

"I'm pleased you can face it with humor."

"Not with humor, Fokas. The situation has reached a dead end. In the beginning there were isolated episodes, now our health is at stake. Take your wife and leave!"

"But we're still looking for a house."

"So hurry it up! It doesn't have to be perfect. It can be something temporary. I'll help you with the furniture—behind your mother's back of course, because you'll leave, but I'll have at least another two decades with her. Do you know what scares me?"

"That Mother doesn't seem to accept the situation?"

"Exactly!" Kyriakos answered. "Instead of slowly coming to terms with the idea and with Julia, she gets angrier than ever. I ask myself what else she'd be capable of doing."

"Well, there isn't much more she *can* do."

"Don't be naive! Up till now the attack has been on the front. What will happen if the guerrilla warfare starts?"

"You're confusing me with your military talk."

"I mean that until now your mother has been attacking your marriage in obvious ways. But what if her treachery becomes sneakier and more underhanded?"

"Where are you going with this?"

"I would be foolish if I thought I could predict Evanthia's way of thinking. She's frightened me in the past. That's why you must leave. At least if she doesn't see you, if she doesn't have the evidence of scandal in front of her, perhaps she'll calm down. And later you'll have a child—and then where else can it go? She'll accept the situation then."

"Why is she so angry with Julia?"

"Because your wife has personality and opinions, and those two things are deadly sins to Evanthia. What's more you chose your wife instead of letting your mother choose for you. So how does her tyrannical disposition deal with it?"

"OK, you're right. I'll take Julia and we'll go as soon as possible."

◆　◆　◆

In the end, the fact that they found an apartment had a worse effect on Evanthia.

"That witch took him from me!" she kept repeating to Kyriakos until he lost his patience.

"Come to your senses, woman!" he shouted. "You knew they were looking for an apartment. So, one day they were bound to find it."

"Yes, but before then I'd hoped to separate them," she admitted.

Kyriakos looked at her with pity. "Evanthia, you were never naive or stupid. How did you get it into your head that two people who are in love would separate because you created a battle of wills with your daughter-in-law?"

Evanthia thought for a moment. "You're right," she murmured. "How stupid I was! I made war with her instead of making him see how unsuitable she was." And with renewed hope and shining eyes Evanthia began pacing the room.

"Evanthia, you're making me nervous," Kyriakos said sternly. "These things you're doing are unnatural. Leave the kids alone. Can't you see how in love they are? How happy our son is with his wife? What's wrong with you?"

His wife gave him a disdainful look in reply. Then she left the room. It wasn't long before Kyriakos heard the front door close behind her.

◆ ◆ ◆

Fokas and Julia moved into their own apartment a month later. On their first night in their new little home, Julia felt as if she were dreaming. She prepared their evening meal with enthusiasm and when Fokas saw the red stew, he smiled.

"Should I dare to try it, or has my mother been by?" he asked and Julia laughed aloud.

Later, lying in bed with the curtains open, they admired the moon, shining down on them like a small offering to their happiness.

"Isn't it wonderful?" Julia asked as she gazed enchanted at the silver disk in the sky.

"You're wonderful, my darling," Fokas answered, and his eyes shone in the darkness. "I'm proud of you and all that you've managed to do since we were married. What do you say we go to the village for a few days?"

"How did that idea come to you now?" Julia wondered.

"I was thinking that it's been five months since you left—maybe you're missing your sisters, your mother?"

"Everything is fine back there. My mother writes to me and I write to her. Besides, you can't be absent from your work like that without a reason. Don't worry about me, Fokas, especially now that we're living by ourselves, I'm completely happy. I don't miss anyone!"

Fokas took her in his arms and, for the first time since their honeymoon, Julia felt completely free to enjoy his love, without fearing an invasion by Evanthia and her sick attachment for her son.

As it turned out, Julia had no reason to fear any intrusions—or even visits—from her mother-in-law. Evanthia never set foot in the apartment, not even when Julia invited her one Sunday for a midday meal. Kyriakos showed up alone, and neither his son nor his daughter-in-law asked where Evanthia was. They understood that her anger continued unabated. When Kyriakos went home, he avoided any discussion with his wife and pretended not to notice her irritated mood.

The next day, Evanthia appeared at her son's office with a box in her hands.

"Mother, welcome! What are you doing here?" he asked cheerfully.

"I came to see you," she answered. "Am I bothering you?"

"Not at all, although you could have seen me yesterday when we invited you over with Dad," Fokas replied innocently.

"Didn't your father tell you that I was indisposed?"

Fokas shook his head and smiled again. "He must have forgotten," he said flatly, indicating that the ruse was up. "In any case, I don't want to put pressure on you. Maybe it will take a little more time for you to understand and admire Julia."

"If you're going to spoil my mood by talking about your wife, I'm leaving."

"OK, OK. Tell me why you've turned up so early in the morning at my office."

"I made a few cheese pies and brought them for you to eat. You always liked my *tiropites*!"

"I haven't even had coffee yet and I'm supposed to eat *tiropites*?"

"Oh, I see—now that you've left home with her, my food isn't good enough anymore?"

Fokas shot his mother an indignant glance, then took the piece she held out, eating it with fast bites. "There! Are you happy now?" he asked with his mouth still full.

"Let's say . . . yes."

"There's something not quite right with the *tiropita*," Fokas observed. "The taste isn't like what I'm used to."

"Well, maybe it's the cheese. I changed grocers and the new one gave me a different one . . . it's not like the one I used to buy."

"So go back to the old grocer. And now that we've exchanged opinions about cheese and grocery stores, I'd better get back to work."

Evanthia left smiling with satisfaction, leaving Fokas to wonder. This wasn't a usual visit, but he couldn't understand what she was up to. Two hours later he was taken to the hospital with terrible pains in his belly, and Julia, notified by his office, ran like a madwoman to find him. She called her father-in-law from the hospital, and he arrived in record time, his face distorted with agony. The doctors diagnosed severe poisoning. They had pumped out Fokas's stomach, but they wanted to keep him under observation for a day. When they'd asked him what he'd eaten, the first thing he remembered was his mother's cheese pie with its strange flavor.

Kyriakos arrived home certain that his son was in no danger, but with a nasty suspicion that seemed inexplicable to him. He found his wife in the kitchen washing dishes. He noticed the baking tray she was holding in her hands.

"Did you make a *tiropita* today?" he asked in lieu of a greeting.

Evanthia looked at him in surprise. "What made you ask that?"

"Did you make it or not?" he insisted.

"Certainly not!"

Kyriakos looked at her now with a dubious expression. "I'll ask you one more time and I want the truth! Did you make a *tiropita* and take it to Fokas this morning?"

"Well then, yes! Is it forbidden to take a little food to my son?"

"And where's the rest? From what Fokas told me you only brought him one piece."

"So you're cross-examining me now?"

"Our son is in the hospital! Do you realize that? Tell me what you did!"

"My God!" cried Evanthia, pale as a ghost. "What happened?"

"What happened was what you fed him! Have you gone mad, woman? Did you try to poison our son?"

Evanthia collapsed on a chair and put her head in her hands.

Kyriakos sat down opposite her. "Tell me, Evanthia, what did you do?" he insisted.

"I did it for his own good—I didn't know, I swear . . ."

"Leave off the swearing, for heaven's sake! What sort of good was poison?"

"But I didn't want that to happen."

"So why on earth did you do it?"

Evanthia looked tearfully at her husband.

"I went to one of those . . . She gave me something to feed him to stop him hanging on the skirts of that useless creature."

"God, you're not in your right mind! Where did you go, precisely?"

"To a gypsy."

"So you went that far. You ran to a so-called witch to destroy your son's marriage?"

"It's her fault. Who knows what she gave me? I'll sue her!"

"Yes, bravo! That's what you should do. So we can look more ridiculous than ever and get mixed up with the police? Go and see a psychiatrist before we get into a bigger mess. Maybe he'll help you. Electric shock, pills—there must be some way to make you recover."

"So you're saying I'm mad?"

"How do you want me to characterize you after your latest achievement? Enough. No more. You're becoming dangerous."

"Me? And what about her, that slut who seduced him, what's she? She took our son and we've lost him. He doesn't even come home anymore!"

"His home is where he lives with his wife, and if you hadn't shown such unjustified antipathy toward the girl, everything would have been all right."

"And I tell you that she gave him something and made him blind."

"At least that's better than what you did. You nearly sent him to the next world. I prefer him blind rather than dead! From now on if I find out that you're still carrying on, I'll go to the police myself and tell them about what you did today! This is the last time I'm telling you this: leave those kids alone!"

Kyriakos went out, slamming the door behind him and leaving Evanthia alone with her thoughts.

The day they celebrated their first anniversary, Fokas bought his wife a beautiful bracelet, and Julia organized a small informal party at their house, inviting two couples that were their close friends. On her sideboard was a vase of flowers that her father-in-law had sent early that morning. No dramatic change had taken place in the relationship between mother and daughter-in-law during the last few months, but there wasn't the same tension that had been there at first. Indeed, under pressure from Kyriakos, Evanthia had invited the couple over one Sunday and she seemed quite calm. Her husband didn't take his eyes off her, to preclude any unpleasantness, but at the end of the visit he had to admit that his wife had appeared to be the perfect hostess.

When Julia returned the invitation two weeks later, and Evanthia accepted, everyone breathed more easily. Evanthia even spoke politely about the apartment that she was seeing for the first time and generally kept her behavior at an acceptable level.

◆ ◆ ◆

In the beginning Julia didn't pay any attention to the charming man she kept running into wherever she went. When she saw him at some shop, she assumed it was a coincidence, but when she found him standing opposite her house she realized that something was going on. She said nothing to Fokas because her instinct warned her not to, but she decided to be more careful.

The first day that flowers arrived at the house without a card, she knew they were from him. She threw them in the garbage but the same thing kept happening every day. And every day when she looked out the window at the street, the man was there. Once or twice he'd even smile cheekily at her. Julia began to be really anxious. If Fokas found out there would be quarrels. He was very jealous; she'd noticed that at the beginning of their marriage. She didn't know what to do, nor could she ask anyone for advice. She stopped going out unless absolutely necessary, for fear that the man would approach her and someone would see them, something she didn't manage to avoid in the end. One day, when she went out to do the shopping, she turned pale as soon as she left the house and saw him crossing the road and coming toward her, smiling.

"Good morning," he said warmly.

"What do you want, sir?" Julia asked, making up her mind to put things in their place once and for all.

"You must know what I want," he answered. "My name is Kimon Alexiadis and I'm enchanted by you!"

"I think you must be out of your mind, sir! You don't even know me."

"But I've been following you for such a long time. From the first minute I saw you, it was impossible to stop thinking about you!"

"Do you do this often? You see a woman, just by chance, and begin annoying her?"

"Since when did admiration become annoyance?"

"When the object of your admiration is a married woman. Since you've been following me, you must know I'm married."

"So? What does that matter? Is it forbidden for a man to admire a married woman?"

"I don't know about you, but for me, yes! Please stop bothering me, stop sending me flowers, and stop turning up all the time wherever I go. Otherwise I'll be forced to tell my husband and you'll be in serious trouble."

"Julia, I'm not some cad. Don't you understand? I'm in love with you."

"You're clearly crazy. Leave me alone!"

Upset, Julia turned around and hurried back into the house. Let the shopping wait! She was dealing with a madman.

Any hope that Kimon Alexiadis would come to his senses and stop disappeared when the bouquets kept arriving, accompanied by fiery notes. Julia, her hands trembling, tore them up into a thousand pieces and threw them into the garbage. One day the wife of one of Fokas's colleagues, who had come for a morning coffee, witnessed this. She rolled her eyes when she saw the flowers arrive and Julia turning bright red. Then she let out a whistle of approval and smiled knowingly.

"What's this I see? So that sort of thing is going on?" she asked.

Julia looked at her guest in despair. Eugenia was the last person who should find out about this. She was quite a bit older than Julia, but superficial, and listening to her talk, Julia had often asked herself if Eugenia was completely correct in her behavior toward her husband. Simos was a very low-key person; he spoke very little and was still in love with his wife after six years of marriage. They had a little boy who was looked after mostly by Eugenia's mother while Eugenia went wherever she wished. Julia crumpled the note up and put it in her pocket. Then, as usual, she threw the bouquet into the garbage.

"What was that?" Eugenia persisted. "Do we have a secret admirer?"

"He's a stupid man and nothing more," Julia said firmly. "A man who harasses a married woman who has given him no excuse can only be stupid."

"And why is he 'stupid'? Is he handsome, at least?"

"What difference does it make if he's handsome or ugly?"

"Oh, I get it! He's handsome."

"So?"

"It's different if a handsome man flirts with you. It's flattering."

"Do I look to you as if I'm flattered? Do you know what would happen if Fokas found out?"

"Why would he find out? Has my husband found out anything? My dear, men are very easy to fool."

"But I don't want to fool my husband. I love him."

"Hmm. You're really naive! A little adventure is always welcome."

"Eugenia, I'm sorry, but I don't see it that way."

"You can take the girl out of the country, but . . ."

"Are you calling me a simple villager?" Julia was beginning to get angry.

"Don't take it the wrong way. Anyway, you are from a village, right? Things are different there." Eugenia was speaking more softly now.

"But it's not a question of what's acceptable in the city versus the country. I love my husband. Why can't I make you understand that? I'm not interested in this man or any other."

"A pity."

"Instead of feeling sorry for me, can't you give me any advice about how to get rid of this nuisance?"

"Oh I can't help you with that. I have all sorts of advice if you want to keep him, but not for getting rid of him."

"Please, nobody must find out about this business!"

"Don't worry. For secrets like this there's nobody more discreet than me. But I advise you to think it over."

Julia's warning expression put a stop to any more discussion on the subject, with no solution on the horizon.

◆ ◆ ◆

That night Fokas's company held a party for their tenth anniversary. Many of their clients were invited, as well as a lot of people from the sophisticated circles of Thessaloniki. Julia was quite anxious about the evening because she had never been to a party. Eugenia's presence was something of a relief for her; at least she'd have someone to talk to while Fokas was busy mingling.

When Julia saw Kimon staring at her from the other side of the room, she looked around in a panic. Fortunately, Fokas was off talking with some people. She felt trapped and wanted to run away but knew that was impossible. Suddenly she felt like she was about to faint. Eugenia, standing close by, noticed her friend's distress.

"What's the matter with you? You look as if you've seen a ghost," she asked. "Do you want me to call Fokas?"

"I need to get out of here."

"Why? What's happened?"

"He's here," Julia explained.

At that moment Eugenia laughed aloud. "You don't say! Who is it?"

Julia looked at her reluctantly. Maybe her help was needed. Discreetly, Eugenia turned and saw Kimon. She turned quickly back to Julia and rolled her eyes.

"Is that the one who's chasing you?" she asked. "That's Kimon Alexiadis!"

"Do you know him?" Julia asked in surprise.

"The whole of Thessaloniki knows him! He's loaded. And I can tell you that your husband knows him too. He's a client of the office and right now he's building another block of apartments and they're designing it."

"My God, it's all over! What am I going to do now?"

"Hey, what can I tell you? And you're saying no to that man? You're crazy."

"Eugenia, do you know what you're saying?"

"Do you know how lucky you are? He's really loaded. Imagine what he can offer you—furs, travel, jewelry."

"Eugenia, pull yourself together!"

"Just look where the good luck goes! If he wanted me and I told you, I wouldn't think twice."

"You don't think much at all, Eugenia. The problem is that he wants me and I don't want him."

Before Eugenia could respond, their husbands returned and the conversation stopped. Fokas immediately noticed the change in his wife's appearance.

"Julia, what's the matter? You look pale. Are you tired?" he asked her anxiously.

"The truth is I'm not used to standing for such a long time, especially in high heels," she explained.

"So let's find somewhere to sit for a while," Fokas suggested. "Unfortunately, we can't leave just yet. You see Mr. Dellis has been calling over to us every few minutes to introduce us to some people, potential clients."

"It doesn't matter, I'm fine," she whispered as she saw Kimon approaching their group.

"Good evening!" he greeted them cheerfully.

"Mr. Alexiadis!" Simos called out warmly, holding out his hand.

"I see that tonight you have the privilege of escorting the most beautiful women in Thessaloniki," Kimon observed and the two men hurried to introduce their wives.

Julia looked like a martyr as she held out her hand to Kimon. Smiling, he bent to kiss it. The young woman relaxed when the men immediately began to talk about business but she felt her heart stop when Fokas and Simos excused themselves to chat with Dellis.

"But there's no need to excuse yourself, gentlemen," Kimon said. "You'll be leaving me with two beautiful women at last. If you had any tact at all, you'd have done that earlier!"

The husbands smiled and hurried off. Complete silence immediately fell on the group. Julia kept her eyes fixed on the floor and didn't utter a word. Eugenia smiled at Kimon, but he kept staring at Julia.

"I don't want to seem rude, Mr. Alexiadis, but I'll leave you for a little while alone with Julia. I noticed a friend of mine a few minutes ago and I must go and say hello to her."

As Eugenia went off, Julia couldn't believe her friend had deserted her.

"Will you stare at the floor for much longer?" Kimon asked.

"I think it's the best thing I can do," she answered abruptly.

"Yes, but it's not the cleverest. You attract attention and I don't think you want to do that."

"What are you trying to say?"

"That your husband himself introduced us, and it won't seem logical to someone who notices us, for you to stand there in silence looking down when one of your husband's clients stands opposite you."

Julia raised her head and fixed her eyes on him. "Then I'll look at you. And I repeat that I don't like this game. I have no desire for a relationship with anyone. I love my husband, I'm happy with him, and I want you to leave me alone. Why won't you believe me?"

"I never said I didn't believe you. However I always get what I want in life. And now it's you that I want."

"And the fact that I don't want you—doesn't that mean anything to you?"

"Absolutely nothing! It's only a matter of time before you realize that with me you'll be much happier than you'd be with an employee in an office who, by the way, could find himself out of work tomorrow."

"Are you threatening me with something or have I made a mistake?"

"I never threaten a woman. I'm simply showing you all the parameters. It happens that people are let go sometimes. It could be your husband, and then you'll understand that I can offer you everything. Come with me, Julia, and the world will belong to you."

"Please, Mr. Alexiadis, leave me alone and find someone else more willing to be offered the world. I'm not interested." Now Julia was in a rage. She left Kimon by himself and found Eugenia.

"Come with me!" Julia said sternly and her friend followed her without any objection.

They found themselves in the restroom.

"Don't ever do that to me again!" Julia snapped.

"What did I do?" Eugenia asked innocently.

"Stop it! You know very well you shouldn't have left me alone with him."

"But what could I do? It was obvious that he wanted to talk to you. So what did you talk about?"

"To put it briefly, he told me that if I don't give in to him, Fokas will lose his job."

"My God! This gentleman is playing rough. What will you do?"

"Nothing."

"Maybe you've taken it the wrong way."

"It's wrong any way you look at it. And I think the time has come to talk to my husband."

"You mustn't do that. It's the surest way for him to find himself out of work. Are you stupid? If you tell Fokas about this, he'll go and demand an explanation from Kimon. You can imagine what'll happen after that."

"You're right, it's dangerous . . . but what else can I do?"

The day after the party, when a very expensive necklace arrived together with the usual bouquet of flowers, Julia felt the blood rushing to her head. Furious, she opened the window, saw Kimon smiling at her, and threw the necklace and the flowers at him with all her strength. Then she slammed the window shut. Trembling with nerves, she collapsed on a chair. She racked her brain for a solution to her problem, which seemed to get bigger and bigger every day. She even thought of asking her father-in-law for help, but she rejected the idea as foolish. How could she tell her husband's father about the dreadful things that had gone on and persuade him that she had no responsibility for them? Nor could her mother advise her. In the letters Julia had written she'd never even referred to the problems she'd had with her mother-in-law, and she didn't want to burden her mother with her concerns now.

She could hardly believe her luck when Kimon disappeared from her life as suddenly as he'd appeared. She guessed that her violent response to the necklace made him finally understand that he was wasting his time with her. Julia felt as if she had recovered from a serious disease. She could now leave the house without constantly looking over her shoulder to see if she was being followed.

It didn't last more than two months, however. Kimon Alexiadis appeared again, and more insistently this time. He even invited them to dinner with Simos and Eugenia. Julia knew it would be impossible to refuse to accompany her husband without raising suspicions. So she obeyed her destiny, knowing it would be a very difficult evening.

Kimon welcomed them to his house, which was a palace in a suburb of the city, clearly designed to make an impression. However much Eugenia showed her frank admiration both for the man and his house, Julia confined herself to the strictly necessary approval of the works of art that their host proudly showed them.

That night Julia found out that Kimon had been abroad for the last two months and she silently wished that he'd stayed wherever he was and left her in peace. She didn't expect things to get worse now that he was back, but she was wrong. Kimon became her shadow. He turned up wherever she went and often approached her, starting up a conversation with some ridiculous excuse. One day when she was waiting for Eugenia at a pastry shop, he dared to sit down at the same table, something that made her so furious that she tipped a glass of water on him and ran off.

The next day she was surprised to see her father-in-law at her door. His grim expression made her heart nearly stop.

"What's going on, Father? Has something happened?" she asked as soon as she closed the door behind him.

"Something's happened and I want the two of us to have a little talk," he answered, and she could hear the sadness in his voice.

They sat in the sitting room and Julia offered him a coffee. The older man smoked for a while in silence. He seemed embarrassed and had difficulty beginning, so Julia, who had never seen him in such a state, began the conversation herself.

"Father, something's happened. Don't keep me in agony, please!"

"Yesterday I had a meeting with someone in a pastry shop in Kypseli," Kyriakos began.

It didn't take long for Julia to understand that her father-in-law had witnessed the scene with Kimon. A feeling of liberation flooded over her. She may not have had the courage to seek his advice herself, but fate had brought her perhaps the only person who could help her.

"Of course! I hope I didn't splash you with water too," she said, unperturbed.

"Julia, I want to know what's going on with Alexiadis!"

"Do you know him?" she asked in surprise.

"Oh, I know all about him—the good and the bad. And you, what do you have to do with such a bastard?"

Without any more hesitation, Julia told him what had been going on for the last few months. She explained all the efforts she'd made to discourage Kimon and the reasons why she'd said nothing to her husband.

"I don't understand how and where he found the nerve to pursue me so aggressively," she said. "Suddenly, one day, I realized that he'd become my shadow. Then the flowers and the notes began."

"I believe you, my girl. I have no doubt that you bear no responsibility. And even if I'd had doubts, yesterday's soaking would have quickly dispelled them."

"So where do you know him from?"

"It's a long story. My brother, the one who came to the wedding, was the reason I met that scumbag. His wife caught Alexiadis's eye more than two years ago. She was younger than my brother and very beautiful. Alexiadis began besieging her. Except that Alexandra didn't have the same strength as you and she didn't love my brother so much. She gave in very quickly and the whole of Thessaloniki laughed behind the back of a man whose only crime was that he loved his wife and completely trusted her."

"And what happened? From what I've heard, Alexandra is dead. Was she killed?"

"That's what we told everyone. But it was suicide. When that bastard grew tired of her, he threw her out like a rag, but it seems that she really loved him. She couldn't bear it and killed herself. The scandal would have come out in the open, and for the first time Alexiadis seemed afraid. But my wife saved the situation. She did everything to cover things up. She hid my sister-in-law's suicide note, and thanks to Evanthia's cousin, who was a prosecutor in the traffic police, the suicide was reported as a tragic accident."

"Unbelievable!"

"There's more. Alexandra was pregnant when she died and the baby wasn't my brother's because he couldn't have children. Alexiadis was the father but it didn't bother him. Evanthia worked a miracle there too. I don't know how, but nobody ever found out. So the one who was really responsible got off and managed with unbelievable audacity to say he owed us a favor. That's why I panicked when I saw you yesterday. I realized that the good-for-nothing has his eye on you!"

"Yes, but why? Just like that? Where did he first see me and how did he find out so much about me so he could begin to pursue me? Something bothered me about his story from the beginning. It's as if someone sent him to me on purpose."

"He has good taste," Kyriakos whispered, as if at a loss.

"He has no taste at all, Father!" Julia said angrily. "If Fokas finds out, I'm finished. Leaving aside the fact that Kimon has threatened me in no uncertain terms, saying that my husband may lose his job if I don't . . . do you understand?"

Kyriakos got up suddenly from his chair. "Don't be afraid; nothing will happen, my girl. Now that I know, I'll help you."

After her father-in-law left, Julia felt she could breathe more easily. At last she had an ally; finally she wasn't alone. She began doing some housework, ignorant of what was taking place on the other side of the city.

At that very moment, taking every precaution, Evanthia crossed Kimon's doorstep. He received her in his living room.

"You've finally come," he said.

"We said we'd avoid meetings. Why did you ask to see me?"

"Because this business has to stop immediately! I'm exhausted, I'm bored, and what's more, there's no result. Your daughter-in-law is a moral rock. Whatever I do, all my efforts come to nothing. Besides, I'm afraid I'll become a laughingstock."

"You nearly became a laughingstock back then, but I rescued you."

"And I paid you back with interest! From the beginning, I didn't like your game, yet I agreed to play it. But nothing's going to happen. The girl is completely honorable and she loves your son, just as he loves her. Why don't you leave them in peace?"

"That's my business."

"Fine. But I think I've settled my account with you. I give up. I'll leave the girl in peace and I advise you to do the same."

"I don't need to be lectured, especially by you. Next you'll tell me that you felt ashamed!"

"Yes, because that's the way it is. I may do whatever I like with women, but with women who want it. Not to mention that cooling my heels under the window of some woman doesn't suit me. Just yesterday she threw a necklace I sent her out the window, and it was really expensive. If anyone had been watching, what would have happened?"

"All right, all right. Stop your whining! In any case, I got what I wanted."

"Maybe I'll regret having asked, but what exactly did you want and get?"

"Photographs."

"Photographs?" Kimon rolled his eyes. "Have you gone crazy? I forbid you to use them!"

"Calm down. No one else will see them except my son."

"Oh, great. Now I'm not worried," Alexiadis shot back sarcastically. "And if he comes to me to demand an explanation? What will I tell the man?"

"Don't worry about that. He won't come to you. I know my son. And if he does, you only have to say that his wife wanted it."

"You're unbearable, Mrs. Karapanos."

"That's not what you said when I saved you from a scandal that would have expelled you from the high society of Thessaloniki."

"At this moment I wonder if it was worth the trouble, now that I've gotten mixed up with you like this. But tell me, what do the photographs show? The girl never did anything reprehensible. Just yesterday she doused me with water."

"We avoided that snapshot. But in all the others it looks as if she's speaking to you in various places and you look like a couple. In one, you even kiss her hand."

"Yes, I remember, and immediately afterward your daughter-in-law nearly scratched my eyes out! But what do you want to achieve with all this?"

"I want my son to see that the girl he married is not for him, that she chased him for his money."

"But Julia doesn't care a damn about all that. She only wants Fokas. It's a shame!"

"So let the shame be on me, Alexiadis; you don't have to get mixed up in it. Remember that I've kept Alexandra's letter where she names you as the reason for her suicide and the death of her unborn child."

"You're a blackmailer!"

"Thank you for the information. The important thing is that I do my work. This village girl is not for my son, and now I have the weapons I need to fight her."

Evanthia departed, leaving Alexiadis to shake his head helplessly. He'd never known another woman like this one, nor did he ever wish to.

◆ ◆ ◆

As soon as Fokas got home, Julia knew that something was bothering him.

"What's the matter?" she asked. "Did something happen at the office?"

"Yes, but it has nothing to do with work. An old friend came to see me. I knew him when I was doing my national service. He's a contractor. He suggested that we work together."

"That's wonderful!"

"Not so wonderful. He's been away from Greece for years. Now he's based in Africa."

"In Africa? And what would you do there?"

"There's tremendous development going on in Cameroon. He takes on various projects, mostly government ones. He suggests I come there."

"To Cameroon?"

"Yes. He tells me I'll make a lot of money. He asked me how long I'll remain an employee on a salary and he insisted that people who dare, succeed. He really got me thinking!"

"So what do you think?"

"I can't leave, Julia. First of all, how can I drag you to Africa, on the other side of the world? Then I have my parents here."

"About your parents, I understand, but don't think about me. I have no problem following you."

"Are you telling me the truth? Would you follow me?"

"What sort of a question is that, Fokas? Of course I'll come! My life is wherever you are."

"But you won't have anyone down there."

"Who do I have here? And you have to admit that it's a great opportunity for you. Think carefully about it and whatever you decide, I'll agree to it."

Julia embraced him and saw that her husband's eyes had darkened quite suddenly and inexplicably.

◆ ◆ ◆

Alexiadis stood like a pillar of salt, staring at Kyriakos Karapanos, who was standing on his doorstep. He suddenly took a step back and Kyriakos entered the house, closing the door behind him.

"And now, the two of us," Kyriakos said angrily.

"I don't understand," Alexiadis stammered in a low voice.

"What business do you have with my wife? Wasn't it enough that you sent my sister-in-law into the next world? Now you have your eye on Evanthia?" Kyriakos asked.

Alexiadis rolled his eyes. "Have you gone crazy, Kyriakos? I have nothing to do with your wife!"

"So what was she doing at your house? I saw her leaving just now with my own eyes. Tell me! Whatever you didn't pay for then you'll pay for in spades now!"

Kyriakos grabbed him by the lapel and shook him. He dragged him into the living room and shoved him into a chair, where he stood in front of him, hands on his hips, and stared at him furiously. When he left Julia a little while earlier, his first thought was a head-on attack on the perpetrator. He didn't expect to see his wife leaving the house, taking extraordinary precautions not to be seen, but when he did, his suspicions were confirmed. Evanthia was behind the plans for seduction, using the past to enlist Alexiadis as an ally. Not for a moment did it pass through his head that there was any sort of bond between his wife and the man who, at this moment, was looking at him in fear, but it was the only way to make him confess.

"So!" he shouted even more angrily. "Are you going to tell me what sort of relationship you're having with my wife and how long you've been making a fool of me?"

"For the love of God, Karapanos! You're making a mistake. I don't have that sort of relationship with Evanthia."

Within a few moments, Alexiadis had revealed everything to him.

"And since my daughter-in-law didn't give in, what does Evanthia have to gain?" Kyriakos asked.

"From what I understand, every time I met Julia, she arranged for someone to take photographs. She's sending them to Fokas—that's what she told me. I swear that this is the whole truth, Kyriakos. I tried to get her to change her mind. She didn't listen to me. She threatened me with that old business. She told me she'd kept the letter from that poor woman and that it revealed everything about us in it. What was I supposed to do?"

"You're a ridiculous man, Alexiadis. A useless bum and nothing more. Stay away from my children and my family. If you don't, I swear to you you'll pay very dearly!"

"I'm already leaving tomorrow for abroad."

"And a good thing too! And when you come back, take care to forget that you know us."

"That's just what I intend too. Enough of the Karapanos family!"

Kyriakos left, having made up his mind not to go home right away. He had to think, and if he saw Evanthia in front of him he wasn't sure he could keep his self-control. He felt partly responsible for what had happened. He should have realized that Evanthia would not have stopped after that fiasco with the "magic spell." He should have realized that her good behavior over the last few months was intended to hide what she was plotting. How could he have imagined that she'd begun to feel some affection for her daughter-in-law? How could he have believed that she'd leave the couple in peace?

He couldn't decide what to do first. Should he go straight to his wife or to his son? And if he chose the first, how could he manage not to do what had never passed through his mind until now and beat the daylights out of her? If he went to his son, what would he say to him? How would he summon up the courage to tell him that his mother was responsible for everything over the last year and a half as she tried to separate him from his wife?

With his head ready to burst, Kyriakos decided to go to his store. Among his accounts it would be easier for him to calm down and put his topsy-turvy thoughts in order. Kyriakos kept a paint store and was proud of the fact that it was the largest in Thessaloniki. Thanks to his efforts, it did a roaring trade.

He arrived around closing time and went straight to his office, where he poured himself a drink and sat down, exhausted.

What he was most afraid of was Fokas's reaction if he found out what his mother had been up to. He was always a strange child, and it wasn't so rare for his reactions to leave them stunned. However much Evanthia tried to train him, he never accepted being a "mama's boy." For a moment, Kyriakos was tempted to not say anything to him about his mother's scheming, but to simply confront Evanthia and force her to promise that she'd never do anything to undermine her son's marriage again. But how could he believe such a promise? He poured himself another drink, but hadn't yet taken a sip when he saw his son walk in, clearly upset.

"Fokas," he said, and shuddered at the coincidence. The answer to all his uncertainties had unexpectedly presented itself.

"Father, something very serious has happened; I need your help!" Fokas told him and collapsed exhausted into one of the armchairs.

Kyriakos filled a glass for his son, and offering it to him, sat down opposite him. "I'm listening," he said calmly.

Fokas began speaking quickly. He explained that something was going on between his wife and a client of the office. Then he showed his father the photographs that had come in the mail. Kyriakos had to admit that Evanthia's man had done amazing work. Anyone who saw those images would assume that the couple in them were lovers—here, they were walking along, here they were looking in shop windows, and here the man is tenderly kissing the woman's hand.

Fokas had said all that he wanted to say and stopped, out of breath, looking at Kyriakos.

"What should I do, Father?" he asked. "I love my wife and I would have sworn that she loved me too! But what's she doing with him? Sure, he's rich, but Julia never showed an interest in money to the point where she would . . . do you understand?"

"I understand, but I'm afraid that you don't. And you should be excused for not understanding."

"What don't I know?"

The moment had arrived for the whole truth to be told. Kyriakos Karapanos told his son everything from the beginning, even about his aunt who had so unjustly died because of Alexiadis. He hesitated for a moment before he relayed the story behind his son's so-called food poisoning, but the knife had to reach the bone. Fokas's face, as his father's story progressed, kept changing more and more.

"Now you know everything," Kyriakos said when he'd finished.

"Damn the moment I asked to find it out!" Fokas gasped and threw back his drink in a single gulp.

Without speaking, Kyriakos got up and refilled their glasses. "I don't blame you, whatever you're thinking at this moment," he murmured and sat down again opposite his son. "Your mother exceeded every limit, and to be honest, I feel a little bit guilty that I didn't tell you then about the magic potion. Maybe, if I had, we would have avoided the present situation."

"I don't think so. My mother, as you said yourself, went beyond all reason, and I intend to do the same."

"I was afraid of that. Be careful, Fokas! Be careful that the punishment doesn't go beyond the crime. Worse things could happen."

"I'm leaving, Father."

"To go where?"

"Someone made me a proposal and I rejected it for the same reasons I'll accept it now: because of my mother."

"What sort of proposal?"

"An old acquaintance of mine named Tayaris is a contractor in Africa, in Cameroon to be exact. He's suggesting that I go there too. There's plenty of work and the money is really good. So I'll take my wife and I'll leave. When the conflicts between my mother and Julia began, you yourself told me to take her and leave, so Mother wouldn't see us every day and would calm down. It seems that the change of house wasn't enough. Now that I'm putting an ocean between us, maybe she'll understand what she's done."

"It's a very harsh punishment, my son, and the worst thing is that there's an unintended casualty."

"What do you mean?"

"Me. I wasn't to blame, but I'll be deprived of you and your family too. The only thing that will comfort me is if this ends up being a good opportunity for you, and not just revenge."

"You mean you think this is a good idea?"

"As a father I find it awful, but logic indicates something different. Still, I wonder if I'll ever see you again."

"When we've set ourselves up down there, we'll come back. I promise you that."

"And I promise that I'll be OK and get on with my life even if you don't come back."

Moved, Fokas covered his father's hand with his palm. When they looked at each other, both of them had tears in their eyes.

"Who will tell Evanthia?" Kyriakos asked sadly.

"I will, but not yet. I want to get everything ready and then announce it to her. Please don't say anything to her. I know I'm asking you something very difficult, but . . ."

The two men hugged each other and parted. Before he left, Kyriakos had another drink. He'd like to have gotten drunk, but he knew he still had to confront Evanthia.

Fokas went home and Julia greeted him as she always did with a smile. He hugged her tightly, to her surprise.

"What's happened to make you nearly squeeze the breath out of me?" she asked cautiously.

At that moment Fokas's face darkened. Then he fastened his lips to hers as he picked her up in his arms and carried her hurriedly to their bed. Julia, almost shocked, watched him hastily undress.

"Fokas, have you gone crazy? The kitchen . . . the dinner . . . it'll burn," she managed to say.

◆　◆　◆

The weeks that followed seemed like a whirlwind to Julia. Fokas had accepted Tayaris's proposal for Cameroon, and they had to prepare everything as quickly as possible: passports, visas, and a heap of other details. Her husband had demanded complete secrecy about their departure. He'd asked her not to say anything to anyone, not even to his mother.

"I promise I'll explain everything to you as soon as we leave," he soothed Julia and she obeyed without asking any details.

They would take very little furniture with them. Tayaris had rented a house for them down there and had shown them some photographs from the faraway, unknown continent that would be their home for the following years. Their house was a little outside Yaoundé, the capital of Cameroon, and Tayaris had bought a map so that they could understand more or less where they were going. The unknown names with their strange pronunciation delighted Julia, who repeated them again and again so as to get used to them. The official language of the state was French, so she decided to learn it as soon as they set foot there. Of course there was a local dialect, but it wasn't the only one. There were two hundred local dialects, Tayaris had said, and Julia's eyes grew wide.

The journey had fired her imagination. She was in a hurry to arrive, although she was glad to learn that there would be other Greeks there. So she wouldn't be too homesick, her husband's colleague had assured her. He was the dark spot in this whole story, but Julia didn't dare say a word to Fokas. She didn't like this man at all. Something in his eyes, and the way he looked around him made her shudder. His opinions about easy profits made her very anxious. He seemed capable of selling his own mother in order to make money. It also disgusted Julia that when he spoke about the local population, his language was disrespectful and racist. For Tayaris they weren't people but animals to do the hard work. Julia had never seen a black person in her life, but she always believed that the color of a person's skin didn't make any difference. The heart and mind were what mattered. Still, she kept her thoughts to herself. She concluded that perhaps she was in a hurry to make inferences about a man she had only just met, and that wasn't right.

When the tickets were in his pocket and all the papers in order, Fokas announced that he would go see his mother and tell her they were leaving.

"But I must come too so we can say good-bye to them together," Julia said.

"Believe me, it isn't necessary. My father will take us to the boat tomorrow and you'll be able to say good-bye to him then," he reassured her.

"I don't understand. How can I leave without saying good-bye to your mother? We may never see her again," Julia protested.

"My darling, I told you I'd explain everything as soon as we leave. Be patient for a little while. For now, trust me! There's no need for you to say good-bye to my mother."

Fokas went out, leaving Julia with a thousand questions.

◆　◆　◆

Evanthia opened the door to her son. She had no idea why he'd come by unannounced at this hour. She also didn't know why her husband happened to be home.

At Fokas's first words, her face darkened. When she saw the photographs of Julia with her apparent lover and heard her son say that he knew that she was behind this dirty business, she paled, but she didn't dare deny anything. She realized from her husband's expression that he also knew what she had done. When Fokas finished, he looked at her sternly, his arms crossed on his chest.

"So—fine!" Evanthia said boldly. "I don't deny it. I tried every way I could to get a woman I thought wasn't worthy of you away from you."

"And despite all your failures in these machinations you set up, do you still think you were right to do so?" Fokas asked her.

"I don't know . . ." For the first time, Evanthia seemed to be at a loss.

"I'm sorry, Mother. I always knew you were pigheaded, but I never thought you would stoop so low in your efforts to have me to yourself. You played your hand and lost, and now the time has come for you to pay."

"Do you want me to ask forgiveness from your wife?"

"Oh no! It's too late for that. I can't go on living in fear of what you might do next to Julia. So I'm taking my wife and leaving here."

"What do you mean? Where are you going?" Evanthia's voice lost its calm tone and her eyes filled with panic.

"I've been offered a chance to work in Cameroon."

"In Cameroon? That's in Africa!"

"Exactly."

"You can't be serious. Tell me that you're saying this to punish me!"

"Tomorrow night we're getting on the boat. Everything's ready."

The next moment Evanthia collapsed. Kyriakos caught her and made her sit down. Sobs began to rack the woman's body, but Fokas remained unbending as he looked at her.

"I'm sorry, Mother, that you brought things to this point. Everything would have been simpler if you hadn't disliked my wife so much."

"Son, please, I promise you that I won't do anything bad anymore! I swear I'll do anything you want. I'll even fall at Julia's feet to ask her forgiveness. Just don't go!"

"It's too late, Mother. Besides, Julia doesn't know anything about all this. I didn't tell her because she has her limits too."

"We have nobody but you! What will happen to us all by ourselves?"

"You're still young and very healthy. And I don't intend to spend my life in Africa. I'll go there to secure my future and I'll come back. Until then you'll have plenty of time to think and to . . . forgive yourself."

Fokas tried to leave but Evanthia suddenly stood up and clung to him. "Don't do this to me," she begged. "I can't bear it!"

Her son gave her a bitter look. Then he pulled her hands off him and turned to his father. The two men exchanged a glance full of understanding.

"We'll talk tomorrow," his father whispered.

Fokas nodded and left.

Kyriakos knelt beside his wife, who was sitting down again and crying with her head hidden in her hands. "Stop crying, Evanthia. Let's ask God to keep him strong, so we'll be hugging him again very soon," he murmured, his voice hoarse with emotion.

"What did I do? What did I do?" Evanthia asked herself between sobs.

"I told you this wouldn't end well, but you didn't listen to me. Now neither you nor I can change his mind."

"You knew everything," Evanthia accused him.

"Yes. A series of coincidences helped me find out the truth about your wonderful scheme, and when the boy came to me, shattered by the apparent infidelity of his wife, I told him everything."

"Why didn't you stop him, Kyriakos? Why didn't you try to make him change his mind?"

"Because leaving may turn out to be for his own good—and yours too. Putting some distance between yourself and a problem makes it seem that much smaller. The distance will make him forgive you sooner, Evanthia."

◆　◆　◆

After a journey that seemed endless to her, Julia wasn't in a state to judge much about her surroundings. After the boat, she didn't remember how many train cars they got into, and she didn't know how many miles they rode. She couldn't remember anything about the changes in the landscape, nor could her mind count all the languages that had reached her ears. But she did remember the first black person she saw. She had widened her eyes a little in fear. The man opposite her seemed very strange to her, and it wasn't long before he became aware of her staring and glared back at her. He turned to Fokas and asked him in English why his wife was looking at him like that. Fokas explained that Julia had never seen a black person in her life and she was simply intrigued.

The man smiled. His teeth flashed blindingly against his black skin and he turned to Julia, who was now really embarrassed. The man looked at her calmly and thanks to Fokas, who acted as their translator, began a conversation with her. He told her that his name was Christian (also his religion, he told her) and that he was married with two children. After introducing himself he held out his hand for her to shake it. Julia looked at the pink palm that contrasted sharply with the rest of his body. When she placed her hand in his, she noticed it was warm and strong and his grip exuded confidence and kindness. Before long they were talking like old acquaintances. Julia and Fokas were enthusiastic when they found out that Christian also lived in Yaoundé. For the rest of the trip Julia managed to teach him a few Greek phrases, but they laughed when Julia tried to say some words in his native language.

Christian turned out to be a wonderful traveling companion, and the information he gave them about his country was really useful. Cameroon, he told them, took its name from Rio dos Camarões, the "Shrimp River," as the Portuguese had called the river Wouri. Nearly half of the country was covered by forests inhabited by various ethnic groups, the chief of them being the Bantus and the black Sudanese tribes. In the southern part, where they would be living, the Bantu people and their various tribes were dominant. He himself was from the Basa tribe. Most of the country's inhabitants, he went on to tell them, lived in villages. The capital Yaoundé was very European, at least in the center. Seventy percent of the country's population were farmers and the area around Yaoundé produced mostly cocoa. Julia and Fokas were glad to hear that the area they would be living in was fairly rainy, with a relatively cooler average temperature of about seventy-seven degrees. Still, it would be humid.

From Garoundere the three travelers took the train that would lead them to their final destination. Exhausted as she was by the heat, Julia managed to stay alert and see enough from the window to realize that she liked this country much more than she had imagined. The landscape delighted her. In some areas the vegetation was really dense, while along the Sanaga River, one of the largest in Cameroon, large areas of forest had been cleared for cultivation and dwellings.

At the end of their journey, Tayaris was waiting to drive them to their house. Julia was annoyed with him when he seemed reluctant to give Christian a ride to his house, which was only a block away from theirs. With Christian out of earshot, she argued with Tayaris. Fokas took her side, so Christian joined them in the jeep, unaware—fortunately—of what had been said.

The house was a pleasant surprise for Julia. A short distance from the city, it was surrounded by other small houses. It reminded her of her own house by the river and her eyes filled with tears. As she looked at the small garden full of flowers, her mother's garden flashed before her. As she climbed the few steps that led to the wooden verandah, she had the feeling that she was treading on the boards where she'd taken her very first steps in life.

Inside, the house had many more amenities than she'd imagined: a large, light kitchen, four bedrooms, and a comfortable sitting room. A very pleasant black girl hurried to make a deep bow when she saw them. Her hair was hidden under a scarf and she wore an unattractive brown dress that was too big for her while her feet were imprisoned in some heavy shoes that were clearly uncomfortable. Her skin was a deep russet color that matched the color of her dress, and her eyes were full of intelligence and warmth.

"Who is that girl?" Fokas asked.

"This is Faida. She'll help Julia with her work," Tayaris answered.

"But I don't need help in the house," Julia immediately announced.

"Faida comes with the house," Tayaris explained. "Besides, no white person here lives without a slave at their service."

"Slave?" Julia said in disgust. "What are you saying? Don't even talk about that. I don't want it."

"All right, all right! I used the wrong word. But if you turn her away, you deprive her of food she really needs, do you understand?" Tayaris said, losing his patience. "If you don't like the word 'slave' call her a 'servant,' call her 'household help,' but don't shame her by firing her. Basically, you'll be paying her. Not much, but she'll get some money from you. She just turned fifteen and she's more or less a burden to her family."

"Burden?"

"Of course. She's one more mouth for them to feed. Welcome to Africa!" Tayaris concluded, smiling now.

"But how will I communicate with her?" Julia added hopelessly in a last attempt.

"It's wonderful here, isn't it, Faida?" Tayaris said, turning to the girl.

"I speak Greek, madam," she said.

Julia couldn't believe her ears. "That's wonderful!" she blurted out.

"Faida used to work for a Greek family who moved to Cairo, so you won't have any problem."

The couple exchanged a defeated look before turning warmly to the girl who, was still smiling at them. When Julia held out her hand in greeting, Faida looked at her in surprise and wiped her own hand before giving it to her, as if it had been dirty. The same scene was repeated when Fokas extended his hand. Then the girl hung her head in embarrassment.

"Faida's not used to these sorts of things. So it would be better for you not to do anything like that again," Tayaris advised sternly.

Julia turned and looked at him coldly. "I thank you for your advice, and I thank you for the house," she said. "But from now on I set my own rules in here."

Tayaris turned to Fokas to back him up, but Fokas just smiled at his wife. So Tayaris whispered some excuse and left.

Faida's help turned out, in the end, to be invaluable. Their first night in the house, she arranged their clothes with lightning speed, cooked them a light evening meal that they enjoyed on the verandah, and served them a dessert of fresh fruits they'd never seen or tasted, but were both crazy about. She left for her house when the couple, satisfied and relaxed, were enjoying their wine and listening to the night sounds mingling with some song that came from a long way off. They of course couldn't understand the words, but it was so melancholy that they knew it must be about someone's pain. The good food and the wine had relaxed them so much that they were in danger of falling asleep on the verandah in their comfortable armchairs. But, with a lot of effort, they finally reached their bed.

"I'm glad we came here," Julia managed to say before she fell fast asleep.

Fokas didn't answer but carefully closed the large mosquito net that surrounded their bed. He had every reason to fall asleep himself with a large smile on his lips.

Julia adapted very easily to her new way of life—much more easily than Faida, who found it difficult to get used to the fact that the lady wasn't like all the others. Faida was amazed when Julia, from the very first morning, insisted that they drink coffee together, sitting opposite one other. Fokas had left very early—Tayaris was waiting for him at the office they shared—and Julia had no desire to spend the whole day without talking to anyone. The young girl obeyed her mistress's orders and sat across from her, but from the look on the girl's face, you would have thought her chair was full of nails. She avoided raising her head until Julia became irritated.

"Faida, I refuse to go on like this," she complained. "I asked you to have coffee with me so we could talk. From now on we'll spend each day together, and I can't go on looking only at the top of your head."

The girl raised her eyes with difficulty. At first, she looked at her mistress shyly, but when Julia smiled at her she returned the smile. It only took half an hour for them to begin to chat. Julia wanted to know all about Faida, who, it turned out, was the oldest of nine children. Julia, in return, told Faida about her own family and her sisters. She spoke to her about Greece, and Faida talked about Cameroon and Yaoundé. Although Cameroon's capital had some European culture, under the surface, the heart of Africa was beating. It was strong and full of passion. But the thorn in Cameroon's flesh was always exploitation by white people. Things might be a little better in Cameroon than in other areas, but even here, some white people saw blacks as beasts of burden, as slaves, and this brought back bad memories.

Julia could do nothing to convince Faida to speak to her using her first name. Rather, the girl insisted on calling her "madam." And Faida nearly lost it when Julia began to take an interest in the girl's clothes. It seemed ridiculous to Julia that Faida should go around the house dressed in such unattractive things. As it turned out, the previous mistress of the house was to blame: she'd asked Faida to dress in "European" clothes and had given her all those baggy dresses. From what Julia had observed so far, the women in Cameroon dressed in bright colors and wore wide, comfortable dresses with lovely jewelry on their arms and necks. So Julia asked the girl to wear whatever she liked from now on.

"But if you really want to dress in the European style, I'll buy you some other clothes that are not so miserable," she said. "As for the shoes, I imagine they must bother you."

"The truth is they hurt me, madam," Faida answered. "And I don't like these clothes. They're hot."

"So from now on, you'll wear whatever you like. Throw out those heavy shoes, and what's more, I'd like you to help me to find new shoes for myself. I don't think mine are suitable for Cameroon."

If somebody had told Julia how much her life would change, and how suddenly, she would have said they were crazy. Yet within a few months she was unrecognizable. The sun turned her skin a golden color and her hair, which Fokas so passionately admired, became even blonder. Her fashion became more varied, with comfortable, cool clothes in bright colors, and she had learned to cook local foods. But her biggest weakness was fruits, and their table never lacked a great variety of them.

The pace of everyday life was a little slower than she was used to, and her own country seemed very far away. She wrote as often as she could to her mother, who didn't want to believe, at first, that her daughter would go to a place she didn't even know existed. She also corresponded regularly with her father-in-law. Every week a letter left from Cameroon and every week one came from Thessaloniki.

Julia had a particularly close relationship with Christian's family. His wife undertook to teach her French, and Christian began to teach her to drive. Her hands trembled when she first took the wheel but after two months she could drive Christian's little truck confidently. Fokas bought her a little car so she could get around. So, with Faida beside her, Julia began driving around the city, but never outside it, because that was dangerous.

Neither Fokas nor his wife understood how the first year of their stay there had passed so quickly. After three years of marriage, Julia was slow to realize that she was finally pregnant, perhaps because her cycle had become quite irregular with the change of climate. Faida was the one who noticed that her mistress had begun to wolf down enormous quantities of grapefruit.

One morning, the girl made up her mind to say something about it. "Madam . . . I think you're going to have a baby."

Julia, who was peeling another piece of fruit, froze with her knife suspended in midair. That's when she realized that her period was more than two months late, and she thought how silly she was to have been so absentminded. She said nothing to Fokas, but found a doctor by herself and went to see him. When he confirmed it, Julia burst into tears of happiness. She had begun to get anxious about not becoming pregnant, although at the beginning of their marriage Fokas had taken precautions because, as he'd stressed, it was too early for them to have a child. Now that their financial situation was sound, however, she knew he'd welcome the news.

She told him that evening, and Fokas was overjoyed. He picked her up in his arms and spun around with her while Faida scolded him for it. He must be careful with "the lady who is having a baby," she said.

The girl had become her mistress's guardian angel. She worshipped her with a passion and there wasn't a moment she wasn't beside her. Julia had met Faida's entire family, who received her with gratitude, and she helped them in every way she could. They lived in a hut; the father was a laborer and never could earn enough to feed the family. Every week Julia sent them baskets of food and when one of the children got sick, she called a doctor, although this terrified Faida's superstitious mother. Julia herself would watch carefully until the child took all the medicine that the doctor had prescribed. After the first illness, Julia made sure all the children in the family were inoculated. She had become the family's earthly goddess and Faida's life began and ended with her mistress.

The pregnancy progressed normally. Julia complained that she had been transformed into a round ball, but Fokas smiled tenderly each time she said it, until she lashed out at him one day.

"Why are you smiling?" she demanded. "Do you find it funny? Given my short height and how wide I am right now, I really am just like a ball. If I lie down I'll roll!"

"But I find you particularly beautiful with your belly, dear Mrs. Karapanos! You were never more beautiful, I swear to you!"

The next moment they both burst out laughing.

It wasn't long before Faida moved into the empty room in the house. As the pregnancy progressed and the hour of giving birth approached, she didn't want to be far away from Julia, and Fokas felt calmer knowing that his wife wasn't left alone for even a moment. Of course he had a telephone installed in the house so that they could inform him right away and he could transport Julia to the hospital as soon as her pains started.

One morning early in her ninth month, when Julia was saying good-bye to her husband, she noticed a few pains in her belly, but didn't say anything to him. It was too early; she couldn't be in labor. Anyway, if something happened, there was always the telephone.

She sat down to drink her usual coffee with Faida, and a little while later, Christian's wife, Helene, dropped by on her bicycle. Helene didn't drive; every effort she'd made to learn had ended in failure. She laughed each time she described how she'd run the car into a tree her first time at the wheel; the second time, it was a wall. The third time she wasn't so lucky and ended up hitting another car, whose driver gave her an unpleasant talking-to. For her good, but also for the general good and safety of the public, Helene had decided she would never drive again.

Julia got up to serve her friend some cake she'd made the day before. It was then that she felt a warm stream wetting her legs. Surprised, she looked at the little lake of water that had formed on the floor.

Helene immediately called out, "Your water has broken! You're giving birth!"

"But the doctor said . . ." Julia managed to stammer and immediately a strong pain cut her off.

Like lightning, Faida was beside her and led her to bed.

"Call my husband," Julia whispered with difficulty. "I'm in pain!"

Fokas was out of the office at some building site, but no one knew which one. In the meantime, Julia's pains came more and more frequently and each new one was stronger.

It was then that Faida jumped up. "Mrs. Helene, you put water on to boil and I'll go get help," she said decisively.

"Where will you find help? You don't know how to drive, and curse my own incompetence!"

"I'm not going far," the girl answered. "I'm going to get my mother."

Faida's mother arrived almost immediately and she brought another woman with her. She looked so old that her black skin was full of folds, deep enough that her face had almost lost its shape. In her hands, with their gnarled fingers, she carried a large, multicolored cloth bag from which she took out dozens of small bags full of leaves of all sizes and shapes, as well as some sort of powder. Without any delay the two women got to work. They stripped Julia and the old woman examined her carefully. She said something to Faida in their own language and the girl ran to bring a glass with a little water in it.

The old woman first emptied a little white powder into the glass, then some red. She approached Julia, who was groaning in pain, and gave her the mixture to drink. Helene drew Faida aside. "Are you sure that the old woman knows what she's doing?" she asked anxiously.

Faida looked at Helene reproachfully. "Imela isn't just anyone," she answered. "She's brought hundreds of babies into the world. Don't be afraid, madam, Imela does it better than a doctor!"

"Yes, but what did she give her to drink?"

"Just something to ease the pain."

Indeed Julia's cries quieted down soon after, but Faida's mother looked anxious. With her few words of French, she explained to Helene that the baby was coming the wrong way around and they had to turn it. Imela opened one of the multicolored bags and withdrew a green ointment, which she used to palpate all of Julia's belly and the point between her legs. Helene watched with horror as the old lady shoved her hand inside Julia, who barely moaned. When Imela drew her hand out, it was covered in blood, but she smiled so broadly it revealed her teeth, which were pure white despite her age. She said something to the women and Faida translated the good news to Helene, who had taken on a deathly pallor.

"Everything's finished! The baby turned, and in a little while it will come," the girl said.

Imela gave Julia another liquid to drink and Faida explained that this was to help the mother give birth more easily. When Fokas and Julia's daughter had finally made her appearance, the old lady handed her to Faida's mother then turned her attention back to Julia.

When Fokas returned to his office and they told him that something had happened at his house, he left like a madman. On the way, dozens of terrible thoughts leapt into his head, filling him with panic. Before the car had properly stopped he jumped out and took the stairs two at a time. He found his wife sitting up smiling in bed with their daughter in her arms, while beside her were Helene, Faida, Faida's mother, and an old woman he'd never seen before. He stood there ecstatic at the sight.

"Welcome," Julia said to him teasingly. "Right on time to meet your daughter!"

Later Fokas learned all that had happened, including the invaluable help of Imela. Despite Julia's pleas, neither the old woman nor Faida's mother would accept any payment. With the help of Faida, the old lady explained why she couldn't take any money.

"This family," she began, indicating toward Faida and her mother, "are my people. I delivered all their children and the parents too. Julia, you helped them and you continue to help them. You've been like a sister to Faida, and this is the only way I know how to thank you. So don't insult me by asking me to take your money."

Fokas and Julia's daughter was named Hara, or Joy, because that's what she brought to their home. The baby looked very much like her mother and her little face was always smiling. Besides her parents, Hara had many fanatical admirers, first among them Faida, who moved permanently into the house. Christian and Helene were the godparents, and their children looked in amazement at the baby's golden hair. Enchanted with her curls, they carefully stroked them with their chubby little hands.

The happy couple took lots of photographs of their baby and sent them home to her grandparents. Theodora took the photograph of her granddaughter in her hands and covered it with kisses before putting it under her pillow. For their part, Kyriakos and Evanthia stared ecstatically at their grandchild, although Evanthia soon burst into tears. Despite her husband's comforting words, she couldn't forgive herself for having deprived him or herself of every happiness.

A year after Hara's birth, Julia announced to Fokas that she was pregnant again. When it came time for the baby to be born, Imela was called, at Julia's insistence, to bring the child into the world. This second labor went much more easily than the first, and when it was over, the couple had a second daughter. They called her Theodora, since Fokas, with childlike stubbornness, refused to give the baby his mother's name, just as he had with the first. He still hadn't forgiven his mother and only wrote to his father. Julia, however, had begun very tentatively to write a few words to her mother-in-law now and then. She was astonished the first time that Evanthia answered, asking forgiveness for all she had done. Julia sat down and wrote back right away, suggesting that they never refer to the past again. Peace finally settled on the relationship between the two women, but Fokas didn't seem to be moved when his wife showed him his mother's letter of apology.

"If my mother thinks she can persuade me to return like that, she's fooling herself," he said. "As soon as she gets her way, she'd start the same things again."

Julia didn't answer; she could see there was no point. Anyway, she herself had no desire to leave Cameroon and all the people she loved there. The only thing that continued to annoy her was Tayaris. Despite the fact that Fokas seldom spoke about his work at home, Julia had discovered that his colleague had provoked a number of problems with his tendency to cheat anyone who naively trusted him. Most of the time, Fokas's intervention had saved them from the worst consequences, but Julia worried about the day when her husband couldn't contain the damage. Despite that, she had to admit that the office was doing extremely well, getting one job after another, most of them government contracts, which meant the profits were large. At the same time there were quite a few private clients who trusted Fokas with the design of their houses.

The situation with Tayaris finally hit a crisis point when Julia was pregnant with her third child. Hara was five, Theodora had just turned three, and Julia was expecting a third baby in two months' time that she fervently hoped would be a boy. One of the biggest bankers in Yaoundé had commissioned Fokas to design and oversee the construction of a villa, which left Tayaris solely responsible for all the other new projects that had come in. One day, a new client stopped by the villa's construction site and asked Fokas to accompany him to his project's site to take some measurements. Fokas agreed, and from the moment they arrived and he saw Tayaris there—with an uneasy expression on his face—he knew something was wrong. Tayaris tried to block him from entering, but Fokas calmly pushed him aside. When he began to examine the columns, he saw that the reinforcement wasn't what he had designed. The iron rods were very thin and there weren't enough of them. These "mistakes" would probably have fatal consequences for the final structure. Fokas turned toward Tayaris, frowning.

"The concrete won't be poured today. Cancel whatever you've arranged!" he ordered. "If we pour now, the columns will bend right afterward and will have to be built again."

"But that's a lot of trouble," Tayaris objected.

"You should have done it right from the beginning. I didn't design it like that. Why did you make changes without even telling me?"

"I thought we were overdoing it with so much iron."

"Tayaris, if you want us to get along from now on, no more changes to my designs!" Fokas shouted. "Do you understand? How much iron did you charge the customer for? Can I see the invoice?"

Even before Tayaris showed him the paperwork, Fokas knew it would be incorrect. His colleague had charged for one thing, but put in another.

Fokas grabbed Tayaris by the lapel. "Were you trying to destroy me?" he asked, shaking him from head to foot. "This is cheating! The man trusted us and we not only cheated him, but we could have killed him with a building that didn't have sound foundations."

Tayaris tried to escape Fokas's grip but couldn't. He looked at him furiously. "Are you really going to do this right now?" he shouted. "The blacks can see us! How can I give them orders after you humiliate me like this?"

Fokas suddenly let him go as if he was disgusted to touch him. "Tayaris, if you want us to continue to work together, what happened today can never happen again, otherwise we'll dissolve the partnership the moment you find someone else to make a fool of. Agreed?"

"OK, friend, I made a mistake," Tayaris replied softly this time. "It won't happen again, I swear."

"For the good of both of us, I hope you keep your promise."

Fokas went home very upset. When Julia saw her husband, she demanded to know what exactly was going on. When he told her what had happened, the blood rose to her head; she turned red and her eyes flashed. Fokas regretted confiding in her. When his wife got into a state like that, she could become dangerous.

By chance, the next day, Tayaris came by the house to collect some papers for the office. Fokas was busy getting dressed for work, which left Julia alone to deal with him.

"What happened?" he said coolly to Julia. "Are you going to have another baby?"

She went up to Tayaris with a threatening air and made him step out onto the verandah, almost pushing him.

"What's the matter with you?" he said. "What sort of behavior is this?"

"You really have to ask? Take care, because I'm not joking. The next time you try to play a game like that under Fokas's nose and you endanger his reputation, you'll have me to deal with!"

Tayaris smiled sarcastically, looking at the short woman in front of him, who'd stuck her neck out like a rooster ready to attack. "Are you threatening me?" he asked.

Julia stretched up onto her toes and cursed her size; even like this she only reached up to his chin. But what she lacked in height she made up for in anger. "Don't mock me, Tayaris, or you'll regret it! I'll send people to deal with you. And they'll all be black. I may not even have to pay them. Maybe they'll do it for pleasure!"

Tayaris seemed at a loss.

"This is something that will stay between us. Fokas doesn't have to know," Julia added. "Just do your work properly and you won't have to protect yourself, at least from me."

Just then, Fokas appeared, putting a stop to the conversation. He looked for a moment in surprise at his wife, who was bright red with anger, and Tayaris, who was clearly embarrassed. Fokas had learned over the years that he couldn't stop his wife from speaking her mind and doing as she pleased, so he decided not to intervene in whatever had just transpired. He was sure that the scene he'd stumbled upon had to do with yesterday's events on the building site, and he could imagine that Julia was angry because someone had upset her husband. She was unbelievable, this woman. Sometimes she reminded him of his mother.

Tayaris took the papers he wanted and left. Fokas followed him, while Julia stayed on the verandah alone with her thoughts. Her words might have been a little exaggerated, but she wasn't wrong about the fact that a lot of people hated Tayaris. First and foremost Faida's father, Abdul. He had worked for Tayaris for a month but had left, unable to bear the man's racist behavior. Every time Abdul thought of Tayaris, his eyes would flash with anger. Christian had told Julia that the name of Tayaris was hated by most of his workers and no one in the business world had much faith in him until he began working with Fokas.

Before long, though, the episode was forgotten as Julia's confinement overshadowed everything else. When the baby arrived—yet another girl—Imela at first laughed heartily, then, unlike at past births, quickly disappeared.

"Just like my mother," Julia said sadly after the old woman had left. "I only pile up girls!"

"And who told you that was a bad thing, my love?" Fokas asked as he held the child in his arms.

"Anyway, I'd have liked to have used your father's name," Julia said, taking a deep breath before she went on. "But this one will have your mother's name instead."

Fokas looked at his wife without any expression.

"Don't look at me like that, Karapanos! It's years ago now and I've forgotten it. Why do you still hold on to it? You can sit down and write your mother the news."

"Me?" Fokas found himself in a very difficult position.

"You. And I won't discuss it further. Enough! It's ridiculous for me to correspond with my mother-in-law while you refuse. You'll sit down and write to her today and I forbid you to make any reference to the past."

When Evanthia opened the letter, she was doubly surprised: her son had finally written to her, and, what's more, announced that the name of her third grandchild was Evanthia. She asked herself if she could hope, now, that they would return home and she would finally see him after so many years.

◆　◆　◆

Julia looked at Imela, unable to read the expression on her face. The old woman had stopped by for no apparent reason, and, now, as Faida translated the purpose of the visit, Julia's smile faded. She suddenly turned pale and her eyes filled with tears. The young mother had complete confidence in the midwife, but she simply couldn't accept her advice not to have any more children. It seemed like silly nonsense that Imela had seen something in little Evanthia's placenta. So Julia didn't say anything to Fokas and was careful to forget what she had heard.

But she was forced to remember it when she became pregnant for the fourth time and nothing seemed right. Faida was very worried, and, as soon as Julia reached her ninth month, Imela came by the house every day, even though she was finding it hard to walk. The delivery was difficult, and as soon as the child was born, Julia knew she would lose it. It was a boy—small, sickly, almost blue, and Julia couldn't help remembering how her mother and grandmother had given birth to strong girls, but with boys they were unlucky. She cried bitterly when the baby died a week later, and she turned to Imela for an explanation.

"I told you, my lady," the old lady said while Faida translated. "Something inside you doesn't make good male children. Have as many girls as you like, but you'll never hold a boy tight in your arms. And since nobody knows beforehand what baby is coming, don't do it again!"

"But you saw from the previous birth that something wasn't right. You said you saw it in the placenta."

"And in this one too, I saw it, my lady. Don't have any more children, because you may be in danger yourself and you have three girls who need you."

Julia hung her head in defeat as she realized how right the old woman was and asked her to forgive her for not having believed her earlier. But Imela just smiled.

"Don't be sorry, madam. I wasn't angry with you. If people don't suffer, they don't learn."

"Strange," whispered Julia. "My grandmother said the same thing."

"All people who have lived a long time, like me and your grandmother, have the same minds, whether they're white or black," the old lady observed, then left.

Julia told Fokas everything that Imela had said and he scolded her for not revealing it all from the beginning, after little Evanthia was born.

"That's enough now!" he said tenderly. "We don't need other children. We're fine with our three girls. The important thing is for us all to be healthy and happy like we are now!"

219

When Hara blew out the twelve candles on her cake, Julia remembered how her mother always said, "When you have children, you don't realize the time passing." She had been so young when she first set foot in Cameroon and last year she had turned thirty-four. Fokas's hair had turned gray and he wore glasses. Faida, who had been a girl when she first met her, now stood in front of her as a real woman, although not yet married. Whatever Julia said, she couldn't persuade her to marry and have her own family. In the end Faida had started to cry and ask her if she didn't want her with them anymore, so Julia had decided not to raise the subject again.

Christian and Helene happily admired Julia and Fokas's children. Their own oldest girl was already engaged. To Julia it seemed as if someone had suddenly moved the clock forward. It had already been some time since she had realized that both she and Fokas had become a part of the local society and that, even more bizarrely, they had somehow attracted the adoration of the locals, which sometimes reached extreme levels. Now she could laugh when she remembered what had happened the previous year, but at the time she hadn't enjoyed it at all.

It was just after Julia had intervened to save the life of a young boy who'd come home with terrible pains in his belly. Faida's mother had run to get Julia, who came and drove the boy to the hospital, where he was operated on for a ruptured appendix. The young man's life was saved and he came home smiling a week later. Julia again found herself with two parents at her feet wanting to thank her—it wasn't the first time she'd saved someone in the village. In fact, it had become an open secret that the white woman who lived nearby was a person with feelings, who cared for everyone and who ran to whoever needed her, just like her husband, who was a good and honorable man.

No one was surprised, then, when one day, two weeks later, Julia found two men on her doorstep holding a big basket of fruit. They explained that it was a gift that would always be there. Julia couldn't understand how a basket of fruit could exist forever, but she accepted it, thanking them. Everyone knew her love of fruit and the fact that she would never say no to it.

She started peeling a piece from the basket when she heard the shouts of Abdul, who called to her from the yard. She was frightened by the panicked tone of his voice as he jumped up and ran to see what was happening. He asked her if she'd been given a basket of fruit, and when she said yes, he asked if she'd eaten any of it. When Julia said she hadn't yet, Abdul seemed really relieved. The fruit, he told her, was poisoned. His fellow countrymen were famous for making strong poisons that they dipped their arrows into to be certain that anything they hunted was doomed.

"And they wanted to kill me?" Julia asked, bewildered. "But why? I thought they liked me."

"That's exactly why they did it!" Abdul explained. "They were afraid you might leave and they wanted to keep you, even dead, in their country."

"But that's terrible!"

"Perhaps for you, who has a different way of thinking. To them, though, you are a sacred woman, and they want to keep you with them to protect them. Don't be angry with them, madam," he begged her. "They didn't do it as a bad thing."

When Fokas returned, Julia told him what had happened. Her husband seemed to partly understand the mentality of the locals. "If they love you like I do, I understand how desperate they are to hold on to you," he said.

In any case they agreed to be much more cautious from now on with whatever the locals offered them.

Meanwhile, quite suddenly, an inexplicable nostalgia for her homeland overtook Julia. Her in-laws were openly begging them to come back. Evanthia and Kyriakos had aged and wanted to see their son and daughter-in-law again. Julia wondered how her own mother was, and her grandmother, and all her sisters. Over the years, their correspondence had dwindled almost to nothing. The children and the rhythm of her life in Cameroon had made her almost forget her own country. There were moments when she was ashamed of that, but however many promises she made to herself to be a more regular correspondent, something always intervened and nothing changed.

She spoke to Fokas about it and for the first time he realized that Africa, even though it started as a temporary solution, had become permanent. With the money they'd saved they had enough for three lifetimes, but everyday life had completely absorbed them, and the dream of return remained a dream until his wife forced him to confront reality. They had stayed there so long—perhaps they should return.

They had begun to discuss it when Fokas's office undertook a large project. It was a bridge, the construction of which would bring a lot of money to the business.

"Two years," he announced to Julia, just after Hara's birthday. "Two more years and we'll leave. We'll go home to our country."

"Are you telling me the truth, Fokas?" she asked, touched.

"I swear to you. This bridge will bring us a substantial profit and then we'll leave. And to show you that I'm serious, I already sent all the rest of our money to Greece."

Julia leapt into his arms. From the very next day, she began to prepare the children for their return. She spoke to them daily about their country, about their grandfather and grandmothers, and promised them that as soon as they returned they'd take a big trip with their father to get to know Greece.

Her greatest problem was Faida. As soon as she heard that they planned to leave, she burst into tears so pitiful that Julia didn't know what to do to calm her down. Finally she promised that they would take her with them to Greece, and only then did the girl stop crying and look at her with gratitude.

"Are you telling me the truth, madam?" she asked, wanting to be reassured.

"Have I ever lied to you? I'll take you with me and I'll see later what you have to say so far away from your family," Julia scolded her affectionately.

"But you're my family now . . . don't you know that?" whispered Faida. Julia, deeply touched, hugged her.

The plans for the bridge were delayed a lot. It was the most demanding project Fokas had ever undertaken, requiring great care and precision. The responsibility was enormous. Of course, Tayaris did nothing but rub his hands together, thinking of the money that began pouring into the agency's account. Fokas hadn't told him anything about his decision to return to Greece after the completion of the bridge, although even he wasn't sure why he felt compelled to maintain secrecy.

After six months, everything was ready for construction to begin. Fokas seemed very anxious, and Julia began to feel a strange uneasiness inside her too. She wished her husband had a different partner. The episode of the iron reinforcement on the building site still haunted. Tayaris had stayed out of trouble, keeping his end of his bargain with Julia, but this time fate was not on their side.

A bad cold forced Fokas to take to his bed. It was impossible for him to oversee the work and so his partner was left with complete control. A few weeks earlier, Fokas had finally announced his plan to return to Greece. Tayaris had seen the company's profits decline as the flow of work that Fokas brought in was suddenly cut off. So, he decided, since this was their last project together, it would have the greatest profit.

He canceled all the first-class materials that Fokas had ordered and replaced them with cheaper materials, pocketing the difference. He reduced the iron and concrete without appreciating how dangerous this was. He cut corners wherever he could, and when the first part of the construction was completed, it collapsed like a house of cards, killing several workers. Tayaris ran to Fokas's house to ask for his help.

Fokas's hair stood on end when he heard his colleague explain what had happened. He grabbed him by the shoulders in a fury. "What did you do, you scum? How could you? We're ruined! Do you understand?"

"I didn't mean for this to happen, friend! I swear. They'll catch us. It was a state project. They'll have informed the police by now and they'll arrest us. We'll have to leave secretly so they won't find us!"

"Ah, so apart from being a crook, you're a coward too!" yelled Fokas. "They'll arrest us, because we'll go and give ourselves up."

"Have you gone crazy, Fokas? They'll put us in jail for the rest of our lives! Think about your children!"

"You even took the trouble to think about them!"

Julia heard what was going on as if she were hypnotized, but at the mention of the children she recovered. She approached the two of them. She spat in Tayaris's face before turning to her husband. "You have to leave, Fokas. This scumbag is right. Hide somewhere until things calm down and then we'll see. I'll find you a lawyer, although I think it's better to leave the country."

"Julia, have you gone crazy? Why would you think that I'd run away as if I was guilty?"

"But for them you *are* the guilty one. You did the study, you're responsible for the bridge collapsing, and you were the cause of people dying."

"And what will happen to you and the children?"

"They have no reason to harm me. I'll collect the children and leave for Greece too. Don't worry about me. I'll manage! Christian will help me. You leave now! Right away!"

But it was too late. Five very tall policemen had just entered their courtyard and their intentions were quite obvious. Tayaris made a run for it but he didn't get far. When three of the policemen moved toward Fokas, Julia felt the blood rising to her head. She let out a cry and leapt toward them. Shocked, they didn't know what to do; they had no idea how to deal with this tiny woman who cursed them in perfect French and kicked their shins. At one point she climbed on one of the police-men, pulled his hair, and scratched his face while she continued kicking the other two. The scene was indescribable. Faida, who heard the shout-ing, ran and jumped on the men too. Between French curses, Julia gave strict orders to Fokas in Greek. "Go, for God's sake, now! You can see that I'm managing here. Leave now!"

In a single bound Fokas leapt over the fence and disappeared. One of the policemen managed to free himself from the women to run after him but it was too late. It was as if the earth had opened up and swal-lowed him. In truth, Faida's father had heard the ruckus and walked toward the house with a cartful of hay, which provided the perfect place for Fokas to hide. As Abdul strolled nonchalantly past the house, push-ing his cart and whistling, the police didn't suspect a thing. After all, the fugitive couldn't possibly be hiding in a cart that was headed right past the place where his pursuers were waiting.

When things had quietened down in the courtyard, Julia very calmly asked the policemen for an explanation, assuring them that it was impossible for her husband to be responsible for the disaster. The policemen seemed embarrassed by her sudden change in her behavior and decided she wasn't right in the head, a fact that Faida confirmed, speaking in their native tongue. She explained to them that her mistress had problems with her nerves and suffered from these crises often. The police said that however things were, the house would remain under observation and Fokas would be regarded now as a fugitive. They went off, leaving one policeman to guard the house. Julia gave him a scathing glance and went inside with Faida following her.

As soon as the door closed behind her, Julia collapsed in Faida's arms. The young woman made her mistress sit in a chair and brought her a glass of water, which she took with shaking hands, spilling half of it. She had to get ahold of herself. She had to concentrate and find solu-tions. She knew that Fokas was in good hands for the time being—she had no doubt that he'd escaped in the cart that Faida's father had pushed past the house a little while earlier. She'd only exchanged a glance with Abdul, but it told her everything she needed to know. Fokas would have to leave the country secretly. Tayaris was capable of putting all the blame on him. He had no moral qualms; she was sure of that. But how was she to manage getting her husband safely abroad? She would need help. She telephoned Christian without saying what she wanted because she was afraid her calls were being monitored, but he knew right away why she'd called. The radio was bombarding people with news of the terrible accident, repeating again and again the name of the engineer responsible for it and declaring that the authorities were looking for him.

When Christian arrived, his face was distorted with worry. Julia explained to him what had happened and what had to happen now.

"This is very difficult, especially now!" he told her. "They're searching for him everywhere—how are we going to get him out?"

"Difficult, easy, it must be done," Julia insisted. "But we mustn't put his life in danger. For the time being he must stay hidden until things calm down. During that time, I'll try to find a way to get him out of the country.'

Fokas never left the country. Christian found him hiding in a deserted area and began to visit him daily, while taking every precaution, to bring him food and tell him about his efforts, with Julia, to get him out of the country. One afternoon, though, wasn't like the others.

When the locals heard what had happened at the bridge site, they knew immediately that the one responsible for the disaster wasn't the husband of the good white woman, but the other one. They found out that Fokas was hiding and that he would leave the country—which meant they would lose her too. The poisoned arrow struck Fokas in the leg. When Christian found him, he understood immediately what had happened. Fokas had managed to pull the arrow out, not knowing that if air got into the wound, the poison would work faster. Death found him almost instantaneously, with the arrow still in his hand.

◆ ◆ ◆

The return journey was an endless nightmare for Julia. Even after some time she had difficulty remembering what had happened after the unbearable and unjust death of Fokas. She only remembered that Christian, Helene, and of course Faida were always beside her, with Faida holding her hand. Her instinct for self-preservation had probably erased from her brain all the painful memories, difficulties, and hopelessness that had overwhelmed her. If it hadn't been for Christian, she didn't know if she would have managed to leave the country.

One of the few memories she could dredge up was the moment of her farewell with Helene and her children, and the guilty expression of Abdul, who hadn't managed to save her husband as he'd once saved her. Perhaps that's why he allowed Faida to leave with her for Greece without any discussion.

Everything seemed different to her when she set foot in Thessaloniki. Fortunately, Fokas's decision to send all their money there before he started on that cursed bridge was a salvation for Julia and the girls. She decided to book them into a hotel, since she hadn't had the courage yet to write anything to his parents.

When she finally lay down on the bed, she slept for almost twenty-four hours. The children stayed completely quiet, realizing how much their mother needed to recover her strength. Besides, they also felt exhausted. After so many hours of sleep, Julia woke up feeling better. She ordered them all a large breakfast, and while they were eating, she tried to organize her thoughts. She looked out of the window. It was winter and the first thing she had to do was make sure they had suitable clothes. They were all wearing summer clothes, and despite the heating in the hotel, they were cold in their cotton dresses. She decided they would go shopping first, then, in the afternoon, she'd go see her father-in-law. She couldn't put it off any longer.

In the store, the salespeople were a little surprised at first by Faida, but her pleasant personality together with the fact that she spoke good Greek soon made them forget the color of her skin and treat her kindly. For herself, Julia chose simple black clothes. She had to explain to Faida that all Greek women who are in mourning wear black, but the girl didn't like it. They came back loaded with packages, ate their lunch, and Julia lay down to rest for a little while. After the difficulties of the last weeks, she tired easily.

She was awakened later in the afternoon by the cries of Faida. It had begun to snow outside and a white mantle had covered everything. Julia watched the flakes falling, enchanted. She had forgotten how beautiful the snow was. But Faida was afraid.

"Madam, bread is falling out of the sky! White bread!" she called out. "What are we going to do?"

Julia laughed. Of course snow would seem like the strangest thing Faida had ever seen. The girls were surprised too. They knew about snow theoretically from school, but they'd never seen it. Julia opened the door and took them all out on the balcony. At first Faida looked at the snowflakes falling on her in a panic, then marveled when she saw them melt a moment later. With great reluctance she let Julia put a snowball in her hand, but then jumped up immediately shouting, "It burns, madam! The white bread that's falling from the sky burns!"

Julia began to laugh and the children joined her. She took the camera that she and Fokas had bought together and began taking pictures of Faida. "I'll send them to your parents," she said. "So they can learn about snow too!"

Faida began to enjoy herself. She even reached the point of lying down on the white mattress that had collected on the balcony and filling her hands with snow. Julia soon called them inside. They had amused themselves for long enough, and she didn't want them to catch colds. Faida and these "African" children were unaccustomed to this weather; the last thing Julia needed now was sickness. Besides, however difficult it might be, she had to go and see her father-in-law.

Her legs trembled as she stood outside his store. From his letters she knew that Kyriakos hadn't retired, that he continued to go every day to his business and that he was still very active despite his seventy-six years. She went inside and saw that the employees were the same. His young lads were now mature men, and his young girls were women of a certain age. With an effort, Julia climbed the few steps to his office and entered without knocking. She found him bent over his accounts as usual.

When he saw her his eyes opened wide and a happy smile spread over his face. He jumped up and Julia disappeared in his embrace. The old man couldn't stop kissing her while his hands kept stroking her hair. "My little girl," he said over and over again. "I see you but I don't believe it. But when did you arrive? Why didn't you let us know? Where is Fokas? Where are the children?"

Julia pulled back from his embrace. "Sit down, Father," she said quietly to him. "I'll tell you everything. That's why I came."

The man's face suddenly darkened. It was then that he noticed her clothes. "Julia, why are you wearing black?" he asked her, very upset. "Who died?" And then, when she didn't answer, "Why don't you speak?"

"Because it's not easy, Father. Sit down and I'll explain everything."

It was much more difficult than she had imagined. Her father-in-law cried like a baby in her arms as soon as he learned of the death of his only son. Julia gave him some water and a cognac and comforted him with words that still sounded hollow and meaningless in her ears but seemed to bring Kyriakos around. He straightened his body, dried his eyes, and looked at his daughter-in-law.

"Here I am, beating my breast and not thinking at all about you, my girl," he whispered.

Julia smiled affectionately through her tears. Even at a moment like this the dignity of this man rose up proudly. "Father," she stammered as soon as she could speak, "we must all be brave. There are the children to think of."

"Where are the children?"

She explained that they were at the hotel. Then, through more sobs, she told him the whole story from the beginning as he had asked her to. He had the right to know how and why his son had died. She recounted for him all their troubles up to the point where they managed to leave the country and explained that Faida was with them. When Julia finished, the two of them were silent, both steeped in their pain.

"Why didn't you come straight to the house?" Kyriakos asked.

"The journey was endless—we were exhausted. And I didn't have the courage to tell you what happened yet. How could I turn up suddenly at your door with the children and Faida but without Fokas? I needed a little time. Do you understand?"

"Completely, my girl."

"But how will we tell Mother? How will I face her without him beside me? What will I tell her about her son?"

"Don't worry about that. We'll tell her together, and then we'll fetch you from the hotel to live with us."

"That's not possible. I have Faida with me."

"So? Do you think that a girl who stood beside you for so many years wouldn't be welcome in my house? She not only looked after you and the children, but also my son!"

"I'm afraid of Mother."

"Evanthia isn't the person you remember, my child. And now . . . after this . . ."

"Exactly because of this! Maybe she'll think I'm responsible for the death of her son."

"Even Evanthia isn't as crazy as that. Before he left, Fokas made the reasons for his decision clear to her. And she knows that you simply followed him. You aren't responsible for any of this. Come, let's go."

The two of them went out into the frigid air. The snow grew heavier as night came on. They walked side by side, not speaking, one supporting the other as tears kept streaming down their faces. As they entered the house, Julia realized she was trembling uncontrollably and not only because of the freezing air.

Evanthia was in the sitting room reading when she saw them come in. A happy cry sprang from her lips. She ran and embraced her daughter-in-law with real delight, which made Julia more upset than ever. She surrendered herself stoically to the kisses and hugs of her mother-in-law so that she could use the time to calm herself. What followed was much like what had happened at her father-in-law's shop, except that Evanthia fainted when she heard the terrible news. They had to give her a tranquilizer as soon as she recovered, but her weeping was like a pitiful lament. Julia looked at the two old people crying in each other's arms in front of her and didn't know what to say to comfort them. She knelt beside them and Evanthia reached out her hand to stroke her hair, at which point Julia too burst into tears again. Her sobs shook her whole body until the two parents embraced her and joined their sobs with hers.

The first to recover was Kyriakos. "We need to pull ourselves together," he murmured, wiping his eyes. "We're not alone. There are three children depending on us. They've been through a lot already!"

Julia dried her eyes too and took a deep breath.

"Where are the children?" Evanthia asked, her voice faint. "Why didn't you bring them? You'll stay here, with us."

Julia repeated everything she had told her father-in-law, that the children were at the hotel and Faida was with them. "Maybe it's better to postpone our moving in till tomorrow," she said. "You're still very upset. And then there's Faida."

She was surprised to hear her mother-in-law say almost the same as her father-in-law had said a little earlier. "We'll all live together," Evanthia declared abruptly. "After what has happened, you and the children are our only joy. As for the black girl, she's welcome in our house just as she was in yours."

Julia stroked her mother-in-law's cheek softly and couldn't help thinking that if Fokas could see them from above, he'd be very happy that the women in his life had finally come together.

The children were very curious to meet the grandparents they'd come to love through their mother's stories over the years. As soon as they entered the house, they dashed into the elderly couple's arms as if they'd only seen them the day before. Evanthia sobbed as she hugged the girls to her. After the first hugs were over, little Evanthia made herself comfortable in her grandfather's arms and soon after fell asleep.

Faida came nervously into the house and sat down on one side of the room near the entrance. Julia called her over to introduce her to her in-laws. The girl didn't know what to do when Kyriakos, as soon as he was introduced, opened his arms and gave her a big hug. Evanthia did the same. Much later, lying on her bed, Julia thought how she used to believe that people can't completely change, but Evanthia was living proof of the opposite. The warm embrace of her in-laws was like balm to her soul, which, after so long, was finally at peace. She felt that she had somewhere to rest and people to look after her, love her, and make the absence of Fokas hurt less.

The next day Julia's father-in-law enrolled the three children in school, explaining the special circumstances to the teachers. He bought another bed for Faida, who had slept on the floor the first night, and before a week had passed, Evanthia, with Faida's help, had arranged the apartment to accommodate everyone. But when Faida explained politely but firmly that from now on she would do all the housework, Evanthia was overwhelmed and turned to Julia for help.

"That's the way it is, Mother, just as she said," she explained. "I didn't want to accept it either in the beginning and even more so now that I've become so close to her. But Faida has very strong opinions about her place and her duties. The salary she gets is almost symbolic, but she would never accept any more, however much I insisted, any more than she would abandon calling me 'madam,' even though it really irritates me."

"But I feel so bad, child! She anticipates my every wish."

"And if you deprive her of that she'll be unhappy. She does the same to me. The girl has been with me since she was fifteen and she seems to have dedicated her life to me and the children. If I hadn't taken her with me, she could have died."

Before two months had passed, Julia felt as if she'd never left Greece. Only the absence of Fokas tormented her from time to time. She tried not to cry in front of the children and her in-laws, and Faida put cold compresses on her eyes when she did cry so the others wouldn't know about it. The young woman never told her mistress that she did the same thing for her mother-in-law, who also hid her tears. Julia had never written to her mother about what had happened. In fact, she had stopped writing to her altogether. She didn't have the courage to tell her how her daughter's life had been ruined. Better for her to live in ignorance.

The children seemed happy with their life in Thessaloniki, except for Hara, who had told her mother that she didn't like the city. She couldn't bear so many cars and wanted to live in a house with a garden rather than an apartment. Julia smiled despite herself. Her daughter wasn't like her. She'd grown up with a longing for the city and always saw her house, the one by the river, as an anchor that stopped her from sailing to other places. Now she saw that her eldest daughter needed precisely that anchor, but Julia couldn't do anything about it. She knew that if she even mentioned going to her village, it would upset her in-laws, who clung to her and would tremble at the thought she might settle there. Besides, there was something that counterbalanced Hara's hatred of the city and that was the grandparents themselves. At fourteen, she and Theodora, now twelve, were like their grandmother's shadow; they followed her faithfully. Evanthia had taught her two older grandchildren to knit and to cook. On Sundays, when they didn't have school, she took the two of them into the kitchen and closed the door behind them. There she sat on a chair and directed them as they prepared the family meal. She only got up to check if the onions had browned as they should, if the rice needed to boil a bit longer, or if the sauce needed to thicken a little more. She also taught them to roll out the dough and make the pies she was famous for.

Nine-year-old Evanthia, on the other hand, was completely and utterly tied to her grandfather. She went to his store with him, and they regularly took long walks together. All of Thessaloniki got to know them; wherever little Evanthia was, there would be her grandfather. He was also the only one she would allow to check her homework, and although she didn't like school much, she studied hard so as not to disappoint him.

That summer, when Kyriakos took her fishing, Evanthia found her destiny in life. From then on she often dragged her grandfather away from his shop so that the two of them could go fish. Julia and Faida observed all this and often laughed about it. By now, these two had taken over the running of the house together and always began their day with the usual coffee, except that their company now included Evanthia. Often daughter- and mother-in-law talked about the old days, and they could now laugh at the past. Only occasionally did Evanthia lament the mistakes she'd made that drove her only child away. Whenever this happened, Faida would always distract her by asking to hear the story of the cup again and they would all end up laughing and hold hands.

They lived like that for three years, and during that time, the wounds that had opened in Cameroon finally closed. The loss of Fokas stopped hurting with the same intensity as it had in the beginning and became a sweet burden on all their spirits. It was a burden none of them wanted to avoid; it was what bound them to him.

It was unexpected, but in reality they should have expected it. It was unbelievably painful, but how else could it have been? Kyriakos

Karapanos took his last breath just before the spring came, thrusting them back into winter. His eighty-year-old heart, already tired, stopped beating during a short time he spent in the hospital. They were all shocked when the doctor announced it and didn't want to believe him.

The children were more upset than anyone. For the second time in their short lives they had lost someone they adored; for a second time they felt the ground give way under their feet.

The house suddenly felt empty as the six females were left behind to weep, and their grief for Fokas returned more sharply.

◆ ◆ ◆

Julia felt as if she were suffocating in the house and went out to walk along the waterfront to get some air. More than a year had passed since the death of her father-in-law and yet the heavy atmosphere didn't seem to lift. Every corner was filled with his presence. The summer was already nearly over and in a short time the schools would open. Everything seemed the same, but nothing was the same. The store had been sold for a very good price, leaving her mother-in-law a serious sum of money, just as Fokas had left a large sum for Julia.

Julia took a deep breath to stop the tears flowing. She didn't know how to go on. Everything around them was full of painful memories, memories that made them suffer more than they could bear. More than anything, she was concerned about the children. They had all changed a great deal. Everything that tied them to the city, which none of them really liked, was lost with the death of their grandfather. Hara seemed to be suffocating more than any of them and quite often she had hinted at the possibility of leaving, but her grandmother's wounded air always made her stop talking.

Julia heard hurried steps behind her and turned to see who it was. She was astonished to find her daughter Hara standing there. "What are you doing here, child?" she asked.

"Don't be angry, Mom, but I followed you."

"And why did you follow me?"

"Because I wanted to talk to you when we were by ourselves. You must listen to me."

"All right, we're alone here. So tell me. What's going on?"

"What's going on is that we can't take it anymore. The younger ones agree with me!"

"About what?"

"Listen, Mom. We came to Thessaloniki after our father died—maybe that's why the city upsets us. Now even more because it's connected to everything bad in our lives."

"But we live well here."

"We lived well as long as Grandfather was alive. But now it's hell here. And all three of us want to leave."

"And where would we go?"

"I think you know . . ."

"And Grandmother?"

"Grandmother agrees. If you'll allow it, she'll come with us. She even helped me decide all this. She wants us to leave if it will make us happy and she knows she can't live far away from us."

"Why does this smell to me like a plot?" Julia asked her, not believing her ears.

"Maybe because that's something familiar to you," her daughter teased.

"Do you understand what you're asking me? Do you understand that things will be very different there?"

"That's exactly what we want. A new beginning in a new place that doesn't remind us of anything but is beautiful. And you yourself have said to me a thousand times how beautiful that corner of the earth is. So? What do you say?"

"Let me think for a while."

Her daughter kissed her and left as fast as she had come. Julia turned her short walk into a long one. Dusk was falling; the sea had darkened but was calm as if it didn't want to disturb the thoughts of this small-framed woman who walked slower and slower until she stopped and stood, looking at the water with a steady gaze. Her whole life passed in front of her like a movie. She had done the only right thing in her life when she followed her heart and Fokas, but she had to admit that she hadn't managed to stop the river from dragging her along. It had taken her countless miles to another continent. Now, it seemed that fate had decided on a different course. If Julia was honest with herself, she had to admit that Hara had only spoken out loud what she herself hadn't dared to say. The desire to go home had been in her heart for some months now. Now, the fact that a whole tribe would return with her, together with a girl of another nationality and color, made her smile. And then Evanthia came into her mind. Who could have predicted that she would return in the company of her mother-in-law? What strange games life plays!

Julia's gaze finally cleared. She'd made her decision. She knew very well what she wanted. She wanted peace, she wanted her home . . .

The house by the river.

ASPASIA

Stavros's house disappointed Aspasia a great deal. It was at the edge of the city and very small, tucked into a courtyard with other small houses around it and lots of neighbors. Stavros seemed to be very popular: when they arrived, everyone was waiting for them in their doorways and started throwing rice at them. Her mother-in-law, Kyria Stella, was very happy to see them and took pride in her beautiful daughter-in-law. They had first met at the wedding, and as soon as Kyria Stella was introduced to her future daughter-in-law, her eyes filled with tears. She hugged her and kissed her and gave her her blessing with all her heart. Kyria Stella also took a warm liking to Aspasia's mother, as the two had a lot in common. Both had grown up in a village and both were simple women whose only interest was the happiness of their children.

Right after the ceremony Stavros, Aspasia, and Kyria Stella left in the car that Stavros's boss, Kyrios Alekos, had lent them. When they arrived at Stavros's house, the three of them went inside. Aspasia looked around her. The kitchen, which also served as the living room, was the largest room. Two bedrooms made up the rest of the house and Aspasia noticed with horror that they were next to one another. Would she spend her wedding night here with her mother-in-law a breath away? She nearly started crying.

With the help of the neighbors, they unloaded Aspasia's things and she started to arrange her clothes in the closet, trying to hold back the tears that had started to fall. She already wanted to go home. At least there they didn't live one on top of the other. The yard at home was a gateway onto nature and the infinite. She could breathe freely there, and she had the river to carry her along on its green waters. Here everything was so small and wretched that it weighed on her spirits.

Stavros found her crying on the bed that his mother had made up with pure white sheets decorated with lace she had crocheted herself.

"What's the matter, my love?" he asked anxiously. "Why are you crying?" His tender voice made Aspasia cry even harder and he didn't know what to do. He reached out his hand and stroked her hair but Aspasia showed no sign of calming down. "If you don't tell me what's wrong, I can't help you," he said softly. "Speak to me, my darling. Why are you suddenly so upset?"

"I want to go home," she stammered between her sobs.

At that Stavros smiled with relief. "Is that all it is? Don't you like the house?"

Aspasia stopped crying and looked at him in surprise. "How did you know?" she asked, wiping her eyes with the handkerchief he gave her.

"It's not so strange. And I don't like the house much either, but it's the only thing I could find. But don't worry. Kyrios Alekos announced that he wants to open an office in the Peloponnese so he'll be sending me there."

"So we won't be staying here?"

"No. In a week or two at the most we'll leave for Kalamata. We'll find a house together there, something more to your taste, and move in as soon as possible. The only thing is that we'll have my mother with us too. I can't leave her alone, Aspasia. I hope you understand."

"Of course I understand," she hurried to assure him. "You made that clear to me from the beginning and I accepted it."

Her look, though, told him that something was still bothering her. "Come on, grouch!" Stavros said with a smile. "Tell me what else is annoying you, because it's not just the house."

Aspasia lowered her eyes in embarrassment. "And tonight?" she asked him softly. "What's going to happen tonight? Is this where we're going to spend our wedding night?"

Stavros started laughing and hugged her. "Silly girl! Where did you get that idea? Did you have so little faith in me? As soon as you've changed and packed a few clothes, we're leaving."

"Leaving? Where are we going?"

"Kyrios Alekos has a house in Tyrnavos. Last year he completely renovated it and he's given me the keys so we can stay there as long as we want. It's not a fancy hotel, of course, but we'll be all alone there."

Aspasia sprang into his arms. She was still crying, but with tears of relief and happiness now.

The house at Tyrnavos was beyond their expectations. They arrived late at night to find food in the cupboard and plenty of wood in the yard for the fireplace that dominated the sitting room. A little while after they entered the house, a roaring fire had filled it with warmth and Aspasia had fried some eggs.

"I'd have liked to make you something better," she told Stavros. "But this was all I could manage tonight."

"Don't be silly. This is wonderful," Stavros replied, smiling and sitting down quickly at the table. "To be honest, I'm starving," he added.

Their meal was made complete by the wine that Kyrios Alekos had left for them in the fridge.

"Your boss must love you a lot," Aspasia observed as they ate. "He went to so much trouble for us."

"The man has a big heart. I've been working for him for six years and I love him very much. He and his wife treat me like a son."

"Don't they have any children of their own?"

"They have . . . a daughter."

"What? You didn't tell me about that."

"There's nothing to tell you. The truth is that they would have really liked to see me with Despina. They'd hinted at it, but she fell in love with a sailor and married. Fortunately—for me, that is—because I'd have been in a difficult position."

"Don't you like their daughter? Maybe she's ugly?" Aspasia teased.

"She isn't ugly, but she wasn't for me. We weren't at all suited. I tried to explain that to Kyrios Alekos but he didn't seem to understand. Later Despina introduced her husband to him and that was the end of the story. The poor man was bitter about it, but relaxed. Still, his love for me didn't change. Maybe it got stronger. As if he felt bad that his daughter went her own way and didn't marry me."

"What did he say about me?"

"He was very happy I'd found the sort of girl I wanted."

The evening continued beside the fire. As the time passed, Stavros's eyes shone brighter and brighter, while Aspasia's embarrassment became more obvious. Stavros felt ready to burst. His mind searched for ways to approach his wife but he instantly rejected them all as being too coarse. Then his eye fell on the radio that was in the room. He thanked his lucky stars that at that particular moment they happened to be playing simple, romantic songs. He reached his hand out to Aspasia and pulled her up for a dance. It was enough.

After their dance, Stavros lifted her in his arms and carried her into the bedroom, where the large double bed was waiting for them. He put her down gently and lay down beside her. Aspasia looked at him. Her eyes were shining like his. The moon peeped in from the window, making her hair look like molten gold as it surrounded her face, and her body looked beautiful on the white sheets. Stavros knew he couldn't contain himself another minute.

They stayed for five wonderful days in that house, and if someone had asked them how they liked Tyrnavos, they wouldn't have known how to answer. They were indifferent to exploring the area. All their interest was directed to each other's bodies. Stavros found it difficult to take his hands off his wife, and Aspasia was curious to explore all the avenues of pleasure with him. They had to return to Larissa eventually—Stavros couldn't stay away from his work any longer. They both knew, though, that these last few days would remain in their memory as the best time of their marriage. From now on they would have to be more careful with their expressions of affection so as not to embarrass Kyria Stella. Or so they thought.

Stavros's mother remembered very well how much she had loved her husband. In the glances that the newlywed couple exchanged she saw the same flame she had experienced and realized that she should leave them alone as much as possible. On the day they returned, as soon as they had eaten, Kyria Stella got dressed and took her handbag.

"What are you dressed up for, Mama?" Stavros asked in surprise.

"Oh, son, I didn't know you were coming back today, and I promised Argyro I'd help her make a jacket for her son," she answered before turning to her daughter-in-law. "Argyro is a friend of mine, my girl, but she has one fault. If you laugh at her it puts her in a bad mood and I can't bear her moods. And she doesn't seem to be able to learn how to sew. So what can I do, eh? Not go to help her? You two shouldn't bother to wait up for me because I might be late."

Then she disappeared and Stavros turned to his wife with a knowing look. "If that wasn't a *deus ex machina,* I don't know what is," he said, taking her in his arms and laughing.

The next day, after Stavros left early for work, Aspasia was surprised when her mother-in-law announced, "Listen, girl. Now you're queen of the house. From now on, you tell me what to do and I'll follow."

"But what are you saying, Kyria Stella?" Aspasia protested in embarrassment.

Her mother-in-law cut her off with a movement of her hand. "Forget the formality, Aspasia. Just call me Mother because we're mother and daughter now. The house is more yours than mine! And the fact that you accepted living with me is a big thing, but it doesn't mean I give the orders. I just help you."

That same night, their second in the house, Kyria Stella got dressed to go out again.

"Where are you going again, Mama?" Stavros asked with obvious curiosity.

"Hmm . . . I'm going to see Kalliope, son," she answered quickly. "She's making some lace for her daughter's dowry and she asked for a little help."

And before anyone could say anything more, Kyria Stella disappeared.

Stavros turned to his wife. "What on earth? Everyone's forgotten how to crochet and they need my mother to help them?" he asked. Stavros had a look of mock disbelief on his face, but the next moment his expression changed as Aspasia's very presence, alone with him in the house, aroused him.

A few days later Stavros and Aspasia left at dawn for Kalamata with precise instructions from Kyrios Alekos. They were to find an office on the port suitable for their work and a house quite nearby for themselves. He provided them with the addresses of some people he knew who would help them. They set out full of high spirits; to them the trip felt like a second honeymoon. The summer had just begun, so the journey was pleasant, and they were full of dreams about what seemed to be a shining future.

They were very lucky to find an office on the first day. It was exactly what was needed for a transport agency and from what Stavros learned, there was plenty of work here and many possibilities if someone was willing to work. He was very eager on behalf of Kyrios Alekos, who had helped him so much. The greatest stroke of luck, though, was the house they found. It was in a quiet neighborhood with a distant view of the sea, which made them both happy. It was quite large, but completely suitable for a couple who wanted to have a family. There were three bedrooms and a large kitchen and living room, and in the yard there were trees and flowers that reminded Aspasia of home. Since the rent was affordable, they closed the deal without any discussion.

The young couple returned to Larissa full of enthusiasm and impatience for their new life. Aspasia could hardly wait. Kalamata was a much livelier city than Larissa and she counted the days until they moved into their new home, far from the courtyard that suffocated her.

As soon as they were settled, Kyrios Alekos made a trip to Kalamata to see the new office and left completely satisfied. Aspasia, who knew how much they were indebted to this man, did everything she could to look after him for the five days he stayed nearby, and Kyrios Alekos was truly pleased by Stavros's good luck, although he couldn't help thinking that if his daughter had more brains in her head, this fine, hardworking young man would now be his son. Together they could have done big things and spread out all over Greece. But instead, the girl had chosen a man she hardly ever saw as he traveled on big gas tankers for months on end, and the time she spent alone drove her to look for company that didn't suit her.

◆ ◆ ◆

It wasn't very long before Aspasia suddenly realized that she was terribly bored. The discovery hit her like a giant wave. Stavros left before dawn each day and often returned late in the evening, leaving her with just her mother-in-law for company and her only amusement a walk to the sea. She had never found it easy to make friends, perhaps because she had sisters. From the time she was very young, she'd always had someone to play with, so she never sought the company of other girls. Later, when she was older, her sisters again took the place of friends as they told her all their secrets, great and small. Now that she was grown and living in Kalamata, she could have sought a companion among her neighbors, but she was still recovering from the claustrophobic feel of their neighborhood in Larissa, so she kept a wary distance.

Her mother-in-law, on the contrary, soon made a network of friends. She often left to have coffee with Aphrodite, who lived next door, or with Katina, whose house was two streets further up, and these women, in their turn, returned the visits. Aspasia usually took care to be out of the house at those times. She got tired of the boring conversations the older women had, about recipes, children, and grandchildren, and she preferred to take her regular walk to the sea. There, looking at the ocean that began at her feet and stretched as far as she could see, the desire for escape came back to her. The ships she saw leaving made her eyes fill with tears; she wanted to board one of them without knowing its destination, so much so that it sometimes felt painful. Kalamata began to feel like her village had—like the heavy ball and chain that prisoners once wore. It weighed down her feet and her soul and chained her to the ground, while she wanted to fly high and far, to see the world and live her life however it came. She didn't dare write about these thoughts to her mother because she knew how she would answer. In the short letters she wrote, she confined herself to daily events.

Songs came back to her lips and with them the desire to make something of her voice, even though she wasn't sure how. At the same time she thought about her husband; he had married to have a family, not for his wife to be a singer. Duty and desire fought each other inside her. So when she discovered, just over a year into their marriage, that she was pregnant, she felt some relief mixed with her joy. The child she was expecting was the distraction she needed to drive foolish ambition out of her heart and root out of her brain every false hope that she might have to one day become a singer.

Stavros was out of his mind with happiness when he found out the news. So was his mother, who impatiently waited for her first grandchild and set about making everything it would need. She embroidered sheets, crocheted blankets and little jackets, but not once did Aspasia tell anyone that she hoped the baby would be a boy so that it would take her husband's name, as was the custom. She felt rather ashamed of this desire. To assuage her guilt, she prayed for hours on end that the child be healthy, whatever it was. Kyria Stella, who had begun to make daily visits to the church, prayed for something else: that this child would bring peace to her daughter-in-law's soul. For some time she had known that Aspasia was a restless spirit. Kyria Stella was afraid when she saw the way the girl looked at the sea. Her desire for escape hadn't gone unnoticed by the old woman and she feared the time when that desire would grow stronger than the feelings of duty that she knew Aspasia had in her.

Stavros and Aspasia's daughter was born a few days before they celebrated their second wedding anniversary and by general admission, she was the most beautiful baby anyone in the hospital had ever seen—completely blond, with a bright little face and her mother's regular features. Very moved, the mother-in-law held her grandchild in her arms and thanked God she was strong and healthy.

The baby swept everything up and changed everyone's lives. Little Stella, as they called her, had very strong opinions about her care and would only calm down in her mother's arms. Aspasia couldn't be away from her for a moment or else the child would make a deafening racket with her cries and sobs. This wasn't unpleasant at first, of course, but soon it began to be a nightmare for Aspasia. Wherever she went she had to take the baby; on her walks to the sea she now had company, and despite the fact that little Stella was quiet in her stroller, Aspasia felt as if she had lost her independence.

As soon as Stella was six months old, Aspasia discovered, this time without any pleasure, that she was pregnant again. Stavros could jump for joy and her mother-in-law could weep with emotion, but she didn't feel the same. She was much more tired than she'd been during her first pregnancy and she wondered how she'd manage if the second child had the same disposition as the first. How much of her would be left?

A second daughter soon joined the family. Even though Aspasia had again hoped for a boy to name after her husband, she was happy to give the child her mother's name. Little Theodora was the complete opposite of her sister. She never cried and showed no special need for much affection from her mother. On the contrary, she seemed very happy and satisfied in her father's arms and got along well with her grandmother.

As the two girls grew, their differences continued to show. Little Stella went wherever her mother was, while Theodora was always with her grandmother. Nevertheless their love for one another was very obvious from the beginning. The little one, in particular, admired the older one and looked at her with adoration, and Stella, when they got a little older, took the blame for whatever mischief they'd been up to.

When Theodora was just eight months old, Aspasia realized that she was expecting a third child. Extremely upset by the news, she had a row with Stavros, their first serious quarrel in four years of marriage.

"I can't go on having a baby nearly every year!" she exclaimed when Stavros tried to hug her.

"What are you saying?" he asked in surprise. "I don't understand."

"That I don't want this baby!" Aspasia shouted.

Stavros's face darkened. "Have you gone crazy, Aspasia? God sends us a child and you resent it?"

"First of all, it's not one child, it's the third. Secondly, the last one isn't even a year old. And finally, I don't think the Almighty has anything to do with your dirty business."

"My dirty business? Is that how you feel every time I touch you?" Stavros was now beside himself.

"That's not what I meant, and you know it. But I can't go on having children all the time. I'm tired, don't you understand?"

"No. But explain it to me so I can."

"I'm trying but you don't want to listen. The children are very young—one came right after the other. I can't even imagine having another child in the house. And basically you're gone all day."

"So what should I do, then? Stay home? I have mouths to feed."

"Yes, you do. Too many in fact, and now we're adding another. You already work from morning till night so I never see you anymore; we don't even go out. And I'm stuck in here all day with two babies and your mother. This is no life!"

"So what did you expect when we got married, Aspasia? Didn't you know we'd have a family? And now what's missing? Whatever you ask for, you get! Did I ever make you do without clothes, shoes, and whatever else you want?"

"And why do I have them? What do I do with them? Do we ever go anywhere?"

"What does that have to do with the child?"

"Just that another child means more expenses and more of being tied down."

"So if you didn't have the children what would you do?"

"I don't know. Maybe I'd work."

"Work? Where would you work then?"

"Somewhere! I'd bring some money into the house and more important, I wouldn't be stuck inside all day."

"Aspasia, are you in your right mind today? When I met you, did you have some plan to work that I didn't know about? Had you decided to study or learn some skill and I got in your way? What's this you're flinging at me without any warning?"

"I like singing and you know I have a good voice. That's what enchanted you back then if I'm not mistaken," Aspasia said bitterly.

Stavros stood looking at her for a moment. "Who told you it was your voice that enchanted me? It was you yourself who enchanted me. I loved you and I thought you loved me too."

"I didn't say I didn't love you."

"Then why are you driving me crazy? And what does singing have to do with this conversation? I married you so we could set up a house, not a bouzouki joint. You're a married woman with two children and you're expecting a third, and we're sitting here talking about what? The possibility that you'll become a singer?"

"It's my dream we're talking about, Stavros! A dream that will never be anything else but a dream in the end!" Aspasia answered as her eyes filled with tears.

Stavros went to her, softer now. "Hey, sweetheart, why did this idea come to you today? All this time you never told me you had a dream like that. And now, instead of being happy because we're expecting a baby, we're quarreling about nonsense."

Aspasia stopped crying and looked at him angrily. "Nonsense? Is that all you have to say about all the things I've just told you? Do you understand me so little? All you care about is having a wife at home to wash and iron and cook for you and to raise the children you make for her. Not to mention that later you'll need her as a nurse for your mother."

Stavros jumped up from beside her in a fury now. "You shouldn't have said that! You're wrong, Aspasia. And my mother adores you—she helps you and she embraced you with real love. How can you think that way about her and me?"

"Of all the things I said, what isn't true?" Aspasia asked. "Do I do all the things I said or not? As for your mother, I have nothing against her, but that is what the outcome will be. So why are you angry? And amongst all these duties, where do I fit in? Where do I exist and when will I ever get to do what I want? When we married you were a simple driver; now Kyrios Alekos is getting ready to make you a partner. Your dreams, your career, everything is turning out as you wanted it. But what about me?"

"What about you? When I married you, you were a village girl who wanted, by any means you could, to escape the life you were leading."

"And end up in a worse one where I have only responsibilities and no rights?"

"I'm not going to answer that because I'll only say things I'll regret afterward. I'm very sorry that you've spoiled an otherwise happy day—I didn't know you felt like this. But there's nothing else I can do, Aspasia. I'm offering you what I offered when we first agreed to marry. Nothing more and nothing less. The only thing I can promise you, now that I know what you want, is that there won't be another child after this. Certainly, if you had said it before, I'd have taken precautions, but I didn't know. It's the only thing I can say I'm sorry about."

Stavros suddenly looked very tired. He left the room and Aspasia heard the door shut behind him. Almost immediately she started to cry. She already regretted all the things she had said. She was ashamed of her ingratitude and for throwing it all so insensitively in his face, and she berated herself for not being happy with her life. Stavros was right about everything he had said and she hadn't had the courage to accept it and say she was sorry before he'd left so bitterly. She thanked God that the children were sleeping and her mother-in-law was out. If Kyria Stella had overheard what she'd said about caring for her, Aspasia would have died of shame. What had come over her?

A little while later, when Stavros came back home, she flung herself into his arms weeping and asking for forgiveness. When Stavros saw the sincerity in her eyes, he hugged her tightly, taking a deep breath as if he'd been drowning.

"Don't do that to me again, Aspasia," he whispered. "I felt as if the ground was giving way under my feet. I thought my head would burst. I love you more than my own life and I try to do the best for you and the children. I understand that you've been lonely here, that we don't go out and have fun at all, but I promise you that these things will pass. Look how successful we've been since we married. In a little while we'll be able to buy our own house. Just be a little bit patient."

"Forget everything I said—I was being silly. Maybe it's the pregnancy. The doctor says a pregnant woman's hormones do all sorts of strange things. That's what's wrong. Do you forgive me?"

His kiss conveyed his forgiveness. Then she led him to the bed and gave herself to him with a passion that reminded her of the first days of their marriage.

Months later, Aspasia's son, unable to survive the difficulty of birth, died before he'd properly come into the world. The house was truly overwhelmed with grief, but Stavros and his mother hid their despair as they tried to help Aspasia, who got worse every day. She forced herself to get out of bed each morning, but even little Stella couldn't attract her attention; as for little Theodora, it was as if she didn't exist as far as her mother was concerned. For hours on end, Aspasia would sit and stare at nothing, and if it hadn't been for her mother-in-law feeding her, she might have died of starvation. At night she hardly slept, and although Christmas was approaching and the nights were chilly, she went outside and sat for hours on the verandah. Her gaze passed over the lights of the town and focused on the harbor and the boats that were anchored there. In time, she came down with a severe cold and was confined to her bed for weeks with high fevers. All the while, her grief persisted. In fact, she cried even more.

In a moment of helplessness, Stavros yelled at her. "Enough!" he shouted one day when Aspasia started crying again. "It's been three months since you lost the baby and instead of getting better, you get worse and worse! Life goes on, Aspasia—you don't seem to understand that! We have two other children who need you. What do you think you'll achieve with this behavior? Will it bring him back?"

"I'm not crying for that," Aspasia answered.

Stavros was thunderstruck. "So why are you crying?" he asked.

"I'm to blame for everything that happened. I'll never forgive myself."

"Forgive yourself for what? Tell me, Aspasia, so we can find some way out. The way things are going, we're heading for disaster. Why do you say it's your fault?"

"I didn't want the child and said terrible things when I found out I was pregnant. And so God has punished me. He took the baby from me before I could hold him in my arms. That's why I'm crying."

"What you're saying is crazy, Aspasia! What fault is it of yours that the child had a heart defect and couldn't survive? Didn't you hear the doctor? Even if the boy had lived, it wouldn't have been for long. Perhaps for a week, perhaps a little longer, but he would have died. It's not your fault!"

"How can you say that after everything I said? The memory of it all makes me want to end it all in the sea."

"Oh, nice words, Aspasia!" Stavros said sarcastically. "And what about our children? They need you. And what's more, I do too. It's not your fault, my darling, that we lost the child. It was the will of God, like so many other things that happen in the world. The important thing is for you to look ahead and offer our girls what they need. And if you want to pray about something, pray that our daughters are healthy and strong. And later on, if you want to, we'll have another child."

Aspasia fell into her husband's arms and began to finally calm down. From that day on she slowly recovered and her mother-in-law hurried to light a large candle in the church as she prayed that her daughter-in-law would find peace.

◆ ◆ ◆

The wedding celebration of one of Stavros's colleagues would put his own marriage to the test, although none of them knew it at the time. No one could imagine that the reception following the ceremony would cause so much damage.

Three years had passed since Aspasia had lost her son, but she hadn't mentioned the subject of another child and Stavros hadn't pressured her. Little Stella had turned six and was going to school, leaving Theodora inconsolable during the hours that her sister was away.

On the evening of the wedding, Aspasia was more beautiful than ever. Her daughters were so dazzled as they watched her and their father leave that they forgot to complain about being left behind with their grandmother. Immediately after the ceremony, the couple went to the nightclub where the reception was being held. It had been years since Aspasia had had any fun and she enjoyed it with all her heart. In her high spirits, she took the microphone from the singer and opened Pandora's box with a single song. It was a tremendous surprise for everyone who knew them, but also for Aspasia herself. Her clear, strong voice blended perfectly with the band and everyone's spirits were lifted even higher. When she tried to give back the microphone, the hired singer refused and begged her to continue as he backed her in harmony. They sang the third song together.

Aspasia was delighted with her success that evening and smiled broadly at the owner of the club, who asked her if they could talk later. His proposal was clear: he wanted her to sing every night at the club for a salary that made her jaw drop. She'd never had money of her own and now she was being given the opportunity to do something she loved as well as make money she could use however she liked. Of course, there was the issue of Stavros. He most certainly wouldn't be pleased with the proposition, but Aspasia had made up her mind to do battle.

They fought for three days, their voices echoing all over the house. Kyria Stella crossed herself and left with the children so they wouldn't hear their parents quarreling. The situation reached an impasse; the atmosphere was unbearable but Aspasia was adamant. When Stavros started sleeping on the sofa, his mother realized she had to intervene. She went to see her son at his office, where they would be alone.

"Sit down, son, because we need to talk," she ordered him quietly and he obeyed.

"What have you come to say to me, Mama?" he asked. "Don't you know what's going on? Don't you hear?"

"I came because I hear and I understand."

"So what can I do? Shall I let my wife sing and have men hitting on her? It's not a job for a married woman with two children!"

"I won't say that you're wrong, Stavros, but you must understand that you can't do anything but give in."

"What are you saying?"

"That Aspasia will do it with or without your permission. I've never seen her like this."

"But what's got into her?"

"I think she had the desire to sing in her long before you met her, but when she met you and had children she put it aside. But you can't hold on to her now, son. If you try, you'll destroy your home."

"And if I do let her go and become a singer, won't that destroy our home?"

"Maybe it will, and maybe it won't. I'm not saying that things are simple, but if you insist on saying no, she'll leave you. Perhaps if she gets into that party world, she'll tire of it at some point and decide that it's better for her to stay home."

The discussion with his mother got Stavros thinking. He had to admit that she was right. Aspasia seemed determined not to give in but his male egotism wouldn't allow him to back down. Meanwhile, the club owner was pressuring Aspasia. For years he'd been looking for a good singer who was also beautiful, and this particular girl was all that. He'd make a lot of money with her, he was sure. He couldn't wait to get started, so when Aspasia delayed, he generously increased his offer.

For the good of everyone involved, a compromise was finally struck. Kyria Stella tactfully suggested to her daughter-in-law that she propose working half time at the club on a trial basis until the summer. This gave Stavros a way to end the crisis without completely backing down.

The first day she got up on the stage, Aspasia's legs trembled a little and her hands were sweaty as she held the microphone. But after the first song, when the tips began to collect in front of her, she let fly, singing the biggest hits of the season and delighting everyone in the room. Nobody, especially his wife, mentioned to Stavros that after her set, as was customary, she sat at a number of different tables to drink with the customers and increase the amount they spent.

Before long, Aspasia was in great demand. At the club, her high spirits seemed tireless, and the late nights didn't seem to bother her at all. At home, though, things were different. On the evenings that she worked and got home at dawn, she slept all the next day, and on the days that she didn't work, she didn't seem to have any appetite for life. The children were no longer among her priorities. If it hadn't been for their grandmother, the little girls would have been growing up almost entirely on their own.

As the days passed, Stavros clenched his teeth harder and his mother grew bitter, but Aspasia didn't see any of it. She only lived for the hours when she was working; nothing else mattered anymore. As she was oblivious to the small-town gossip that centered on her, she had no idea how difficult it was for her husband to restrain himself when he heard the rumors about the crazy parties she attended each night. Nor was she aware of the embarrassment she caused her mother-in-law. Wherever Kyria Stella went, conversations were quickly cut off so that she understood they'd been discussing how she raised her son's children while her daughter-in-law sang and had a good time nearly every night at the bouzouki club.

When she got up on the stage, Aspasia saw people singing and having fun with her, she heard the applause caressing her ears, and her heart swelled with joy. When she saw the plates smashed for her, a traditional show of appreciation and celebration, she felt like a queen on an invisible throne. When she saw the boxes of champagne that the waiters brought onto the stage and heard the pop of a cork and saw the golden liquid filling a glass, she thought this was her destiny in life. She was born for this work. She no longer wrote to her mother. Rather than tell lies, she preferred silence.

Just before Easter, Aspasia was offered a summer gig at a club in Rhodes, along with a very high fee. Elated, she hurried to accept it before she talked with Stavros. She knew he'd just refuse, and she had no intention of backing down. The confrontation was intense and this time even her mother-in-law lost patience. Faced with a united front of mother and son, Aspasia dug her heels in even more. The words she exchanged with Stavros were the worst that had ever been spoken in the house.

"You're not going anywhere!" Stavros declared for at least the tenth time.

Aspasia looked at him derisively. "If you think you're the sultan and I'm a slave for you to order around, think again. I'm a free person, Stavros. I can do what I want."

"You're a married woman and you've got duties. How dare you ask me to go away for a whole summer?"

"But I'm not asking you," Aspasia answered calmly. "I'm simply telling you that they're offering me a really good job, the pay is very high, and I'm going."

"So, in other words, you're defying me?"

"When you tell me that you're going to Tripoli to transport goods, are you asking my permission? No. You simply announce that your work is sending you there and you go. Well, my work is sending me to Rhodes."

"That's different!"

"Don't tell me that a woman's place is in the home, because I'll tell you to go and look at a calendar. We're living in the twentieth century, not the nineteenth. Anyway, you don't seem to mind the money I make too much."

"To hell with the money! Don't you realize you've destroyed our home? The children hardly see you—my mother is bringing them up. Even when you *are* home, you might as well be away. And now you tell me you're going to be gone for three whole months. You've really lost it!"

"Is that what annoys you, that I'm not home? Or is it the fact that I earn more money than you do and have more success?"

"You should be ashamed of yourself for saying things like that, Aspasia. Wake up before it's too late! Where is the woman I married? We dreamed about a family, remember?"

"Fine. I made you a family; I had two children—what more do you want?"

"I want you. But in your place. And with your head on straight!"

"My head is just fine! As for my place, I finally found it, and I have no intention of returning to your service. If you want a servant, you should hire one. But I'm a woman, Stavros, and I'm clever. I'm going to achieve what I always dreamed of."

"Aspasia, do you love me?" Stavros suddenly asked.

Surprised by the question, she hesitated.

Stavros pressed on. "I'm asking you something. Can't you answer?"

"What sort of question is that now?"

"A very simple one, if your feelings are clear."

"Of course I love you. What's that got to do with what we're talking about?"

"If you love someone, you want to be with them as much as possible and you try not to upset them. Instead, you and I are becoming strangers, and every day you fill me with bitterness!"

"It's the same for me. You know that I love what I do and despite that, you put pressure on me to give it up. Why do you do that? Because I'm a woman? If it was your work that sent you far away I'd have to sit quietly and wait for you, however long you were gone, without complaining. But you don't do that. With the money I'm making we'll be able to buy the house we've dreamed of a little sooner, but your masculine ego won't let you accept that. You don't see that singing is a job like any other."

"Aspasia, things aren't that simple. You have two children. What will happen to them while you're gone?"

"I have faith in your mother. Don't you?"

"This isn't about my mother but the children. They need their mother, don't you understand? My mother is getting old; she can't take care of two small children for so many months."

"Would you prefer that I take them with me?"

"Are you out of your mind? How would you look after them? You work at night and sleep all day!"

"I'll find a woman there."

"So you're not even thinking about the possibility of not going to Rhodes? Instead, why don't you take the children to your village for a while and see your family—give Theodora a chance to get to know her grandchildren."

"Are you crazy, Stavros? I'm supposed to pass up the opportunity I've been offered and go ruin myself in the village instead?"

"I don't know what to tell you, Aspasia. You're walking with mathematical precision toward a catastrophe and you don't want to see it. You're destroying our marriage."

"Wrong! You're destroying it with your nonsense. We're doing fine and you're trying to spoil it."

"We're fine? How do you figure that? Do I even have a wife anymore?"

"That's not what you were saying yesterday or the day before, I believe," Aspasia said sarcastically.

Stavros looked at her with disappointment. "A marriage isn't only about sex, Aspasia. If you don't understand that, you can't understand anything anymore. I'm sorry."

Stavros left the room quietly but this time Aspasia didn't cry, nor did she regret anything. Instead she began to pack.

◆ ◆ ◆

Aspasia was as successful in Rhodes as she'd been in Kalamata, only now she felt different. Living on her own for the first time, she had a unique sense of freedom. She didn't have to account to anyone for her movements, nor did she have to hurry home to duties awaiting her. She'd spend all night partying with the musicians, then join them for morning coffee afterward. Often she didn't get to bed before noon. Her communications home were rare. They didn't have a telephone in the house, so she'd call Stavros at his office, and occasionally he'd bring the children with him so they could speak to her too. That summer was the best of her life. She learned to swim—something she had always wanted to do—and enjoyed the sea with all her senses.

Stelios appeared in her life just two weeks after her arrival on the island. He was a customer at the club and from the beginning he was drawn to the beautiful singer. He was about forty, presentable, very rich, and determined to win her. From the first evening that she caught his eye, the fuss he caused in the club was impressive. Aspasia's boss told her that she'd hit the jackpot with this one, but she just smiled cynically; this man wasn't the first and he wouldn't be the last, she said. Before long, she'd run out of space in her dressing room for all the bouquets Stelios sent. When the flowers weren't enough to persuade her, he began to send her jewelry, which she politely but firmly returned.

Still, he'd achieved what he wanted. In spite of her refusals, Aspasia often found herself thinking about the man who threw a fortune at her feet every night. She'd gone to his table once after the steady siege that had gone on for so many days. It impressed her that he had behaved like a real gentleman, without any crude suggestions, and she didn't have to cunningly avoid his hands, as she'd had to do with others. He bought her a drink, asked politely about her impressions of Rhodes, and offered to give her a guided tour of the island whenever she wished.

Aspasia kept her defenses up for as long as she could. The thought of Stavros held her back and reminded her that although she was living like a single woman, she wasn't one. She had a husband and two children and she had come to Rhodes to work, not to get mixed up in an affair. So she avoided the charming Stelios as much as she could.

That morning she was enjoying the sun and the sea as they drove every thought from her mind. A little while earlier she had spoken to Stavros and they had argued again. He'd complained that she didn't communicate regularly with him, and accused her of not caring about anything except singing. He'd also questioned her, not very tactfully, about her other activities on Rhodes, and Aspasia had ended the conversation by hanging up on him. Suddenly she was aware of a presence beside her and she turned around angrily, but as soon as she saw Stelios smiling at her she sat up, quite uneasy.

"What are you doing here?" she inquired.

"Do you have to ask? It's summer, it's warm, it's paradise here. And this particular paradise has an angel who interests me."

Aspasia had to admit to herself that he was a very handsome man. "Yes, but the . . . angel you are talking about wants to enjoy the sun and the sea in peace," she answered flatly.

"So? Who's stopping you, gorgeous? If you don't want to we won't speak at all. I only want to look at you."

"That's all?" she asked sarcastically.

"I could tell you the rest, but I'm afraid I'd shock you."

"So don't do it," she said sharply. "Stelios, we need to talk, and talk seriously."

"I'm listening." Stelios sat down next to her and looked at her with interest.

"You have to understand that I came to Rhodes to work and not to get mixed up with someone."

"And am I stopping you from doing your work?"

"Don't pretend you don't understand, please. What you don't know is that back in Kalamata are my husband and two children. I have two daughters."

"May you enjoy them—and your husband! What do I have to do with them?"

"Nothing. But you do want to have something to do with me. And I'm explaining to you that it can't happen."

"In my life I've discovered that everything can happen. You just have to want it."

"Yes, but I don't want it. That's what I'm trying to tell you."

"But sweetheart, I didn't say I wanted to separate you from your husband. You're a stranger here. You'll only stay for a while. Is it a bad thing for us to spend time together? Have I asked for anything more?"

"The truth is that . . . you did behave like a gentleman when we spoke at the club."

"So? Do you want me to be your guide for however long you're here? Rhodes is really beautiful and nobody can show it to you better than someone who knows it like the back of his hand."

"All right then. But be careful. I can only be your friend."

"I never take anything unless it's given to me," Stelios said quietly, and his gaze met hers.

Aspasia felt something strange inside her, as if a small alarm was ringing, but she chose to ignore it.

Stelios kept his word. With him, Aspasia got to know and love Rhodes. The Palace of the Knights in the old city enchanted her, even though she was tired from the hours of sightseeing. Stelios teased her, saying that no one goes on a tour wearing high heels. But Aspasia hesitated to take them off and walk barefoot beside him. The village of Afandou reminded her a little of her village, invisible as its name suggested, and deliberately built not to be seen from the sea. They passed through it on their way to Lindos, where Aspasia loved the white houses and courtyards paved in pebbles from the beach.

The little harbor of Agios Pavlos, where, according to the locals, Apostle Paul disembarked when he arrived to teach Christianity, looked like a painting by a great artist. In its calm waters, boats and small craft were anchored, and Stelios let Aspasia admire them at leisure while he observed every movement, every expression of her face. This woman was really his type. And the fact that she wasn't like all the other singers who were immediately flattered by his interest and succumbed eagerly to him made her still more desirable. She didn't seem to be impressed either by the gifts he sent her, or by the money he spent on her, or by his very expensive car. Her eyes lit up only when he told her the historical details of someplace interesting he was showing her. As the days passed and nothing in her behavior toward him changed, he became more determined.

It was inevitable that everyday contact and the endless walks would lead Aspasia to open up more to Stelios, but she was surprised at how easily she could speak to him about herself. Stelios listened to her with genuine interest, while keeping his word and behaving only like a friend. Eventually, she found herself waiting impatiently for their daily trips, and one night, when he didn't come to the club, she realized she was disappointed. The two had fallen into the habit of comfortably chatting each evening in the cozy warmth of her dressing room, and his absence spoiled her mood.

The next day she waited for him for their daily walk but again he didn't appear. She went by herself to the beach but she took no pleasure in it. On the contrary, she spent most of her time looking around her in case she saw him. Finally she left in disappointment, went back to the boardinghouse she was staying in, ate very little, and lay down to rest. But it was no use. She gave up and started walking up and down in her room, full of irritation. She went to the club in a bad mood and the other employees, who'd been working with her for a month now, were surprised; they'd never seen her like that.

When Stelios didn't appear at the club that night either, Aspasia nearly wept. For the first time, singing seemed unbearable, the high spirits of the customers disgusted her, and the hundreds of plates they smashed only provoked repugnance and more irritation. Afterward, the room she was staying in seemed particularly small and suffocating. She was surprised at herself but she had to admit that she missed Stelios terribly. Unfortunately, she had no idea where to find him.

She passed the next day again by herself, without any news of him. She left for the club much earlier than she usually did and shut herself in her little dressing room, wondering how she would pass the time until she was due on stage. She undressed and put on her robe as usual. At least she could start getting ready.

She was so absorbed in her thoughts that she hardly heard the knock at the door. When she saw in her mirror that Stelios had appeared in the open doorway, she didn't know what to do. He came in and closed the door behind him. Aspasia quickly stood up, ready to shout at him for his disappearance. Through her open robe, Stelios could see her beautiful body and was enchanted by the sight. He snatched her in his arms and without saying a word placed his lips on hers. When he sensed no resistance on her part, he lost all control. The small space around them suddenly filled with the energy of their hungry kisses and urgent embraces, and in the fire that burned between them, Aspasia felt the passion of love as she had never known it.

When it was over, she looked around, bewildered. There were bottles thrown on the floor and the room had literally been turned upside down. Stelios was still half-dressed, and when she saw him she was overwhelmed with guilt. She hid her face in her hands and burst into tears.

Stelios looked at Aspasia in amazement. He didn't expect this reaction from her. This woman had hot lava inside her, he thought. It had burnt him, it had nearly destroyed him, and despite the intensity, he wanted her again. But she was crying like a baby in front of him, with a despair that moved him.

"Aspasia," he said. "What's going on, sweetheart? Why are you crying? Aspasia!"

"What did I do? What did I do?" she kept repeating, refusing to raise her eyes and meet his.

Stelios took her gently by the chin and made her look at him. Her eyes were bright red, her hopelessness written all over her face. "What do you mean, 'what did I do?' You did what you wanted to do. You wanted it as much as I did. So why do you feel such despair now?"

"Don't you understand? I'm married! I had no right."

"Sweetheart, the body doesn't know anything about marriages and relationships. It speaks its own language. Don't spoil it now."

"Stelios, please leave," she said, her voice breaking. "I need to be alone . . . to think . . ."

Stelios looked at her, smiling affectionately. "Fine. I'll leave, but I'll be in the club. I need a drink."

"No! I won't be able to perform tonight if you're there and I see you."

"All right. I'll do what you ask, if only this once."

After that he slowly finished dressing while Aspasia pulled her robe tightly around her with trembling hands.

She had never sung like she did that night. The passion in her voice moved the audience and a mountain of smashed plates stood at her feet by the time she was finished. After the show, she pretended she wasn't feeling well and left the club early. She walked back to her room as a light breeze cooled her flaming cheeks. Her thoughts made her head nearly burst. She didn't recognize herself anymore. She was ashamed but at the same time she wanted to run like a crazy woman to him and relive, moment by moment, again and again, all the passion that had poured out of her as soon as he touched her. The sudden thought of Stavros made her feel even worse. Her stomach was churning; she stopped and leaned against a tree to recover. How could she go back to him? How could she look him in the eyes after what she'd done? She went into her room exhausted but determined not to see Stelios again for as long as she was on Rhodes.

He was waiting, sitting on the balcony outside her room.

"What are you doing here?" she asked, almost afraid. "How did you get in?"

"Do you really think a small detail like that would stop me from seeing you?" he answered as he approached her.

Aspasia took a step back but he grabbed her and pulled her into his arms. His lips sought hers and when they found them, all her previous decisions were forgotten. Minutes later, they were lying naked on the bed with his body covering hers.

Aspasia managed to put her guilt aside. From now on, her body would govern everything. As the days passed, Stelios became the center of her world. She couldn't wait to be alone with him, and whenever they were together, he would lose himself in her embrace. The little dressing room, which used to be filled with their laughter and conversation, was now filled with the sounds of their lovemaking. Her colleagues laughed knowingly as they passed by, especially when the couple's passion became especially loud.

As the final days of summer neared, they knew their time together would soon end. And the nearer the moment came, the more insatiable their passion was. Each night after the show, they would practically run to hide in her dressing room. Even a chance touch led to erotic delirium. When her contract finally ended, Aspasia delayed her return home by three days so they could take a farewell trip together. She wondered at herself. She had been aware all along that this relationship had an expiration date, and, having accepted that, she had no regrets. Yet this acceptance sometimes made her feel depraved. If she had felt some sort of emotional attachment, this would have given her an excuse for what she'd done. As it was, she had none.

When she returned home, her children threw themselves longingly into her arms and wouldn't leave her side. Stavros kissed her passionately and she responded easily. That night, in his arms, she felt as if she was coming back to a familiar and peaceful harbor. As the days passed, life resumed its usual rhythms. That Aspasia would work again was a foregone conclusion that they all accepted without discussion. She herself, however, decided she would only work Friday, Saturday, and Sunday, and Stavros felt relieved because at least the children would have their mother with them a little more.

Spending the summer on his own had given Stavros time to think, and he realized that his feelings for his wife had begun to change. At first Aspasia's departure hurt him deeply, but as time passed, the pain grew less, and he got used to the fact that she was away. When he took her in his arms that first night, he recognized the change in her. The woman he was making love to wasn't his wife, not as he knew her. She was full of passion, but also of experience that he hadn't taught her in all the years of their marriage. He felt he was sleeping with a stranger and his anger was stronger than the pleasure this other Aspasia could give him.

He spent that night awake, at first sitting on the balcony while Aspasia slept. The thought that his wife had given herself to another man drove him crazy, and he couldn't get it out of his mind. When he eventually returned to the bed, Aspasia was sleeping, still naked, and the image of her body in somebody else's arms made him groan like a wounded animal. He wanted to hurt her, but at the same time he wanted to take her in his arms and make her forget whoever had touched her. He began to tremble and fell violently and frantically on top of her. Aspasia immediately woke up. She seemed to accept this new side of her husband that gave her painful pleasure and they both reached climax very fast.

Fortunately this change in their marriage wasn't obvious to those around them, even Aspasia's mother-in-law, who watched the situation with her ever-vigilant eyes. At night, when Stavros came to bed, he was violent and demanding; his lovemaking didn't have any sense of love about it, but only the instinct of a wounded animal. Sometimes he reached the point of being crude. Still, the more he behaved like that, the more his wife seemed satisfied. It was true: Aspasia liked this side of her husband. Stelios had been completely forgotten. Stavros was her new passion.

Instead of being satisfied with this new development in his marriage, Stavros seemed to suffer more each day. This wasn't his wife. This was a being insatiable for sexual pleasure and she displayed it in a way that seemed disgusting to him, even as they both abandoned themselves with no limits. He left home on a business trip to Tripoli and, in a hopeless effort to rid himself of his sickening obsession, he went to bed with the first available woman he found. But Aspasia still haunted his whole being. He came back to her even worse, thirstier than ever, incapable of resisting her, while at the same time, he almost hated her for what he was certain had happened on Rhodes.

When the next summer came, Aspasia told her husband she had an offer to sing again on Rhodes.

"Will you go?" he asked, his heart leaping in his chest.

"Of course. Why shouldn't I? The money we made was good. And the girls are just fine with your mother," she said, then added, "Will you manage OK without me?"

Stavros looked at her with a blank expression. "As well as you do," he answered. "Isn't that right?" He ground his teeth in fury and his look darkened as he began to approach his wife. But, at the last moment, some remnant of decency pushed him to turn and leave before he said and did something he'd later regret.

◆　◆　◆

When Aspasia arrived on Rhodes, Stelios was waiting for her with renewed interest. Instead of renting an apartment, she moved into his house. She also asked for and was given two evenings off from the club each week, so she could indulge in their affair as intensely as she wanted to. Stelios was delighted with the changes in Aspasia. Last year she had behaved more modestly. In fact, her inhibitions had tired him sometimes. But this year she was unrestrained and much readier to experiment in lovemaking, to give and take everything.

Back in Kalamata, Stavros felt at first as if he were recovering from a serious illness. Far from the influence of Aspasia, he began to regain his balance, but the thought that she was almost certainly with someone else still drove him crazy. With a great deal of difficulty, he persuaded himself not to go and see her. From time to time he thought that he was living a nightmare. He remembered how Aspasia was when he met her, and wondered whether that shy, wholesome girl was still hidden deep inside this other woman, who was only ruled by her passions. He tried to drown his pain at parties in Tripoli and in other women. He allowed another self to swallow him, a person he sometimes couldn't bear, but the deeper he went into this other self the more her absence hurt him. His children were the only thing that brought back the old gentle, calm Stavros, so he tried to spend a lot of time with them, stealing a little of their innocence. Only then, when he heard their laughter, did he feel at peace.

As Aspasia's return date approached, he was so anxious that he couldn't eat or sleep. He hadn't touched her for three whole months and he felt like he was losing his mind. When he met her on the doorstep, it took all his self-control not to snatch her in his arms. He accepted her conventional kiss and returned it, then waited patiently as she greeted the children and heard all their news, while his mind made plans. He wanted to take her away somewhere that very night. He felt ill from her absence and wanted to be alone with her in a place where he could feel free to let himself go.

Aspasia agreed without any objection when Stavros announced that he'd arranged for them to go away for a few days by themselves. That very night they drove to the first hotel they found and hardly came out of their room, to the point where the owner assumed they were newly-weds and strictly instructed the staff not to disturb them. When they returned home, Stavros now knew what was happening to him. Aspasia had chosen her road and either he had to follow her or go very far away. But he didn't have the strength to leave. Apart from the suffering he would feel, he had to think of the children, who weren't to blame for anything. And he had to admit that now that Aspasia was doing what she wanted, she had become a better mother. She devoted her free time to both girls, even though her weakness for the older girl was still obvious. She played with them, chatting happily, and she seemed generally more sociable.

The winter passed very quickly and Stavros waited for the moment when his wife would tell him she was leaving again, but something else happened instead, and it changed everything. Completely out of the blue, shortly after Easter, his mother passed away in her sleep—as peacefully and discreetly as she had always stood beside him in life. Stavros again lost the ground under his feet; his world was shattered and for the first time he felt enveloped in loneliness. Aspasia also seemed to be at a loss. Her mother-in-law had stood by her all these years, a calm strength always ready to help, a rock to lean on. Her loss now seemed very strange to her. The children were the ones who were most upset at losing their grandmother, who was a second mother to them in every sense of the word. They were too young to understand why she'd left them so soon. For the first time in so long they became a family again. They clung to each other for comfort and their spirits came together.

◆　◆　◆

Aspasia didn't want to admit that she was bored again. At first she thought she was just feeling tired. Later she realized that the past had awoken again in her, and the need to escape came back with urgency.

She was angry with herself because nothing seemed to satisfy her anymore. Even her husband seemed predictable, and therefore boring, to her, and the girls drove her crazy all the time. In the afternoons she felt as if she would go insane shut up in the house. At night, when Stavros had fallen asleep in her arms, she would get up silently and go out onto the balcony for some air. She'd look at the lights of the city and know that somewhere among them were the lights of the clubs, where she longed to get up on stage with a microphone in her hand. She'd look at the sea and know that crossing it held adventures that she was greedy to live. Sometimes, when logic took over, she'd ask herself what sort of stuff she was made of, and why what she had wasn't enough. Her girls were growing up; they were beautiful and she was proud of them. But motherhood only satisfied one piece of her and the rest, the larger part, made demands. She could see there was no way out, and however much she persuaded herself to calm down, the other Aspasia became more demanding, more impatient, readier to leave.

Stavros knew that his wife would have to leave again. This time, the offer came from Crete. He couldn't believe his ears when he heard Aspasia announce that everything was arranged, and that she had even hired a woman to look after the house and the children while she was away. She was completely honest with him. She made it clear that she couldn't bear it anymore, that she was suffocating, and that unless she left she would lose her mind.

"And the children?" he asked. "How will they feel with a strange woman looking after them?"

"The children are growing up," Aspasia answered, her mind made up. "They have their school, their lessons, and Sophia will cook for them and look after the house. In three months I'll be back."

"Why, Aspasia?" he complained.

Aspasia answered him honestly. "I don't know, Stavros. Really I don't. I tried, though. You saw that I tried, but I didn't manage it. I think this must be the way I'm made. It's not that I don't love you and what we've made together. But if I don't leave I feel as if I'll go crazy. The house stifles me, the girls tire me, and you . . ."

"And me? What am I to you, Aspasia?"

"Do you want the truth?" she asked. When Stavros nodded his head, she continued, "You're my husband and when I leave you I love you more than ever. I miss you and I count the days till I'm with you again, but if I have to stay with you for a long time, I can't wait to leave again. You suffocate me too. Let me leave, Stavros. When I come back I'll be much better. If I stay I'll hate you."

She stopped talking but continued to look at him. Stavros's eyes filled with pain.

"Go, Aspasia. It's not your fault, it's my fault that I didn't understand what you really wanted when we married. Now I have to pay for my mistake. Only please telephone the girls regularly. They need you."

Aspasia pressed her lips to his. Now that she knew she would leave, she was in love with him again.

Stavros pulled back and looked at her. "What's this?" he asked grimly. "My payment for letting you leave without a quarrel?"

Aspasia didn't answer him. She smiled and began to undress, and Stavros stretched out his hand to stroke her breast. Then, as if the touch had burned him, he pulled back and ran out of the room as if he was being chased. Quite unexpectedly, as she stood there alone, half-naked in the middle of the room, the stern face of her mother appeared in front of her. She heard the words Theodora had said to her before she left the village:

"I know your restless spirit, your sharp mind, and your passion for singing. You have to calm all those things, my daughter, and be satisfied with what your husband's love offers you. And if the trials are very strong, remember that here, in this corner of the earth, is the river. Dive into it to purify yourself again!"

Aspasia didn't know if one dive into the river would be enough to cleanse her. So many things had happened. She didn't want to think about what her mother would say if she ever found out what she'd done. So she drove those thoughts away and began to pack her suitcase.

This time, her farewell with the children pained her. Stella didn't say anything when she heard that her mother would leave again, but her eyes were very eloquent. She was thirteen now and understood much more than she let on. As for little Theodora, she avoided her mother's kiss. Instead, she clung to her father, who also kept a cool distance from his wife. From the day that she announced she was leaving again, Stavros systematically avoided Aspasia. He came home late from work and slept in the sitting room. However many efforts she made to pull him into her arms, they came to nothing. Still, it was quite clear what it cost him to refrain from touching her.

Aspasia's sadness lasted as long as the journey to Chania, which was her destination. When she got there she forgot everything as the city itself enchanted her. She never tired of looking at the beautiful buildings. The sea seemed to gently embrace the shore and the streets were full of people. The club she was to sing at was among the best and most popular. The house she was staying in was small but lovely, and all the people were warm and friendly. From her balcony she could see the harbor, the best gift of all, because the view of the sea always calmed her.

Aspasia threw herself into her work. The club was due to open in a week's time to meet the demand of the island's rapidly expanding tourist industry, and the rehearsals were exhausting. From the first moment she first saw him perform, the "star" of the club made an impression on her. Christos was a little older than Aspasia and the most handsome man she had ever seen. He had already begun to make a name for himself in Athens and was preparing to release his first record in the fall. All the other singers wanted to sing with him; to them, he was their ticket beyond anonymity. But Aspasia was indifferent to all that. The only thing that moved her were his eyes, which were the color of the sea. Whenever they rested on her, she'd become tongue-tied, like an inexperienced young girl.

It was Christos himself who suggested they sing a duet, something that automatically made the other girls dislike her, although she didn't care. She liked this man. The blood flowed faster in her veins when she was near him, making her feel like a woman again. For his part, Christos was intrigued by the beautiful singer. Approaching her midthirties, Aspasia was more striking than ever. She may not have realized it, but her behavior, which showed quite clearly that she was ready for any-thing and everything, made her even more desirable. Christos had a permanent relationship in Athens with a woman named Myrsini, but he knew from experience that summer jobs were more enjoyable when you added in a love affair. The other singers didn't interest him; he knew they saw him only as a way to Athens, and he didn't want to risk his relationship with Myrsini, who, apart from being young and beautiful, was also very rich.

Aspasia was a different case, though. She couldn't care less about the nightclubs of Athens. It was quite clear that what interested her was his bed; her eyes told him that plainly. But Christos hadn't calculated the imponderable factor: that his love of Aspasia would make him lose his mind. Never in his life had he met a woman who was a living volcano, as incredible and daring as any man could be. Nothing concerned her except being in his arms. Her erotic games were extraordinary and made all his fantasies seem like adolescent daydreams.

She was dynamite on stage too. The customers of the club were soon crazy about her. When she performed, they couldn't take their eyes off her, which pleased the club's owner. Aspasia had paid off as a real moneymaker.

Aspasia had come to understand the duality she possessed. As she saw it, there were two women inside of her. One was the housewife from Kalamata, the mother of two girls. The other was a woman completely devoted to satisfying her own body, which seemed to be insatiable, and to feeding her hungry soul. Whenever she left her home, she left the housewife behind, and the other woman awoke inside her.

While on Crete, Aspasia slept very little. In the mornings she would wander around Chania and the surrounding countryside. In the evenings she would set the club alight with her high spirits. And in the intervals between her shows, she was always in Christos's arms.

Myrsini's visit to Chania was unexpected and very annoying. She would stay for five days, and during that interval Aspasia couldn't see Christos at all—he had made that clear to her. But after the second day he himself realized that the narcotic called Aspasia was much stronger than he thought. He missed her terribly. Myrsini, who never left his side, stifled him with her presence and when he and Aspasia went up on stage to sing together, it nearly caught fire from the glances they exchanged. By the third night Christos felt ill. As Myrsini slept beside him, his body burned at the thought of Aspasia. He couldn't contain himself. So he snuck out and went to her house. He knew that Aspasia always slept with her balcony doors open, so he carefully climbed up to her room, where he found her sleeping half-naked because of the heat. He undressed and lay down silently beside her. At first she was startled, but as soon as she realized who the man in her bed was, she laughed happily.

They were lucky. Myrsini hadn't noticed Christos's absence. When she woke the next morning and found him sitting on the balcony drinking coffee, she thought he had simply woken up early. She never imagined that he was trying to recover from the unbelievable night he'd spent with Aspasia.

Shortly before the summer was over, Christos asked Aspasia to follow him to Athens.

"Listen to me for a little while without interrupting," she said. "I won't come to Athens. We've never spoken about our lives. Of course I know about Myrsini because she came here, but you don't know anything about me."

"I know as much as I need to know, Aspasia, and it's enough to know that I can't lose you."

"I asked you not to interrupt me," she scolded him tenderly. "Christos, things aren't so simple. Back in Kalamata there's a man waiting for me—my husband!"

"You're married?" Christos's eyes opened wide in surprise.

"I have two daughters too."

"So what are you doing here in Crete? Are you two separated?"

"No, and I'm not about to be. I met Stavros when I was still almost a child. I didn't know then that singing was more important to me than marriage, so this is where life led me: In the winter I change back into a wife and mother, but in summer . . ."

◆　◆　◆

When Aspasia arrived back home again the girls greeted her warmly. During the months of separation, they'd put aside their objections to her trip. Stavros, however, had changed; that was quite obvious. His greeting was formal and slightly cold, and when Aspasia realized later that evening that he now slept in the room that had belonged to his mother, she was surprised.

"Are you going to sleep here?" she asked as she stood in the doorway of her mother-in-law's old room.

"I've slept here since you left," he answered.

"Yes, but now I'm back."

"For how long? It's just a matter of time before you leave again, isn't it?"

"I don't know, but what does it matter? I'm here now and I missed you."

Stavros gave her a hard look and began to undress in front of her, then lay down and covered himself with the blanket.

"And I missed you—in the beginning," he said. "But then I got used to it. I don't want to go back to how I was, Aspasia."

"And how were you?"

"Sick with you. As if I was drugged, dependent on your body and your love. I can't go through that again. After the death of my mother I thought that the two of us had found our way back to each other, but then you cured me of that illusion when you told me about Crete. I realized then that there was no possibility for us anymore."

Aspasia was at a total loss. She couldn't believe what she was hearing. "What are you saying, Stavros? I'm your wife, don't you remember?"

"Of course I do. But you left without caring how any of us felt and now you come back and you're claiming what? My presence in your bed?"

"Naturally."

"Can't you manage without that, Aspasia?" he asked, and the sarcasm in his voice stung her. "Why are you surprised? Do you think I don't know that when you go away it's not only for the love of singing, but because other people also enjoy your company in bed? And do you know what's worse? That *you* enjoy them even more. I don't know what sort of perversion you have hidden in you but I don't want to share it. I refuse to sleep with a woman who has just gotten out of another man's bed!"

Aspasia had to support herself on a chair so as not to fall. She couldn't take in what she was hearing. She looked at her husband, shaken.

"You didn't expect such a reception, of course," he said unkindly, smugly.

"No," she whispered. "And I can't say you're wrong. It's true, Stavros, but you don't understand me."

"And I don't want to. Just as you don't want to understand what you're doing. One day you'll recover. I don't know what it'll take to make that happen, but I hope it doesn't break you at the same time. You can do as you like from now on, so long as you don't drag my name and the girls' through the mud. I could ask for a divorce, but the children aren't to blame for anything. So we'll remain husband and wife, just as a formality, and we'll behave like a loving couple in front of others and the children. And you . . . do your dirty business discreetly a long way from here, as you have until now, and never ask me to come to your bed again. It's just too crowded in there! Good night, Aspasia." And with those words Stavros rolled over and turned out the light.

With her head hung in shame, Aspasia slowly left the room and dragged herself to her bed, where she lay down, still in her clothes. She felt as if she'd been beaten. Everything that Stavros had said was true and the truth hurt. But even more painful was the fact that she couldn't regret anything, nor could she promise to change.

Everything happened as her husband had described. From that day on, he was quite affectionate to her in front of the children, but when they were gone, he didn't speak to her. If she touched him even by accident, he stiffened and pulled away with a dark look. On many evenings he would come home very late or not at all, with the excuse of some work in Tripoli or elsewhere, but she knew he was out partying.

One night when he came home very drunk, Aspasia reminded him sharply that he had insisted they be discreet. They argued and for the first time Stavros raised his hand and slapped her. Then he threw her on his bed. Aspasia had never felt cheap, but she did now. As soon as he took his hands off her she left, crying, with her clothes torn and her body covered in bruises. The next day she hoped he would apologize, but Stavros only appeared at her door, his expression dripping poison.

"If you were expecting me to say sorry for last night, you have another thing coming!" he lashed out. "You got what a woman like you deserves. And however often it happens, it'll happen like that. If you liked last night's performance, I'm always at your service. From what I understand, you only like it like that."

When he left the room, Aspasia felt so dirty that she ran and stood under the hot water, but it didn't help. She came out of the bathroom feeling worse. She sat in front of the mirror and looked at herself. She couldn't blame anyone but herself for the destruction of her marriage.

She had wounded her husband and distanced herself from her children, who had grown up in her absence. Singing had become her whole life— a life that suited immoral women, cheap women. How had she allowed herself to be dragged away like that?

The river came into her mind again. She had become a branch on the current, just as her mother had feared. After so many years, Aspasia finally wanted to go home, but she couldn't. She knew she wouldn't have the courage to look her mother in the eye. In spite of her longing, she had cut all ties and burned the bridges of return.

◆ ◆ ◆

The next summer it was Patras. Aspasia went without thinking about it, but this time everything was different. She was always perfect in her work, but she seemed to be punishing herself. She drank a lot and in the morning she couldn't remember who she'd slept with. She felt like an object without any feelings, but she continued her behavior with an unhealthy persistence, without caring how much she was humiliating herself.

However much Aspasia drank, she couldn't forget that her oldest daughter had given her an ultimatum just before she left. When Stella had found out that her mother planned to go away again, as she'd done in previous summers, she exploded.

"That's enough!" she had shouted. "Every summer for years now you've disappeared. Don't you think you'd better stop this stuff at some point?"

Aspasia looked at her, unable to accept that this angry creature in front of her was the daughter she'd always favored. Her heart felt heavy with sadness.

"Why are you speaking to me like that?" she asked. "It's only for a little while. Most of the rest of the year, I'm here with you; you know that!"

"Yes, but a mother's job isn't something you do in your spare time. You can't be gone for four months and spend the rest of the time here. We need you all year. And Dad—don't you see how hurt he is every time you leave?"

"But it's my work," muttered Aspasia. Even to her own ears, this seemed a feeble excuse.

"Don't give me that! You're a singer in bouzouki clubs. It's not like you're world-famous. To be honest I don't think the evenings would suffer much if you didn't appear, and you don't do it for the money."

"Stella, you're still young, and you don't understand."

"But it's because I'm young that I want my mother. And Theodora is very young and you pay no attention to her."

"Now you're wrong. When I'm here, aren't we together all the time? Don't we read and play and don't I do what you want?"

"You said it yourself! *When* you're here! In summer, when you're not here, we're all by ourselves. It's not enough!"

"What are you asking me, child?"

"Not to go away again. I understand that you have no choice this time; you've already signed a contract. But I want it to be the last! Put an end to all this!"

Stella had left, crying, and Aspasia felt as if she would collapse. The last thing she expected was this attack. All summer long, as she drifted between the stage, the drinking, and the meaningless beds, she couldn't forget her daughter's look. The margins were shrinking. This summer would be the last one like this. Life as she had been leading it would have to come to an end.

◆ ◆ ◆

Two months later, when Stavros called to tell her in an unsteady voice that Stella was in the hospital, Aspasia raced back to Kalamata like a madwoman. When she got there, she found Stavros on the point of collapse. He had refused to share all the details with her until now, but the doctors were quite clear: it was cancer. The girl only had a short time left.

The shock was terrible. None of the doctors they saw could explain where such a terrible thing had come from. There is no explanation for this disease, they all said. And nobody gave them the slightest hope. The enemy was especially aggressive—it was a form that spread rapidly. Unable to accept what was happening to his child, Stavros arranged for them to all leave for London, convinced that there, Stella might get better care.

They arrived in the foggy city in a daze, but wasted no time; every minute lost might prove fatal. The English doctors operated on her and bombarded her with radiation. They did everything they could, but Stella seemed to be slipping through their hands like sand. In the months they spent there, Stavros and Aspasia watched their daughter fade into her bed while Theodora wouldn't leave her sister's side. She spent the whole day holding Stella's almost transparent hand in hers and murmuring loving words.

Aspasia became a shadow of herself. Her eyes swimming with agony, she looked at the emaciated face of her daughter and tried to give her strength through her gaze. She wanted to scream, to order the sickness away from her child, to beg God to take *her* instead. All the while, her lips remained frozen in a reassuring smile so Stella wouldn't be afraid. For hours Aspasia spoke to her, even telling her the stories she hadn't told her as a child; she'd sing to her until she lost her voice and Theodora took her place.

Stavros spent hours in silence, staring at his daughter's chest, which rose and fell with difficulty. He counted her breaths by the second, the minute, and the hour. As long as his child breathed there was hope. The doctors wondered how Stella continued to live. She hardly communicated with the world around her, breathed with difficulty, and needed tremendous effort to say just two words, and only to her mother. Afterward she would sink back into the bed, exhausted.

One night Stella opened her eyes and saw her mother looking at her. She smiled weakly.

"What do you want, my child?" Aspasia whispered.

"Why aren't you sleeping?"

"I can't sleep. I look at you and I can never have enough," Aspasia said, her voice breaking.

"We never had enough time, the two of us," murmured Stella, and with a great effort, she stroked her mother's cheek.

"Don't talk and tire yourself, my darling." Aspasia felt the tears burning her eyes.

"Yes . . . I'm tired," the girl said. "You know, I want to leave now, Mama . . ."

"No my darling! It's too early. You have your whole life in front of you. Hold on, Stella! You'll get better."

"No, Mama, I won't get better . . . I know now. I want to leave but I don't want to leave you. That's why I'm holding on. It's the first time I've felt you were mine, only mine . . . and I don't want to lose you. I also don't want to hurt you. That's why I'm trying to stay, but I feel so tired."

Stella's eyes closed again. Aspasia broke out into a silent weeping that shook her whole body. When her husband's hands gently touched her shoulders, it frightened her. Stavros had heard the whole conversation. Aspasia leaned against him and continued to cry.

In the morning, Stella's condition had become even worse. Her breaths came out with a whistling sound that was frightening. Stavros led Theodora away from her sister's bedside. She was crying and didn't want to leave, but Stavros insisted that she go for a walk in the care of a woman he'd met in the hospital.

Then Stavros turned to his wife. "The time has come, Aspasia," he said, but she shook her head. "Yes," Stavros insisted. "You and I both heard what the child said last night. As long as you're beside her she won't die. She's holding on so as not to hurt you. It is a shame, though, because she's suffering herself. Let her rest now."

"How can you ask me such a thing?" Aspasia demanded, crying. "She's so young. It's a crime! We shouldn't lose our child, Stavros! If she's still living because of me, that's fine. Maybe my presence will give her the strength to fight and win."

"If there was the slightest hope, do you think I'd be talking to you like this? Don't you see her? Don't you hear what the doctors say? Enough, Aspasia! Let her go—she's suffering, don't you understand? It's not God's will for her to survive."

Aspasia looked her husband in the eye. Then she turned to Stella and took her in her arms. She sang her a lullaby for a while as she had done when she was a baby, then she laid her back down on the bed, covered her up, and kissed her tenderly. She left the room with her head high.

An hour later Stavros came out.

"She's gone," was all he said.

Aspasia blinked as if she'd been shot, then collapsed at his feet.

◆ ◆ ◆

It could have been a nightmare but it wasn't. They came back home, a sad trio with a coffin, all of them tragic and white. Stella would be laid to rest beside her grandmother. All of Kalamata attended the burial, but Aspasia had never made friends in all the years she had lived in this town, so no one felt comfortable enough to approach her and offer a few words of comfort.

Stavros, on the other hand, was surrounded. Even Kyrios Alekos came with his wife and daughter. As the procession moved toward Stella's gravesite, people offered the grieving father their support and hugged Theodora as she huddled beside him. All the while, Aspasia walked alone, looking straight ahead, her eyes red from crying.

She was almost startled when she felt a warm hand squeezing her own. As she came to her senses, she turned and saw her youngest daughter.

Theodora had been scanning the crowd for her mother, and when she saw her walking alone, she went to her. Mother and daughter looked at each other and Aspasia pulled her child close and hugged her in despair. From then on, Theodora didn't leave her mother's side. When the white box disappeared into the earth, Aspasia broke down, and if it hadn't been for Theodora she would have fallen into the great hole that had been opened to receive her firstborn. The little girl embraced her mother with all her strength and called her father for help. Stavros pulled himself from Kyrios Alekos's arm and ran to his daughter. The two of them managed to hold Aspasia back as she howled in pain. A few minutes later she fainted in their arms and despite all their efforts, she didn't regain consciousness. They took her to the hospital, where the doctors said it was the result of severe shock.

Aspasia remained in the hospital for two days. When she finally returned home, as soon as she stepped inside, painful memories of her child returned with even greater intensity. When she burst into pitiful crying, Stavros gave her a strong sedative and made her lie down, just as the doctors had ordered. A week later she was still hovering between semiconsciousness and reality. Theodora stayed with a neighbor, whose daughter was a friend of hers, but she asked for her mother every day. Stavros finally realized they were doing more harm to the child by keeping her away and brought her home. Before that, though, he spoke to Aspasia.

"Aspasia," he said softly. "Drink your coffee—it'll make you feel better. We have to talk."

She gave him a confused look and nodded her head. Then she drank her coffee with slow sips. "Give me a cigarette," she said in a broken voice.

Without saying a word, Stavros lit a cigarette and put it in her mouth. Aspasia took a long drag, coughed a little, then continued to smoke without speaking.

"You've started smoking?" he asked, more to say something than out of interest.

"Yes, in Patras," she answered.

Silence fell on the room again. Stavros took a deep breath and Aspasia finally looked at him with clear eyes.

"You told me you want us to speak," she said. "What do you want to tell me?"

"Aspasia, you have to get over this, and you have to do it quickly."

"Do you think that's easy? I lost my child! How can I recover?" She began to cry again.

Stavros looked at her sympathetically for a moment, but then slapped his hand loudly on the table. Aspasia sat up, frightened.

"What do you think it was like for me? Wasn't she my child too?" He raised his voice. "But in case you don't remember, I must remind you that we have another child."

Aspasia looked at him as if she was seeing him for the first time. "Where is Theodora?" she asked softly.

"She's at Aphrodite's house. But what am I saying? How would you know who Aphrodite is? Did you ever bother to find out who her friends are? Did you ever concern yourself with anything to do with her?"

"Stavros, please! I know I wasn't a perfect mother—"

"You weren't a mother at all!"

Aspasia looked at him with a wounded expression. She lowered her head and broke into sobs again. When she spoke, her voice could hardly be heard. "Yes, I'm to blame for everything. I left you . . . the children . . . I never had time for them, and now Stella's gone and I can't do anything to make it right. Why didn't God take me, Stavros? Why the child?"

Stavros looked at her bitterly. "We don't choose. I'm sorry I spoke to you like that, Aspasia. It's not the time to relive the past. We have to think of Theodora. She's only a child, and her sister's death has hurt her much more than us. I sent her to stay with her friend because you were in such a state but she's asking for you—she's afraid she'll lose you too."

"You're right. Go and get her."

"I can't do that when you're in this state. That's why I said you must pull yourself together. We must put our pain to one side and look after the child. We must help her get over it. Life has to go back to normal. School starts soon. How can she go like this? Do you understand?"

"Yes, but how can I pretend that I'm all right? I can't laugh as if nothing happened."

"I'm not asking you to do anything like that. I'm asking you to take our child in your arms and comfort her, and through the child we'll comfort ourselves. At the least, you owe her that. You've always ignored her. The small amount of time you devoted to the children always went to Stella first."

"And she was the very one I lost," Aspasia said in a low voice.

"Yes, but it's not Theodora's fault that she lived and Stella died."

"You shouldn't have said that!" Aspasia's anger flared.

Stavros was almost glad to see his wife angry. Anything was better than the apathy that the tranquillizers only increased. "Prove to me that I'm wrong, then," he said. "Support your child as she deserves. For once in your life, be a good mother!"

Aspasia looked at him intently and then got up. Before she left the room she said, "Bring her to me at lunchtime."

That afternoon, when Stavros returned to the house with their daughter, he was very anxious. He didn't know what state he'd find his wife in, despite her promise that morning. As he closed the front door behind him, he looked around. The house appeared to have been cleaned and there was a smell of cooking in the air. He didn't dare believe it. Suddenly, Aspasia appeared. She'd had a bath and tied up her hair with a black ribbon, and her eyes were no longer red. Stavros also detected a little makeup on her face to hide the pallor. He noticed how thin she'd become—she'd needed a belt to pull in her black dress—but her face radiated a calm that he hadn't seen in years.

Theodora looked at her mother with longing, but didn't know what she should do, so she simply stood still beside her father. When Aspasia opened her arms, the little one ran and hid herself in the warm embrace. Aspasia could feel her daughter's heart beating fast. She pulled back and looked at her as if she was seeing her for the first time. She stroked her blond hair, which was just like her own, and her fingers wandered over the girl's beautiful face, like a blind person whose touch has replaced her sight. As the girl looked delightedly at her mother, Aspasia hugged her again and cursed herself. What a crime she'd committed all these years! How could she have ignored one of her own children? Even little Stella, who Aspasia had had such a weakness for, had never gotten all the love she deserved. Aspasia swore she'd be a better person from now on, in every way she could.

A discreet look from Stavros brought her to herself. She smiled at her daughter. "We lost track of time," she said to her tenderly. "And Daddy is probably hungry. Come, wash your hands and I'll be waiting for you in the kitchen."

Theodora left quickly and Stavros followed her.

"A good performance!" he said drily on his way out.

Aspasia looked at him, wounded. "What performance? What are you talking about?"

"All that affectionate behavior and the hugs and caresses—what was that? I didn't expect so much coming from you. And don't tell me that you suddenly discovered some motherly instincts. In any case, I have to admit, it was good for the child."

They didn't manage to say anything else because Theodora came into the room, sat down, and began to eat hungrily. From time to time she looked at her mother, who had to make a big effort to swallow a few mouthfuls. Aspasia understood that she would need all her strength from now on. She may have begun to win her child back, but she had more work to do if she wanted to regain her husband's trust.

◆ ◆ ◆

Stavros looked at Despina, who was sitting opposite him and watching him without speaking. "I'm not very good company," he murmured.

"I wasn't just looking for company when I called," she said. "I wanted to see you—to speak to you and find out how you are."

"And in the end we're sitting here not talking."

"Even that, if it helps you feel better, is good."

He never expected that Kyrios Alekos's daughter would return to Kalamata to see him a month after little Stella's death, but here she was. In keeping with custom, they had planned a memorial service several weeks after the burial. As the date approached, the atmosphere in his house had become heavy again. Aspasia was making ambitious efforts to stand on her feet again and help Theodora, but Stavros questioned how long this change would last. His wife got up early every morning, prepared breakfast for everyone, and went out with her daughter. For the very first time, she'd bought her all her school supplies and spent hours covering textbooks and decorating exercise books. She wrote Theodora's name with pretty lettering on the labels and did everything else a mother did in those days. The child thought she was dreaming. Yet often, without an obvious reason, Theodora closed herself off and hardly spoke. Even then, though, Aspasia stayed close to her and invented dozens of excuses to draw the child out of her isolation and silence.

At the same time Aspasia had transformed herself into a perfect wife. She cooked food that she knew Stavros liked, she always asked him about his work when he came home at lunchtime, and when he had a very busy day and couldn't come home at midday, she took food to his office. In the evenings she sat with him but not close. Stavros had to admit that she was very tactful. She never touched him, even by accident, and she never asked to return to his room. This new Aspasia, however, frightened him even more. All this obedience, this desire to be useful, to do everything before she was asked, made him anxious at first. Then it became annoying.

Stavros became angrier and angrier with her. He spoke to her nastily and dismissively, but never in front of the child. As long as Theodora was with them their exchanges were polite, but as soon as the child said good night and went to her room, Stavros's expression darkened. He avoided looking at his wife and answered her only in monosyllables until Aspasia understood and stopped talking.

Despina's visit made Stavros feel better. She had also changed a lot. The carefree young girl who had dreamed of adventure had been transformed into a beautiful woman, calm and always smiling. He watched her again as she absentmindedly drank her coffee.

"What are you thinking about?" he asked.

"I was just trying to think of a subject that would interest you so that we could talk about it," she answered, smiling. "But my brain isn't being very cooperative with me today."

"I suppose I'm not very helpful either. My daughter's memorial service is in a few days, and I can't think of anything else."

"That's not surprising. How is Theodora?"

"Much better . . . school has helped her forget."

"And Aspasia?"

"Despina, please, let's not talk about Aspasia."

"All right. What do you want us to talk about?"

"About you! You haven't told me anything about your life during all the years since we last saw each other. How is your husband?"

"I think he's fine. We separated, you know."

Stavros's eyes opened wide. He sat up and looked at her with interest. "You separated? When? Your father never said anything to me."

"It wasn't long ago. Officially, that is. Unofficially things weren't going well for a long time."

"Do you want to tell me about it, or is it still too painful?"

"No! Not anymore. Besides I share a lot of the blame. I thought I wanted something and when I found it, I realized I had made a mistake. I thought that a carefree life suited me. I thought we'd travel together all over the world, but I soon got tired of it. I wanted a family and he didn't. His love for the sea was greater."

"You didn't have children?"

"I tried, but I miscarried. And then he didn't leave anything to chance—you understand? He made it plain that he didn't want children. He was gone for months on end, and when he came back he wanted me to be like the lovers he found in the ports, and to live the life they had lived there. We ended up arguing every time he came back and after every argument he stayed away longer."

Despina's confession made Stavros relax, and he suddenly found himself talking about his marriage, telling her every detail. His voice was flat and he kept his eyes fixed on his hands that were constantly holding a cigarette. He didn't hide anything from her and often Despina was embarrassed by the frankness of his descriptions. When he finished, he realized how much he'd said and was ashamed.

"I'm sorry," he muttered, still looking down. "I've put you in a difficult position."

"When my husband left me for months at a time, I made a lot of mistakes too. I thought that nothing could surprise me, but I have to confess that I'm shocked. Aspasia seems to have gone further than me, given the fact that she had two children. And now? Where are you now?"

"Nowhere. Since Stella's death, she's changed into a perfect mother, a model wife, an admirable housekeeper. Do you believe it?"

"The important thing is, do you believe it?"

"No, not anymore. I don't believe anything about her. In the past, she made some efforts too—not a lot, but some—but after a while, she'd always get bored again and her other life would drag her far away from us. I won't suffer through that again. I'm finished with Aspasia for good. Whatever she says, whatever she does, I won't ever believe that she's truly changed."

"And what if it is like it seems? If the death of your child was such a big blow that it managed to sweep all the bad things out of her? If it's as you say, it's as if she's asking forgiveness, as if she wants you to start over."

"I don't know, Despina," Stavros answered. "Aspasia has managed to make me forget all the beautiful moments we shared together. Now, when I see her, I don't feel anything."

Despina tried to soothe him. "It's early. You'll see yet that slowly, one of you will approach the other," she said.

◆ ◆ ◆

The memorial service was an agonizing event that scratched still-open wounds. This time Aspasia held back her emotions with superhuman effort. Her first concern was Theodora. Holding her tightly by the hand, she cried quietly without letting out any sounds so that the child wouldn't be frightened. Immediately after they came back from the church service she gave her something to eat, put her to bed, and sat beside her until she saw her eyes close. Only when she was sure that the child was fast asleep, exhausted by the ordeal, did she go out into the garden, despite the fact that it was raining hard. There she wept for the child she had lost. Her lament joined the sound of the thunder as she knelt in the mud, begging God to give her the strength she would need.

No one knew how hard Aspasia had struggled in recent weeks to regain her peace of mind. She'd faced her mistakes quite honestly. She'd counted them and was shocked by the number, but she didn't hurry to justify them as she had once done. Instead, she remembered every detail, and if it hadn't been for Theodora, she would have condemned herself to death. It would have been quite easy to end the life that she herself had wasted so far, but doing so would have further injured her one remaining daughter. Suicide would only add to the desertions and irresponsibility Aspasia had exhibited in the past.

She got up, covered in mud, and went inside to clean herself up. When she came out of the bathroom, she was the calm Aspasia, her eyes still red from crying, but determined to go on without any more mistakes. Despite her husband's cold demeanor lately, she was hopeful she could persuade him that it was worth the trouble to rebuild their family for the sake of Theodora.

When Stavros returned that evening, Aspasia dared to approach him and kiss him on the cheek but was frightened by his response. He pulled away abruptly and gave her a hostile look.

"Don't do that again!" he shouted. "Don't touch me ever again!"

Aspasia looked at him, hurt. "I'm sorry," she whispered. "I didn't do it to harm you. I felt the need to kiss you without any ulterior motive." She was close to crying but held on to herself.

"It doesn't matter to me why you did it," Stavros said, still angry. "But I'm asking you not to do it again because you're not going to like the way I respond. And you should know that having you in this house is very difficult, but I'm doing it for the child. Don't make me do something that I'll regret. Do you understand what I'm saying?"

"Yes. I didn't realize you felt like that. Now that I know I'll stay away. But I thought . . ."

"What did you think? That I believe the act you put on with the child? That I'm so stupid that I believe that you've become a human being again? No, Aspasia. I know you too well."

Aspasia looked at him in horror. "Is that what you think of me, Stavros?" she asked in a voice that came out with difficulty. "Then there's no hope for us. I must leave."

"Ha! So you've found an excuse now? You've gotten tired of playing the good mother and the model wife so quickly? Who's made you an offer? Who are you in a hurry to fall into the first bed you see with? Will it be in Rhodes? In Crete? Maybe in Patras? Or maybe you'll set sail for somewhere else? Greece is full of bouzouki clubs . . . and beds."

"It can't be you who's talking like this," she responded calmly. "Once you loved me and even I, who made all the mistakes, loved you. And I still love you. We lost our child and you think I want to leave to sing? I'm finished with all that. I'm really sorry that I did what I did, but I can't turn back time and wipe it all out. I can make a new start, though."

But Stavros just continued his tirade. "You might try the theater now. You have a talent for that. Leave me, Aspasia, and stop thinking you can fool me! The Stavros you knew doesn't exist anymore. Your victim, which is what I was, can't be persuaded this time. And if I decide to take you back when you return, know that it's for the child. Even a useless mother is better than nothing."

Stavros left and didn't come back all night. In the morning, Aspasia lied to their daughter, telling her that her father had left very early for work.

◆ ◆ ◆

Despina stared at Stavros with an expression that seemed to be scolding him. "I think that you overdid it," she said. "You shouldn't speak to her like that."

"You don't know how I felt when she came up to me and kissed me. She doesn't hold anything sacred, that woman! A few hours after the memorial of our child and she . . ."

"First of all, I don't think she had anything calculating in mind when she kissed you on the cheek. You're exaggerating. You're not the only one who's mourning the child; she's a mother and what's more she must have a lot of guilt."

"Aspasia feel guilty? Despina, you're a very good person at heart."

"I'm just more detached than you and I see things more clearly. Aspasia is suffering and she's suffering a lot. But for you to react like that means that your wife has the power to really upset you, even with an innocent touch. You love her, Stavros, and you'd better accept it."

"It's not love, Despina, it's a sickness. She arouses me, but in the wrong way. When she kissed me and I felt her near me, it didn't evoke love and affection but something else. An animal instinct. I wanted to fall on her and humiliate her, to make her feel what I felt for so many years. And then I got angry. I was angry most of all with myself. I don't like the person I become when I'm near her. Do you understand?"

Despina covered his hand with hers and Stavros immediately seemed to calm down. The lines of his face softened. After the fight with Aspasia, he'd left the house so as not to do something bad. He drove like crazy and without understanding how, he found himself knocking on Despina's hotel room door, even though it was late. She opened it right away—it was obvious she hadn't been asleep. She gave him a drink and listened attentively. Before long, he was sleeping in her bed while she watched him tenderly.

When he woke up the next morning Stavros looked around him in surprise. "Did I sleep here?" he asked in embarrassment.

She smiled at him. "Don't worry! You were a gentleman. Whatever I did, I didn't manage to drag you into debauchery."

"Now you're making me feel even worse."

"Not a bit! Last night you were worse. Now I see you looking fine. And I'm quite serious! You came here in an awful state. You told me what happened. I gave you a drink and you slept soundly all night."

"Despina, I'm sorry if I bothered you. I didn't know where to go last night."

"You did the right thing to come here. That's what friends are for. Come on now, get up and we'll have some coffee before you leave for work."

"I don't feel like working today," he said, rubbing his still tired eyes. "What time will you leave today?"

"To go where?"

"Home, I suppose."

"I think I'll stay a little longer in Kalamata. I like it here, and what's more I have a friend who probably needs me."

Stavros looked gratefully at her. They spent that day together. They went for a long walk around town, then ate dinner at a quiet little restaurant. Afterward, Stavros finally went home to see his daughter.

Theodora welcomed him lovingly. "Where were you all day, Daddy? I missed you," she said as soon as she saw him.

"I had a lot of work, sweetheart . . . I'm sorry," he whispered sweetly to her and hugged her. "What did you do today? Did you go to school?"

She smiled slyly and exchanged a glance with her mother. "You won't believe it, Daddy," she said happily. "I skipped school today."

"Skipped it?" Stavros looked confused. He looked at Aspasia, but her expression was impossible to read.

"Yes," Theodora went on. "I played hooky with Mama! We went for a walk, we ate out . . . it was wonderful." Her face darkened for a moment. "Mama told me I could miss school just for today because yesterday was Stella's memorial and we were both in a terrible state. Are you angry, Daddy?"

"No, darling. Mama knows best what you need and since she arranged it, you did the right thing!"

Stavros avoided his wife's eyes and concentrated instead on his daughter. As soon as she went to sleep, without saying a word, he shut himself in his room. He heard Aspasia's door close and it took all his self-control not to go to her room. It didn't make sense and he knew it.

◆ ◆ ◆

Three months had passed since Despina had come to Kalamata, and still she didn't seem to have any immediate plan to return to her family in Larissa. Stavros finally stopped asking her and simply accepted her company.

Every day that passed he was more aware of how much the superficial young girl he had known once had changed. Every day she became more necessary to him than he was prepared to accept. He now spent very few hours at home and only at those times when he knew his daughter would be there. He and Aspasia rarely spoke to one another, and only then when the child was present. His wife never asked him where he disappeared to all day, and she never complained when he left, even on weekends, supposedly for work. During the endless hours of solitude when her daughter was at school or doing her extracurricular activities, Aspasia read or went for walks; on the weekends, she took her daughter to the cinema.

Immediately after the holidays, Despina found a little house—she now planned to live permanently in Kalamata—and Stavros became her regular visitor. They listened to music for hours, played backgammon, and rarely went out. Only in that house, full of companionship, did Stavros feel relaxed.

One afternoon Stavros came home unexpectedly and found Aspasia talking to a stranger. He quickly realized that he was a club owner who had come to offer her work. As he felt the blood rise to his head, he shut himself in his room in a vain attempt to recover his self-control. He didn't expect Aspasia to follow him.

"Why have you shut yourself in here?" she asked.

"So as not to disturb your . . . negotiations!" he said with difficulty. "Where was the offer for?"

"Crete."

"Very nice! Your old haunts. And when, may I ask, do you leave?"

Aspasia looked at him without any expression. "And what does it matter to you?" she said coldly. "You don't even know I exist anymore."

"Oh, I do know very well that you exist. And I know why you exist. To torture me as you always do!"

Stavros was beside himself. He knew that he would regret it but he couldn't help himself. He approached his wife with rapid movements, grabbed her, and fixed his lips on hers. He felt like an addict who, after a long period of deprivation, was taking his desired drug again, even though the dose could be fatal. Aspasia immediately came to life at his touch. She wound her arms around his neck and clung to him with longing. It didn't matter to her that he hurt her; it didn't bother her that his caresses came from anger and not from love; it didn't matter that the only thing he wanted to do was to humiliate her. She let him do what he pleased. But she couldn't bear the way he looked at her afterward, his eyes full of disgust. He got up and for a moment she thought he was going to spit in her face. Instead, Stavros dressed and left like a madman. Aspasia got up, feeling her body in pain. She saw everything around her smashed to pieces. There was no hope—not after that. She must make up her mind.

Despina wondered why Stavros had disappeared from her life. For a week he hadn't stopped by the house, nor had he called her. She gave him his space and didn't stop by his office. She waited for the time when he himself would come looking for her. He finally did one night when he was very drunk. With great difficulty he told her what had happened and began crying when he explained how disgusted he was with himself. His last encounter with Aspasia had convinced him that he'd never be able to see her as a woman who deserved his respect and love.

Despina put him to bed, stopping his raving, but she herself stayed awake. She had come to Kalamata not knowing what drove her here, but she knew very well why she had stayed. She had never been indifferent to Stavros, but in the craziness of youth, he had seemed boring to her, and the other man so attractive that she'd married him without a second thought. After so many years and so many mistakes, she had thought all roads were closed. Stavros was married. She had honestly tried to help him as a friend, even if she didn't feel like that, and she had never wanted to come between him and his wife. But now? What exactly would she be destroying that wasn't already destroyed?

In the morning, Stavros woke up in a bad mood and with a terrible headache. Again, he felt embarrassed in front of Despina.

"Forgive me," he said.

"Forgive me, Father, for I have sinned," she replied. "Enough of your apologies, Stavros! I'm beginning to feel like the archbishop. Are we friends or not? Where else would you go in the state you were in?"

"It's not right to burden you all the time. To be honest, I don't know why you don't get fed up with me and leave so you can have some peace."

"Maybe peace is not what I'm looking for at this particular moment." Then Despina looked him in the eye.

Her look confused Stavros. He lowered his eyes, certain that last night's drunkenness had made him imagine things. The day passed very peacefully. Despina made him some soup to calm his stomach. After lunch she forced him to take a nap, and when he woke up in the afternoon Stavros felt better. Still, Despina's look wouldn't leave his mind. It couldn't be true, what he saw in her eyes.

"Aren't you going home?" she asked at one point during the evening.

Stavros noticed she'd avoided looking at him when she asked and he felt an inexplicable agitation. "Are you in a hurry to send me away?" he said. An embarrassed smile was the only answer he got.

"Despina," he began in a low voice.

Despina finally raised her eyes and finally looked at him, and the love he saw there overwhelmed him. He reached out his hand and stroked her cheek, which burned as if she had a fever, and her lips attracted his like a magnet. It had been years since he'd felt like this as he kissed a woman. As they moved next to the fire and continued their exploration of each other, he heard himself moan almost painfully and at the same time he felt as if something bad was leaving him.

Finally he had found paradise again. However unbelievable it seemed, as he watched Despina sleeping in his arms, Stavros couldn't help but accept that he was happy again. He couldn't even remember the last time he had embraced a woman to show her love instead of disdain. Nor could he remember when he had begun to think of love as an act of punishment and humiliation, so far had he degraded its importance. Now, however, everything had changed. The ghost of Aspasia faded inside him; the thought of her didn't provoke anger or pain. His blood didn't boil when he remembered her. Even that last cursed evening only aroused sorrow and shame for having abandoned himself to something so unhealthy.

Despina moved a little, then woke up. They looked at each other and she smiled.

"Are you going to ask me to forgive you now?" she said mockingly.

"If you think I should," he answered.

"If you do I'll hit you," she said, pretending to be serious.

"How long have you loved me so much?" he asked.

She didn't lower her eyes but continued to look at him. "I think from the time that I met you."

"So why did you marry the other fellow?"

"If I hadn't married him, would you have asked me?"

"To be honest, no. I took you for a superficial girl who wanted to have a good time and not marry."

"And I saw you as an inexperienced young man who would have married me so that he could become a partner in my father's business more quickly."

"We're even then," Stavros said and kissed her.

"Stavros, I haven't denied that I love you, but you . . ."

"If you're asking me how I feel . . ."

"I don't want you to feel I'm putting pressure on you."

"The answer you're seeking from me isn't easy. I feel as if I've recovered from a serious illness and to be frank, I feel so calm for the first time in ages that I don't want to spoil it, I don't want to think of anything."

"I understand. Don't say anything, then. Let yourself enjoy something you were missing. We have time."

When Stavros bent to kiss her again, she pulled him down on her. He enjoyed every moment that followed without hurrying. Despina responded to his every touch with ineffable sweetness. With every kiss he felt himself becoming young again, while his wounds stopped hurting.

Aspasia saw the change in him, and although at first she thought she might be imagining things, when she observed him more carefully, she was certain of it. His face was more relaxed, and the wrinkles around his eyes, which had recently become very deep, had softened; suddenly he seemed younger. But what made the greatest impression on her was his behavior toward her. After that terrible evening he had disappeared for days. When he came back he was much nicer to her. He didn't seem absentminded when he spoke, and he didn't look at her with dislike. Aspasia took heart. Perhaps after that violent outburst and the pain it caused her, which she endured and answered only with love, he understood that his wife still loved him. Perhaps everything wasn't lost.

As for Theodora, she had begun to show her mother more trust, talking to her more and sharing innocent secrets. When the girl told Aspasia about the joke that all the students had played on the mathematics teacher whom they didn't like, she was surprised and delighted by her mother's happy laughter. But she felt the ground slip from under her feet when her father asked Aspasia, "Well, are you going to Crete then?"

Aspasia was confused. "Why would I go to Crete?" she asked her husband.

As she listened for a response, Theodora held her breath.

"Last week, if I remember rightly, you told me you'd been offered a chance to sing in Crete again!" Stavros answered.

"You remember correctly—as I do," Aspasia said. She fixed her eyes firmly on him, but Stavros didn't look away. "I didn't ever say I'd go."

"So you won't go?" Now it was Stavros who was confused.

"Of course not. If you hadn't rushed to shut yourself in your room that day, you would have heard me making it clear that singing doesn't interest me anymore and that my decision not to take it up again is final."

Theodora couldn't contain herself. She ran to hug her mother, who continued looking at her husband. Stavros couldn't believe his ears.

"I didn't know," he said in a soft voice. "I'm sorry, I rushed to conclusions that day."

His apology was sincere, but Aspasia smiled bitterly. "It doesn't matter," she said. "You weren't very wrong to imagine the worst." Then she turned to Theodora. "Sweetheart, can you leave us alone for a little while? We have to talk."

The child, reassured that she would not lose her mother again, kissed her and disappeared. Aspasia turned to Stavros.

"I don't want you to feel bad about what you did that day," she said quietly. "It hurt me very much, I can't deny that, but I've forgiven you. I've done you a lot of harm too. From the time we lost Stella I've tried to show you that I've changed, but you didn't believe me, again with good reason."

"Aspasia, I'd rather we stopped here."

"Don't worry, I won't make you angry again. Nor will I push you to behave like you did before. I'll never give you again the opportunity to push me onto the bed like an animal and have me come out covered in bruises. Once you taught me to have sex as an act of love, but later you made it a punishment. Not that I didn't deserve it. I was the one who first betrayed what beauty we two had. I was once cheap, I don't deny it, but I'm finished with all that for good. Do you remember what you told me when I came back from Crete? That you hoped I'd recover, but also that the reason for my recovery wouldn't break me. In the end I had to be broken to pieces so as to pick them up one day and go on. Now the question is whether you can forgive me so that we can go on together. Can you, Stavros?"

Rather than answering, he left without giving her a second glance.

◆ ◆ ◆

As soon as she saw Stavros on her doorstep, Despina knew something had happened.

"Stavros, what happened? Don't tell me you did it again," she said in an agitated voice.

"No, nothing bad, if that's what you're asking. I didn't touch her, we didn't argue, I haven't been drinking."

"So why are you like this? Something happened."

"We talked. Aspasia told me she was finally finished with singing and with the past. She meant it, Despina. What happened that night was wrong. She had already refused the offer from the club owner. And I . . . the more I think of what I did to her, I'm ashamed. I'm more ashamed of that moment than you can imagine."

"I won't say you're wrong to feel some shame. The two of you have done a lot of harm to one another. So what are you going to do now, Stavros?"

"What do you mean, what am I going to do?"

"Your wife has become what you wanted her to be, you have a child together, and she's asking you to start over again—isn't that right?"

"She told me that she's completely finished with the past and I have to think about whether I can forgive her so that we can move ahead. She stood in front of me without offering any excuses for what she did. She took full responsibility. She was the Aspasia I once knew . . . calm, strong, able to look me in the eye again. She looked just as beautiful as she did then."

"So what is there to decide? Whatever the two of us have, with Aspasia you'll always have something more—your child."

"I can't do it, Despina. However much I want to believe her I can't go back. I don't love her anymore. Over all those years, day by day, any feeling I had for her died."

"Did you tell her that?"

"No, I wanted to think. I've been wandering around the streets for hours asking myself if I have the slightest trace of feelings left for her, something that would allow me to hope. There's nothing."

"And the child?"

"The child will come with me, of course."

"Are you sure?"

"Completely. However hard Aspasia tried with Theodora—and I won't say she didn't make up for some lost time—the girl won't want to live with her mother."

"You sound very sure. But . . ."

"Would you like to live with me and help me raise her?"

Despina tried to hide the longing in her voice. "What are you suggesting?"

"I won't lie to you, Despina. I love you. Maybe not in the same way I loved Aspasia once, but I'm certain about one thing: I want to live with you. You make me feel as if I'm getting better. I feel calm beside you, I miss you when I'm not with you. Is that enough for you to agree to be my wife?"

The answer came in the form of an embrace and warm kiss.

Stavros now had to speak to Aspasia, but he wanted to wait until they'd gotten beyond the first anniversary of Stella's death. Nothing would change, of course. Neither of them would ever get over the death of their child, but he still thought it would be best to tell her the day after the ceremony.

Aspasia seemed ready. They'd sent Theodora to play with her friend, and now they sat like duelists, one opposite the other.

"So the time's come," she said, without a trace of bitterness in her voice.

"I think so, yes," he replied. "We left the conversation half-finished, and I didn't think it was right to continue it before the anniversary of Stella's death."

"I respect that. But I think I already know what you want to say. We're finished, aren't we? Isn't that what you wanted to tell me, Stavros?"

"Yes. I thought about it very hard. It's not that I don't believe that you've changed, but . . ."

"But you can't forget."

"No, I can't. Also, I don't feel anything anymore, Aspasia. There's nothing left in me."

"I didn't leave anything in you."

"You could say that. Regardless, I don't want to put more blame on you. When you get down to it, we said all we had to say; in the end, there was just no way to fix this."

"You're right. For a little while, recently, when you began being nice to me, I thought that things were going to turn around for us. But now I understand. There's another woman in your life, isn't there, Stavros?"

"What does that have to do with it?"

"So she does exist. Don't worry, I won't provoke anything that would make us enemies again. I had accepted the fact that we won't be together again before you told me. Even I have instincts. So, are you going to reveal who she is?

"Despina."

"Despina? Kyrios Alekos's daughter? But she's married to a sailor."

"Yes, but they've separated. Some time ago. For the last year she's been living in Kalamata. But I only recently realized . . . I mean, it's only recently that we've been together."

"Yes. But it's an irony of fate, isn't it? If you had discovered that you were suited to one another back then, you wouldn't have gone through all the suffering I've caused you."

"You speak as if it doesn't bother you."

"It bothers me, but not so much. I love you of course: you did nothing to change my feelings, but I can accept that it's better like this. We've done a lot of harm to each other—"

Stavros cut her off. "I know what you mean. The strange thing is that Despina said the same thing."

"Will you get married?"

"Yes. That is, I asked her and she accepted. What will you do?"

"I don't know yet. What will happen with the child, Stavros? Who will Theodora live with?"

"Do we even need to discuss that? Naturally, she'll live with me. I've already spoken to Despina. She knows we'll raise Theodora together."

"Does that mean that you've made up your mind to take her away from me?" Aspasia's voice sounded strange.

"Just wait a minute, because you've caught me unprepared. Do you mean that you want her with you?"

"How can you think that I don't want her? The best years of her life passed without my knowing she existed, and now that I've struggled so hard to get close to her, you want me to leave her?"

"Aspasia, I think you're overlooking something. However hard you struggled—and I know you struggled—the little one is closest to me. And what do you intend to do? I mean, where will you go? Where will you work? How will you raise her?"

"I don't know yet. I haven't had time to think. You see, you've already made your decisions, you've discussed them with your future partner. But I guess I hoped until the last moment . . ."

"Have you thought about going back to singing?" he asked.

Aspasia couldn't understand why it felt so difficult to answer. "I told you I was all finished with singing!" she finally declared.

"Yes, but now that you're free, I thought . . ."

"You thought wrong. I already made it clear that I'm entirely done with singing and the life I led. I didn't just say that to save our marriage, although I hoped it would. I decided to give it up for myself."

"And how will you live? I'm ready to help you, to give you some support."

"I won't accept a penny from you. I have some savings from my time in the clubs, and I'll see what else I can do. As for the child . . ."

"Aspasia, if we want to make sure that we're doing the right thing, we can ask her."

"Why would we put her in such a dilemma? Why would we make her feel guilty over who she decides to leave? No, Stavros. I'll accept this, as I've accepted all the rest. I had everything and I lost it on a roll of the dice, like a bad gambler. I only ask that I can see her now and then."

"I promise you I won't do anything to stop you from seeing her."

Aspasia stood up. She looked very tired. Stavros stood too, and they looked into each other's eyes. Quite spontaneously, he stretched out his arms and hugged her. They stayed like that for a few minutes, and when they separated, Aspasia's eyes were filled with tears.

"I'm truly sorry," she said quietly.

"I am too. I'll always remember the Aspasia I knew and loved; I'll remember only our good moments."

"Yes, do that. It will be a relief to me to know that you're thinking of me without hatred anymore. And I want to believe . . . I'll pray to God that Despina gives you all the happiness that I couldn't give you."

Aspasia dared to kiss him tenderly on the cheek, but Stavros neither pulled away nor did he seem to be angry. She smiled sadly at him and went to her room until she heard the front door close behind him and realized that Despina was waiting for him.

◆ ◆ ◆

Theodora looked at her father in surprise. The two of them were in the house alone, as Aspasia had made some excuse and then gone out so they could talk. She didn't have the courage to be present at such a discussion.

"What do you mean when you say we'll leave this house?" Theodora asked. "And what about Mama?"

"Theodora, you're a big girl, so you can understand. Your mother and I can't live together anymore."

"Don't you love her? Is that it?"

"No, not in the way a man should love his wife."

"Do you love someone else?"

Stavros looked at her bravely. "I won't lie to you. Your mother and I understood some time ago that we couldn't live together. We were patient in case something changed . . . but during this time, another woman turned up in my life who loves me and I love her."

"And will we live with her?"

"Yes."

"And Mama? Will she live by herself?"

"Yes, unless she finds someone else. She's very young and still very beautiful."

"And the other one, the woman we'll live with? Is she young and beautiful?"

"Yes, she is."

"More beautiful than Mama?"

"What does that have to do with it?"

"If she isn't more beautiful than Mama, why are you marrying her?"

"It has nothing to do with beauty, darling. Despina is very nice; she knows we are all going to live together and she can't wait to welcome you into her house!"

"Despina? Is she the daughter of your partner, Daddy?"

"Yes. And whenever you want, you'll go to see your mother. You won't be losing either of us. I promise you!"

"Daddy, why are you doing this? I know you used to be angry with Mama when she went away, but now she's always here. So why are you angry with her?"

"Who told you I was angry with Mama?"

"So why are you separating? Is it because we lost Stella? I'm here and I don't want you to separate!"

"I know, sweetheart. That's why we were patient, why we tried, but it didn't work. We're very young to stay together without wanting to. When you grow up a little, you'll understand."

The girl was silent. A deep wrinkle appeared between her brows. She looked at her father thoughtfully. "Do I have to come with you?" she finally asked.

Stavros's eyes opened wide. "What do you mean?"

"When two parents separate, the child has to go with one or the other. Is that right?" she continued.

"Right."

"OK. Well I want to go and live with Mama," Theodora announced, straightening her body proudly.

"But, my child, I want to say . . . you and your mother . . . that is, I thought . . ." Stavros was at a loss. "I want to say that with Mama, we decided . . ."

"Do you mean to say that Mama agreed to let me live with you without any discussion?"

"The truth is that I told her that's the way it would be, because I thought you'd want to stay with me. You and your mother mended your relationship only very recently, and I never imagined that you'd want to go with her."

"It's very bad that you didn't ask me before you made decisions that concern me."

"Your mother didn't want to put you in such a dilemma."

"But there's no dilemma for me. I love both of you but my mother needs me right now."

"I need you too."

"But you'll have another woman beside you and Mama will be by herself! No, Daddy. I'm not going with you. I'll come and see you as often as I can, but my place is with my mother."

"Theodora, are you sure?"

"Absolutely! Do you know something? When we lost my sister I felt very much alone. You see, for me, Stella wasn't just my sister; she was much more. Mama was away, and even when she was here it was as if she was away. But later she changed. At first I didn't dare to believe it. Every day that went by I thought it would be our last together; I thought that she'd leave me again. But eventually, I realized that it wasn't like that. She'd come back to me forever. If this had happened a few years ago I'd have come with you without any discussion. But now that Mama has changed, now that she seems to regret everything, I won't turn my back on her. All people deserve another chance—that's what our literature teacher at school says, and now I know she's right. You understand, don't you?"

Stavros looked at his daughter, very moved. "When did you grow up so much?" he asked.

"Probably right now, at this moment. You won't be angry with me, will you, Daddy?"

"How could I be?"

"And you'll let me go with Mama?"

"How could I do anything else?"

◆ ◆ ◆

Aspasia walked like an automaton along the road without seeing where she was going. She had no idea how long she'd been out, but she didn't want to go home and hear her death sentence. And that's what it felt like. When Theodora would go to live with her father, she'd take all her mother's strength and vitality with her. The wheels of the cars passing Aspasia seemed very tempting; one step and she'd be saved forever from the pain she carried inside her. But reason stopped her. No, she wouldn't do that to her child. She would let her go and then she'd disappear forever without her daughter ever knowing that she'd fled from a life that had no meaning anymore. If she did it any other way, the child would be full of guilt that she'd carry with her for the rest of her life.

She entered the house exhausted and only when she had closed the door did she allow her tears to flow freely. Complete quiet reigned. She took two steps forward and was startled when she saw Theodora reading a book.

As soon as she saw her mother she smiled. "You've finally come home!" she said. "I've been waiting for you for an hour!"

"Where's your father?"

"Daddy and I had a big discussion and now he's left. He went to Despina, who is waiting for him."

Aspasia looked dazed.

Theodora continued, "Like I said, I talked to Daddy. I know that you're separating. I found out about Despina, and he wanted to take me with him to meet her but I told him I wanted to talk to you, and so Despina will have to wait to meet me another time."

"What do you want to say to me? If it's about you, I know . . ."

"You think you know, just like Daddy."

Aspasia felt her heart leap and sat down in an armchair so as not to collapse on the floor. It wasn't possible—she must have made a mistake.

Theodora came over and sat on the arm of the chair. "We'll leave together, Mama," she said. "Because we will be leaving, won't we?"

Aspasia couldn't even move now. "Did you tell your father you want to stay with me?" she asked in a voice that could hardly be heard.

"Of course!"

"Why?" Aspasia dared to ask, her eyes brimming with tears. "Why do you want to live with me? I wasn't ever . . ."

"Once, you weren't a mother to me. But now you are, and I'm not going to leave you alone."

Aspasia couldn't hold herself back anymore. Shaking all over with sobs, she hugged her daughter, who responded with delight.

Theodora recovered first. She pulled away and looked at her mother. "Mama, enough tears," she said, wiping her mother's eyes.

"You're right! Now we have to think about what we'll do, where we'll go."

Holding hands, they talked for a long time, suggesting and rejecting cities where they could live. In the end, neither of them knew how a river came into the conversation, a river that flowed calmly. Its waters ran beside a house that was embraced by two chestnut trees, like two tender sentinels. The decision to return excited them both. Recently Theodora had heard her mother talk about the village tucked away below Mount Olympus. Enchanted by everything her mother described, she was dying to go there and to meet her grandmother whose name she carried.

Aspasia, with a tender smile on her lips, remembered her mother's words. *"And if the trials are very strong, remember that here, in this corner of the earth, is the river. Dive into it to purify yourself again!"* The hour of return had come and with it the hour of her expiation. The river of her life had dragged her along, but now she would go against the current, holding her daughter's hand tightly, and return to where she had begun, knowing that she never wanted to leave again. And so, back to the house . . .

To the house by the river.

POLYXENI

Squeezed between boxes and costumes, Polyxeni kept holding her breath until they were far enough from the village. She didn't want anyone to discover her until they were so far that they couldn't throw her off the truck and send her back. From what she'd heard before they left, the troupe was heading for the Peloponnese to give its next performances. When she stowed herself away, she didn't know exactly why she was doing it or how she would manage without a penny to her name. The only thing she knew was that if she didn't leave the village, she would go insane. She had taken a few clothes with her, only what was strictly necessary. Now, sitting in the hard back of the truck, she thought about what she'd say to the traveling players when they found her. Would they let her stay with them or kick her out? If they allowed her to stay, how could she earn her keep? And if they sent her on her way, where would she go?

Polyxeni once again imagined herself standing on the stage, wearing beautiful clothes and with a crowd of people applauding. Her daydream, together with the rhythmic movement of the truck, lulled her sweetly to sleep. She woke up hungry a few hours later. She crawled to the side of the truck and lifted the tarpaulin a little to see where they were. They were coming into Almyro, which meant that they'd been traveling for hours. She went back to her place and opened her cloth bag. At the top was a piece of bread wrapped in a napkin. She pulled off a small piece and began to chew slowly. Her imagination helped her transform it into smoked salmon. Somewhere she had read that the rich ate smoked salmon and caviar at the parties they went to, and she was determined to eat the same thing one day. She didn't know how, but she was sure of one thing: she would become rich and famous, no matter what it took. She would dress in very expensive clothes, wear marvelous jewels, and have people wait on her.

She looked around the dirty place she was sitting in and shuddered. Suddenly tears came to her eyes, but once again she used her imagination to escape. Nothing around her was real. This was a stage setting and she, as the leading actress, was playing the role of a persecuted woman. In her mind she began to set up a dialogue, to answer imaginary characters, and she only stopped when she felt the truck braking. She carefully looked out and realized that they had reached Kamena Vourla and had stopped for food.

Besides the little truck, there was another car belonging to the troupe. Old and broken down, it passed in front of Polyxeni as it carried the other members of the group to a cheap restaurant a few meters further on. Polyxeni knew she had to come out of her hiding place. She really needed to stretch her cramped legs and breathe some fresh air. When she'd made sure that everyone was seated in the restaurant, she took her bag and stepped down.

She hadn't managed to hit the ground before she felt two hands lifting her, as if she weighed nothing more than thistledown, and standing her up. She raised her eyes and saw one of the men of the troupe. He was the oldest, and in the plays she'd seen them perform he always played the role of the father or the grandfather.

"If I'm not mistaken, we have a little stowaway here," he said to her, smiling. "What are you doing in our truck, miss?"

"Let me explain . . ." Polyxeni began in a weak voice.

But before she could go on, the tall man pulled her into the restaurant and showed her to the others. "Look what I brought you instead of cigarettes!" he announced and everyone turned and looked at her. "She traveled in the back of our truck," he clarified.

"Let me explain . . ." Polyxeni repeated, ready to burst into tears. Now they would leave her here and she'd be all alone in a strange place.

"We're listening," the man prompted her, crossing his arms on his chest. "What business do you have in our truck?"

"I wanted to come with you," the girl answered softly.

"We understood that. It's the *why* we want to find out!"

"I want to be an actress," she said with some confidence now. But her statement only provoked loud laughter from the troupe. Polyxeni straightened her shoulders and looked at them disdainfully. "I can act better, much better, than most of you," she said drily and the laughter broke off. "You only have to let me audition, then you'll see."

The tall man looked at her more carefully now. Undoubtedly she was very beautiful. Very tall, with fine features and long blond hair. She'd certainly have success with the men if she could say her lines right. For a long time he'd been missing a young girl in his troupe. But first he needed to find out a few things.

"Before we have you audition for us, what do you say we all have some food together? Sit with us and we'll talk later!" he suggested, and they all made room for her.

At first Polyxeni sat quietly with an almost aristocratic air about her. While they ate, she observed the others without speaking. In the village, she'd only seen the players on their rudimentary stage in their theatrical costumes, whereas now she saw each one as an ordinary person. The impression they gave her was depressing. They all seemed sad, worn out, and very hungry. It scared her the way they ate, dipping into the oil and sauces and licking their fingers. Only one woman sitting opposite her behaved differently. She looked about forty, was beautiful, and from what Polyxeni remembered, she was more talented than the others. She sat in her place with dignity, ate very little, and always used her fork, something that raised Polyxeni's opinion of her. Polyxeni hadn't realized that the woman was observing her with half-closed eyes, not missing a single movement. She was the only one who didn't snicker at the girl as she ate with a knife and fork, cutting her food into very small mouthfuls so as not to fill her mouth.

After the meal, most of the group lit cigarettes. It was now time to hear some details about Polyxeni. The girl had already decided that whether they took her with them or not, they must not learn who she really was.

"So," began the man who had discovered her. "Are you going to tell us who you are?"

From the beginning, Polyxeni had understood that he was the leader of the troupe and that her fate depended on him. So she looked at him with confidence and smiled. "My name is Xenia Olympiou," she answered. She had no difficulty thinking up a name that would follow her from that moment on. Olympiou was of course inspired by Olympus, which she had just left behind. And half of her first name was better than all of it. "As I told you, I want to be an actress, and I'm sure I have talent!"

"So why didn't you come and find us in the village and ask us to take you with us? Maybe you ran away and they're chasing you? Because I don't want to get mixed up with any police."

"I'm an adult, sir. I can decide for myself and I did. Nobody is likely to chase me. My family knows that I followed you, even though they don't approve, of course. But that's not at all important."

Lambros Pagonis, the leader of the troupe, looked carefully at the girl in front of him. She was a real windfall, and since she herself was prepared to starve with them, he had no objection. She might even, if she had talent as she said, be good for the troupe. For years now he'd been traveling all over Greece. He had given performances in cafés, in the open air, even in barns. Once, when he was young, he had begun his career with lots of dreams, and he'd played beside some serious actors of the day. He'd managed to make a name for himself, but he very soon started to get into the drink. The beginning of the end had arrived, but he hadn't understood it at the time. He began to forget his words onstage and to delay his entrances, creating gaps in the performance. Soon he stopped being in demand.

When he met Zoe, he stopped drinking, but it was too late. Nobody trusted him, nobody would offer him even a small role. But the bug for acting didn't leave him. He formed his own troupe and from then on he traveled around the countryside. A lot of people had been with him and moved on. Some were real actors and some didn't want to believe that they would never become actors. Very occasionally, real talent had appeared beside him, but precisely because of that talent they always left for some theater in Athens. He had suffered hundreds of humiliations. Frustrated by the troupe's poor performances, audiences often threw whatever they found at them, forcing the show to end. And it wasn't so unusual for them to have to flee from a village in the night so that the disgruntled locals, who felt they'd been cheated after such a bad show, didn't beat them up.

Tickets were often used to barter for eggs, honey, corn, even vegetables—the important thing was for the troupe to eat. When they were lucky, though, they ate in a restaurant. They'd been able to do so today because the tour in Pieria had gone very well thanks to Martha, the woman who was observing Polyxeni so carefully. Lambros had to admit that her acting had saved the whole troupe. She'd been with them for two months, and things had gone quite well during that time. If the girl he found in the truck proved to have talent, as well, maybe he'd manage to buy new costumes, or even pay his actors a little more.

"Fine then," he said to Polyxeni. "We'll try you out right now. And if you're as good as you say, you'll come with us . . . as long as you realize that things aren't always easy. The life of a traveling actor comes with hunger and hardship, Miss Xenia."

"Xenia" smiled at him with understanding and Lambros introduced her to the other members of the group. Apart from himself and Martha there were six members. There was Paschalis, a young man with greasy hair and a slimy smile who played the handsome lead. Then there was Markos, a forty-something actor who also served as the troupe's electrician, prop master, and whatever else they needed. Markos was married to Pelagia, a short woman with a nice figure who always muddled her lines and was given only very small parts (her real talent was cooking, so she was generally in charge of feeding the troupe). Polyxeni already knew Thomas, a short, fat man of around fifty who'd made an impression in the village with his comic roles; Thomas only had to appear on stage to make people laugh. Then there was Zoe, Lambros's wife, an occasional actress and magnificent dressmaker who had taken over the preservation of the troupe's worn-out costumes. Finally there was Sotiris, a true savior. His role was not on the stage but under it, where he quietly called out the lines when the actors forgot them, something that happened often, because the featured play was always changing, often on the same day. When the audience was dissatisfied with a performance, the players had to switch to another play immediately so as not to lose them. On other occasions, even though the group had arranged to perform one play, the audience would demand another before the show even began, forcing a last-minute change.

As Polyxeni listened to the troupe talk of frayed costumes and angry audiences, she was disappointed, but she knew that all this was only the beginning for her. At the first opportunity, she would go to Athens to try her luck in a real theater. The group walked her down to the beach, a little way from the restaurant, where Lambros gave her a worn-out old script to read, a scene from *Romeo and Juliet*. Martha would play the nurse. Polyxeni had read the play in the village. Her literature teacher at school had lent it to her and she knew it well. She had been so moved by the classic love story that she'd played the role of Juliet dozens of times in front of the mirror.

When Polyxeni began to read her lines, Lambros saw her transform into Shakespeare's heroine. Her face assumed the tenderness of a young girl in love, yet her voice was strong enough to be heard clearly on the deserted beach. He noticed that the girl hardly looked at the script, a sign that she knew the role well. Together with the rest of the troupe he lost himself in her performance. His eyes shone. Finally. He had pure gold in his hands.

For the rest of the trip to the Peloponnese, Polyxeni sat between Martha and Zoe, and as the car groaned, eating up the miles, she thought about the future. They would give their first performance in a village outside Nafplion, and Lambros had announced that she would act in the performance, with Martha playing her mother. He had, of course, given Polyxeni the script to study as they went along. It was a mawkish, sentimental piece, the origin of which she didn't know. That didn't matter at all, though. What mattered was that she would be acting. Finally she would set foot on the stage, and it would be in her hands whether she heard applause or not.

Xenia Olympiou's debut took place in a small café in front of a small, poorly dressed audience, and at first the leading actress was very disappointed by the crowd. But her imagination came to her rescue again. When she started to act she didn't see wooden chairs but velvet seats, and the spectators turned into men in smoking jackets, while the headscarves of the women transformed into diadems adorned with precious stones. With a dignified air she got up on stage and played her role in an affecting way. And although at the beginning whispers and laughter reached her ears, after a few minutes there was complete silence; the audience was enthralled and followed the scene with interest. In the end, the performance was satisfying, even for Polyxeni. The applause was loud and warm and the voices enthusiastic.

The crowd may have been small on that first day, but that wasn't the case for the rest of their stay. Soon, Lambros was rubbing his hands together with satisfaction as he thought of the money the troupe was making thanks to Xenia Olympiou, who with each performance made everyone in the smoked-filled interior of the café cry. For the first time the players stayed for fifteen whole days in the same place. People even came from the surrounding villages to see their shows, and when the troupe got ready to leave, everyone in town protested. So the company changed the play and stayed another fifteen days.

Polyxeni looked at the money in her hands. It was the first money she'd had of her own. Lambros had given it to her, happy that after so long, he was in a position to pay his actors. He also managed to buy quite a few yards of material so his wife could sew new costumes for the play they would perform in Gytheio. The play was a French farce and the role Polyxeni had been cast in fit her like a glove. She was especially happy in the pink dress that Zoe had sewn for her. Martha played her older sister, and they had a delightful dialogue that made the audience clap enthusiastically. This time they stayed two whole months in the area. The café where they played was quite large and its owner was pleased with the crowds the troupe brought in.

Boredom struck Polyxeni before she realized what was the matter with her. She felt as if she was suffocating; the hour before the performance seemed endless, and when she got on stage she mechanically acted out her lines. She woke up every morning before everyone else, and as soon as she had drunk her coffee, she wandered around the area and admired the landscape. After the first two weeks of performances, the locals began to recognize her and smiled when they saw her, which Polyxeni liked. She also liked it when the owner of a pastry shop, who also recognized her from the play, wouldn't take her money. But celebrity in Gytheio had a price; when some local men acted a little too friendly, because she was an actress and, in their minds, must therefore be ready to give herself to anyone, Polyxeni became annoyed. She wondered how these uneducated and uncouth villagers, with their heavy work boots and rough hands, dared to bother her.

Lately, Polyxeni had begun to think seriously about her future. Lambros's troupe had been her ticket out of the village, but it could also be a quagmire that would swallow her, and she had no intention of growing old as she played indifferent parts in traveling theaters. Besides, she had wanted to get away from the countryside, and here she was, back in the country and living in conditions much worse than she had known at home. There, at least she had a room of her own. Here, at best she could expect to sleep in a dirty hotel, at worst, in a tent. There, she ate in a warm kitchen. Here she ate food of doubtful quality in cafés and cheap restaurants. In addition, she had no friends. She rarely chatted with the members of the troupe, and her frozen expression toward anyone she was speaking to usually put an end to any desire for further conversation. She knew that behind her back, they all gossiped about her, but she didn't care. She'd heard them refer to her as "countess" many times, but it pleased her rather than annoyed her.

When she heard they would be leaving Gytheio, Polyxeni drew a deep breath. Finally something new was coming; finally the routine would be broken. They left for Kalamata, but Lambros soon found out there was another traveling troupe there and he didn't want to compete with it, so they continued to Kyparissia instead.

Polyxeni was enthralled by the beauty of the landscape in Kyparissia. The beaches seemed endless, and the hues of the foliage merged with the blue of the sea and the sky. Polyxeni's delight was further bolstered by the fact that the space they were performing in here was the best she had seen until now. It was a new, very large café, and the owner, having seen their performances in Gytheio, welcomed them very happily. He also owned a hotel, so they all slept in fine rooms. Polyxeni quietly hoped that they would stay in this town for a while. For the first time she was nervous about the performance going well, so she decided not to leave anything to chance. She would talk to Lambros about the show.

When the troupe gathered together that evening, everyone was shocked to hear Polyxeni speak. It was so rare for the "countess" to open her mouth they all stopped to hear what she had to say.

"Lambros, what play do you plan for us to open with?" she asked in a voice slightly tinged with sarcasm.

Lambros had just lit a cigarette. He looked at her carefully through the smoke that flowed lazily from his mouth. "Why do you want to know, Xenia?" he asked. "Since when have you been interested in what we play?"

"Since today," she answered in a sharp tone. "I'm tired of doing the same thing all the time. Besides, look around you! It's a nice place, well built, and the town has a lot of people—we'd better do our best."

Silence fell on the room. Lambros's eyes narrowed threateningly. "Listen, Miss Xenia. The only thing that should concern you is that you act well. The rest is my business."

"I always act well," Polyxeni said slowly. "But it is essential that an actress also have a good script in her hand in order to create, and so far, I haven't been satisfied with the works you choose."

"Then go and find yourself something better, my lady!" Lambros shot at her, stubbing his cigarette out fiercely. "And if you think that because you can say a few words you've become an actress, then think again! You've got a long way to go before you start being one. You may be playing the leading lady for me here, but you try playing in a real theater company and see what sort of roles you get. Pull yourself together, why don't you, and get your nose out of the air!"

Everyone held their breath, but Polyxeni continued to look at him unperturbed. "Whether I'm an actress or not you know for yourself, now that you're finally seeing an audience at your performances. As for a real theater company, I may be playing bit parts but at least one day I'll be treading on the stage of a theater. You can mark my words!"

Lambros jumped to his feet, red in the face, his eyes flashing in fury. Martha appeared at his side and put her hand firmly on his shoulder.

Lambros turned around abruptly, ready to attack her as well, but her calm eyes stopped him.

"Sit down, Lambros," she advised. "We won't get anywhere like this."

"But didn't you hear her?" he shouted furiously.

"I heard you *both*. So sit down and let's speak nicely like the cultivated people we are, and in particular like artists who love what we do!"

Lambros looked at her for a moment, undecided, then sat down with a scowl on his face and lit a new cigarette.

"So," Martha began. "Xenia is right in one way. Our repertoire has been stagnant for some time now and we have to do something about it."

"We're a handful of people and we don't have unlimited strengths!" Lambros objected. "You talk as if you don't know that, Martha!"

"I do know that. But the works we perform don't help us at all. I don't know where you found them, but they make matters worse."

"And where am I going to find something new now?"

"I have something myself, and don't ask where I got it. It's my business."

"Why didn't you tell me about it before?"

"Because we didn't have Xenia, that's why. The work is completely suited to a young girl. I've made some adjustments, I'll admit, so that it fits the strengths of our group, but it's ready."

All disagreements were forgotten. Martha began telling them the story, which was a comedy with a clever plot, and soon after they began their first reading. It left them all satisfied, particularly Polyxeni. The bulk of the play fell on her shoulders. The dialogue was smart, especially a scene with Lambros, who would play her father, which soon transformed everyone's smiles into laughter. The way Martha had adapted it, the costumes didn't require much alteration, and the scenery was ready, since the entire play took place in a restaurant.

They all immersed themselves in learning their parts and in three days they were ready to perform in front of their public, which filled the café to overflowing. It was years since they'd had a theater troupe in the region and the owner of the café had done a lot of publicity. Polyxeni surpassed herself that evening. She was coquettish and charming in her role and the scene with Lambros provoked a storm of applause and laughter from the audience. By the end of the night the troupe knew they had a triumph. Differences had been forgotten, and Lambros himself hugged and congratulated Polyxeni when she came off the improvised stage.

"You were magnificent, Xenia!" he shouted. "And about what we said . . . all that is water under the bridge. I hope you don't hold it against me."

Polyxeni looked at him, satisfied. "I don't remember anything after tonight's show," she answered. "Do you?"

"Not a word."

They both smiled. A bright period began for the group and everyone recognized it. From the very next day they began turning people away from their sold-out performances. The café owner's till was full and the actors finally had money in their pockets. Polyxeni didn't change her way of life at all. Every morning, after her coffee, she walked around the area. When one of the locals suggested she see the enchanting sunset, she skipped dinner with the troupe, set off for the place she'd been told about, and waited patiently for the miracle to occur. The description she'd been given was hardly adequate. The air was so clear that she didn't miss the smallest detail. She saw the fiery disk sink slowly, while the sky filled with colors that no painter could copy. The few clouds had descended very low, almost touching the sun like fine lace hurrying to wrap itself around its shoulders. Then suddenly, in a magical way, everything around her was on fire. Polyxeni had the feeling that if she stretched out her hands she could touch that scarlet color, and she herself would take on a little of the sun's brilliance, so she opened her arms like a child. Later, when dusk turned to dark, she stayed in that spot with her head bowed, contemplating the wonderful experience she'd just had.

She came back to the village in a distracted state, determined to go again the next day to wrap herself in the sun's rays once more.

She arrived a little earlier the next evening but she wasn't alone.

"Martha! What are you doing here?" she asked when she saw the woman sitting on a blanket in the spot where she'd planned to sit.

"You're not the only one who wants to admire the sunset," Martha answered smiling and moved over, making room.

Polyxeni hesitated at first. She wanted to be alone; she had no desire for meaningless conversations but she couldn't leave yet. So she sat down with a sulky face next to Martha.

"Kyparissia has a long history," Martha began. "Even Homer refers to it in the *Iliad*. It was part of King Nestor's kingdom, which took part in the Trojan War. During the Byzantine period it was called Arcadia, perhaps because of the many Arcadians who came here to save themselves from the Slavs. When the Byzantine Empire ended it was occupied first by the western Europeans and then by the Ottomans."

"How do you know all that?" Polyxeni asked, now interested.

"I read it. Do you like history?"

"It was my favorite class in school."

The two women were silent for a while. Polyxeni looked secretly at Martha, who was sitting motionless, her back straight. A strange woman, who didn't fit in with the rest.

"How did you come to be with Lambros and his troupe?" The question just slipped out of Polyxeni's mouth. "If you don't want to, don't tell me . . . I understand."

"I have nothing to hide. I was in love with an actor who traveled around with the troupes. I met him one summer when my family and I were on vacation in a village, and of course my parents didn't want to hear a word about it. I was born in Athens. My father was a lawyer—we were a rich family with a pedigree, as they say. My family hoped I would marry someone whose social position matched our own, some lawyer or doctor—not a failed actor."

"And what happened?"

"They refused to give their blessing, so I left home and followed him."

"It took a lot of courage to do that."

"And stupidity."

"Did you ever regret it?"

"How could I not have regretted it? In the next town we came to he fell in love with another girl, and then another."

"Why didn't you go home then?'

"Because my father had cut off all communication with me. He had disinherited me and made it clear he no longer had a daughter. He left all his fortune to my sister, who married a man they had suggested to her. I lived alone, without any money. I couldn't live in Athens—a lot of people there knew me and my story. In my helpless state I met an old friend from my time with the actor I had loved, and he suggested I follow him on a tour they were doing in northern Greece. I'd been in some plays and I knew I could act. Somehow while I was traveling I met Lambros, and the rest you know."

"It seems unbelievable to me. Even though I knew from the beginning that you were different from the rest."

"And you too," Martha responded and looked directly at Polyxeni.

"What do you mean?"

"That Lambros and his troupe are very small for you."

Polyxeni looked at Martha in surprise. How did she know what she was thinking?

"I know that you've thought about it too," Martha continued. "You have a quality that would be a pity to waste, buried in the countryside playing silly parts in a café. With a little help you could rise very high."

"But where would I find that help?" Polyxeni dared to ask.

"I'll help you."

"You? But if you could help me, why didn't you help yourself all these years?" Polyxeni burst out, then bit her tongue.

"Because I didn't have your beauty or your talent! And what's more, recently I've acquired an admirer."

"An admirer? What sort of admirer?"

"The sort that will help me in my plans for you."

"If you think that I'm ready to sleep in anyone's bed . . ."

"No, silly girl! I'm not trying to be a pimp. I want to help you."

"And what would you gain from that? Why are you so concerned with my success?"

"Whatever happens will happen with a view toward profit, young lady. I'm talking about work. So calm down!"

"Sorry, that's not what it sounded like."

"You're my golden opportunity to stop knocking about in the countryside. I'm looking to make money off of you and your work. But you must be prepared to work hard and do what I tell you. I don't mean anything funny. Who you put in your bed is your own business."

The sunset came, quieting their conversation as it bathed the horizon in crimson. Somewhere among the fiery clouds, Polyxeni saw herself dressed in beautiful clothes on large stages, performing important plays in front of well-dressed people. The setting sun seemed to her, at that moment, like a crown destined for her head. These were the dreams she'd had when she left home; they were the only reason she had hurt her mother so much. She knew very well that after she'd left, Theodora had shed enough tears to make a second river next to the one that already ran beside the house.

When the sun had fully disappeared from the vault of the sky, Martha began collecting her things. The two women walked back to the hotel in silence. Polyxeni didn't dare to ask anything else, but questions were pounding at her brain. How would all the things Martha promised come true? How would the two of them set out and when?

That evening it took all of Polyxeni's self-control to play her part correctly. Afterward, she tossed and turned all night, sleepless in her bed, and the next morning she had no desire for her regular walk. She found the group sitting in the spring sunshine drinking coffee, but Martha wasn't there. Polyxeni listened patiently for quite a long time to the mindless conversations before she dared to ask Thomas, who was sitting next to her, "Thomas, where's Martha?"

"She left really early," the fat man answered. "She told us she'd be gone all day but back in time for the performance."

"Where was she going? Didn't she tell you?"

"I think I heard something about going to see someone in Patras, but I'm not sure. Why are you suddenly so interested in Martha?" Thomas wasn't used to having the "countess" addressing him or anyone else.

"Oh, it's nothing. I just didn't see her and I was surprised."

Her heart was beating hard now. It couldn't be a coincidence. Certainly it wasn't a coincidence. Martha must have gone to see her admirer. The one who would help her.

◆ ◆ ◆

Martha got up from the bed unconcerned by her nakedness. She put a robe around her shoulders in a leisurely fashion, then lit a cigarette. Stathis watched her until she caught his eye and smiled.

"What are you looking at?" she asked.

"I'm not just looking—I'm enjoying the sight. You're a very beautiful woman, Martha!"

"Yes, for my age, I'm well preserved!"

"For your age? Huh, I didn't expect to hear something like that from you."

"And why not? I know exactly what I am and how old I am. Come, enough of this laziness. Get up, I'm dying for a coffee!"

They sat on the verandah of the hotel to drink their coffee. After the first sip, Martha lit another cigarette, then turned to Stathis.

"So, will you help me with the plan I told you about?" she asked.

"About the girl, you mean?"

"Yes, about her. Without you, I can't do anything, and an opportunity like this shouldn't be missed."

Stathis looked at her carefully for a while. "Why so much trouble for an unknown girl?" he asked.

"I thought I'd told you. Xenia is my ticket to leave the traveling theater."

"You have another ticket, except you won't accept it. We've been together for a year. I've asked you at least five times to be my wife and you keep refusing without giving me a valid excuse."

"Stathis, do you know how old I am?"

"Do you think I don't know? The very first moment you met me you were careful to tell me without my having to ask."

"Do you think, then, that at nearly forty I want to make a move that might be another mistake?"

"Why would it be a mistake? I love you. I've told you that every way I can. For a year now I've been going all over Greece following the Pagonis troupe just to steal a few hours with you here and there. What more do I have to do to show you that I love you?"

"Why do we have to start this conversation again? I asked you to help me with Xenia. You told me that if I wanted, you could help me find work in a theater in Athens. So if you can, I'd like you to do that for Xenia."

"And what will you gain out of all this?"

"I'll take a percentage on the work I get for her. From what you've told me, Athens has begun making heaps of films. The girl's got talent, I'm telling you. I don't want to see her end up like I have, traveling endlessly and performing only in backwater towns and cafés. She'll save herself, and me too!"

"And what will I get out of this?"

"I don't understand. Don't you want money too?"

"I want you."

"But you have me."

"Not like this. I want you to be my wife."

"The same thing again! Why do you insist? Aren't we fine as we are?"

"No, Martha. We're not. I want you beside me all the time. I want to wake up in the morning and see your face. I want us to sleep together, to hold you in my arms. I want to go around with you, not for us to run and hide away in some hotel. I know that you weren't lucky in your relationships in the past. I understand your fears, but you must know what sort of man I am."

"I can't disagree with you, but what will your circle of friends say? Have you thought about that? You're rich; a man of forty like you can marry a younger woman who will give him children."

"I'm not interested in children, and as for my circle, I don't care what they think. If they don't like my choice, they can go to hell. We'll make our own circle. As for this girl you're hung up on helping, I know that when something catches hold of your brain, it doesn't let go. So I'll help you. I'll move heaven and earth and I'll promote her. We'll make her a star of the highest order. On one condition, though."

"What sort of condition?"

"As soon as your protégé is standing on her own two feet, you'll give it all up and marry me. Otherwise I won't do anything at all."

"That's extortion," Martha said accusingly.

"I don't disagree, but there's no other way with someone like you. Do you accept or not?"

Martha put out her cigarette and stood up. Stathis watched her every movement. When she went inside and headed for their room he followed her.

"You're certain you'll succeed, otherwise you wouldn't have made such a condition," she said.

"Exactly! In six months, the girl will have a career in her hands, and you'll be my wife. Agreed?"

❖ ❖ ❖

Martha arrived back in Kyparissia just ten minutes before the performance began and found the whole troupe in a panic over her absence.

"I'd like to kill you for what you did, but I don't have time now!" Lambros shouted at her as they were getting dressed. Martha stuck her tongue out at him playfully.

When the performance began, she managed to say to Polyxeni, "Do your best tonight, Xenia."

With Martha's words in her ears, the girl got up on stage and acted her part exceptionally well, raising a storm of applause. Stathis, who had come back with Martha to see the show, was impressed. Martha was right, after all. The girl was very beautiful. With a little care from specialists, she'd be dazzling, and her acting could stand up in any professional theater company, and in any large role. If she was photogenic, as he suspected, film directors would worship her.

Right after the performance, Martha brought Polyxeni to the table where Stathis was waiting.

"Xenia, I want you to meet my good friend. Mr. Stathis Syrigos came to see you tonight. Stathis, Miss Xenia Olympiou."

Polyxeni was overwhelmed. She hadn't imagined that Martha would act with such lightning speed. "How do you do?" she said as she extended her hand, and then sat down opposite him.

The couple immediately started making plans regarding Polyxeni's future. But she didn't quite understand everything they were saying, so she decided to intervene.

"Mr.—" she began.

Stathis cut her off. "It's better if we start with first names," he said. "We'll be working together and I can't deal with formality when I'm working with people."

"All right, but there's still a problem," Polyxeni went on.

"What problem?"

"I've been listening to you talking about things that I don't completely understand. But I do understand one thing: you'll need money to do this and I . . ."

Stathis interrupted her again. "And who said anything to you about money? Listen to me carefully, Xenia. We're gambling on you—we're investing. Do you understand?"

"No."

"To us you are a business venture, and in a business that is starting out, you must put money in if you want to take more out later. Now do you understand?"

"More or less."

"You'll understand better as it goes along. For now, all you have to do is trust us and do what we tell you."

"I want to be clear. I told Martha already, I don't want to . . ."

This time Martha intervened. "Don't be afraid. When Stathis tells you to do whatever we tell you, it will have nothing to do with your morals."

"Of course that's right," Stathis hurried to reassure her. "We won't interfere at all in your personal life, so long as it doesn't harm your career. When you become famous, you'll choose who you want beside you."

"So, shall we move ahead?" Martha asked.

"In order to move ahead, you'll need to tell Pagonis that you'll be gone in fifteen days. Both of you," Stathis said.

"So soon?" asked Polyxeni. "I mean, he won't be able to . . ."

Stathis stopped her again. "If you want to get ahead in this business, Xenia, you'll need to leave your feelings behind sometimes. Now, we have a lot of work to do, and we don't have time to waste."

◆ ◆ ◆

Two months later, Polyxeni felt as if she had found herself at the center of a cyclone that threatened to break her to pieces. Everything around her happened with astonishing speed. Every night she fell into bed exhausted and despite her efforts to put some order into her thoughts and write down the things that had happened that day, or count the new faces she had met, sleep came before she could manage to even form a picture in her tired brain. The Pagonis troupe, which she'd been traveling with such a short time ago, was already a dim memory.

Their departure from the troupe would bring disaster to Lambros. Polyxeni knew it and felt very uncomfortable about it. For that reason she'd left it to Martha to tell him the news. The director exploded with anger. Lambros was famous for his temper and in the face of the ruin he knew would follow, he became terrible. If it hadn't been for Sotiris intervening, Polyxeni was sure he would have hit Martha. The next day, the two women collected their things and left in a hurry. Stathis was waiting with his car and they all set out for Athens, where he put them into a good hotel. He himself had a large house in a suburb that Polyxeni heard them refer to as Patissia, but naturally they couldn't stay there; it would have given people an excuse for gossip.

On that first evening, Polyxeni felt lonely for the first time. Stathis had followed Martha to her room next door, and after a while, the girl, sitting on the balcony outside her own room, began to hear the tender sounds of lovemaking. As the time passed the sounds grew more intense and upset her so that she didn't have the courage to get up and go back inside in case they became aware of her. Step by step she listened to an act of love that was an unknown experience for her, and which, until that moment, she'd had no desire to know. But when the cries of the couple at the climax of their lovemaking reached her ears, she jumped up from her chair and ran to hide away in her bed in a very disturbed state. She had lived with her sisters while they fell in love and made their secret rendezvous, but she herself had never felt any desire for things like that. She wondered what it was that made Martha cry out like a wounded animal. She tried to imagine her in Stathis's arms and immediately felt ashamed of her thoughts, so she wrapped herself in the soft covers and tried to sleep. She was surprised by the tears that began flowing down her cheeks and wiped them away angrily.

Polyxeni wasn't silly enough to get mixed up in love affairs, nor would she ever become a plaything in the hands of any man. When she chose somebody it would be because he could assure her of everything she wanted. She knew her weapons and she would use them to reach her goal. She hadn't left the village to fail or to fall in love. She could have done that there. Before she fell asleep she decided that she owed her mother, at the very least, a card, to tell her that everything was all right, without adding any other details. Yes, that's what she owed her.

◆ ◆ ◆

The image that her mirror reflected was Polyxeni, but at the same time it wasn't. The beauty salon that Stathis had chosen had taken up a whole day, but it was worth all the trouble. She was dazzling. She smiled in satisfaction at her image, while Martha looked at her in approval, but there was no time to lose. Now they needed to acquire more clothes and shoes. Polyxeni had to admit that Stathis wasn't at all cheap. Her closet at the hotel was already filled with all sorts of beautiful things.

The photos they had taken later by a professional photographer were sent to a director and a manager. Both were impressed by the young actress's appearance, and Stathis's carefully considered comments led to a professional offer ten days later.

Polyxeni couldn't believe her ears when Martha told her she would be playing a small role in a film.

"Of course it's nothing big," Martha said as the three of them went for a drive to Faliro. "But the important thing is for you to get your foot in the door. If you succeed, then . . ."

"But I don't know anything about films," Polyxeni protested.

"It's not so different from what you've been doing in the theater troupe," Stathis explained patiently. "You'll stand where the director tells you to and you'll say the lines they give you. That's all. Don't be frightened, Xenia; you'll manage it. You must manage it!" he said, looking meaningfully at Martha.

That night and the next, Polyxeni didn't sleep at all. She read and reread the script they had given her. She only had two lines, but her mind was already racing. She imagined herself as a leading actress, giving interviews to journalists and being photographed constantly.

When she arrived at the shoot nobody paid any attention to her. They were all in a hurry and distracted, and they talked about things that she didn't understand. After a while she was ready to cry. When she stood in front of the camera she felt awkward. The lights really bothered her and she was sweating with anxiety. But despite everything, they got the scene the director wanted in just two takes.

Polyxeni came back to the hotel, tired and disappointed, but Martha was beside her to give her encouragement.

"But what did you expect?" she said. "You're not a leading lady yet."

"I know, but I didn't like it. In the theater it's different. You've got people in front of you, you hear them breathing, and you feel that they're hanging on your every word! Here you're in front of indifferent people and machines and lights that blind you."

"Be patient, Xenia," Martha said soothingly. "It's the beginning and the beginning is difficult. A day will come when they'll all be hanging on you. They'll pamper you and beg for your attention. Be patient!"

That same day, the producer of the film asked to see all the material that had been shot. It was something he did on a regular basis. He had put his own money into the production and wanted to be sure of the result. When the scene with Polyxeni came up, his curiosity was aroused.

"Who is she?" he asked the director with interest.

"Stathis Syrigos introduced her to me. Her name's Xenia Olympiou. She's good, and she says her lines."

"Is that all you have to say! Look at the screen, my friend, and tell me you haven't lost the ability to see a star in front of you. The girl shines. She steals the shot!"

"She's a little cold, isn't she? And then there's that rural way she talks. Will she go over with the audience?"

"The audience will see a beautiful girl and nothing more. And the colder she is the more passion she'll ignite. Come on, you're not a newcomer to this job. In the next film, give her a bigger part and let's see how she does."

As the days passed, Polyxeni's irritation grew. The hotel suffocated her, Athens annoyed her, and the hours refused to pass quickly enough. When Stathis appeared before her, a smile on his face and the script of a new film in his hands, Polyxeni couldn't believe her eyes. Nor could she believe the size of her role.

"It's big, Stathis," she said, and for the first time since he'd met her, Stathis heard her voice rise.

"It seems as if the producer likes you, and from what my friend the director said, he wants to give you a chance, to see what you can do. And not only that. Right now I'm negotiating a part in a play for you."

Polyxeni looked at him, her eyes wide. "Are you telling the truth?" she asked, hardly able to breathe.

"Naturally. It's not anything very big, of course, but as a beginning, it's just right."

Polyxeni could have been satisfied with everything that followed, but she wasn't. All her plans had begun to fall into place, but it wasn't enough. Despite the fact that her second movie was successful, despite the fact that some critics had written about her, despite her first appearance in the theater having made an impression, Polyxeni couldn't see herself emerging from obscurity.

"Could you stop being in such a hurry, please?" Martha shouted when Polyxeni shared her frustrations. "You've only just begun. Look how far you've come. You're young and beautiful and you have all the time in the world in front of you."

"It's precisely because I'm young and beautiful—and *unknown*— that I need publicity. At the premiere, not a single reporter approached me!"

"But why would they approach you when there were such famous people there and everyone was frantic to get a photograph or a statement? Are you crazy?"

Polyxeni didn't answer. A review in a newspaper she was looking at had stolen her attention: *Miss Xenia Olympiou, despite her honorable intentions toward the audience, failed to persuade us that she was a young girl in love, as the role she played demanded,* the reviewer wrote. *Very "starchy," very prim, very artificial in her love scene. Perhaps Miss Olympia should seek experiences so that she could act better in roles that are otherwise consistent with her appearance . . .*

Polyxeni read the review again and again and had to admit to herself that the critic was right. She was lacking in experience, particularly in the realm of love. But love was the last thing that concerned her at that moment. She was an artist, not some silly young girl who dreamed of romantic assignations and white bridal gowns. And besides, even if she had been interested in finding someone, she wouldn't know where to look. No one in the cast of her current play seemed suitable. The men in the company were all older and married. Given how her life was structured, how could she ever be expected to find a likely candidate?

The answer came from the theater, but not from the stage. Leonidas Argyriou was a handsome young man of about twenty-five who was charmed by Polyxeni's flawless beauty the very first night he watched her from the audience. He attended her performances nightly for a week before very shyly sending a bouquet of flowers to the dressing room that she shared with the other girls in the cast. Polyxeni was amazed. She'd never received flowers before, and she had no idea who the man was who had sent them, but she thought it was a nice custom. When flowers began to arrive on a daily basis and the other girls teased her about her admirer, Polyxeni became curious to meet him.

"If you'd looked a little around the theater you'd have seen him!" a red-haired girl who was putting on her makeup beside her remarked.

"What do you mean?" Polyxeni asked.

"You poor thing—when you come out to say your lines, look down a little. The same young man has been sitting in the first row for the last ten days, and from the moment you come out he doesn't take his eyes off you. He's the one who's sending you flowers."

"Oh, I've seen him too," another girl joined in. "He's dreamy."

The girls moved on to talking about their own experiences with admirers, but Polyxeni didn't listen to a word. Perhaps this man could help her gain the knowledge of love and passionate experiences that seemed so essential to her career as an actress. Stathis had brought her a new script in which she would play a young girl in love with a wealthy man; Polyxeni wanted to be prepared.

That night she came out on stage and searched the front row to see if she could recognize the person of interest. It wasn't difficult. The dark man didn't take his eyes off her and Polyxeni risked smiling at him. The result was immediate. Leonidas was surprised, but he smiled back at her. She almost expected him to come find her at the end of the performance, and she wasn't disappointed. Holding a few flowers, Leonidas stood at the entrance of the theater after the show was over. As soon as he saw her he approached her.

"I decided that today I would present the flowers myself," he whispered shyly.

"You did the right thing," Polyxeni said, looking him in the eyes. He wasn't ugly—on the contrary. His face was bright, his eyes large and clear, and more importantly, full of admiration. Judging by his clothes, Polyxeni surmised that he was also rich. Better still.

"So?" she said, smiling. "Are we going to stand in the street for long?"

Leonidas seemed unable to believe his luck. "Do I dare to suggest that we go to have something to eat?" he asked in an almost inaudible voice.

"The truth is I am hungry. Yes, why not?"

His car was large and expensive and Polyxeni was impressed, just as she was impressed by the expensive restaurant where he ordered them champagne. She had never drunk alcohol in her life and she enjoyed the slight dizziness it induced. She felt relaxed and her smile became less frozen. It was obvious to her that Leonidas was swimming in an ocean of happiness. He looked almost worshipfully at her and told her all about his life. He was the son of a very rich family and had studied law, but he preferred writing poetry. He had no brothers or sisters. His parents had him when they were quite old, so not surprisingly they had a great weakness for him.

Everything she heard suited her nicely. Leonidas, on the other hand, learned very little about his date for the evening. Every time he tried to ask her questions about herself, he hit a wall. It was obvious that the girl who had unexpectedly agreed to eat with him wasn't inclined to reveal anything about her life, but that didn't bother him. He was madly in love with her already, and it was enough for him to just be sitting with her.

When he accompanied her to her hotel, he dared to kiss her hand and to ask her out again for the next evening. Polyxeni accepted, but the truth was that Leonidas had begun to get on her nerves. He reminded her so much of Julia's dog when they threw him a bone. Except that he didn't pant with his tongue hanging out. *If he'd had a tail he'd probably have been wagging it,* Polyxeni thought.

She went up to her room, trying to put some order into her thoughts. Leonidas didn't mean anything to her, but she was determined to go ahead with it just the same. Perhaps she would feel something along the way. In any case, he was so rich.

The next evening she took more care with her appearance and rehearsed in front of the mirror. Her look had to be one that would give him courage to go forward. She didn't want to waste all her time on mouthwatering looks and mindless hand kissing. He was waiting for her again at the entrance of the theater and drove her in his expensive car to a magnificent club, the likes of which Polyxeni had never seen. Still, she hid her impressions under an indifferent expression. All through the meal she ate heartily while he looked adoringly at her.

"Leonidas, what you're doing isn't polite," she finally said in a scolding manner. "It's not pleasant to always feel like you're watching me."

"I'm sorry," he stammered, upset. "I don't want to displease you, but you can't imagine how I feel. I can't believe that I'm here, near you, and that I can talk to you and see your eyes looking at me."

"You can do something else, though," Polyxeni said, softening. She wanted to provoke him, not put him in his place.

"What do you want? Tell me, and it's done this minute!"

"Can you dance with me?"

Leonidas looked at her, not believing what he'd heard. The very thought of holding her in his arms made his eyes fill with tears. He jumped up and held out his hand. When Polyxeni realized he was trembling, she almost laughed, but held herself back. He led her onto the dance floor and she thanked her lucky stars that Stathis had insisted that she learn to dance. The melody was passionate and Polyxeni felt Leonidas's hot breath, but no emotions overwhelmed her. His hands, holding her so lightly, made no impression on her. She felt as if she were far away from her body and followed the scene like an onlooker. Fortunately he didn't seem to notice.

When they went back to the hotel, she didn't hurry to get out of his car, giving him the opportunity to kiss her at last, but Leonidas hesitated. The moments that followed seemed endless and Polyxeni's irritation increased. She finally gave him her hand to say good night and in the darkness she heard his breath coming with difficulty. He rested his lips on her fingers almost worshipfully, then Polyxeni leaned in slightly toward him, but Leonidas pulled back.

"So," Polyxeni began, trying to hide her annoyance at the failure. "Thank you for the lovely evening."

"The pleasure was all mine," Leonidas said in an unsteady voice. "Dare I ask you to go out with me again tomorrow?" he asked shyly.

Polyxeni moved her body a little toward him again, knowing that in this position the cleavage peeking out of her low-cut dress would be hard to ignore. She looked at him intently and finally Leonidas seemed to make a decision. Very slowly he began to approach her until his lips covered hers. At first Polyxeni was surprised by the contact, even though she had provoked it, and froze, but she forced herself to relax and abandon herself to his kiss. So long as he met no resistance, Leonidas became more daring. His arms embraced her and held her tightly against him while he moved his body closer to hers, but Polyxeni pushed him gently away.

As if he were ashamed, Leonidas pulled back quickly and looked at her with shining eyes. "I'm sorry," he whispered. "I didn't mean to make you feel embarrassed."

"I don't feel embarrassed," she said evenly. "But it's late—I must be going."

"Tomorrow?"

"I'll be waiting for you," she said and got out of the car.

Later, lying on the bed, Polyxeni thought about what had just happened. The kiss wasn't unpleasant, she decided, although nothing seemed to awaken inside her. At least nothing that would make her sigh as Martha had done in Stathis's arms. Regardless, she waited impatiently for the next evening, when she hoped that Leonidas would be more decisive and dynamic.

She wasn't disappointed. After a delicious meal at a restaurant, Leonidas didn't hurry to take her back to her hotel but drove to a deserted beach instead. The night was balmy and they began to walk silently along the pebbled shore. Leonidas put his arm around her shoulders and at some point he stopped walking and embraced her. This time he didn't hesitate for a moment. His kiss was more daring, his hands pulled her toward him forcefully. Polyxeni smiled encouragingly as he released her but she froze as soon as she heard the words he spoke next.

"Xenia, I love you!" he said with passion.

She remembered the instructions of the director in the film she had made: *"When he says, 'I love you,' lower your eyes bashfully."* So she did. "It's very early still, Leonidas," she murmured in a low voice.

Leonidas took her by the arms and shook her, forcing her to look at him. "It doesn't bother me," he said, still more urgently. "I've been crazy about you since the first moment I saw you. Tell me you feel something for me too!"

"The fact that I'm here with you must tell you," Polyxeni answered calmly. "But it's too early for anything else."

Leonidas kissed her again and this time his kiss was full of passion, intensity—and hopelessness.

"I love you," he told her again. "I can't live without you. Every moment away from you is hell!"

❖ ❖ ❖

The next day, when Polyxeni played the scene in which she had to kiss her leading man, her director was delighted.

"That's it, Xenia!" he shouted as soon as they finished the shoot. "You were just how I wanted you. In love and abandoned. That kiss will be a sensation!"

Polyxeni accepted his congratulations without any shame and in her mind a single word went round and round: *abandoned*. So that was the secret. A woman in love gives herself up.

She went back to the hotel when it was nearly lunchtime and found Martha and Stathis waiting for her.

"Finally," said Martha, smiling. "It's been days since I've seen you. What have you been up to?"

"I have the shoot, and then there's the play . . ." Polyxeni began.

"Yes, but after each performance, you disappear, and that's not usual for you," Stathis added cheerfully. "What should we suspect, Miss Olympiou? Is there someone in your life?"

Polyxeni looked at them without any expression. "Although I don't think it concerns you . . . yes. There's someone."

"Sneaky girl! And you were hiding it from us," Martha teased, ignoring her frozen expression. She was used to that from Xenia.

"It's only been a few days."

"And who's the lucky man?" Stathis asked.

But there was something in his expression that Polyxeni didn't like. "What's going on, Stathis? Are you cross-examining me?"

Stathis became serious and approached her. "Xenia, you know very well that we don't get mixed up in your personal life unless there's a reason. But I've heard some rumors that I don't like at all."

"Why? I haven't done anything bad, and the person I've been going out with isn't some bum," Polyxeni objected.

"Who is it, Xenia?" Martha asked.

"Is he by any chance Leonidas Argyriou?" Stathis gave her a piercing look.

"How do you know him?"

Stathis slapped his forehead in despair. "It's him! And I'd hoped that the gossip was just nonsense."

"But what's wrong with Leonidas?" Polyxeni demanded.

"Do you love him?" Stathis continued, and when Polyxeni didn't answer, he grabbed her by the arm and shook her. "Xenia, don't even think about telling me that it's not my business, because by God I'll beat you! Tell me: do you love him?"

"No, certainly not! It's just that he likes me and he can give me what I want."

"Are you after his money?" Martha asked in surprise.

"For the moment, I need something else," Polyxeni answered as she pulled herself away from Stathis's grasp. She looked at the two of them defiantly. "Leonidas can provide me with the experience I need to play my parts better. How can I act the part of a woman in love when I don't even know what a man is?"

Silence followed her declaration.

Stathis seemed stunned. "What did you say?" he murmured in a voice that could hardly be heard.

"I think I made myself clear. After that review, when they wrote that I'm not believable when I play a woman in love, I thought that I needed a man to . . . learn."

"Good Lord! Are you using the man as a guinea pig?" Stathis shouted.

"I wouldn't put it like that. Probably 'teacher' would be more correct. I have to say he's too soft for me, but he's young and handsome. What's the crime?"

"It's a crime to use any man like that, but especially so in this case. Do you know who you're making a fool of?"

"Leonidas. And I'm not making a fool of him. I'm simply learning. Now, if he's in love with me . . ."

"Is he?" asked Martha.

"He couldn't be more so," boasted Polyxeni. "He says he can't live without me."

"That does it!" Stathis exclaimed.

"Why?"

"Because he means it, you stupid girl. Leonidas Argyriou is a very sensitive boy, and he has shown that he is capable of dying because of a woman. He's tried twice. His parents only helped him escape death by the skin of his teeth."

"What?"

"You heard me. The first time he was in love with a fellow student, and when she left him he tried to commit suicide by taking pills. Last year he was madly in love with another girl who also left him for someone else and the young fellow slit his wrists."

"That's too much. I mean, *he's* too much. I've gotten myself involved with a crazy person!"

"You've gotten involved with a very sensitive person. And he's fallen madly in love with you, while you're using him for one reason: to find out what love is. Do you really think you're going to learn what love feels like from this? Basically, the only thing you'll learn is how far this man will go when he's tragically in love with you."

"It'll still do me good," Polyxeni declared coolly.

Stathis looked at her in horror. "Do you understand what you're saying? When you take your precious experiences from Leonidas and leave him, he is capable of dying. Do you understand the scandal that would erupt? Do you understand that it'll be your fault?"

"You're exaggerating, poor Stathis. Just because he's already made two attempts doesn't mean that he'll make a third for my sake. And basically, at this point, what happens, happens. Whether I leave him now or later, the same thing will happen in the end."

Martha approached Polyxeni with a sad face. "You have no right to play with people like this, Xenia," she said. "This is life; this is reality.

The leading man won't stand up alive again when the director calls 'cut.' Do you understand that? Find some nice way so you won't hurt him, and leave him in peace."

But Polyxeni was defiant. "Don't talk like that! Leonidas is young, handsome, and rich. I may not even have to leave him. Maybe I'll marry him! And now, could you please leave my space, because I want to sleep a little before tonight's performance!"

She opened the door herself and the couple left without a word. As if nothing at all had happened, Polyxeni took a bath, then lay down, completely calm.

In the next room, though, Stathis was walking irritably up and down the room.

"You won't find a solution pacing back and forth," Martha said quietly.

"But do you understand what might happen? Our Miss Xenia will enjoy him as long as she needs him and then, when he's given himself completely up to her, she'll throw him away. What do you think a young man as sensitive and in love as Leonidas Argyriou will do? Martha, maybe it's time for us to leave. Marry me and we'll live in my house, far away from the theater and from this girl!"

"What are you saying? We're only just beginning to make some money from the work she's been getting."

Stathis walked over to her and grasped her by the arms. "Is that what you think? That I did what I did to make money? I helped her so you would get her out of your head. I did it so you would say yes to marrying me." He began pacing again. "Your Xenia has found her way. And if she's not a star already, with the mind she has, she very soon will be. She has no ethical inhibitions, no boundaries, and the only thing that interests her is herself. Don't worry about her succeeding. Let's just leave! Please."

"All right."

The answer came so fast, so quietly, that it surprised him. He turned as if he couldn't believe his ears. "What did you say?" he asked in a trembling voice.

"I said yes . . . that I'll marry you."

When Stathis started crying, Martha was taken aback. She hadn't expected such a response. They embraced and he began to say "I love you" without stopping, like a needle stuck on a record. His lips covered hers, and a little while later, their bodies joined together in a union filled not only with passion, but with a new kind of love and tenderness.

"What made you say yes so easily?" he asked afterward.

"I'm tired, Stathis."

"Is that why you're marrying me? You're tired?"

"You didn't understand me. I'm tired of listening to my logic and not my heart. I love you. I want to live with you and grow old with you. How long am I going to let the past forbid a future for me? However many men were close to me, they never saw the person in me. They saw the body and that's what they claimed. But you were different. I saw it from the first moment and I'm ashamed that I didn't want to accept it."

"I think I must be dreaming! When do you want the wedding to be?"

"As soon as possible. First, however, I'm going to have a conversation with Xenia."

The discussion didn't take place until four days later. Polyxeni was busy with the theater, the film shooting, and naturally, Leonidas, who, drunk with love, took her in his arms every evening when they said good-bye but was incapable of asking whether he could come up to her room. That morning Polyxeni had a shoot and was enjoying her coffee beforehand and watching the heavy rainfall from the window of her room. She was in a good mood, as she'd seen the first photograph of herself in a magazine. A photographer had caught her with Leonidas at the restaurant where they had eaten a few nights before. Now her smiling face was featured along with the caption:

The beautiful, up-and-coming actress Xenia Olympiou in a romantic rendezvous with lawyer Leonidas Argyriou.

At last! She had begun to be someone.

When Martha arrived, Polyxeni was delighted, as she wanted to share her pride in the photograph with someone. But when she showed it to her, Martha just sadly shook her head.

"But aren't you pleased for me? Finally the magazines are starting to take notice of me. In a little while I'll be famous! The director told me that in the next film, I'll have the second leading role. Do you understand what that means? I'll begin to make money! I'm even thinking about renting a house and leaving the hotel. It'll be the first time I've lived in a house since I left the village. Aren't you pleased for me, Martha? You helped me to get here."

"With a view toward my own profit," Martha answered.

"Oh, stop that! You didn't even take a third from me. That's nothing compared to what you spent when we first came to Athens. Besides, I know you didn't just do this for the money. I do understand that not everything is about money."

"Yes, you're right. Even though you . . ."

"I'm not ungrateful, Martha. I know what I owe to you and Stathis."

"Xenia, I came to tell you that I'm leaving."

"Leaving? Where are you going?"

"For some time now, Stathis has been asking me to marry him. I've accepted."

"Oh! You scared me for a moment there! Of course you should go and marry Stathis. You're doing just the right thing. Stathis is rich; you won't have to get by without anything ever again."

"A little while ago you told me that not everything is about money."

"Yes, but marriage is. Why would you want to marry someone if he couldn't offer you a good life?"

"Are we going to overlook the fact that some people might marry for love?"

"Completely. A man who's poor and can only offer you misery— how long could you bear to love him?"

"Certainly . . . that's an opinion. What I want you to know is that from now on you are on your own. Stathis and I won't interfere with your career. Now that the road is open, you can go wherever you wish."

"But we have an agreement. I still owe you a lot of money."

"At the risk of being tiresome, I'll remind you that you said it yourself: not everything is about money. I hope you learn just how true that is, and soon."

"What do you mean?"

"Xenia, I don't understand what goes on in your head and I never really did. You only seem to focus on the superficial, and that won't do you any good in life. I'm not just talking about Leonidas, even though you haven't taken Stathis's advice on that topic at all seriously. You allow yourself to be seduced by things that don't matter in the end. Instead, try to strive for something beyond the superficial. Don't let life flow like a river beside you without diving in."

"The river . . ." Polyxeni whispered, as if she was talking to herself.

"What did you say?"

"Beside my house there's a river. Our mother always told us to be careful because life is like that river and can carry us away."

"Your mother was right. You left—you did something that no young girl would have dared to undertake. You cut all ties, but now you have to sit and think. You're chasing a chimera. Trust me, I know. I made the same mistake years ago."

"So what are you saying? To go home? To go back to my village?"

"I'm asking you to keep your village—and all that it taught you— with you. Happiness isn't found in fame or in money."

"And yet, they're the only things I want," Polyxeni answered almost solemnly.

"Then I hope that you're ready to pay the price."

Martha stood up and Polyxeni followed.

"It feels strange that you're leaving me," the younger woman said.

"My house is always open to you. Come and see us, even though I'm sure we'll find out all your news from the magazines."

Polyxeni smiled and for the first time, Martha dared to hug her. Then she left, very moved.

◆ ◆ ◆

The feeling of freedom was new to Polyxeni. She looked around as if she was seeing the room she had been living in so long for the first time. Her first job would be to find a small apartment. No more hotels for her!

That evening Leonidas seemed distracted and Polyxeni was anxious. He looked at her with an inscrutable expression and spoke very little. She asked him many times what was bothering him, the last time outside her hotel just as he was dropping her off for the night.

Instead of answering her, Leonidas kissed her passionately and as soon as he pulled away he told her, in a trembling voice, "Xenia, I can't bear it anymore. I want to hold you in my arms, I want to come up to your room tonight. I don't want to go home alone and dream of you all night long!"

Polyxeni looked at him thoughtfully. So the hour had come! "Come up," she said softly.

Leonidas looked at her as if he didn't believe his ears, but Polyxeni got out of the car and signaled to him to follow her. As soon as they entered her room he looked around him.

"Is this where you live?" he asked.

"Yes. But I'm thinking of finding a small apartment. I'm tired of living in hotels. Would you like something to drink?"

Leonidas nodded and Polyxeni poured one for him and one for herself. She didn't feel any embarrassment, any shame, only curiosity about what would follow. She took a small sip of her drink and then, excusing herself, went to change.

Leonidas couldn't breathe when he saw the black nightgown she wore when she returned. Through the sheer lace he could see that she was quite naked underneath. He stood for a moment, gazing at her like a statue, then gulped down his drink. He put down his glass, then loosened the tie that was choking him. He approached her and, incapable of holding himself back, enclosed her in his arms.

Polyxeni abandoned herself to him, determined to set herself free to enjoy the moment. Still the burning kisses of Leonidas and his hands caressing her whole body failed to give her any delight. Much later she wondered what had gone wrong. Leonidas's lovemaking left her completely indifferent. Not a cell of her body responded. Perhaps for one or two moments she felt pleasant, then nothing more.

What moved her, though, was not the young man's love, but the surprise that awaited her five days later. He picked her up from the set and drove her to an elegant apartment with fine furniture and a view of the Acropolis. Polyxeni looked around, confused.

"What's this? Whose house is it?" she asked.

"It's yours, my love! Didn't you say you wanted to leave the hotel? I put my agent onto it and he found it. I furnished it and I'm handing it over to you. If you want, we can buy it later."

Polyxeni froze for a moment. She couldn't get it into her head that finally she had her own home. She had escaped from the cold hotel—she was independent. Then she remembered that she should thank Leonidas, so she turned to him. She knew what her payment should be. With slow movements, and without taking her eyes off him, she undressed until she was completely naked. He grabbed her abruptly, picked her up in his arms, and headed for the bedroom. Without having the patience to undress, he fell on her, kissing her all over, and her lukewarm response was enough to make him lose control. Carried away as he was by his love, he didn't seem to notice that the object of his passion didn't return his feelings with the same warmth.

◆　◆　◆

Polyxeni's new life suited her very well. Her career had finally taken the path she wanted. In the theater she was no longer just another face in the crowd. She now played opposite famous actors. And after so many minor roles, a producer from another company had offered her the second lead in an upcoming play. Full of enthusiasm, she raced to Martha's house to tell her.

Martha and Stathis had married and were living happily in a house in Patissia, but Polyxeni didn't often see them. There were her professional responsibilities, of course, and Leonidas took up all her free time. When she did visit them, they never asked about her relationship, and when they found out about the apartment, they politely wished her well without any further comment. This suited Polyxeni because she wouldn't have known what to say.

The truth was that Leonidas had begun to annoy her a lot. His endless love, the worship he offered her without any demands, and most of all his meaningless lovemaking, had all begun to tire her. She had to admit that she had succeeded in mastering the art of playing a woman in love, but that was partly her own achievement. Her ability to detach her mind from her body during sex and coolly observe every detail of the act like a spectator had proved very useful. Sometimes she would even correct her acting partner, which earned her praise from the director, who admired her well-honed observations.

That afternoon, when she arrived at Martha's house to tell her about the new role, a surprise awaited her. Martha announced that she was expecting a baby. She was radiant and very happy, despite the doubts she was having about giving birth to a healthy baby at her age.

"But the doctor's assured me that I'm completely healthy and I'll manage it," Martha said.

Polyxeni had never seen her friend like this. Her face had softened; her eyes shone with a strange light and a permanent sweet smile seemed to be painted on her lips. "You've changed," Polyxeni said.

"I'm happy, Xenia. Stathis is everything I ever dreamed of, and the only thing I curse myself for is that I didn't marry him earlier. You can't imagine what it's like to have the love of such a man."

"To be honest, no. I can't imagine feeling so satisfied by a man's love."

"Have you never been in love?"

"Never. And I don't know, that is, I don't think . . ." Polyxeni stopped in confusion.

Martha sat down beside her and took her hand. "Tell me, Xenia. I'm your friend—perhaps the only friend you'll ever have. Don't hide what you're feeling inside."

"I don't think you want to hear it, and you certainly won't understand it."

"Try me. We're alone—Stathis is out. Talk to me."

With difficulty, Polyxeni began to describe her relationship with Leonidas. She described their lovemaking as if she were talking about the weather, completely indifferent. She confessed that she didn't understand anything about the great wonder she was supposed to feel.

She stopped when she had said everything, then looked at Martha, whose sad expression annoyed her. "I told you that you wouldn't understand," she said sharply.

"Who said I didn't understand?" Martha rejoined. "It's precisely because I understood that I'm feeling such sorrow."

"For me?"

"For you and for him. What do you want from life, Xenia? Have you thought about that?"

"I don't know. Nothing gives me any pleasure except my work. When I'm on stage I feel alive. When I come down from there I become a spectator of my own life and nothing touches me, nothing moves me or affects me in any way. When I'm in front of the camera shooting a scene, I feel everything that the woman I am playing feels. In my own life, though, I feel nothing."

"That's not good."

"But that's the way I'm made, Martha. Why can't you accept me the way I am?"

"I've never met anyone like you, despite the fact that I've known a lot of people in my life, including actresses with dreams and ambitions. You're living half a life—crippled, without feelings. And what about Leonidas? How does this affect him?"

"He's in his own world. He's happy just because I'm in his bed."

"You speak cynically. This is not love, my girl."

"That's why I'm thinking of putting an end to this relationship. And besides, it's been going on for too long."

"You got what you wanted," Martha stated bitterly.

"You could put it like that."

"And what will happen to Leonidas?"

"Mercy, Martha! What am I supposed to do? Stay with him out of pity? Basically, if he doesn't understand that not all relationships lead to the altar, perhaps it's time he learned."

"All the gossip magazines say you're heading for marriage."

"You read them too? They've finally begun to take an interest in me!"

"Be careful, Xenia."

"What should I be careful of?"

"Everybody knows about your relationship. If Leonidas does some harm to himself, they'll all blame you."

"So? I'll go down in history as a fateful woman."

Martha looked at her, shocked.

"You said you wanted to hear what I'm thinking, what's going on inside me. Now you have to put up with the consequences. I never speak freely to anyone anymore, but you insisted."

"You're right. And I still prefer you tell me what you're thinking rather than keep it to yourself. But when you do, you'll have to accept my criticism and advice."

"Fine. But that doesn't mean I have to act on it."

"Agreed."

Polyxeni left feeling lighter than when she'd come, and she had to admit that she was breathing more freely. It had been years since she'd revealed herself to someone just as she was, and she still wondered how she had done it. Perhaps it was Martha's calm voice and the sweet atmosphere of her house.

The decision to separate from Leonidas was delayed. A week after her conversation with Martha, he turned up with a signed contract for the purchase of the house. Polyxeni didn't know what to say. She looked at his face, bright red with happiness, and wondered why she couldn't love this man who offered her everything she wanted before she'd even asked for it. She did feel happy to finally have something of her own, a whole apartment that was entirely hers. She let Leonidas lead her straight to bed, where she became totally unaware of what her body was doing. Like a piece of wood, like a dead thing, she abandoned herself to his hands.

◆ ◆ ◆

When Polyxeni realized that she and Leonidas had already been together for a year, she knew that she couldn't delay their separation any longer. When her producer told her that he was taking her to a film festival in Thessaloniki for a few days, she decided it was the right moment.

"And how many days will you be away?" Leonidas asked sadly when she told him about her departure.

"Four—five at most," she answered coldly.

"Shall I come with you?" he suggested longingly.

"No, of course not. I'll have lots of things to do there and I won't have time to pay attention to you."

"Then when you get back, I'd finally like us to talk seriously about our future."

"And I think we should do that now."

"Even better," Leonidas said, taking heart. "I say that, when you get back, we announce our engagement and arrange to have the wedding before Christmas. My parents are very anxious to meet you."

"Have you spoken to your parents about us?" Polyxeni's voice didn't hide her displeasure.

"Yes. But they'd already seen us in so many magazines! They knew we were going out together, and now they know that I love you and want to marry you."

"Yes, but it's not enough for only you to want it."

"But I told you. My parents have no objection."

"Have you asked me?"

The curt phrase made Leonidas lose all his color. "What are you trying to say? Don't you love me anymore?"

"Did I ever say I loved you in the first place?"

Leonida was completely overcome. "But we've been together for so long—we have a . . . relationship!"

"And does that oblige us to marry?"

"What are you saying, my love? I feel as if you're joking."

"I'm not in the habit of joking. Listen, Leonidas. The truth is that you've been very good to me, and you've even given me this apartment, but I don't think I want to marry you."

"But why? Would you rather we go on as an unmarried couple?"

"I don't want that either."

Leonidas tottered as if he'd received a strong blow to his face. "Xenia, what are you saying?"

"I think you understand. I'm sorry Leonidas, but I want it to end here."

"This can't be true! You can't be telling the truth! Xenia, I love you. I can't live without you!"

"I'm afraid you'll have to. I'm leaving for Thessaloniki in the morning and when I come back, I don't want to see you again."

"But why? What did I do to you? Is there someone else? Tell me the truth!"

"Don't be ridiculous! Of course there's no one else. I have no desire to get mixed up with someone else—I haven't got out of this yet."

"Is this how you see me? Someone you got mixed up with? How is that possible? Only yesterday you were sighing in my arms."

"It was probably you, sighing in mine, that you heard. If you were more perceptive you'd have seen that I never felt anything for you. I tried, because you're a good person, but . . ."

Leonidas looked at her as if he didn't recognize her. He rushed at her and grabbed her by the arms. He shook her, howling her name, trying to kiss her, but her lips remained closed and frozen.

Polyxeni looked at him with an empty gaze. "If you want to become violent, I won't fight you," she said coldly. "But whatever you do won't change the fact that we're finished."

Leonidas pushed her hard and she fell on the carpet. Her coolness made him even more furious. "I'll kill you!" he screamed.

"And that's the way you'll make me yours?"

"Afterward I'll kill myself!"

"Not even in the next world will I be yours. Accept my decision and go, Leonidas! When you calm down, you'll meet another woman who'll love you."

"Never! There'll never be another!" he yelled, then left quickly, as if he were being pursued.

Polyxeni sighed with relief. After an entire year she finally felt free. Without any delay she began packing her bags. She wanted to dash out and see Martha before she left town. Martha's pregnancy was progressing normally and she had begun to show. Stathis kept teasing her about her belly and laughing happily. Polyxeni was glad for her friend, but she didn't envy her at all—in a little while she'd be stuck with diapers and pacifiers.

It was dark when she stepped outside to hail a taxi to go to Martha's house, so Polyxeni didn't see him immediately. When the taxi stopped in front of her, Leonidas appeared on the opposite sidewalk. She looked at him then got into the cab without paying him any further attention. As the car pulled away, he howled her name. As soon as the sound of his voice had faded behind them she heard the shot.

A nightmare—that's what it must be—it couldn't be true. Yet Leonidas was lying on the sidewalk in a pool of blood from the bullet that had penetrated his skull and killed him instantly. The taxi driver thought he had a flat tire and stopped. People from the building began shouting. A woman shrieked.

"Something's happened," said the driver, shaken, as he got back into the car. "It wasn't a tire. It was a shot!"

"Whatever it was, I don't have time—I'm in a hurry," Polyxeni said sharply. "Please, let's go!"

The driver hesitated at first. But then he realized the police would be coming soon, and he didn't want to get mixed up in anything. So he drove off quickly.

As soon as Polyxeni got to the house, she collapsed in Stathis's arms. Her reserves of self-control had evaporated. Stathis led her half fainting to the sofa while Martha ran to fetch water and smelling salts. With a great effort, Polyxeni explained to them what had happened in the afternoon when she ended things with Leonidas. When she got to the part about the suicide, Martha let out a small cry and collapsed in an armchair.

Polyxeni turned to Stathis, who looked angrily at her.

"I told you!" he yelled. "I warned you that he wouldn't be able to bear losing you."

"Stathis," Martha intervened. "There's no point in attacking her now."

"Do you realize what she's done? She sent a man to his death in cold blood!"

"I didn't believe he'd do it," Polyxeni said in a quiet voice. "A lot of people separate, and none of them die."

"None of them except Leonidas. He has a history of suicidal tendencies. I told you that."

"If I hadn't been the reason for it to happen, someone else would have."

"Perhaps someone else would not have aroused such a great love. But you were the love of his life and you know it. You slept with him for a year. You drove him crazy!"

"Is there any point in our saying this now?" Martha intervened again. "The point is to decide what we'll do now that this has happened."

"We can't do anything," Stathis argued. "Nor do we have anything to do with this. But her? Can you imagine what will happen when the newspapers find out? Their relationship was known to everyone. He blew his brains out right outside her door!"

Polyxeni got up and began pacing nervously. "It's not my fault if Leonidas didn't know how to take rejection. I couldn't stay with him any longer because I was afraid he might do the crazy thing he finally did."

"Well now you'll have a lot more to be afraid of," Stathis warned. "Especially when it comes to your career. All those people who know you as a tender, loving girl—do you think they'll accept the fact that you drove a man to suicide?"

Polyxeni's panic began to rise. "What shall I do? What shall I do? I wanted us to separate, not for him to die."

Martha got up, stood beside her, and put her arms around Polyxeni's shoulders. Then she looked pleadingly at her husband. "Will you help her?"

Stathis, for a moment, thought of refusing, but his wife's look changed his mind. He took a deep breath before he spoke. "I must think up a story for the press. If you appear in public as you are now, it'll all be over for you."

"What do you mean?"

"You have to look as if you're in shock. You have to present your separation as a tragic disagreement that poor Leonidas misunderstood, then killed himself in despair. The newspapers and magazines worship great love stories. You'll be the heroine in a tragedy and that will save you from a lynching."

"So what am I to do? I'm flying to Thessaloniki tomorrow."

"That's impossible. Forget about it! You can't make a promotional appearance at the same time as your lover's funeral."

"I can't go to his funeral!" Polyxeni protested with horror.

"You won't need to. I'll arrange it with a doctor and we'll announce that you've had a nervous breakdown. Then you'll wait patiently until the story's been forgotten. That way there'll be no danger of ruining your name. If the press describes you as a hard, unfeeling woman who drove someone to suicide, you're finished."

"I'll do anything you tell me. I'll call my director, the producer."

"Are you mad?" Stathis scolded. "You're not supposed to know anything about the tragic event. You left your house to come and see us, and he did what he did behind you, without your knowing. I'll drive you home now. The press will probably be waiting outside. You'll act as if you don't know anything."

"I can't do that."

"You can. You're an actress. So play the scene to save your neck."

The next hours were a bad dream for Polyxeni. Stathis took her home and, as he'd predicted, a swarm of reporters was waiting outside.

"As soon as you hear the news, faint!" Stathis ordered her through clenched teeth.

That evening Polyxeni gave the best performance of her life. As soon as somebody asked her what she had to say about Leonidas's suicide, she persuasively feigned ignorance. And when they explained to her what had happened, she collapsed in Stathis's arms. He lifted her up and took her to her apartment. Later he came out to learn the details. Leonidas had left a note that they had found on him. The only thing he said was that he couldn't live without his beloved. When Stathis finally permitted the reporters to come up to her apartment for a brief interview, he stood beside her like Cerberus.

Polyxeni explained that she loved Leonidas, that there'd been a misunderstanding, an argument, and he, thinking he had lost her, did what he did. Finally she burst into loud weeping. It was the excuse for Stathis to dismiss the reporters, telling them they must leave Miss Olympiou to lament the loss of her beloved.

When he closed the door behind them Polyxeni looked at him, wiping her eyes and completely under control.

"How do you think it went?" she asked.

"From the first moment I saw you perform, I said you were a good actress, but in fact you've become much better," he answered coldly.

"So what do we do from here?"

Polyxeni's casual attitude infuriated Stathis. "I'm asking myself, finally, what sort of person you are," he shouted at her. "Do you understand what happened tonight? A young man died and what was his crime? That he loved a heartless bitch like you!"

"Would it make any difference if I was crying and beating my breast?"

"At least you could show some remorse for what you provoked."

"I didn't tell him to go and kill himself! You'd think the world was running out of women."

"What can I say to you that you could possibly understand?"

"I just want to know what to do now."

"Call the director and tell him what happened. Tell him you're not going to Thessaloniki."

"At all?"

"Xenia, you will be in bed recovering from a nervous breakdown. Stop worrying about attending the premieres at the festival. You'll find yourself at many more from now on. Your star is in the ascendant. May God pity your suitors and whoever loves you!"

Polyxeni ignored the insult. "And what will you do now?" she asked.

"I'll contact my doctor and he'll send an announcement to the papers about your condition. You, for the time being, will shut yourself up in the apartment. Martha and I will come to see you and bring you whatever you need. Are you happy now?"

"Let's say, yes. And when will I be able to leave the apartment? My next shoot begins in ten days."

"Don't worry. By then you'll be free and your admirers can stand in line to see their sad heroine. And you can expect a leading role very soon."

Stathis was completely right about everything. Beside the headlines announcing Leonidas's suicide, the papers featured a photograph of Polyxeni fainting in Stathis's arms. The captions pleased her: *Miss Xenia Olympiou distraught about the unfortunate death of her beloved,* one wrote. *Miss Olympiou collapsed when she was told about the unfortunate death of her lover. The cause was a misunderstanding,* another one informed the public.

Naturally, she didn't appear at Leonidas's funeral, but Stathis attended it, even though he felt like an accomplice in the young man's death. For a week Polyxeni didn't stick her nose outside her apartment door. The gossip magazines all wrote about her nervous breakdown, and the director informed her that the production offices had been overwhelmed by letters of sympathy and support for her. Dressed in black, she finally emerged from her home to go to the shoot, where everyone greeted her with words of understanding and the director praised her for her professionalism in coming to work despite her situation.

The film was a sensation. Even though she didn't play the lead, everyone ran to see the girl who had lost her man in such a tragic way. Her photograph ran on the covers of magazines, and everyone begged her for an interview. Following Stathis's orders, she always spoke very tactfully and cautiously to the press. As was expected, she played the lead in her next film and also took a leading role in the theater. The theater director had tapped into a vein of gold and he knew it. Polyxeni was like a magnet, drawing an audience that filled the theater every night. The show was sold out for a month in advance.

Xenia Olympiou was a star.

◆ ◆ ◆

Martha glanced at her daughter, who was playing with her dolls on the carpet, then turned back toward the woman she was talking to. Several years had passed since the tragedy of Leonidas's suicide and Polyxeni, sitting opposite her, seemed to remember nothing about it. On the contrary, more beautiful than ever, she was basking in the glory of the films she'd made one after another, as well as her success in the theater, where she'd been playing leading roles for some time. Polyxeni was on top of the world.

"So," Martha said as she returned to their conversation. "What are you doing with your life?"

"Haven't you been reading the papers?" Polyxeni asked, smiling with self-satisfaction.

"I was asking about your life, not your career."

"But my life is my career."

"From what I read, you're not seeing anyone these days."

"No—I have no desire to get mixed up with anyone. I'm just fine."

"Everyone says that you can't forget Leonidas."

"Yes, isn't that funny?"

"I wouldn't put it quite like that. Someone else in your place might have been psychologically wounded by such a great love."

"Yes, I dare say, but in this case we're talking about me, and I was never in love with Leonidas. You know that."

"Still, it's been a long time. Has no one turned up who interests you?"

"No one. We covered all this back then."

"And nothing's changed since that time?"

"Martha, I know you worry about me—I can see it in your eyes."

"Shouldn't I worry? You're young, beautiful, successful, rich . . . and completely isolated."

"If I wanted love, I'd be looking for it."

"But doesn't every living being want intimacy and love?"

"OK, fine. Go ahead and say what you like. Say what my worst enemies say, that I'm a cold, heartless mannequin, that I'm not even alive. Maybe they're right. I feel as though I died when I was born. And if my body didn't, my soul certainly did."

"Were you always like this, Xenia?"

"Why do you ask?"

"I can't imagine you as a little girl in the village with your mother. Do you have brothers and sisters?"

"Four sisters, but I don't know where they are."

"And your mother? Do you know how she is?"

"No. From time to time I send her a card so she knows I'm all right."

"Why, Xenia? What happened to make you leave home and abandon everyone you left behind?"

"Don't get it into your head that there was some tragedy, because there wasn't. The village always stifled me and at the first opportunity, I left to save myself from the boredom and routine there. That's all there is to it."

"And all these years you never wanted to find out if your family was all right? You didn't want to see them?"

"The very idea of going back makes me shudder. I'm fine here, especially now. Do you know they're talking about casting me in an Italian coproduction? Do you realize that I may have an international career ahead of me?"

"It's quite probable. I was asking about something else, though."

"Why are you so interested in my past?"

"I want to find out if you were always so . . ." Martha tried to find a word that wouldn't offend her.

"So cold? Is that what you mean?"

"Yes, why not? Before you joined the troupe, for example. What were you like?"

"I don't remember, Martha, and I'm telling you the truth. It's as if a sponge passed over all the years I lived below Olympus and wiped them out."

"Is Xenia Olympiou your real name?"

Polyxeni was silent for a moment. "No," she answered.

"I thought not. Don't worry, I'm discreet. I won't ask you anything else because it's clear you don't want to tell me."

"It's not that I don't want to because I don't trust you. You're the only person who knows what I'm like and still accepts me. But I truly don't remember the past. It's as if it was someone else who sat on the banks of the river by my house, looking at the water and wishing for a boat so she could sail to wherever the river ended. And now that it's happened, thanks to you, you're asking me to go against the current and turn back, if only in my memories. I can't do it."

"All right. I won't go on anymore. But you should know that I'm really worried about you. I'm afraid that at some point the actress will finally get a taste of what real life can be like, and she won't be able to bear it."

"Fine, if that happens, I'll run and hide in my house again," Polyxeni said. "My mother said the same thing to my sisters who got married. She told them that if they ever felt like life was dragging them away, they should come back. That only there, in our home, they would be cleansed again."

"I hope you won't need to do that."

Just then Stathis returned, interrupting their conversation. The smile on his face froze as soon as he saw Polyxeni.

"Bah! You're here too," he said with annoyance.

"And I was so pleased to see you!" Polyxeni replied sarcastically and stood up. "Don't try to insist that I stay, I must go—I have work."

Martha looked at her friend apologetically, but Polyxeni just smiled. She absentmindedly stroked the little girl's hair and then left, winking at Stathis instead of saying good-bye.

"Really, can't you even go through the motions when she's here?" Martha scolded as soon as they were alone.

"After what she did, I can't even pretend to bear her presence. I wonder why she even comes, Martha."

"Because however much it annoys you, I'm the only friend she has."

"Friend! Does a creature like that even know what friendship is?"

"Not all people are the same, Stathis. I accept her as she is."

"But she isn't even a human being, she's so cold and heartless. She's like a mannequin!"

"Strange. That's just what she said about herself. Still, one day she'll fall in love."

"She, fall in love? You're dreaming, my love."

"Maybe. But if it does happen, Hell itself will open its doors and say to her: 'Come in!' Women like Xenia can fall in love, even if they don't know it. But they love only once and sometimes it's in a catastrophic way. I almost hope it doesn't happen to her."

"If she does fall in love, I hope she pays with the same price that poor Leonidas did."

◆ ◆ ◆

When Polyxeni left Martha's house, she headed toward the theater. She liked going there early, before the others arrived. Sometimes she went on stage and looked out at the dark auditorium with its empty seats, listening in her imagination to the applause that would soon flood the place. At other times she would sit in the front row and imagine seeing herself act. Mentally she would correct any shortcomings or mistakes, then she would do the same thing from the back row. Her acting, which grew more perfect each day, must move even the farthest-away spectator.

Her fellow actors, even the ones who didn't like her, knew it was admirable, the way she controlled her acting. They recognized that she was completely professional. Often, they had stood back to watch how easily she acted a feeling that they knew she had never experienced in life. She was always cold, always distant. They had never seen her be moved by anything. In fact, it was rumored that this poisonous woman had driven a man to suicide several years earlier. After that, the press had tried to dig up details on her personal life, and some of them followed her very closely, but they only saw her coming and going from her house alone.

The coproduction Polyxeni had told Martha about finally got the green light, sending the young star happily to Italy. It was a story about two friends who loved the same man, and it ended with one tearing the other to pieces until they both lost their great love. Her colead was very beautiful and already famous in her own country, which Polyxeni didn't like. Her envy was tempered, however, by the fact that she had aroused the admiration of the male lead, a charming Italian with black hair and dark eyes. For the first time since Leonidas, she considered going to bed with someone just to see how it felt. Besides, she would be staying in Rome for three weeks, and it wasn't fun to be shut up alone in a hotel room, even the most luxurious one. There was of course the problem of language, although the Italian knew a little English, just as she did. But in the end she didn't want him for conversation.

The shoot was a new experience for Polyxeni, who saw that Italy was more advanced in the field of moviemaking than her home country. The studio was much better equipped, the cameras more sophisticated, and the organization was perfect. When the director ordered the man in charge of the temperature inside the studio to match it to the climate depicted on screen so that the actors wouldn't perspire, Polyxeni was amused. In her last film in Greece, she'd had to wear a low-cut dress despite the very chilly temperature inside the studio, causing her to shiver so much that her voice trembled when she said her lines. Fortunately, this had worked, as her character was supposed to be in distress.

Polyxeni impressed everyone on the set. She was always on time and always prepared, in contrast to the Italian actress, who wore everyone out with her whims. As a result, Polyxeni charmed the director and the producer and stole some extra scenes from her fellow actress. This infuriated the Italian, but she couldn't do anything about it.

On the third day of the shoot, Polyxeni wasn't surprised when she found a large bouquet of flowers in her dressing room. Before she even looked at the card, she knew it was from Giovanni, her leading man. She smiled with satisfaction, then got into her bath, which the maid had scented with bath salts. That evening, the production company was hosting a dinner, and she wanted to be dazzling. Naturally, this wasn't difficult for her to achieve. She had just the right dress in her suitcase.

At exactly seven o'clock she came down the grand staircase wearing a gold dress, and everyone turned to admire her. She soon found herself surrounded by every guest in the room, and the satisfaction she felt made her eyes shine more brightly than the outfit she wore. Giovanni managed to separate her from the throng and lead her to the dance floor. The photographers' cameras flashed as the two danced together. Both their smiles were dazzling, but as soon as the cameras withdrew, their eyes met and the heat between them was almost palpable. They whirled around for hours, and Polyxeni caught herself feeling impatient for what was certain to follow. Perhaps this handsome Italian would finally teach her the pleasure of love.

Three hours later, with great discretion, they disappeared into her room. They didn't want anyone to see them, although everybody knew that the arms of the Greek actress wouldn't be empty that night. As soon as the door closed behind them, Giovanni went to the bar and poured a glass of champagne. When Polyxeni put out her hand to take it, he shook his head and smiled. He circled around her and when he was behind her he unzipped her dress so that it fell like a mountain of gold at her feet.

"The champagne is for me," he said to her in English, speaking slowly so that she would understand. "But I don't like drinking it out of the glass."

His next move took her by surprise. Very slowly he let the golden liquid run down her body and Polyxeni let out a little cry, partly because of the temperature of the chilled wine. Immediately Giovanni began to busy himself licking the rivulets that had formed on her and for the first time Polyxeni felt her heart race. She turned and embraced him but he was not in a hurry. He wanted to taste all of the drink, wherever it had flowed. Then the Italian indicated that he wanted her to take off his clothes. Polyxeni obeyed. She hurried, her hands trembling as she relieved him of his last items of clothing, but he continued to be slow, to the point where she wanted to howl. With indolent gestures he laid her on the bed, where his hands traveled all over her, followed by his lips. Polyxeni was surprised when she heard herself groan. Her body felt like a musical instrument that gave out soft notes when played by a virtuoso.

In the end, nothing was the same as it had been with Leonidas, and yet—something was missing. She had experienced sexual pleasure for the first time in her life, but her instincts told her there was something else, something strong that was hidden inside her and hadn't yet come to the surface. She finally knew what it was to enjoy making love, but . . . This *but* was still going around in her head when Giovanni, not fully satisfied or tired, laid his body on hers again and she experienced the same pleasure once more.

Polyxeni didn't know that news of her affair with Giovanni had reached Greece thanks to her own producer, who'd tipped off the press. Having purchased the rights to the film, he wanted publicity. Had she known it, it wouldn't have mattered. Giovanni had swept her off her feet, and she asked for nothing more than the hours they spent in her room. They both knew that it would end when she finished her work and went back to her country, and neither of them had a problem with that, something that made Polyxeni feel completely free. She had become even better in her role and the love scenes with Giovanni caught fire on the screen. The director nearly cried out for joy. He knew that this sort of chemistry always brought people to the box office.

When Polyxeni returned to Greece, she finally learned of the media frenzy her relationship with the Italian had caused. With an inscrutable expression, she said that the rumors were unfounded. She and her leading man were and would remain good friends, and she was grateful to him for showing her the beauties of Rome. Also, she added, she would enjoy seeing him at the premiere of the film in Italy that winter.

"I want you to tell me the truth," Martha commanded two days later when Polyxeni visited her. "This story about friendship is for the reporters!"

"OK, OK. I wouldn't lie to you anyway. What do you want to know?"

"Everything."

"It might shock you."

"Coming from you, nothing would shock me. So, did you have a good time?"

Polyxeni told her friend everything, without hiding the feelings that Giovanni had aroused in her. She also confessed her suspicion that something was missing, something hidden that she hadn't yet discovered. When she stopped she saw Martha looking at her and smiling.

"Why are you smiling so condescendingly?" she asked, ready to be angry.

"Because you finally understand the difference between sex and love. It's one thing for the body to be satisfied; it's another thing entirely when the soul is involved too. Young and inexperienced as you are, you've only satisfied your body so far."

"But with Leonidas . . ."

"Leave the boy alone, wherever he is. The poor lad didn't even manage to satisfy your body. But the Italian, from what you've described, was unbelievably experienced. Love, for him, was a science and he shook something up in you."

"And real love? What's it like?" Polyxeni looked at her curiously, like a child who wants to learn a secret from a grown-up.

"Ah, love! Love is a mysterious rite, my dear. It brings you Hell and at the same time you realize that Paradise must be something like it. It burns you alive and yet you find yourself refreshed by its fire."

"Martha, I don't understand a word of what you're saying."

"That's because you've reached this age without your heart breaking for someone."

"But is it good, then? The way you put it, love sounds like a complete disaster. It destroys you."

"Yes, but through it you're reborn again. Without the object of your desire, you don't live. You have no air to breathe. To have the man you love embrace you is like a journey that you hope will never end."

"You sound like a romantic."

"My dear, at your age, you should be the one who is a romantic, not me. At my age, love is like a precious thing on display in a store window. You look at it, and before you decide to go inside and see it up close, you think of the pros and cons. Because when it comes to love there's no room for second thoughts. But you . . . now that I think about it, I'm asking a lot of you. You don't manage to feel other things—simpler things, more everyday things."

"What do you mean?"

"Xenia, you promised to always tell me the truth; I'm doing the same for you now. Leave love aside for the moment. Because it's like asking you to walk before you've managed to even stand up."

"Is it riddle day today? You're confusing me again."

"My dear girl, look around you a little. Experience simple feelings first—joy, sorrow. Let yourself approach people; listen when they talk, just as you listen to your director. Soften your unbending soul a little and then everything will come to you. Move your eyes away from the distorting mirror so you can see the world as it really is."

"Like the fairy tale . . ." whispered Polyxeni thoughtfully.

"What I told you isn't a fairy tale."

"No, no, I'm talking about something else. Somebody once told me a fairy tale about a mirror that broke and some shards of glass got into the eyes of a man, or a woman, I don't remember, who from then on saw everything around them coldly and distantly."

"So you do understand what I'm saying."

"I don't know if I'll be able to do it, though."

Vassiliki interrupted their conversation by throwing herself into her mother's lap, crying, with her favorite doll in her arms. A tragic accident had separated the head from the body and the inconsolable child had run to Martha for help. With sure movements, Martha put the head back in its place and handed the mended doll to her daughter. The little girl's eyes sparkled, a smile lit up her face, and two little arms wrapped themselves around her mother's neck. Vassiliki thanked her mother with a tender kiss before running off, completely ignoring Polyxeni.

Martha turned to her friend. "That's a moment of happiness, Polyxeni. Inexpressible happiness. A creature that you love more than yourself needs you and has complete trust in you. She offers you her love and you accept it, like the earth accepts the rain, and give it back because that's all you can do. Just love without any limits and without seeking anything in exchange."

"Mercy, Martha! Don't tell me I have to have a child to become human," Polyxeni replied.

"I don't think it would help in your case," Martha answered sadly. "If you don't mature emotionally, a child will do you more harm than good."

Polyxeni left her friend's house confused. When she got home, for the first time in so many years, she allowed the past to visit her thoughts. She once again became the little girl living below Mount Olympus; she remembered her sisters and especially her mother. She closed her eyes and saw herself barefoot on the banks of the river, playing with Julia and Melissanthi, one splashing water on the other, with Aspasia sitting a little farther away, squealing every time drops fell on her, and Magdalini clapping her hands excitedly. She was moved when she realized that she felt almost happy with her memories. Outside, it had started to rain and a flash of lightning was followed by the roar of thunder, a sound that reminded her of an evening when little Magdalini, frightened by a storm, had run and jumped into her bed, shaking.

"What are you doing here?" Polyxeni had asked her little sister.

"I came so you wouldn't be afraid by yourself," the child had answered. Then Polyxeni had hugged her, smiling at the innocent lie that hid the little girl's fear. She could almost feel the warm, childish breath on her face; in her arms she could feel the little body trembling uncontrollably.

Unconsciously she touched her hair and the memories rose up again. She saw her mother with a comb in her hand and a small bowl of water beside her. Every morning Theodora had followed the same procedure. Sitting in front of the fireplace, with her five daughters waiting their turn, she dipped the comb in the water and then began combing their hair, one by one, then plaited it into tight braids and tied them with big bows that looked like butterflies with open wings. As soon as Theodora had tied the last ribbon, she would make the sign of the cross over all of the girls, kiss them one by one, and say "Good morning." Then she would look at them with pride. This routine lasted until Melissanthi, the oldest, rebelled against it. Only Polyxeni was sad when it stopped. She adored the feeling of her mother's hands in her hair and that first kiss of the day.

Irritated, Polyxeni got up from her seat and turned on the radio. What was wrong with her tonight? Why such an onslaught of memories apropos of nothing? She had chosen her way of life—nobody had imposed it on her. And there was nothing she could remember that would encourage her to go back. She was Xenia Olympiou, the famous actress: the dream had become reality.

She wondered if the news of her success had reached the village. Then she realized how ridiculous the question was. Of course it must have reached them. She remembered the traveling cinema people who would show up in the village with whatever films they could find and project them on the white wall of the school. After all these years, things must have improved; there must have been progress. Her mother and grandmother must have seen her films, and perhaps even her sisters had too. And where were they? Where had the river carried them? Years ago all contact had stopped. Her mother had sent notes full of complaints, but since Polyxeni never answered, Theodora finally gave up.

That night, Polyxeni slept very comfortably and woke refreshed and in good spirits. A new script was waiting for her, and at the theater, after so many rehearsals, a new work that she had loved from the first time she'd read it would begin. Everything in her life was going wonderfully; her account at the bank kept growing, and next month she would travel to Italy for the premiere of her latest film. At Christmas there would be a premiere in Athens and perhaps Giovanni would come.

Her producer traveled with her to Italy, where Polyxeni gave dozens of interviews and did a photo shoot for a magazine. The producer's mouth fell open when she arranged the session for three o'clock in the morning.

"We take off for Greece at 8:00 a.m.!" he protested.

"So?" Polyxeni asked. "They're paying me well. Why should I lose out on so much money?"

"But, my girl, after the screening there'll be a reception!"

"Which will last until twelve or, at the most, one!"

"And when will you rest?"

"Don't worry," Polyxeni answered. "I didn't come here for a rest—I came to work." Then she just smiled and walked away. If Mr. Stefanos knew what else she had arranged for that evening, he'd be much more worried.

❖ ❖ ❖

Giovanni appeared at her door on time holding a bouquet of red roses and ready to give his best to their encounter. As soon as Polyxeni felt his hands on her body she realized that she had missed making love, at least the way the Italian did it. His lips, which reached every corner of her body, sent electric shocks up her spine. Polyxeni trembled as she heard her own voice, as if it came from far away, begging for more. She felt as if she were made of clay. Her legs were amazingly supple, wrapped around his body like tentacles in an effort to bring him closer to her, but he didn't hurry. Unless he first heard her cry out, he didn't allow himself to be free.

The photo shoot that followed was unique. Surfeited by love, Polyxeni had an obvious energy. Her eyes shone and her lips, still swollen from Giovanni's kisses, were a provocation to the lens. The Italian photographers were stunned by the results. All of her breathed an eroticism that wouldn't leave any reader of their magazine unaffected. They were assured of success and they knew it before the film was even developed. This woman was made to be in front of the lights. Polyxeni slept all the way back to Greece and naturally, as soon as she reached her house, she closed the shutters and lay down exhausted on her bed. That night she had a performance and she had to regain her energy.

The premiere in Athens was another success. The film had been very well publicized and Stefanos had done surprising work. There wasn't a day when some so-called "exclusive" piece of information wasn't leaked to the press, and Polyxeni was always ready to accede to everything they said to make everyone talk about a film they hadn't even seen. The press worshipped her; she was their beloved child, and nobody put her in a difficult position by asking her questions that didn't pertain to the film. Her personal life, which seemed to be nonexistent, was always the subject of media interest and investigation, of course, but apart from the Italian, and enough had been heard about him, nothing else turned up in the life of Xenia Olympiou.

Giovanni's arrival in Athens for the premiere intensified the gossip. The couple was obliged to make joint appearances to promote the film, and the camera flashes lit up the fancy clubs where the two of them went, sometimes by themselves, sometimes with the producer and the other actors. Polyxeni's female costar hadn't come, supposedly because of other responsibilities, but Polyxeni knew that was an excuse. The Italian actress might be the center of attention in her home country, but in Greece that game would be completely lost, and she knew it.

However much Polyxeni was in a hurry to be alone with Giovanni, she was very careful. There would be no evidence of what the press, who were now following her everywhere, had suspected for so long. Even though they chased her, she managed to escape them and spend a whole night in his bed. They both knew it would be the last. Their ways were separating and neither of them was sorry about that. They simply celebrated, in their own way, their meeting and its ending, without regretting it. How lovely it was while it lasted!

◆ ◆ ◆

As Polyxeni approached thirty, she felt a little strange. For the first time in her life, she was aware of the years that had passed, and the panic she experienced sent her straight to Martha. She found her reading with her daughter and without wishing to, she remembered sitting at her own family's large kitchen table as a child, struggling with difficult math problems, and how Melissanthi would try to help her. Her sister's voice always became indignant when little Polyxeni forgot how much that cursed seven times eight came to.

"Hello there," Martha said, getting up to greet her.

"Don't stop because of me. I'll wait until you've finished. I'm not in a hurry."

Polyxeni sat down opposite Vassiliki, who greeted her politely.

"Good evening Miss Olympiou," she articulated shyly.

The girl avoided, as much as she could, her mother's distant friend, who had never paid her any attention. She thought the woman was very beautiful but her behavior gave the impression that she found children annoying. Now, though, the distant lady was looking at her with interest.

"What are you two doing?" Polyxeni asked Vassiliki.

The child showed her the book. "I'm trying to doing some reading with my mother," she said with a sad expression. "But the letters get mixed up . . . as if they're dancing and in a hurry to come out of my mouth, so no one understands what I'm reading."

"Oh, that's not so serious," Polyxeni said cheerily. "The secret is to read slowly and to breathe properly. To give your brain some time to put some order into those naughty, hurrying letters."

"Really, miss?" asked the girl hopefully.

"Of course. Then what's important is practice. The more often you read, the better you'll get."

Martha watched Polyxeni talking to her daughter with amazement. The young woman had never spoken to the girl before, and now she spoke to her with so much understanding and tenderness. Martha kept watching, while opposite her, the conversation continued.

"How do you do with arithmetic?" Polyxeni asked now.

"Everything's easy there," the child answered enthusiastically.

"You see? You're lucky. I hated numbers and I couldn't keep them in my head no matter how hard I tried. My poor sister spent hours standing over me so that I learned addition, and even worse, multiplication!"

"What's your sister's name, miss?" Vassiliki was curious to know.

Polyxeni seemed to have difficulty for a moment. "Melissanthi," she finally said softly.

"What a beautiful name," the child replied admiringly.

"Melissanthi?" Martha repeated. "An uncommon name, but I've heard it somewhere. Where does your sister live, Xenia?"

"Why do you ask?"

"Is she here in Athens?"

"I think so."

"Is she, by any chance, the wife of a tobacco merchant?"

"My brother-in-law's name is Fatouras," Polyxeni recalled with difficulty.

"Bravo! Melissanthi Fatouras. I know her."

"Where do you know her from?" Polyxeni managed to ask.

"I met her at a party I went to with Stathis. We were introduced, we exchanged a few conventional words, and that was all there was to it."

"How is she?" Polyxeni's voice could hardly be heard.

"She seemed to be fine. A really beautiful girl. And now that I remember her, you look alike. But why . . . ?" Martha suddenly realized that her daughter was following the conversation with interest and stopped. "Miss, I think these grown-up conversations don't concern you," she said sweetly but firmly. "And since my friend is here, why don't you take a break, like the lucky girl you are, and we'll talk when Miss Xenia has left."

The girl hurried off. But, then, as if she'd forgotten something, she came right back and stood in front of Polyxeni. "Thank you for your help, Miss Xenia," she said politely and quickly as if she were ashamed. Then she kissed Polyxeni on the cheek and ran off.

Polyxeni's hand covered the spot where the child's lips had rested. She turned to look at Martha, but her friend just smiled.

"Hasn't a child ever kissed you before?" she asked.

Polyxeni, still shocked, shook her head.

"Now you know what you've been missing for so long," Martha teased. "And now that we're alone, Miss Leading Lady, tell me why you don't go to see your sister since you live in the same town. Leave aside the others—you don't even know where they live. But with Melissanthi, why don't you go and find her so that you have someone of your own?"

"It's been so many years . . ."

"So? Did you have a fight?"

"No, never."

"Well? The same blood flows in your veins! And even if you did have an argument, by now she would have forgotten."

"We wouldn't have anything to say to each other, though. Each one of us took our own path. Anyway, if she wanted to find me it would have been easy. She must know about me. Leave it, Martha, it's better like this."

"Whatever you think. But I believe you're making a mistake. As for other matters, how come you're taking an interest in the child? What's gotten into you? Until today, you've never known she existed."

"You're wrong, now! I never forgot her birthday."

"Yes, but as an obligation."

"Are you putting me through psychoanalysis again?"

"In a way, yes."

"Maybe this isn't the best time. I can hear her coming back."

Vassiliki entered the room again and sat down beside Polyxeni, where she began reading her lesson loudly and clearly, stopping to breathe as she'd been told, and leaving Martha speechless again.

"How did that sound to you?" the girl asked her mother's friend.

"I think you managed it wonderfully!"

"Thanks to you, miss," the child murmured shyly.

"Yes, but I don't like this 'miss' at all."

Vassiliki seemed prepared. "So then I'll call you auntie," she declared quickly.

"That sounds just fine."

"Can I also tell my friends that Xenia Olympiou is my aunt?"

"Of course!" Polyxeni agreed.

Vassiliki began jumping up and down happily while behind her back her mother crossed herself.

"Now I can say that I've seen everything in life," Martha said, looking upward as if she was speaking to God.

The next hour was full of surprises. Polyxeni continued listening with interest to the child and answering every question she asked; she even held Vassiliki's favorite doll at the girl's request and dressed it in the clothes the child picked out. While they were playing, Stathis arrived and it was his turn to be astonished as he watched Polyxeni outfitting his daughter's doll in a lacy dress with infinite patience.

As soon as she saw her father, Vassiliki ran to him and told him in a single breath everything that had happened on that strange afternoon. "I'll call her auntie from now on," she concluded. "And they'll all be amazed at school when they find out I have Xenia Olympiou for an aunt!"

Stathis smiled at his daughter and sent her to fetch his slippers before he turned to Polyxeni.

"What sort of new game is this?" he asked accusingly.

"I don't understand," Polyxeni answered.

"Neither do I, but be careful. Stay away from my kid!"

"But . . . what did I do?"

"Don't give me that! Since the day she was born, you've ignored her, and suddenly today you become 'Aunt Xenia.' Do you expect me to believe that you've finally begun to behave like a human being?"

Martha tried to intervene. "Stathis, dear—"

But Stathis stopped her with a look. "Martha, not a word! I won't let your friend play with our child the way she played with Leonidas. What's happened, Miss Olympiou? Did they give you a role where you have to play the mother? Are you looking for experience again?"

His tongue dripped poison and his eyes radiated fury. Polyxeni felt a lump in her throat and her eyes welled up with tears.

"Stathis, you're very wrong about me," she said, trying to calm him down.

"Like you were with him."

"So you still don't forgive me."

"Nor is it likely that I will. Just as I don't forgive myself for not leaving you behind with the traveling players! Perhaps the boy might still be alive. But I repeat: stay away from our child! I won't let you play with her sensitive soul for as long as you . . . collect experiences, and then wound her with your indifference because she's no longer necessary to you."

"You're wrong, Stathis, but I can't persuade you. I don't blame you, of course. I'd better go."

Polyxeni left before anyone could say anything.

Behind her, an argument broke out.

"You're unbearable!" Martha shouted at her husband. "How can you behave like that toward her at the very moment when she managed to feel something for someone apart from herself?"

"So you believe she's sincere?"

"Completely! And I'm not stupid or easily fooled. I know Polyxeni better than you. Something has begun to change in her and if you've stopped it, I'll never forgive you. Even her expression isn't so cold anymore. And her voice! It's become lively, and she's lost that apathy that used to only disappear when she was playing some role. You know she's begun to talk about her home, about her family?"

"She has a family?"

"No, she was planted like seed. Of course she has! Four sisters."

"Oh, I didn't expect that. So why doesn't she have a relationship with any of them?"

"That's another issue. For months now, I've been trying to make her feel an emotion of some sort, and today, when she finally and unexpectedly behaves in a human way you rudely sent her away. Ah, Stathis!"

"It's the child I want to protect."

"The child is in no danger from Xenia. Please—I understand how much what happened to Leonidas upset you."

"That's not the only thing that upsets me. It frightened me the way that creature reacted. Or rather *didn't* react."

"Yes, but people change."

"And she's changed?"

"She's begun to change. There's already a small crack in her armor and it'll soon be shattered. So long as she doesn't meet someone unsuitable. Not now, at least."

◆ ◆ ◆

Fate has its own plans for people, and they aren't always the best ones.

Petros Glinos had only been back a month from his long vacation in Paris. He had been bored to death there, just as he was in Athens before he left. He could have had a career as a model or even an actor, but the enormous fortune he'd inherited prohibited him from discovering an interest in any sort of work. His father tried in vain to persuade him to occupy himself in the family business. Imports were burgeoning and Mr. Glinos was getting old and tired, but Petros showed no interest in taking over. He occasionally showed up at their luxurious office, worked for a few weeks, and then, when he got bored, he would disappear for months, leaving his father bitter. The elder Glinos and his wife both asked themselves what mistake they had made in raising their son that he was so uninterested in everything. He was very handsome, but that permanently aloof manner of his kept everyone at a distance, even his parents. From time to time they heard of his multiple successes with women—his indifference seemed to provoke their interest—but Petros quickly tired of them and soon left them inconsolable.

Polyxeni met Petros at a party and was immediately attracted to him. It wasn't just his appearance but more his demeanor that caught her eye. There was also something else about him that was completely unexpected but hard to define. When they were introduced, Petros already knew who she was. He had seen her recently in an Italian film and really liked her. Up close, she was even more beautiful, and the look in her eyes clearly conveyed that she was available and interested, but also very independent and strong. This last quality intrigued Petros even more. He was tired of women who always tried to tie him down. When he kissed her hand, he gave her a meaningful look.

"So, I see tonight is my lucky night," he said.

His voice was deep and velvety and matched his appearance perfectly. "Why do you say that?" she asked, smiling.

"Because when I was invited, I never imagined that I'd meet you here. I just saw your latest film a few days ago and it made a tremendous impression on me because of you. You were . . . dazzling!"

Polyxeni smiled at him again. "Thank you for your kind words. Apart from being dazzling, was I also good in my role?"

"Your beauty didn't allow me to pay attention to anything else—I'm sorry."

Petros suggested a dance and she followed him onto the floor. In his arms, Polyxeni felt her heart pounding. The intoxicating scent of his cologne was making her crazy and she had great difficulty preventing herself from resting her lips on his neck. His hand, resting on the small of her back, sent little flames throughout her body. His breath softly caressed her ear in the same way she wanted his hands to stroke her body. She was almost disappointed when the music stopped, but holding her by the hand, Petros led her to the verandah. The lights of Athens looked like a film set.

The young man took out a cigarette case and offered her a cigarette, but Polyxeni refused.

"I don't smoke," she said softly.

"Now that's something I didn't expect."

"Why?"

"These days, smoking for women seems to be nearly synonymous with their femininity. And you being an actress . . ."

"Don't believe everything you hear about women in the theater. The world imagines us as daring creatures—provocative, without any moral principles."

"And aren't you?"

"No. At least not all of us are. We work very hard and most of us don't have time for a personal life."

"You're painting a very tragic picture. It can't be that bad. You, for example, are young, beautiful, and famous."

"Fame isn't always good. You lose a lot of your freedom when you know that someone is following you even in your private moments."

"Why did you become an actress, Xenia?"

"Because I've loved acting since I was a child. I caught, as they say, 'the acting bug.'"

"And are you happy with your choice?"

"'Happy' is a very strong term. And you? What do you do with your life?"

"I have a good time."

"Just that?"

"For me, that's what's important," Petros answered.

"And how do you manage to always have a good time?"

"Come with me and I'll show you," he suggested.

"Are you in a hurry, or am I imagining it?"

"Oh, don't tell me you're going to make this difficult," Petros said impatiently.

"Maybe I am. It seems that you didn't take what I told you seriously and you continue to believe what you've heard about actresses. When you change your mind, we'll talk again."

Polyxeni gave him a friendly but dismissive smile, then returned to the party inside. She felt as if she was suffocating among all the people, so she said her good-byes to the host and hostess and went home. If Petros Glinos thought she'd go to bed with him to liven up a boring evening, he was deceived. An alarm inside her warned her to stay far away from the dangerous charm of this man, especially after he made it clear that he was ready for an affair and nothing more. For some time Polyxeni had been aware that she wanted something permanent, something stable and meaningful. The affair with Giovanni had tempted her. She wanted something in her life that would absorb her completely. The years were passing and she wasn't getting any younger. Perhaps it was time for her too to start a family. Unconsciously she touched the place on her hand where Vassiliki had kissed her. A child—why not?

She poured herself a drink and drank it down in one gulp. She hardly ever drank, so the alcohol quickly dulled her brain and made her whole body begin to feel numb. She lay down on her bed and immediately fell asleep.

The next evening a bouquet of flowers arrived at her dressing room. The accompanying card had only two words written on it: *I'm sorry.* So, Petros Glinos was still interested. When she got on stage, she only had to glance out at the audience to see that he was sitting in the front row. The strange effect this had on her made her uneasy; she didn't like losing her composure at all.

After the performance, she expected him to come find her, but Petros was nowhere to be seen. She went home, ready to cry. What had she done wrong? After the bouquet with his apology, she thought he would want the two of them to go out. Why had he come to see her if he didn't want their evening to continue? She escaped, again, with alcohol. She needed its warmth and the sleep that she knew was unlikely to come without it.

For a whole week, Polyxeni didn't see Petros at all. However much she searched the theater during the performance, however much she looked for him afterward, he was nowhere to be found. Every night she returned to her empty house, where her only company was melancholy and a bottle of whiskey.

When she finally ran into him one night waiting for her outside in his car, she thought her imagination was playing strange tricks on her. He got out of the car and opened the passenger door for her. With only the slightest hesitation, Polyxeni slid into the seat. They set off at a fast pace into the dark streets. They didn't speak; she didn't ask him anything, even where they were going. It didn't bother her. It was enough for her that she was finally beside him, that she was breathing in his scent. She was surprised when she saw him stop in front of a hotel on the beach, but she still didn't say anything. When he led her inside through a secret entrance so she wouldn't be recognized at reception, she felt relief, but also a sense of humiliation that threatened to bring tears to her eyes.

When they reached their luxurious room, Petros poured himself a drink and half reclined on the bed. Standing a little distance away, she looked at him without any expression.

"What have we come here to do?" she asked.

"Sweetheart, even though I shouldn't believe everything I hear about actresses, don't tell me you're so naive that you don't know what a man and a woman do in a hotel with such a big bed."

"I didn't expect this of you," Polyxeni retorted disdainfully.

"Xenia, skip the melodrama, at least with me. We're big kids now. I want you and I know you want me. So instead of playing at hiding, let's get on with the main course that I know we're both impatient for. You're no naive little girl, nor am I an inexperienced young man who trembles at the sight of his beloved and doesn't dare touch even her hand."

"From there to where we are, there is a middle way!" Polyxeni was now so annoyed that she shouted at him.

"Which doesn't interest me. When I lose time, I'm bored and it's not worth it. I like you a lot, I want you, and because you're an experienced woman, you don't need the fairy tales I usually use for the others. At least you can admire my honesty."

"You're crude, when you get down to it."

"I'm sorry you see it like that. But I have to tell you that I get tired of things quickly and you've already bored me. So, my love, either get undressed and we'll have a good time, or leave. I won't be annoyed with you but you can be sure I won't bother with you again either. You're not the only woman on earth."

For Polyxeni, it was as if he'd slapped her. Her sense of reason told her to leave immediately. But the whole past week that she had spent embracing a bottle came into her mind. She thought of the complete silence of her house, and she knew she couldn't bear it. She watched Petros taking a sip from his drink and loosening his tie at the same time. She fixed her eyes on him. Her hands began automatically unbuttoning her coat, which she let fall to the floor. Still watching him, she continued with the rest of her clothes until she was naked under his gaze, which had already darkened with desire. She heard him breathing more deeply and was rewarded by a little satisfaction. So the gentleman wasn't as cold as he wanted to appear.

She approached the bed, took the glass from his hand, and finished the drink. He hadn't even touched her but she felt herself melting as she'd done in Rome, in Giovanni's hands. Petros reached out his hands and pulled her onto the bed while his lips covered hers. Polyxeni groaned loudly when they descended to her neck and he let out a small laugh.

"I knew I was dealing with a volcano," he whispered to her. "Now, let's see how strong the eruption will be."

What followed was unlike anything Polyxeni had ever known. She shattered. Like glass, her body became a million pieces scattered all over the room. A thousand times she thought she had died and as many times she was sure she'd been resurrected. Every touch from Petros shot her into the sky, his every kiss made her sob. Her nails dug into his back. She scratched him all over. She heard him shout her name and at that final moment Polyxeni's cry brought his release.

Petros, who'd left her out of breath and nearly fainting, slid in beside her, as he too struggled to catch his breath. In the complete quiet of the room, sounds were distorted. Polyxeni stared at the ceiling, her eyes wide open, and tears welled up from the bottom of her soul. So love could be like this! Now she understood Martha completely. Petros was the man of her life and however strangely this story had begun, it must never end. Otherwise she herself would die.

Petros sat up now and looked at her. "Why are you crying?" he asked quietly.

"Even if I told you, you wouldn't understand," she said as she went to get up.

Petros stopped her. "Don't leave. I owe you an apology."

"Better skip it. Last time you gave your apology in writing, and this humiliation followed it. What could be next?"

"Do you call what we experienced humiliation?"

"I'm talking about the way we got here. And now? What do you want to happen from here on?"

Her voice sounded steady but inside she was trembling as she waited for his response. She wanted this man and she would win him— otherwise she'd lose herself.

Petros looked at her hard before he kissed her. Again she felt herself dissolving. Again she lost control.

❖ ❖ ❖

Martha looked at Polyxeni inquiringly before she smiled. It had been almost a month since she'd seen her friend, in spite of all the telephone messages she'd left for her. When Polyxeni had finally arrived that afternoon, she was disappointed to discover that Vassiliki wasn't there. She had bought new clothes for the girl's beloved doll and she was in a hurry to see the child's smile, but Vassiliki had gone out with her father.

"Will she be long?" Polyxeni asked Martha.

"Don't worry, you'll catch her. But first, I want the truth."

"About what?"

"Enough of that innocent expression! Tell me. What's happening in your life that makes you glow?"

"Martha, I'm in love," Polyxeni confessed.

Her friend looked at her with her mouth open. "It's not possible," Martha murmured, at a loss.

"I said the same thing myself, but it's true. It's the first time I've felt like this. Now everything that you told me about love makes sense. He's perfect. He's the man I've waited for all my life."

"Good Lord! One thing at a time, my girl, because I'm dizzy. For a start, who is he?"

"His name is Petros Glinos."

"How would I know him? What does he do? What's he like? Does he love you?"

Polyxeni looked down when she heard the last question and Martha grew serious.

"What's going on, Xenia? Why don't you answer me? Does he love you?"

"I don't know. That's the truth."

"I don't believe you. There are things that a woman's instincts tell her before she ever hears them from the lips of her lover."

"Neither instinct nor reason have remained standing, Martha."

"A classic case of love of the heavy variety. Is he good to you, at least?"

"I can't even tell you that. The only thing I can ever think about is being with him."

"You're not telling me everything straight."

"I'm telling you how things are. Martha, he takes me in his arms and I melt. When I'm away from him I can't breathe. When he looks at me I feel twenty years old again. My heart feels as if it's breaking, I cry when we're making love. Do you believe it?"

"Hold on, Xenia, because I'm beginning to worry. You . . . all that's fine, but what about him? What does he do?"

"You mean aside from waiting for me outside the theater every night?"

"I can't believe the reporters haven't caught on to this."

"Ah. We don't go out much."

"So where do you go?"

"To a hotel near the beach."

Martha was silent for a moment. "All this time together and he takes you to a hotel? That's not very flattering toward you, Xenia. If anyone found out . . ."

"But he doesn't like publicity."

"Yes, but I don't think that if you went out to eat, for example, anyone would be shocked. I don't want to spoil this for you, but be a little careful, Xenia. Don't surrender yourself unless you're sure that he feels the same as you do. Have a little backbone!"

"I'm afraid, Martha!"

"What are you afraid of?"

"That I'll lose him. I can't bear to lose Petros. Don't you understand?"

Their conversation came to an end as Stathis and Vassiliki arrived back home. As soon as she saw Xenia, the child let out a happy cry and ran into her arms.

"Auntie Xenia!" she shouted. "When did you come? Why didn't you tell me, Mama, that Auntie was coming? I wouldn't have gone out—I would have waited for her!"

"There wasn't any reason for you to miss your outing," Polyxeni answered tenderly. "I waited for you. I brought you a present."

Vassiliki opened her eyes wide at the sight of the little wooden trunk full of clothes for her favorite doll. With hands that trembled a little she touched her new treasure and then wrapped her arms around Polyxeni's neck, kissing her tenderly on the cheek.

"Thank you, Aunt Xenia! Everything is so beautiful. My Evalina will go crazy, she'll be so happy."

While Polyxeni was busy with the child, Stathis, irritated by the young woman's presence, stared hard at Martha. His wife looked worried, which only further provoked his anger over the visit. Who knew what trouble Xenia got into this time? He made up his mind to sort things out with Martha. This time he wouldn't lift a finger to help her friend. He waited patiently for Xenia to leave, and only when his daughter went to try the new clothes on her doll did he open up the discussion.

"So, will you tell me what happened while we were gone?"

"What do you mean?" Martha asked, pretending to arrange some flowers in a vase.

Stathis went up to her and took her hands. "My dear, for years you've known that you can't hide anything from me. As soon as I saw your eyes I knew there was a storm going on inside you, and I'm talking about a real hurricane this time. Tell me."

"Xenia . . ."

"What did that heartless monster you call your friend do this time?"

"First of all, she is my friend—let's not talk about that again. And the heartless monster, as you call her, has fallen in love."

Stathis stood looking at his wife, as still as a pillar of salt, before breaking out into loud laughter. "Good for you, my girl," he managed to say in a wheezing voice between laughs. "You've made my day! That's not news, it's a story. Miss Ice has fallen in love. Is that what she told you, and you believed it?"

"It's my fault for even talking to you. You're wrong, Stathis!" Martha said angrily.

The next moment Stathis grew serious. "Now what? Are you serious?"

"Yes. And if you want to know, I'm worried."

"And I'm worried for the poor fellow who's gotten mixed up with her."

"I'm really worried about Xenia. Things are very serious, Stathis. She's fallen head over heels, and she doesn't know about those sorts of things."

"And who's the unlucky 'lucky fellow'?"

"I don't know him. His name's Petros Glinos."

As soon as he heard the name, Stathis was stunned. Looking at him, Martha didn't know what to think.

"Stathis, why are you looking like that? Do you know him?"

"Very well."

"And isn't he nice? Maybe there's something negative about him? Tell me!"

"One thing at a time, my dear. First of all, he's from a very good and wealthy family. They don't even know how much they have."

"That doesn't interest me."

"It may interest your friend, though. Maybe she's after a big fish."

"You don't know what you're saying. She doesn't care about anything except to be with him. Can you imagine, the only place they've been to is a hotel room near the beach. Can you imagine? Xenia! In a hotel room like the last whore on the street!"

"Quiet, love! The child's in the house. Don't shout."

Martha sat down in a chair, exhausted. "I'm very afraid that he just wants to have a good time."

"You're right to be afraid. That's how he is," Stathis said.

Martha turned and looked at him hopelessly. "What else do you know about him? Tell me, Stathis!"

"What should I tell you? What all of Athens knows? A badly brought-up bastard is what he is. His father works while he spends the proceeds. He travels often because he gets bored; he changes women more frequently than shirts. I'd say, without a trace of hostility, that Xenia has found the male version of herself."

"Yes, but Xenia isn't the same person she was. She's as fragile as precious crystal."

"Then I'm sorry, but he will break her into pieces, and without any shame. Maybe it's true, in the end, what they say: everything gets paid for! Don't you remember Leonidas?"

"Even if I wanted to, you wouldn't let me forget him. But whatever you say, Xenia is my friend; I love her."

"You can't do anything to help her, though, my dear. Whatever you say to her, she won't believe you!"

"Yes, I know, and if I do tell her, she'll hope she can change him because she loves him."

"Exactly. And anyway, we don't know anything. Maybe he has finally met his match. The only thing we can do is wait for things to evolve."

◆　◆　◆

Most people were astonished when they found out about the romance. The couple began to cautiously circulate publicly after Polyxeni insisted.

At first Petros didn't like it, but after a while he began to enjoy the fact that wherever they went they were the center of attention. Shallow as he was, he began to borrow a little light from Xenia Olympiou, and was proud of the fact that everyone recognized them and that they always had the best seats at the clubs. With Xenia he'd met all the stars of the day. It seemed like a dream when Kokotas or Zampetas greeted them from the stage. It flattered his vanity to go around with a famous woman and sit at the same table with performers he had only admired on the screen or at the theater, and for them to speak to him like a friend. His face appeared beside Xenia's nearly every day in the gossip magazines, and people began to recognize him even when he was alone.

Fame, even borrowed fame such as this, flattered Petros, and he had to admit that his life had acquired some interest thanks to Xenia. The only thing that bored him unbearably was Xenia herself, who seemed to be completely dependent on him. Sex with her, it was true, was always exciting, and he had to confess that for the first time he hadn't gotten tired of a woman in bed. She was full of invention and ready to try anything, as well as to give him everything. When the two of them were alone she was like a wild cat. She carried him away with erotic surprises he didn't expect, and he liked that, even though he was often afraid they would be caught in the act—something that made him even more eager.

Nobody who knew Petros expected that the relationship with the famous actress would last so long. Yet, it had been nearly a year and they were still together. Certainly no one, especially Polyxeni, had realized that Petros wasn't monogamous. With great care and discretion, he had illicitly tasted the fruit that some young starlets of the day offered him in the hopes that they might get a larger role through Olympiou's influence. She was the only one who didn't have an exclusive contract with any of the studios; she could work with them or not as she pleased. If she liked a script, and of course the fee, then she'd make the film. Because she was so popular with audiences, all the studios fell over each other to cast her.

It's possible that the relationship had lasted so long because of Petros's cheating. He was able to have all the variety he needed, and Polyxeni, who had complete trust in him, never suspected a thing. Blinded by love, she didn't notice anything strange. She never knew how many times Petros had gone to the dressing room next to hers, and in that narrow space, offered complete pleasure to her fellow actress.

Uneasy, Martha followed the story of the relationship in silence, not daring to imagine what would happen if Petros left her friend. With every day that passed, Polyxeni seemed more in love. She had even begun talking of marriage and a child. Martha didn't dare tell her of her fears; she only very discreetly tried to warn her. From Stathis, who kept some relationship with that circle, she continued to hear about Petros's misbehavior, and she trembled at the thought that Polyxeni might be told about it.

When the end finally came, it happened very quickly. When the young couple first met, Petros's parents hadn't been bothered—after all, Petros had made them accustomed to odd things. Besides, how long could it last? But the time had come, they decided, for them to intervene. They had no desire to have an actress as a daughter-in-law, especially one who was over thirty years old, and recently the press had been talking more and more about an impending wedding. The Glinoses agreed that their son should get married, but to someone from their circle, a young girl who could have children. They had no trouble finding a suitable girl, and the knife was held swiftly and decisively to Petros's throat. Either he leave the actress and marry Miss Papalambrou, or he wouldn't see a penny in future.

With the sword of Damocles above his head, Petros didn't have to think hard. However much he liked his life with the stars, however much Polyxeni gave him a good time in bed, he had no desire to be penniless because of her. He chose the worst possible way to break it off. He took her to the hotel again and devoted himself to her body all night, giving her so much delight that she couldn't bear it. He nearly made her weep and beg him to stop, while at the same time she pleaded with him to continue driving her to an erotic frenzy. At dawn he got up and dressed, while Polyxeni looked at him in surprise.

"Are we leaving?" she asked. "I thought we were staying here again tonight."

"You can stay," he told her calmly. "I'm leaving."

"I don't understand." Polyxeni sat up.

"It's quite simple, my love. This was our farewell. We're finished!"

Polyxeni looked at him for a moment as if she hadn't heard. Then she smiled uncertainly. "Petros dear, what are you saying? Do you think this is the right moment for a joke?"

"I'm not joking. I mean it. We're breaking up."

Unconsciously, Polyxeni put her hand to her chest as if she'd been shot. "But why? What did I do?" she asked in a voice like a whisper.

"Did I say you'd done something? We've been together for more than a year—it had to end sometime. I had a good time, you had a good time, so what more do you want?"

"But have you gone mad? How can you say we're separating after a night like that?"

"I told you already—it was a farewell party."

"Petros, tell me you're joking. Please!" she pleaded. "If we'd had problems, I'd understand, but just like that, without any warning, people don't separate."

"Sweetheart, don't make things end in tears. I'm telling you simply and nicely that we're finished."

"We can't be! I love you, Petros! I thought we were going to get married."

"You and me? Did I ever tell you I'd marry you? Is it possible that I, Petros Glinos, would marry an actress? It's one thing to have a good time in bed with you, my dear, and another to marry you. Besides, since you brought up the subject—I'm getting married."

"What?"

Polyxeni felt like she was bleeding now from every pore in her skin, but Petros wasn't about to drop the knife in his hand. Completely cold, he finished dressing without even looking at her.

"That's the way it is, my dear," he said. "I have a name to uphold; a tradition must be maintained. We had a great time, but next month I'm marrying a rich heiress of twenty-three and I don't want my fiancée to find out I haven't finished with you. Anyway, I'll miss you. I don't imagine the young lady will get up to your tricks with me, but one can't have everything in life. Good-bye, darling. Maybe, after the wedding, we'll talk again."

He placed a kiss on Polyxeni's motionless lips, as she sat naked, like a statue, her soul mortally wounded. Then he left. The sound of the door closing behind him was the final shot. Polyxeni collapsed in a faint on the bed.

Martha paced up and down in the room, her anxiety written on her face. It had been fifteen days since she had communicated with Polyxeni, because Vassiliki had been ill. Shut up in her house, she hadn't asked herself what was going on with her friend and she wouldn't have found out anything if Stathis hadn't come home looking worried, with a newspaper in his hands. In a calm voice he had read the news item: Miss Xenia Olympiou had fainted at the end of her performance and the doctor had diagnosed a nervous breakdown. The strange thing was that when Polyxeni recovered, she disappeared. Nobody knew where she was. Her performances were canceled and the film she was making had been delayed. Her house was closed up and she didn't answer the telephone.

"But what happened? Did something happen to her?" Martha asked and asked, speaking to herself.

While he was trying to find Polyxeni for his wife's sake, Stathis had also been making inquiries about what happened. He came home scowling.

"The news isn't good," he told Martha soberly.

"Did you find her?" Martha asked in agony.

"No. Xenia has disappeared. But I did find out why she left. Petros Glinos announced his engagement to Miss Papalambrou, from the well-known shipping family!"

"The bastard! He left her."

"From what I found out, it wasn't his idea. His father demanded an end to the relationship and acted as the matchmaker."

"And he sold her out without a second thought."

"Something like that. What did you think? That he'd choose to be broke, even in Xenia's arms? I told you, Martha."

"Yes, you told me, but after a whole year . . ."

"Which he spent very nicely with Xenia, but also with a few others under her nose. What did you expect? That he loved her?"

"You're right. But what do we do now? Where's Xenia? What if . . ."

"Don't let it cross your mind."

"Didn't you say that everything in life is paid for?"

"Yes, but I didn't mean that. No, I don't even want to think about something like that!"

"So where is she, Stathis?"

"I don't know, my dear. I went again and again to her house. I nearly broke the door down, knocking, but no one answers. The shutters are closed tight—what can I say?"

Martha rubbed her forehead thoughtfully. Then she looked up decisively. "Let's go!" she announced to her husband.

"Where are we going?"

"To her house. We'll break down the door. I have a premonition that Xenia's there but she's hiding."

"But how can we break down someone else's door?"

"I'd rather do something illegal than waste precious time. Will you come, or shall I go myself?"

Stathis had learned over the years to bow before the inevitable; when his wife got something into her head it was completely useless for anyone to try to change her mind. But Martha was right. They forced the door open and found themselves standing in front of a human rag who shuffled around a dark apartment. Polyxeni was unrecognizable, as if she'd aged suddenly in a few days. She was stumbling around with a half-empty bottle of whiskey in her hand. The light that Martha switched on obviously pierced the young woman's eyes like a hot needle. She closed them, groaning. Stathis was horrified when he saw her. With her hair dirty and full of vomit, he didn't recognize her. This couldn't be Xenia.

Martha took action immediately. She grabbed the bottle violently from Xenia's hand, and with Stathis's help, put her in the bath. As if she were dealing with Vassiliki, she shampooed her hair and washed her. She wrapped her in a towel and Stathis picked her up in his arms to put her to bed. Without opening the windows, so as not to give any sign of life, they cleaned the house and threw out the empty bottles as well as the full ones. Martha sent Stathis out for groceries so she could make some soup. Then they waited patiently for Polyxeni to wake up.

The following days were a nightmare for them all. Polyxeni suffered a lot and the alcohol, which was so important to her, was nowhere to be found. Keeping watch day and night, Stathis and Martha never left her alone for a moment and as soon as she recovered enough that she wouldn't shock little Vassiliki, they took her home.

The press was on her side again. Petros's forthcoming marriage had made them lash out against him and drag up the old story of Leonidas so as to demonstrate "how unlucky Miss Olympiou was in her personal life." Polyxeni herself didn't show any interest in what was going on around her. Shut up in Martha's house, she devoted herself completely to Vassiliki. She played with her for hours on end, sitting next to her while she did her homework, and the girl began to bond very closely with her.

Yet again, Stathis had arranged everything. He persuaded the producer to postpone the shooting of Polyxeni's next film a little longer, pointing out that after the publicity surrounding Xenia's separation, the movie would have tremendous success and repay him for the delay. He also arranged for Xenia to play in a summer theater. Once he'd arranged his own affairs, he took his daughter, his wife, and her friend abroad. Petros's wedding was approaching and Xenia should not be a witness to it, even in the newspapers. Besides, everyone had found out that she was staying with them and the telephone didn't stop ringing all day.

They returned two months later, having traveled through most of Europe. Xenia had just about managed to get back on her feet. Her troubled heart had opened like a rose under the rays of a sun that was called Vassiliki. Even Stathis had to admit that his daughter was in no danger from this once-heartless woman. Xenia loved the child passionately, and she also loved Martha. As for Stathis, she clearly respected him, and his opinion was law to her. Polyxeni's transformation would only be witnessed by them, though. For the outside world she became the old Xenia Olympiou again, even more remote and cold than before.

Polyxeni returned enthusiastically to the set, and just as Stathis had predicted, the film was a wild success. The producer was elated—that is, until he heard the fee Xenia was demanding for her next film. But he didn't dare to try to bargain. The star brought in money—so she should get what she wanted. This was the unwritten law. Polyxeni was so popular that endless lines formed for her new play, and at the intermission there was a solid mass of people outside her dressing room wanting her autograph. The young girls became almost hysterical when they saw her in the flesh in front of them; many started crying with joy because they could touch her.

Polyxeni hadn't run into Petros, even by accident, but just to be safe she avoided the theater's public exits. Of course she'd heard about the wedding but she forbade herself any memories. She continued to sleep at Martha's house. Her friend hadn't allowed any discussion about this and Polyxeni was grateful. The complete silence of her own house would have driven her mad, and she knew it. Besides, she couldn't bear to spend a day without seeing Vassiliki.

Martha's concern for Xenia persisted. Superficially she might have calmed down, but a storm was brewing in the depths of her soul. Martha saw that Xenia carried out her professional obligations, but immediately afterward she would lose all her energy. Only Vassiliki exercised some influence over her, but it wasn't enough.

"So what's going to happen?" Martha asked her one day.

Polyxeni looked at her sadly. "What do you mean?" she asked.

"Someday you'll have to live normally again."

"I've tried to, Martha, but it hasn't worked. I can't bear pain like that. I'm better off by myself. Anyway, what can I say? I feel so tired."

"From what?"

"From myself, probably. It's myself that's making me tired."

"Why don't you go away for a while?"

"And go where?"

"Home, to your village."

"Where did you get that idea? My home isn't really the village, it's that river. And it would probably drown me, if I didn't jump in to drown myself. Right now my home would only manage to wound me, not to save me."

◆ ◆ ◆

Two years had passed, years that seemed endless. That morning Polyxeni looked at herself in the mirror. She was in her early thirties, but her face looked much younger. Still, she was tired of everything. She was tired of trying to stay at the top, she was tired of the films, the theater, the publicity—everything. The actress had begun to withdraw. She said no more often than yes to new roles. As television had made its appearance, the theaters had begun to decline. She'd been offered the lead in a television show that paid very well, but she didn't have any desire to do it. Even Martha failed to recognize her. Stathis watched her transformation and was also puzzled. The only person who was pleased was Vassiliki because the more often her beloved aunt said no to new work, the more time she spent with her.

When Polyxeni finally accepted a television role, she did it for one simple reason: she had nothing else to fill up her day. The shooting was in the morning when Vassiliki was at school and Martha had her own things to do, so she was alone.

The show was a success. Polyxeni was a hit playing a dynamic lawyer who tried the most difficult cases. Television antennas, which slowly began to fill the flat roofs of houses like trees with strange branches, indicated that this new medium had a future. From infancy it would grow up fast. At first it would be a companion, but there was a danger of it becoming a tyrant. The romantic followers of the cinema undervalued it, but the more farsighted decided to conquer it forcefully and become themselves the creators of its success. In the beginning they followed what they had seen before, then they progressed with determination and imagination to realize their own creations. Xenia followed the progress of the new medium unconsciously rather than with real interest, but it worshipped and glorified her. Almost everyone in the street recognized her and often they would speak to her with a familiarity that embarrassed her. She had come into their houses; she was their person. She wasn't distant, like she had been on the screen or on the stage. Rather, she came to their homes once a week.

◆ ◆ ◆

It was wrong. Everything could have gone so well but fate had her evil schemes and decided to intervene in human lives. She chose at random who to put in her sights and didn't care if she had any past dealings with the person. In her bad mood, she didn't understand that she was destroying others that she shouldn't harm.

That night, Polyxeni had happily accepted to stay with Vassiliki while Stathis and Martha went out. It wasn't the first time she had done it. It was summer. She had no performances because during the last years, she had taken a vacation every summer, and the shooting of the television show had finally finished, although they were talking about continuing it the next season. She hadn't decided yet whether she would accept the offer. She wanted to change her life; still, she couldn't see how to manage it. That night, though, she was particularly happy. She would be with Vassiliki. They would play Monopoly, which they both loved with a passion, and although they'd stay up late against Martha's orders, they would pretend to be asleep as soon as they heard the car, just like they did every time.

But things didn't turn out like that. Vassiliki was so tired she fell asleep, but the couple didn't come home, even though it was late. At first Polyxeni didn't worry. She put the child to bed and sat down to study her part for the play she would be in that fall. But when the clock struck three, she really began to worry. By four o'clock she was pacing the room, not knowing what to do. The sound of the telephone made her catch her breath. She had always been afraid of the sound of the telephone at night. She lifted the receiver without knowing that the nightmare was beginning at that very moment for herself and for the beloved little girl who was sleeping unaware in her bed.

Faulty brakes were the cause, they told her. A truck whose brakes weren't working when the driver saw Stathis's car. The couple met their death instantly in the tangle of crumpled metal. Polyxeni felt as if lightning had struck every cell of her body; she thought she would go mad. The child, who didn't know she'd never see her parents alive again, had nobody else in the world. There were only some distant relatives on Martha's side and on Stathis's. Polyxeni put down the phone without making a sound. Tears started streaming from her eyes without her being aware of it. Her head was buzzing. She raised both hands and squeezed her head in an effort to hold her brain in its place. Her gaze fell on the bottle of whiskey but she immediately closed her eyes. It had been years since she'd had a drink. No . . . she didn't have the right. She had to remain sober, she had a lot to think about and even more to do, and she was alone. That scared her. How would she manage? She collapsed into an armchair and tried to put her thoughts in some order. Where should she start and in what direction should she go?

Even years later, Polyxeni had difficulty remembering exactly what followed. A gigantic effort was required on her part to get through the greatest storm of her life. She had to stand on her feet at the very moment when all she wanted to do was curl up and cry for her dearest friends, the people who'd been her support. But she didn't have either the right or the luxury of doing it. Vassiliki was the great victim of the tragedy and the one who suffered most, even though Polyxeni struggled to prop her up. The girl's brain seemed to stop when she found out what had happened, and after the cry she let out, no sound passed her lips again. The doctor who attended to her diagnosed severe shock and Polyxeni nearly lost her wits. Apart from keeping Vassiliki out of an orphanage, she now had to worry about the child's health.

Fate, however, had changed her mood. Perhaps she regretted the harm she had done. Stathis's best friend, one of the biggest lawyers in Athens, became the protector and guardian angel of Vassiliki and Polyxeni. He quietly arranged everything. Polyxeni adopted the child and would oversee and disburse the parents' fortune until the girl came of age. There were rumors about the will, which turned up as if by magic, and decreed that things would go just like that. Only the lawyer knew the truth. Stathis, who'd once helped him to study and achieve his career, had been the brother he never had and now he could repay him.

As Vassiliki's muteness continued, Polyxeni called the best doctors for the child, and all advised her that the situation required patience.

They didn't add "love" because that already poured from the eyes of the famous actress. She canceled everything. She would devote herself to the child, who was hers from now on. The news that Xenia Olympiou was withdrawing completely from the scene exploded like a bomb.

After that, that house became hell again. The telephone never stopped ringing. The reporters waited outside for a statement, and even ordinary people turned up to speak to her. The decision was made quickly, and with the help of the same friend of Stathis, Polyxeni and Vassiliki left for a long trip. Holding each other's hands, they went everywhere. Strangers among strangers, they slept in each other's arms and tried together to heal the wounds that had so unexpectedly opened.

It took three months for Vassiliki to open her mouth. When she did, she said the only word she needed to say: "Mama."

Polyxeni felt the ground slip from under her feet and she embraced the child with all her heart. From then on, progress was rapid. From the moment Vassiliki began to talk she didn't stop. The two of them had long conversations, often until late at night. At first, they spoke of the two people they loved only hesitantly and painfully, and then they began to talk constantly about them, since it was the only way they could keep them close. They went back to Athens, knowing that more pain awaited them there; the house was still overflowing with the deceased couple's presence. Polyxeni didn't dare suggest to Vassiliki that they go to live in her house instead, because she was afraid the child would feel she was being separated from the place where she had grown up. She enrolled the girl in school again and tried to organize their life in whatever way she could.

A year later, though, things had not improved. Neither she nor Vassiliki were happy. They hid it from each other, in an attempt to give courage to one another, but this just made the situation even harder. Vassiliki had lost all interest in school. She had no friends and always looked unhappy. Seeing this, Polyxeni didn't know what to do. It had been two years since she'd withdrawn from the scene, but she was still getting offers, which she rejected without a second thought. The very idea of returning to her work was repugnant to her. She no longer recognized herself, but she liked this new Polyxeni who she had become. Relieved of all the "musts" of her work, she had calmed down. Life had taken on new dimensions in her mind. Now she was capable of being happy with little things, simple things, everyday things, while the continuous preoccupation with herself had been replaced by her care of Vassiliki.

The day Polyxeni found Vassiliki crying secretly in her room, she decided she must have an honest conversation with her. She went up to the girl and hugged her, while the child tried, however she could, to hide her tears.

"It's not bad to cry," Polyxeni said softly. "Crying often saves our minds and it certainly lightens our spirits."

"Mama," Vassiliki whispered. That's what she continued to call her after that first time. "I don't want to make you sad. You've done so much for me."

"Not even half of what you've done for me. And you don't make me sad because you cry. I cry too, now and then, because I miss them and I'll always miss them. People like your mother and father are never forgotten. I loved them very much and sometimes I think the nightmare will end and they'll come back to us and never leave again."

"Mama, I don't want to stay here," the child said softly as if she were talking to herself.

"Are you telling me the truth?" Polyxeni asked. "I feel the same myself, but I didn't want to take you away from the house you'd grown up in."

"It's not the same without them, though, and it's not only the house. It's the whole city. When we were away abroad it was better. I could breathe. Here it's as if something is weighing my heart down."

"Do you want us to leave?"

"More than anything!"

"And where will we go? Abroad again?"

"No, no. I like Greece, but Athens . . ."

Polyxeni opened her arms and embraced her treasure. In a low voice, full of nostalgia that even surprised herself, she began to talk to Vassiliki about a village that stood under the shadow of a mountain where the gods once lived. She told her about the tall trees and the steep gorges. She described the white lakes between the rocks where the goddess Aphrodite used to bathe, the water mills that gave life to the region, and the air that smelled of burning wood and earth. Finally, hesitantly, she dared to speak of a house embraced by two old chestnut trees and a river that ran quietly and listened to her confessions when she was a child. For her daughter's sake, she brought every memory to life and then realized that she herself was no longer in pain. Like an old remedy of her grandmother's, these memories had soothed the wound, and when she stopped speaking, she smiled.

"Mama," the child said shyly. "It sounds so beautiful. And you . . . I've never seen you look so happy, so peaceful. Let's go and stay there! Do you want to?"

Polyxeni look into Vassiliki's eyes. "I want to," she answered.

The time had come for her to make peace with the past. For the longed-for peace to return to her soul. No, the years she had lived were not wasted. Without them she would never have understood what she wanted in life. She would never have become the person she was now. She'd made mistakes, endless mistakes that filled her soul with bitterness, mistakes that had even dirtied her hands with blood, but now she knew what she must do. She would go back; she would throw the past into the river and she'd never see it again. The river would carry everything away, and she and her daughter would begin a new life beside people who loved her despite her mistakes.

Back, then . . .

To the house by the river.

MAGDALINI

Everything was enormous in this country—the buildings, the roads, the distances. A crowd of people traveled on the buses, more people than Magdalini had ever seen. The shops had windows with all sorts of treasures in them, and there were thousands of cars. Her aunt's house in Chicago was also enormous: two stories with a well-kept garden and a fountain in the entrance that made a big impression on her because she had never seen anything like it. The interior of the house left her with her mouth gaping. Modern furniture, thick carpets, pictures on the walls, and big windows with heavy curtains.

She followed her aunt up the wide staircase, dazzled as she looked around her, but at the sight of her room she let out a small cry. The bed was very big, but despite that, it hardly disturbed the enormous space. There was also a bookcase and a small desk, and some small chairs to sit in.

"What's this?" she dared to ask.

"Your room."

"Do you call a whole house a room here?" Magdalini wondered, stroking the dark wood of the desk in delight.

Her aunt came and embraced her. "Magdalini dear, I know everything will seem strange to you, but you'll get used to it. I want you to feel at home!"

"It's a little difficult, Aunt. Everything's so different."

"I understand, but I'm sure that in a little while you'll feel like you've lived here all your life. Do you miss your home? I want you to tell me the truth."

"Since we left so much has happened, and I've seen even more, so I haven't had time to think at all about the village or my mother. But I keep thinking I'll go back and when I imagine it, I see her standing beside me."

Theodora was very far away, though, and at times Magdalini felt her absence very strongly. Anna's husband, Peter, came home late in the afternoon to meet his niece. Magdalini examined him with interest. His hair was gray and cut short. He wasn't very tall, his expression was friendly, and he had a pleasant manner. His clothes were expensive, which impressed Magdalini. He welcomed her, drawing on his nearly forgotten Greek, but most of the time he spoke to his wife in his own language, which Anna translated continuously for her niece.

The first evening she lay down on the soft bed, Magdalini had difficulty sleeping. Her brain could barely hold everything that had happened in the last few days. There would be challenges ahead, the first of which seemed insurmountable to her: the language. She would have to learn it as fast as possible or she wouldn't be able to learn anything else, or even study physics.

Anna, however, was prepared. The next day, at breakfast, she spoke to her husband before Magdalini came downstairs.

"You didn't tell me how my niece seemed to you," she began as soon as she'd had her first mouthful of coffee.

Peter looked at her good humoredly. "She's certainly very beautiful, and she seems like a good girl. Are you happy to have her here with you?"

"Very. I feel as if I have a purpose. Does that make sense?"

"Completely. If there's anything I'm sorry about, it's that we weren't able to have children. So let's say that God remembered us and sent us the child . . . Magdalini?" He tried to pronounce her name and smiled. "I'm really afraid that the first thing we'll have to do is change her name. It's a little difficult for us."

"That's the least of it. We'll find something simple. The most important thing is for her to learn the language. She wants to study, Peter. That's why she's here."

"But of course! Whatever she wants. I even know a teacher. I'll call him today. In the meantime, show her around. Go shopping together—surely she'll need clothes. Go and enjoy yourselves together. Make her love Chicago—that'll make it easier for her."

A little while later, after Peter had left for work, Magdalini came downstairs and found her aunt sitting at the table reading the newspaper. She couldn't believe her eyes when she saw how much there was for breakfast.

"Good morning!" Anna welcomed her. "I hope you slept well and got over your tiredness. Sit down and have some breakfast."

"Do you have all this for breakfast?" asked Magdalini. "In the village, we just have a glass of milk and a slice of bread and cheese, and nothing else."

"Yes, I remember something like that. But it's different here. Breakfast is the most important meal of the day."

"And what do you eat in the middle of the day, Aunt? Because if the breakfast is like this, I can only imagine the lunch."

"Ah, at lunchtime we eat something light—a salad, or a sandwich."

"What's a sandwich?"

"Two slices of bread with cheese, ham, some sort of dressing . . ." Anna noticed her niece's sad expression and smiled. The girl didn't understand anything yet, and it obviously upset her. "My dear, be a little patient and you'll learn everything."

"First I have to learn the language, Aunt. When you talk to my uncle, I don't understand anything. How can I go out? How will I study?"

"Don't hurry and everything will happen. I spoke to Peter already and he'll send us a good teacher so you can learn the language. As for our way of life and our customs, you'll need some time for that too."

◆　◆　◆

The changes in Magdalini's life were sweeping. New experiences came to her like sudden downpours, altering everything she knew. Anna never left her side, standing beside her with tenderness and real love. Like a mother teaching her child its first steps, she took her by the hand and taught her to walk in her new life. The first change was in her appearance. Her aunt spent a small fortune dressing her in the season's latest fashions for young girls. In the beginning Magdalini tried to persuade her aunt not to buy all the clothes, shoes, handbags, overcoats, but her protests fell on deaf ears. Before she had been there a month, nothing distinguished her from the American girls she saw on the street.

The teacher who Peter brought home was a man of about fifty who had a daughter the same age as Magdalini. They didn't have any trouble communicating because his family was Greek, so he spoke a little of Magdalini's native tongue. When Mr. Jordan saw Magdalini's determination, he was amazed. She spent hours and hours with her books. She sat up in the evenings reading and rereading words that seemed to her difficult, strange, crazy, until she slowly began to get used to them. Anna complained that she would get sick the way she buried herself in studying, but Magdalini was determined to speak the language of her new country, and to speak it correctly. Meanwhile, Peter had undertaken all the paperwork necessary to make her stay permanent.

Magdalini demanded that her aunt and uncle speak no Greek to her and that they correct every mistake she made. She made a particular effort when it came to pronunciation. She didn't want anyone to make fun of her; she didn't want to appear to be an immigrant. In the evenings, shut in her room, she wrote long letters to her mother, describing every detail of the changes in her life, and not failing to mention how kind both her aunt and her uncle were to her. She also sent home a lot of photographs of the interesting sights she had visited with Anna. Magdalini knew that her mother would read every letter carefully before she put it under her pillow and eventually among the household icons. She smiled each time she remembered Theodora's box of icons. In the beginning it was a small box, but just before Magdalini had left, the village carpenter had built her mother something larger to hold all the letters and photographs, the reminders of her loved ones who were far away from her. Every night Theodora prayed to the Virgin to kiss her children.

In her mind's eye, Magdalini could see her mother saying her prayer each evening and stroking the beloved paper faces that smiled at her, soulless but adored. Quite often she cried, her heart aching from their absence. Magdalini understood how much her mother loved her. She often thought of going back, of accepting defeat and returning to her mother's embrace, which she missed so much. Sometimes she would stand up, determined to announce her decision to return, but she never managed it. Her aunt would have arranged some walk, some outing, some new experience to replace her old ones, and everything would have been turned upside down, all decisions postponed.

◆　◆　◆

It took Magdalini a whole year to adapt completely and to learn to speak English with ease, although she still had difficulty writing it, which made her study even more intensely. At some point she had to be ready to enroll in the university, otherwise what sense was there in her being uprooted? She still hadn't decided what she would study; that was proving to be the most difficult thing. Every time she tried, she was overcome by uncertainty, but Anna and Peter would be there to calm her down.

"Don't be in a panic, Lyn," Peter would tell her cheerfully. "You're very young still. You have all the time in the world in front of you. First, you'll get used to things, then you'll study."

"Lyn" was her new name, although she herself couldn't get used to it and didn't like it. Still, she had to accept that "Magdalini" was long and difficult for Americans.

With her English skills nearly mastered and nothing else to do, Magdalini began to feel as if she were suffocating. The boredom and the loneliness struck her at once and she didn't know which of the two was more painful. She didn't like anything and it seemed as if the house was dangerously confining. The hours refused to pass and the days hid no surprises. In the beginning, she was amused that she didn't have any work to do, since her aunt had two large black women to look after the house and a Mexican woman to cook. It seemed strange to her that by the time she'd had her breakfast and looked at the newspaper, her bed was made and the clothes she'd worn the previous day were taken care of. She was a little ashamed that other people were washing her clothes. And while the washtub back home in the village had seemed a misery to her then, now, as she remembered it, she smiled tenderly. She almost desperately wished there weren't people around to do all the household chores so that she could do something herself. She couldn't even busy herself in the garden—there was a gardener.

When she timidly asked her aunt if she could help out in some way, Anna objected strongly.

"I didn't bring you here to be my servant," she said. It was clear that she didn't understand her niece's objection or where it was coming from.

"Aunt, I didn't say that, but it wouldn't be so bad for me to make my own bed. They even bring me my coffee."

"That's their job, my love."

"The thing is, Aunt, I don't have any work to do," she explained, but she had gotten the message that it was useless to insist.

When Anna told Peter about the conversation, he smiled understandingly.

"The girl's right," he said.

"But do you know what she asked me? If she could work in the garden!"

"It's natural. I don't imagine they had a gardener where she lived."

"But she's been with us for a year and a half. She should be used to it by now."

"Anna, I'm afraid you've forgotten what you yourself once went through. When I could finally stand on my own two feet, when money stopped being a worry for us and started to amuse us, when you stopped working—do you remember what you went through? You fixed up the house, and as long as you were doing that, things were fine. After that—do you remember?"

"Do you mean to say that Magdalini is bored?" Anna began to understand, and her face brightened.

"Bored to death, my dear. See, now you understand. She's alone, Anna. As you said yourself, she's been with us for a year and a half and her only company is you and your friends. She needs girls her own age, boys to flirt with, fun."

"But she's completely inexperienced. She might get into trouble."

"My dear, I know that you're nervous, but you can't keep Lyn here in the house forever."

"So what should I do?"

"Your friends have daughters, but you've never let them approach Lyn. When Charlene suggested her daughter take Lyn out for coffee, you refused."

"How do you know that?"

"She told me so herself. Accept the fact, my dear, that you've been rather selfish. You keep Lyn for yourself and you don't want to push her to make friends with other girls."

"But Charlene's daughter is . . . so lively!"

"Judy's a fine girl for her age. Lively and social. She'll introduce Lyn to a whole lot of people."

Anna lowered her eyes and Peter got up to sit next to her. He put his arms around her shoulders and his voice became loving.

"You can't hold on to her anymore, my love. I understand, but I must warn you that you're in danger of losing her completely. The way she's feeling, it would be easy for her to decide to go back home. Lyn is like the child we never had, but if she were ours, I'd tell you the same thing. Besides, don't you want to see her happy?"

Peter was right. Magdalini had begun to think seriously about her future and the thought of going back to her village was gaining ground inside her every day. However much she loved her aunt, however much she recognized what Anna and Peter had done for her, she didn't see any light on the horizon. The isolation was getting to her. After such a long time in Chicago, she hadn't succeeded in making a single friend, and she missed the company of people her own age. Especially since she had grown up with her sisters. She wondered why Anna's friends didn't put their daughters in touch with her, unaware of the many efforts that had been made and rejected by Anna herself. Magdalini imagined that the girls didn't want to have a relationship with an immigrant, and she was hurt by that, but she didn't say or show anything to anyone.

University and her studies seemed completely uninteresting to Magdalini, while in contrast, the village had acquired mythical dimensions. Whatever she remembered she liked. She was dying to see the tall trees again; she longed to see her house and to throw stones in the river. When she thought about her mother and grandmother her heart leapt. American food, which she had liked in the beginning, seemed tasteless to her now and there were moments when she thought she could smell the fresh bread that Theodora had baked. Although Magdalini didn't fully realize it, the decision to return had begun to take shape inside her.

One morning, when Magdalini came downstairs for breakfast, she was surprised to find that her aunt wasn't waiting for her alone as usual. Two other people were sitting at the table. One she knew—it was Charlene, her aunt's friend, who'd visited the house often. The other one was a stranger. She was a girl of Magdalini's own age, who got up happily as soon as she saw her.

"Finally! We've been waiting for you for ages," she called out.

Magdalini smiled awkwardly and turned to her aunt. Anna stood up and came over to her. She took her by the shoulders and pulled her closer.

"Judy is Charlene's daughter. She's come to meet you. Now that you speak English better, I think you should meet some girls of your own age," she explained.

Magdalini was at a loss, but Judy was a happy creature with an inexhaustible fund of things to talk about, and what's more, she'd been prepared by her mother and by Anna. She had often seen Magdalini from a distance, but her aunt's denial of any friendships had hindered her from approaching, despite the fact that she liked the look of the Greek girl. Magdalini felt a little dizzy, but she was happy to answer Judy's questions about her country, as it gave her the opportunity to observe the girl at her leisure.

Judy was a pretty girl with blond, almost white hair and light-brown eyes that always seemed to hide a smile in their depths. Her voice was childish and she spoke very fast, as if she were afraid of being interrupted and unable to finish what she wanted to say. Within a few minutes she'd told Magdalini her whole life story and described all her friends. Anna saw with relief that her niece smiled at everything she was hearing. When Judy asked her to go for a walk, she accepted without a second thought and the two girls left.

Anna's emotions were conflicted. On the one hand she was pleased because she saw her niece's expression coming to life again after such a long time; on the other hand she felt she was suddenly alone.

Charlene looked at her, smiling. "I understand how you feel about that girl, but she's grown up, Anna. She must find people of her own age."

"Peter thinks the same."

"Then I'm sure you understand that you've done the right thing. Judy knows who she should meet and where to take her. Don't be afraid."

"Now I understand the responsibility I took on when I took her from her mother. What will I tell her if . . ."

"Anna!" Charlene interrupted her abruptly. "What on earth is the matter with you? The girls have gone for a walk—they're not going to war!"

"Yes, but this isn't Greece, it's Chicago."

"So? Has anything ever happened to you during the years you've lived here? It's the middle of the day and they're not going anywhere dangerous. They'll eat an ice cream and drink a cup of coffee. You can't keep her under lock and key, Anna."

Anna was silent. She knew that her friend was right, but she didn't feel at all reassured. The time Magdalini was away seemed long to her and when the girls returned, she had to hold herself back so as not to reveal her anxiety. To her surprise, Magdalini's cheeks were bright red, her eyes shone, and she was smiling happily.

"I had a wonderful time, Auntie," she shouted and hugged her. "Judy's a marvelous girl. She introduced me to all her friends and tonight we're going to a party! They get together at a house, she told me, put on records, and dance. I don't know how to dance, of course, but Laura—one of the other girls—told me it's not difficult and she'll teach me. Stephen, who is Karen's cousin, asked me to save a dance for him, otherwise he'll be angry."

Magdalini stopped, out of breath, and Anna had trouble holding back her tears. She finally understood just how unhappy her niece had been. She had never seen her so poised, never had her voice sounded so happy, never had her eyes flashed like this.

"I'm so pleased you like Judy and her group of friends," she managed to say and she kissed Magdalini.

"What shall I wear, Aunt?"

Anna took her niece by the hand, pulling her up the stairs. "Let's go and look in your closet," she proposed happily.

Magdalini's social life finally began, and it was intense, which worried Anna at first, although Peter kept her on an even keel. The girl was with Judy every day; the two had a lot in common and really loved each other. When Alex asked Judy to marry him and she accepted, Magdalini cried for joy. Her friend's engagement had a strange effect on her, though. The woman in her had begun to awaken, demanding attention. In the two years she'd been in America, no one had flirted with her, but she hadn't really thought about it until Judy got engaged. The way Judy's eyes shone strangely each time Alex was beside her, the adoration as she gazed at the man she would marry—all this kept Magdalini awake for hours every night, thinking. Something inside her told her that there was magic hidden in the moments when Alex and Judy wanted to be by themselves. For her, a mysterious veil still hid the relationship between a man and a woman. Theoretically she had learned a lot since the day she left her village, where such discussions were forbidden, but she understood that theory must be light years away from practice.

◆　◆　◆

For the first time in their lives together, Anna began to worry about Peter. Recently he seemed very anxious. Every sound made him jump. He avoided going out alone, and he shut himself up for hours in his office. When some people she had never seen before began to visit him at the house, she didn't like the looks of them. She had never wondered about her husband's work, and now she was annoyed with herself because of it. Peter was supposed to have an import business, but she didn't know what the agency imported or who he collaborated with. When she realized that her husband was using armed bodyguards, though, she decided that the time had come to speak to him.

That evening she waited for Magdalini to go out and then went into Peter's office, determined to clear the situation up. She found him bending over some papers. He was surprised by her entrance. Anna never disturbed him when he was working.

"Has something happened?" he hurried to ask.

Anna noticed that her husband discreetly covered the papers he was reading. "You tell *me*," she answered calmly and sat down opposite him.

"But my dear, you came and interrupted me, so you must want to tell me something," Peter observed, smiling at her.

"Peter, you've never underestimated my intelligence. Why are you doing it now? Something has been going on lately, and I want to know what it's all about. There are armed bodyguards outside our house who follow you in another car when you go to work. Am I correct? Up until now, I've never met any of the people you work with, and suddenly our house has become a center for people passing through, and what's more their faces shout from a long way off that they're dangerous men. What are you mixed up in?"

Peter broke out in a smile but Anna remained serious.

"What on earth are you thinking?" he asked, in a voice that pretended to be cheerful. "Yes, I admit that I have protection, but my business is expanding—we're living in Chicago!"

"But we've always lived in Chicago and you've never had armed guards to protect you."

"Yes, but as I told you, lately my business has gotten a lot bigger. Charley, my competitor, is mad because I took a job right out of his hands, and his people are following me in case I step on his turf again."

"Peter, do you know what all this sounds like? Dangerous! This Charley must know that there are upsets in business. He's a professional, not a gangster . . . unless . . . Peter, tell me you haven't gotten mixed up with the Mafia!"

Anna had jumped straight up from her chair. Peter came up to her, smiling calmly, and took her by the shoulders.

"My dear," he began, "I think you've been watching too many American movies lately. I'm your husband, not Al Capone."

"That's what I want to know."

"If I'm Al Capone? Have you gone crazy, Anna?"

"Peter, please, tell me the truth!"

"But what should I tell you?"

"How did you suddenly make so much money?"

"Now, you're asking? It's been years, Anna."

"Yes, and I never asked. My mistake. In the beginning we could barely get by. We both worked like dogs, and there was never enough. Then suddenly everything changed. Back then, in my joy, I put it down to good luck. Now, with all this . . ."

"My dear, you're worried about nothing. We're not in danger!"

"Then why the armed guards outside our house, Peter? Then there's Magdalini. Is the child in danger?"

"Anna, you're letting your imagination run away with you. They're protecting me because I usually carry a lot of money around with me in checks, or I meet with businessmen who need protection. Do you think I'd endanger the life of my wife and Lyn?"

"This Charley, what is he? Who is he?"

"He's a competitor. I told you. He's also in the import business. He's been in it longer than I have, and he took it very badly when I took a job away from him."

"And is he so dangerous that you need protection?"

"I don't know, my love." Peter seemed to have lost his patience. "These are precautionary measures. To put it simply, the guys I've hired exaggerate a little and they make an impression. They're doing their job. Charley, who's getting old, wants to pull back and hand the work over to his son. Of course it annoys him that his son will have a serious competitor, whereas he himself had a monopoly."

"And that doesn't remind you of the Mafia?"

"You're really not in your right mind!" Peter was indignant and raised his voice, which made Anna even more concerned. The only time her husband shouted was when he felt he was being squeezed and he couldn't slide out of it.

Their conversation hadn't reassured her at all. On the contrary. She began to be more observant, and she soon realized that in addition to watching Peter, guards also watched the house and herself—even Magdalini. Still she didn't say anything to Peter. Meanwhile she was filled with anxiety and fear. She was almost certain that her husband had gotten mixed up in something, and the fact that the Mafia had spread its tentacles everywhere was an open secret.

On New Year's Eve they were invited to the house of some people Anna didn't know, something that also made her anxious. For years now, they'd spent New Year's Eve with friends and neighbors. But Peter had announced the invitation quite a while before Thanksgiving and he had given precise instructions to his wife about their dress. It would be a formal party, and they'd find themselves among some government people as well as artists, so it would be quite different from their usual parties. Aunt and niece wore their feet out trying to find suitable evening dresses. Although she usually enjoyed shopping with Magdalini, Anna, her head full of unpleasant thoughts and her heart overcome with fear, felt dissatisfied. The girl looked like a movie star in a pale-yellow evening gown that she had fallen in love with at first sight and bought, but Anna hardly noticed. Peter, on the other hand, sighed with satisfaction when he saw his niece wrapped in yellow lace with her hair up, a fact that didn't escape Anna. A nasty foreboding began to grow in her. Peter's sigh was unwarranted. His look confused her. It wasn't admiration she saw in his eyes. Her husband behaved to her as if he were reviewing some merchandise, as if he were expecting to make a great deal . . . but how? She began to be annoyed with herself for her suspicions. She reached the point of asking herself if she was losing her mind and seeing bad things all around her, so she tried to drive away her concerns but it proved impossible.

Peter had hired a huge limousine for the evening and Magdalini laughed happily when she saw it. She sat on one of the comfortable back seats and accepted the glass of champagne that her uncle offered her from the bar of the car.

"Uncle, is there anything in America that's small?" she asked him, wrinkling her nose at her first contact with the bubbly drink.

Peter smiled broadly at her. "Hmm, let me think. No, I don't think so. Everything in America is big, Lyn. Even dreams. If you're satisfied with small dreams, your life will be small, and that doesn't fit with the country." He then turned to his wife, who was looking absently out the window. "What do you say, Anna?"

"What? I didn't hear what you were saying."

"What's the matter, Auntie?" Magdalini asked. "You look so beautiful, everything's so lovely, but you're not in a good mood."

Anna hurried to reassure her niece. "No darling, I'm not in a bad mood—I'm just a little confused."

She realized that her suspicions were spoiling the family's fun. She looked at her husband, who was now talking to Magdalini about the evening ahead. It had been a long time since Anna had seen him so relaxed—and the strangeness of it made her even more uncomfortable.

The limousine stopped in front of a huge, brightly lit house. Neither Magdalini nor her aunt had ever seen anything like it.

"What's this?" Anna asked her husband.

"The house where we'll welcome in the New Year," he explained cheerfully. "Didn't I promised you a New Year's Eve out of a fairy tale?"

"Yes, but this is even more than a fairy tale. Who does the house belong to, Peter?" Anna's voice didn't hide the fact that she was unhappy.

"You don't know him. His name is Matthew Bowden, and he's regarded as the king of gold."

"And how do you know him?"

"Just what is all this, Anna? Are you interrogating me? Do you think you should already know all my friends and colleagues?"

"So do you work with this Bowden?"

"This whole game is becoming tiresome, my sweet. Shall we get out, or will we wait for the New Year in the car?"

Peter got out of the limousine without saying any more, then reached out to his wife to help her down. At first Anna hesitated, then she took her husband's hand and got out of the car. Behind her, Magdalini was still looking, enchanted, at the palace that awaited them. The inside really dazzled her. She had to half close her eyes at the brilliance of the reception room that seemed endless, it was so big. Great chandeliers hung from the ceilings, which were decorated with gold leaf. The furniture was also decorated with gold, the wooden floor shone, and wherever there were carpets they were so thick that Magdalini wondered how far her feet would sink if she trod on them.

The host and hostess greeted them at the entrance. Bowden seemed to be impressed by Magdalini and gave an inquiring glance at Peter, which Anna noticed. A small wrinkle of dissatisfaction formed between her eyebrows. She decided not to take her eyes off Magdalini the whole evening. These two men shared some secret, and it must concern her niece. Nor did she like Bowden. After the necessary introductions and greetings, they moved into an enormous room full of people. Some of them didn't make a good impression; in particular the ones who approached her husband worried her. Despite their formal attire, she recognized quite a few who had crossed her doorstep, and their carefully groomed appearance didn't improve the opinion she'd formed of them.

Magdalini seemed to be living in a mythical world full of princes and princesses. She looked around her, intrigued. Her face glowed, and Anna could see how unbelievably beautiful she was that evening. None of the other guests compared to her beauty in its youth and freshness.

"I've never seen anything so beautiful," Magdalini gushed as she took in the room.

"I knew you would like it," Peter answered. "What do you say? Will you dance with your old uncle and give me the satisfaction of being envied by everyone in the room?"

Magdalini laughed happily and gave him her hand so he could lead her onto the floor. They began to whirl around to the sounds of a waltz and indeed, all eyes were fixed on the beautiful girl that old Peter was holding in his arms. When they returned to Anna, both smiling, she felt bad that she couldn't enjoy the moment. If it were up to her, she would have taken Magdalini out of here by now. Everything in the place seemed suspicious to her. An alarm was sounding in her head and wouldn't stop.

When Franco approached them, Anna wanted to start shouting for reasons she couldn't explain. He was surprisingly handsome, she had to admit, even if such good looks in a man were too much for her taste. Very tall, with a muscular body, black hair, and intensely black eyes, he must have been a little over thirty. His movements had something cat-like about them. Bowden stood beside him, ready to make the introductions. Franco Giotto—that was his name—greeted Peter formally, Anna politely and respectfully. But when he turned to Magdalini, he seemed to be dazzled. He appeared mesmerized by her blond beauty and transparent white skin. And Anna noticed unhappily that Magdalini didn't seem indifferent to him. Her eyes lit up and her mouth half opened in a sweet smile. At that moment she looked just like spring, filled with juices and perfumes.

As the men conversed, Anna was able to observe them at her leisure. Bowden and Peter talked about the stock exchange in a satisfied way that gave her the impression they shared some sort of success she knew nothing about. It was quite obvious that Franco was half listening to the conversation. His glance kept resting on Magdalini, and Anna realized that whatever secret the other two were sharing, he was on the outside. For the time being she relaxed. Her mind kept returning to his surname, which she seemed to recognize, but she couldn't remember where from. Finally she gave up.

"Excuse me, gentlemen, but I think we've been ignoring two beautiful ladies for quite a while now, and it's a shame." It was Franco who'd spoken, and immediately afterward he turned to Magdalini. "I hope you'll agree to dance with me," he said, and held out his hand to her.

Magdalini had the impression that if she touched his hand, she'd catch fire. Her heart was beating loudly and she knew she was blushing, so, although she was dying to be held in his arms, she hesitated.

Peter extricated her from this difficult situation. "Franco's right. We came here to have fun and we forgot ourselves, talking about work. Come on, Lyn. Don't keep Franco in agony. Go and dance, and when I've excused myself from Matthew, I'll follow too, with my beautiful wife."

Matthew nodded in agreement and moved away, while Peter led Anna onto the floor. But Franco and Magdalini remained in the same place, his hand still outstretched toward hers. Time seemed to have stopped, the people around them disappeared. Only the sweet music succeeded in breaking the spell, provoking them to embrace. As they danced, Magdalini was grateful for his strong lead—otherwise she wasn't sure she would have been capable of taking a step. Her feet didn't obey the dictates of her brain, which only followed the beating of her heart.

The couple whirled on the dance floor with all eyes fixed on them. They were beautiful together and well matched by their contrasting features—she tall, delicate, and blond, like a wood nymph; he tall, muscular, and dark. He held her tight, his lips resting in her hair, and he seemed intoxicated by her smell. He didn't dare look at her. If he had seen her face so close to him, he couldn't have resisted kissing her. He wanted to touch her lips; he knew they must be sweet. Magdalini was still holding her breath. She was trying to commit to memory the feel of his hands on her body and his scent. They understood that they were both on fire, and hoped no one else in the room had noticed it. She prayed for the dance not to stop, for the music to last an eternity. When it did stop she wanted to cry, but despite the fact that not a note could be heard, Franco didn't let her out of his arms until a new piece began, then he continued to lead her to its tune. She dared to look at him and he smiled meaningfully at her. For the first time in his life he felt his heart ready to stop from his desire for a woman; for the first time, burning lava ran through his body. And although she was like cool water in his arms, he couldn't drink greedily like he wanted to.

"Maybe you're tired?" he asked her in a low voice. "Do you want us to stop?"

It was only a simple question, but he understood that her answer would determine whether he lost his reason or not. He didn't know what he'd do if she answered yes, if she left his arms, if someone else claimed the privilege of holding her close and smelling her perfume.

"No," Magdalini replied. "I'm not tired at all. It's so beautiful here tonight."

"Beautiful? In here, the only truly beautiful thing is you," he whispered.

Her long eyelashes tenderly swept downward over her golden eyes; a little lower down, her rosy lips half opened softly. Franco felt as if he was losing his mind.

The host provided a solution to the impasse. He interrupted the music and invited the guests to follow him into the garden. The New Year was close and the fireworks would signal its entrance into their lives. Franco led Magdalini out onto a small balcony, far away from the others. He wanted her only for himself during those magic moments when the tired old year would give way to a small, newborn year which, the pages of its days unwritten, would begin its journey. Without speaking, the two of them knew that nothing would be the same for either of them. That evening had changed everything, sweeping it away.

Magdalini was trembling, but it wasn't from the cold. She wondered what it would be like if he kissed her. Franco put his arm around her shoulders a few seconds before the dark sky exploded with fiery flowers, colored umbrellas, and golden ribbons, transforming it into a rare spectacle.

"Happy New Year!" he wished her gently.

"Yes," Magdalini stammered softly. "Happy New Year!" The words came out with difficulty.

He couldn't hold himself back any longer. He bent toward her and kissed her. His lips made hers catch fire as if she were one of the fireworks that still shook the air. She felt as if an explosion had dissolved her. She clung to Franco and his kiss became harder, his hands held her tightly to him. He felt as if he was drowning and only she had the necessary oxygen that would allow him to go on living. Magdalini pulled back first, not because she wanted to but because she was suddenly ashamed. What sort of behavior was this and how could she have acted so outrageously? Her aunt and uncle would certainly ask her why she was kissing a man she had only met a few hours earlier.

"I'm sorry," Franco murmured, but the word sounded so silly in his ears, so false. What was he saying sorry for? Because he was thirsty and drank water? Because he was drowning and she gave him breath?

Magdalini looked pale now, as her eyes rested on the marble floor of the terrace. "I think . . . I think we had better go back inside," she suggested in a low voice. "My family will be looking for me. It's not right."

"Lyn, look at me." His voice ordered her, but at the same time an almost imperceptible tone pleaded with her. Magdalini slowly raised her eyes and stopped when they met his, which even in the dark were shining. "Do you feel bad about what happened?" he asked her tenderly.

"I think we got carried away," she answered honestly. "We only just met tonight. It wasn't right . . . I don't know."

She was ready to cry and Franco was even more shaken. Her honesty wasn't in doubt, but the extent of her innocence seemed unreal in the world where he was accustomed to living. He raised a hand and touched her cheek. The feeling of velvet extended from the tips of his fingers to his brain.

"I wasn't just carried away," he said softly. "From the moment I met you I wanted to do that. But if I offended you, I'm sorry. Will you forgive me?"

Magdalini nodded and a shy smile adorned the corners of her lips.

Franco took a deep breath. "You're right, Lyn. We had better go inside. If we stay out here alone, I'm not sure I won't do something that I'd have to apologize for again."

Magdalini hurried to transform herself before they went back into the brightly lit room, her heart still beating disobediently and an imperceptible sadness in her eyes for something that had stopped and might never happen again. She rejoined her aunt and uncle and felt bad when she saw the uneasiness on her aunt's face.

"Where were you, my girl?" Anna called out as soon as she saw her. "We've been looking for you for ages. Where did you disappear to?"

She wasn't sure she could answer without the tremor in her voice giving her away. She thanked Franco with a glance as he undertook very calmly to explain.

"I'm sorry we frightened you," he said cheerfully. "Mr. Bowden announced the New Year very suddenly and we hurried to go outside. We found a balcony where we could watch the fireworks. Lyn's fine, even though she may have a cold tomorrow. We didn't have time to get her coat."

Magdalini could only nod her head in agreement, and making a superhuman effort, she managed to smile. When Franco said good night and left her side, she felt like everything had lost its luster, its beauty, becoming dull and uninteresting. Before her eyes a distorting mirror made the room stifling and tasteless, the voices and laughter echoed loudly and annoyingly. Fortunately Anna asked to go home. She had put up with this crowd long enough. Peter agreed to leave without any discussion.

Only afterward, sitting in the dark and quiet of her room, did Magdalini have enough time to go over all that had happened on that strange evening. The sky was clear, and in her imagination, she replayed on it, minute by minute, all those fireworks. She could feel all the sensations that his kiss had provoked, and she analyzed all the changes that their meeting had brought about. No one had ever kissed her. She'd never wanted anyone to touch her, and yet Franco had changed all that. She didn't know if she would see him again. He hadn't asked to see her; he hadn't even asked her where she lived or what her telephone number was. Maybe, for such a handsome man, she was just a momentary amusement. She happened to be next to him, so it was she that he kissed. But for her, the simple memory of that kiss made her whole body come alive; she certainly wouldn't forget him. The woman inside her had woken completely and was asking for more, for everything.

In the next room Anna was awake, tossing and turning, to the point where Peter sat up in bed irritably.

"Really, what's the matter with you?" he asked his wife. "What's making you worry so much?"

"Do you really have to ask, after what happened tonight? Magdalini disappeared with that fellow who we don't even know, and when she came back she looked as if she'd seen a ghost."

"I don't agree. Lyn was fine!"

"Peter, you're playing the fool again. That Franco Giotto doesn't seem like much of a trustworthy type to me."

"You're not being fair to him. He's a nice fellow—good looking, educated. And if he singled out Lyn—and he was quite right about that—it's not such a bad thing. She's a young woman. It's time she had a friend. Apart from Judy and Alex, who does she hang around with?"

"Where do you even know this gentleman from?" Sitting up with her arms crossed on her chest, Anna seemed to be annoyed now.

"I've heard a lot about him from Matthew."

"And how do you know Matthew and for how long?"

"Not this again! I'm in the import business. I know lots of people. What's gotten into you?"

Suddenly deflated, Anna fell back on the bed. "I don't know, Peter," she answered sadly. "I have the feeling that something is happening around me, and I can't understand what it is. I feel something bad surrounding us and I can't intervene and stop it from hurting us."

"What are you saying, my dear? What bad thing? We've never been better. And if Franco, as things appear, is interested in Lyn, you should be pleased. They're young. Love is the air that young people need. Don't you remember how we were, once upon a time?"

Peter put his arms around Anna and she curled up against him, tired.

"If I could believe you . . . if I wasn't afraid you were hiding something."

"There's no reason to be afraid, Anna. Everything will be fine."

Franco got up naked from the bed and lit a cigarette. Linda, who was still lying down, supported her head on one elbow and looked at him in surprise.

"What's the matter?" she asked. "I don't recognize you tonight."

When Franco didn't answer, the girl got up and went over to him. Her hands moved over his naked back. Then she hugged him and breathed in his smell.

"Come back to bed," she whispered. "We've left a conversation in the middle, I think . . ."

"Linda, get dressed and leave!" Franco said abruptly. "I don't feel like doing any more tonight."

"But other times we've made love all night," she complained.

"Tonight's not like other times."

"Franco, what's happening to you? Are you sick?"

The man pulled away and went to stand by the window. Outside, Chicago was all lit up, but all he could see were her eyes. Three days had passed since that evening, and he couldn't forget her. In an effort to think about something else, he'd invited Linda over for some company. He'd tried to drown his need for her in Linda's perfumed body, but he only felt worse.

"Maybe I'm sick," he murmured, as if he was talking to himself.

"I don't understand," Linda went on. Then her face brightened. "There's a woman involved! Isn't there, Franco?"

She was hoping he'd deny it, but he just looked at her without any expression.

"I think I told you to go!" he said suddenly.

"Just imagine! Franco Giotto is thinking about a woman, and he's lost his appetite for fun because of her."

"Linda, you're beginning to irritate me, and when I get mad, I react badly."

"But put yourself in my place for a moment. I'm amazed. You, in love? Unbelievable! I've known you for a year, and I've asked myself many times if you even have a heart, if there's anyone, apart from yourself, that you care about. And tonight I see you unable to function because of a woman. And I thought I'd seen everything in my life!"

"If you don't leave right now, you'll see more, and much worse!"

"Yes, I know . . ."

Linda began to dress while Franco poured himself a glass of whiskey and drank it in one gulp. When she finished, she went up to him. "I'm leaving," she said flatly. "I suppose we won't see each other again. There's not a woman on this planet that you can't have. Not that faithfulness is one of your virtues, but something tells me that things are different now."

"Things are different. And much more confusing."

"I don't know whether I should be sorry for you or remind you that everything gets paid for. You were awful to everyone who slept with you—hard and unfeeling. You didn't have the decency to make us feel like we existed as anything more than a body that offered you pleasure."

"Do you have much more to say?"

"No, I'm leaving. I feel sorry for the woman you're wanting right now. She doesn't know what's waiting for her."

Linda turned around and left the room quietly. She hadn't yet finished with the Giotto family for the night. Soon she hoped she would free herself from their clutches. She crossed the fancy corridor and knocked softly at another door, then entered before anyone answered.

Charley Giotto was waiting for her. Wearing his robe and smoking a cigar, he was quite good-looking for his sixty-five years, not overweight and with only a touch of gray in his hair. The repellent thing about him was his eyes. They were so like Franco's but at the same time quite different. Completely black, with a look that didn't remind you of anything human. When he looked at someone, sharp daggers shot from their depths, and now these blades slashed the tender flesh of the girl standing in front of him.

"Finally!" he said, his voice in perfect harmony with his expression. "I've been waiting for you for an hour already."

"It's not my fault, Mr. Giotto. You son just now threw me out!'

"What happened?"

"What did you want to happen? Why did I go? Don't you know?"

"When I ask, you won't answer me with questions! How was my son with you? Like he usually is?"

"Yes. That is . . ."

Charley Giotto slapped her, leaving a bright-red mark on her cheek. "That may loosen your tongue!"

Linda rubbed her cheek, holding back her tears, and looked at him. "I don't know what you're trying to find out," she said. "But Franco was different tonight. He seemed absentminded. He was in a hurry to throw me out, although other times I've stayed all night with him."

"Damn it!" he shouted and Linda cringed even more. "Maybe he said something about another woman?"

"He didn't have to. When I suggested he was mixed up with someone, it was obvious I was right. He basically admitted it."

"That's what I was afraid of! They were right. That bastard Bowden arranged it and my idiot son fell into the trap. They got me, using my son. They'll pay dearly for this!"

"I don't understand," stammered Linda.

As if he'd just remembered he wasn't alone, Charley turned to the woman. "It's not necessary for you to understand. I don't have you around to understand, or to think!" His glance traveled over her and the girl shuddered. "Get undressed and into bed!" he ordered her. "I need to relax a bit."

Linda took a step back. "But Mr. Giotto, I only just got out of your son's bed!"

Charley Giotto was enraged. He went up to her and started hitting her, then grabbed her and tossed her like a sack on the bed. He threw himself on her and in his fury tore off her clothes like some beast from the jungle tearing at its prey. She had never hurt so much or felt such disgust for what a man could do to her body. His rage gave him unusual strength for his age, and Linda thought her ordeal would never end. When Giotto's men had picked her up off the streets and made her work in one of the clubs he controlled, she thought she had found paradise. But in three years on the streets of Chicago, not one of her customers had ever used her like this.

She stayed still until she heard his breath deepening, indicating he was asleep. With difficulty she dragged herself to the bathroom and the image she saw made her cry out softly in fear. Her lips were torn from his blows, her body was covered in bites and bruises, and his smell on her skin disgusted her. She bent over the basin and emptied her stomach. When she stood up, sweating, she had made her decision. Her little hometown in Kansas that had once seemed like a prison was now her only escape. Her parents had lost all trace of her, but she would fall at their feet and ask them to forgive her and let her stay with them. Why not? Anything was better than the hell of Chicago and Giotto.

She tiptoed out of the room, got into her car, and disappeared as the dawn was breaking.

◆ ◆ ◆

Franco drove without seeing the beautiful landscape around him. It had snowed and it was as if a soft white cloud had left the sky and settled lightly on the streets, the roofs, and the trees. His mind traveled faster than his car. Last night was the final blow. Linda was a girl who always managed to satisfy him, but the only thing she managed to do last night was to make him remember *her*.

After that night, he hadn't called her, he hadn't sent flowers. He knew there'd be no turning back once he started and the road that opened ahead frightened him. He wasn't used to a woman controlling him so completely, especially one who'd never been in his bed. That virginal innocence of hers, so foreign to him, drove him crazy. All his life he had fallen into bed with experienced women who knew they were there solely for his entertainment. He didn't care if they enjoyed themselves or not. All that mattered was his satisfaction. With Lyn, though, things would be different. He understood that with her it wouldn't only be their bodies that spoke but their souls, and he didn't know if he was ready for something like that. He had never shared his thoughts or feelings with anyone. He had lost his mother when he was five years old, and the strictness with which his father had raised him, the way of life he'd taught him, didn't leave any room for sensitivity. Then there was the other, more important thing: Lyn must never learn about their work. The Mafia, and the veil of secrecy and fear that covered it were not suitable subjects for conversation.

When Franco finally looked around to see where he was, he was shocked to find himself right outside her house. He had gotten her address from Bowden, but he never imagined he'd drive there unconsciously. He couldn't believe his luck. Magdalini had just come outside and it was obvious that she was about to go for a walk. He realized his heart was beating unevenly and, angry with himself, he took a deep breath to recover. Magdalini had now walked out of the gate and was moving quickly, almost dancing, as she headed away.

Franco let the car roll slowly forward until he caught up with her. She turned toward the vehicle, assuming that the driver had stopped to ask for directions, and her face lit up when she saw who it was. He got out of the car and approached her. Small blond curls escaped from the cap she was wearing, and her cheeks had begun to go red. Franco thought she was even more beautiful than he'd remembered.

"I didn't expect to see you outside my house," she said cheerfully. "What are you doing here?"

"Waiting for you. Are you going for a walk, or are you meeting someone?"

"No, I'm not meeting anyone. But it was so beautiful with the snow that I couldn't stay inside."

"Can I join you? Perhaps we can go somewhere together?"

"In the car?" she asked, and a tone of disappointment crept into her voice.

"Of course not," he hurried to answer. "Since you're going for a walk, I'll walk with you. I don't get outside and walk enough these days."

"So what do you do when it snows? Don't you come out to enjoy the special smell of the snow?"

"Nobody ever told me that the snow has a smell," he observed, smiling.

"Maybe not here," Magdalini accepted, "but in the place I'm from, everything smells lovely and special when it snows. The mountain above the house seems to breathe. I came out to find that frozen breath."

Her eyes were full of nostalgia and despite himself, Franco reached out his hand and touched her frozen cheek. As if she had come to her senses, Magdalini looked at him in embarrassment.

"I'm sorry. I got carried away by memories. If we don't start walking to warm ourselves up, we'll freeze," the girl added happily.

They began walking side by side and Franco asked her to tell him about her country, something that Magdalini had no difficulty doing. Her soft voice was like a caress in his ear; he watched her secretly as she spoke of the people she loved. She behaved as she would to any friend she'd met by chance. In fact, despite the dozens of women who had passed through his life, he'd never taken the trouble to understand any of them, or find out how they thought as people. He couldn't imagine what an enormous effort it took for Magdalini to behave like this. Her heart had missed a beat when she met him. Putting great pressure on herself, she tried not to let her eyes show what she was hiding in her heart, and she kept talking to him about her house and family because it was the only way she knew to keep him at a distance. It was as if the memory of her mother protected her from something she shouldn't do, something she was dying to do but was afraid of at the same time.

Magdalini finally broke off her monologue and stopped to look at him. "Have I bored you?" she asked shyly.

"No, nothing that you could say would bore me. But you speak with such love about your home that I wonder why you left and came to a foreign country."

"That's another long story and I'm very afraid that if we stay out in this freezing air any longer we'll both catch cold. What do you say? Shall we go back?"

"No," Franco said suddenly before he could control himself. He wasn't ready to say good-bye yet. "There's a café a little farther down. Shall we drop in for some hot chocolate?"

Magdalini seemed to hesitate at first, but soon nodded her head in agreement. With relief, Franco took a breath. With quick steps they reached the café and hurried into its warmth. As they sat together with their scalding chocolate in front of them, they both seemed embarrassed. Suddenly there was nothing to talk about and they weren't quite brave enough to raise their eyes and meet each other's gaze. Things were at a stalemate.

"So . . . now that we're not in the cold anymore, will you tell me why you came to Chicago?" he asked, continuing with a subject that seemed safe.

"Because I'm silly, I suppose," answered Magdalini. "The village was suffocating me. I wanted to see a new place—most of my sisters had already left and my aunt was able to offer me something different."

"Don't you like America?"

"They say it's the land of opportunity, of wealth. But I see it as a country of loneliness. Everyone is running to catch up—they don't have time to talk, to live, to breathe. And Chicago reminds me of a volcano."

"A volcano? Why?"

"Outside, it's just another peak. But inside, lava is boiling and at every moment it's ready to erupt. In the newspapers I see, they write terrible things. The Mafia has spread its tentacles everywhere; even the politicians obey them, people who should be above suspicion. Every now and then there's a murder and they say the Mafia is behind it. It's like an open secret, and that makes me furious."

Franco swallowed his mouthful of hot chocolate, then coughed nervously. Magdalini looked at him, frowning.

"What's the matter?" she asked. "Did I say something wrong?"

"Of course not. I just choked a little. You're right about everything you said, but all that's in the underworld. What do our lives have to do with all that?"

"It's not so simple. When the corruption is so widespread, no one can sleep peacefully in their beds. You meet a person who seems decent and you ask yourself if he's really like that or if he just acts that way to hide how deeply he's involved in something illegal."

"So if you feel that way, why do you stay?"

"I don't know," Magdalini answered, and her voice revealed a sad resignation.

Franco reached out his hand and covered hers. He felt it trembling slightly and without a second thought he brought it to his lips. The atmosphere suddenly became electric. Her thick eyelashes dropped down over her honey-colored eyes again, and he fixed his eyes on her half-open lips. The desire to cover them with his overwhelmed him.

"Lyn," he whispered. "I want to know. Do you feel like I do?"

She didn't ask him what he meant. She only nodded her head yes. When she looked up, her eyes were damp. "I'm afraid," she stammered in a voice that sounded like that of a frightened child.

"I swear to you that whatever happens, I'll never hurt you," he said. "Just let me stay beside you. I won't pressure you about anything. Just say that you're mine, otherwise I'll go crazy."

They came back when it was already getting dark and the snow had begun to fall again. Softly, like white butterflies, flakes fell on their shoulders and hair. Like shooting stars, the snowflakes gleamed pure white before they melted, leaving only a small drop of water to remind one of their presence. Franco and Magdalini looked at each other for a second. Invisible threads drew one to the other and it didn't take long before they embraced. His lips sought hers and she offered them willingly. His kiss was tender at first, but, as if he wanted to drink her in completely, it soon became deeper and more demanding until it left them breathless.

"When will I see you again?" he asked.

"When do you want to?" she replied softly.

"I'll come tomorrow night to pick you up. We'll go for dinner," he said to her, trying to control his voice. "I hope your aunt and uncle will let me take you out."

"I don't think they'll have any objections."

"Tomorrow then," he repeated and bent toward her again, but this time he held himself back. His kiss was gentle and he pulled back before he could be carried away.

As he walked to his car, his steps were as heavy as lead. He thought about running back, snatching Magdalini, and making love to her on the snow. He felt as if he had a fever. He was shaking, but at the same time he was sweating. He jumped into his car and left as if he was being chased.

Magdalini stood and watched the lights of his car disappear before she went inside. She needed a little time to recover before her aunt saw her flushed like this. She was madly in love despite the fact that everything she felt scared her. His embrace was the only place where she belonged. Only in his arms did she feel alive and happy.

She found her aunt waiting for her with anxiety written all over her face. "For God's sake, Magdalini!" she shouted as soon as she saw her. "Where were you? You went out for a little walk, and you were gone for four whole hours."

Magdalini looked at her watch and was herself shocked by how long she'd been gone. "I'm sorry, Aunt. I didn't realize so much time had passed."

Just then Peter came into the room. He didn't seem upset, like his wife. Instead, he was smiling. "What happened, young lady? You frightened your aunt! Did you get lost?"

"I went out for a walk, and I met a friend by chance. We went for hot chocolate. I didn't realize it was late . . . I didn't notice."

Something about the girl's tone made Anna suspicious. "Who did you meet, Magdalini? Does this friend have a name?"

"Um . . . I met Franco a little way down the street," she admitted, then stopped.

"Ha! Of course. And completely by chance, I suppose, he passed through our neighborhood." Anna's voice was full of cynicism.

Peter walked over to Magdalini and put his arms around her shoulders before he addressed his angry wife. "Hey, Anna, it seems to me that you're overdoing it. Lyn didn't commit a crime. The truth is she's a responsible person, and you're treating her like a teenager. And she didn't go out with a bum."

"We don't know that!" Anna was furious, and Magdalini looked at her in surprise.

"Do you know something and you're not telling me, Aunt? Maybe Franco—"

Peter cut in. "Your aunt, my dear, is overanxious. You're young and beautiful, just as he is young and handsome. Love needs soil to flower. And being older, I say, live it up, my girl!"

Magdalini approached her aunt, who was looking sadly at her. "I'm in love, Aunt," she explained. "Franco is everything I dreamed of, and I think he feels the same. Can you understand that?"

"Much better than you think," Anna answered bitterly.

"So, can you be happy for me?"

Anna looked tearfully at her niece. She stroked the girl's hair gently and nodded. "I hope you're happy with him," she said softly. "But be careful, Magdalini. You don't know him well yet. Don't be in a rush."

The next evening seemed very far off to Magdalini. The hours seemed to drag by, and her stomach was in a hard, painful knot. Franco arrived exactly on time, offering flowers to the two ladies in the house and accepting the whiskey that Peter poured for him. Anna didn't notice anything strange in the young man's behavior apart from the fact that he seemed very constrained toward Peter, while her husband did everything he could to impress him. The couple left after a half hour, followed immediately afterward by Peter, who said he had some business meeting to attend. He left his wife buried deep in her fear and her thoughts.

Franco had chosen a very fancy club for the evening, but Magdalini would have preferred something simpler without so many people or so much noise. Still, she didn't say anything to Franco, who behaved perfectly toward her all night. Only when they got up to dance did his uneven breath on her hair whisper what she wanted to hear.

◆　◆　◆

When Peter arrived at Bowden's office, Bowden greeted him with a glass of whiskey in his hand.

"So, my friend, I think we've managed it," Bowden announced triumphantly as soon as they sat down.

Peter nodded. "Tonight they went out together; yesterday he was waiting for her outside the house."

"So our fish bit, then. Not that I expected anything less with bait like that."

"Matthew, I don't feel so good about this."

"What nonsense! You're not grateful to me for my plan? We've taken his son hostage with love. Charley doesn't pose a threat to us anymore!"

"So the end justifies the means?"

"Would you prefer some of Giotto's thugs riddle you with bullets?"

"And now? What do you think's going to happen from now on?"

"Old man Giotto can't do anything."

"But doesn't he know what's happened with my niece?"

"Sure, he knows, but he's waiting. The boy was always very casual with women. Charley thinks the girl is just like the others. But he's lost the game. In a little while the market in Chicago will be ours and just in time. In a month a shipment's coming and Charley won't be able to stop us from disposing of it—he'll be so busy with his son's love affair."

"Yes, but what's going to happen to Lyn?"

"What do you think is going to happen? She's hit the jackpot! She's found herself a strong, very rich man who, as I understand it, she loves, and even better, he's in love with her. She'll have a fairy-tale life!"

"I'm not sure a story written by the Mafia is going to have much fairy-tale magic in it."

"Why not? Look at your wife. Or mine. What they don't know can't hurt them, my friend. And the little one doesn't ever need to know what sort of work her boyfriend does."

"I'm not so sure. Anyway, I don't want her to get hurt."

"Peter, my friend, you're a fool! Franco isn't likely to hurt your niece because he's very much in love with her. He'll marry her very soon and she won't believe her good luck. Listen to me because I know a thing or two. He was always busy between the best legs on the market, but he has no idea what someone as pure and untarnished as your little Lyn is like. It's her virginal charm that will throw him into the trap and hand him over to us unarmed."

"But doesn't Franco know who I am?"

"Up until now, the jobs we did under Charley's nose were small. It's unlikely that he's spoken to his son about little flies like us. He had people watch you mostly to know where you were, not because he was scared of you. But now, with the cargo we're bringing in, we're getting into a tough game. If Franco wasn't besotted with your niece, we'd be in big trouble. But the unsuspecting Franco is powerless now, and his father's completely boxed in. And where are we? On top! Come, have a drink, Peter! Tonight we should be celebrating!"

◆ ◆ ◆

Franco spent every evening with Magdalini. His father didn't appear to know anything, but in fact, he followed all his son's movements closely, and the more he learned, the more he was confused. For the first time in his life, he didn't know how to proceed. On the one hand, he couldn't speak to his son, because he was afraid of the young man's ego and he didn't want to clash openly with him. On the other hand, the girl didn't seem to be anything serious. And yet Franco hadn't been to bed with her yet, which confused the old man all the more. That wasn't his son's way. The photographs that his people had supplied showed a girl of rare beauty. Logically, Franco should have had his fill and moved on by now. Except for dinners at expensive clubs and a little dancing, Charley's people had nothing more to report. Franco picked her up early from the house and took her back early too, without even keeping her in his car for long.

In any case, time was running out and the old man couldn't wait any longer. He'd speak to his son and tell him whose niece this Lyn was. There were rumors about a shipment that would arrive in a few weeks, and if Peter were allowed to distribute it undisturbed, he'd break their monopoly in the area. He had his suspicions that behind this idiot there must be some antagonist of his from the west. Someone wanted to destroy him, but he wasn't about to allow it.

◆ ◆ ◆

Franco parked his car outside the house and switched off the engine. This was always the most difficult moment. He had to say good night to her in the most formal way. He had to hold back his passion, to limit himself to some burning kisses, even though he wanted something else.

"Here we are," he said sweetly to her.

"Yes, I noticed," she answered, and something in her voice made him look at her in surprise.

"Tomorrow again?"

"No, I don't think so," Magdalini said in a steady voice. "For a month, you've been coming here every evening and taking me to expensive clubs, although I've been trying to tell you tactfully that I don't like them. However big Chicago is, I can't imagine there are any clubs left that we haven't been to."

"And where would you like me to take you, Lyn?" he asked with a touch of bitterness in his voice.

"Somewhere where we can talk and get closer to each other!"

"Didn't it cross your mind that that's exactly what I'm avoiding? Do you know how hard I have to try to control myself so as not to . . ."

"What?" Magdalini asked.

"Lyn, try to understand, sweetheart. I don't want to scare you. But if we're not always with people I don't think I can control myself. I want you so much. At night I imagine you naked in my arms and I want to hit my head against the wall!"

"Why do you think I feel differently?"

Franco looked at her as if he were seeing her for the first time. He could hardly breathe. His hands reached toward her, although it was unnecessary, since her body had already moved toward his. Her perfume surrounded him like an intoxicating mist. He felt her trembling, and before he lost control, he pulled away carefully.

"Lyn, are you sure?"

She answered with a single nod of her head.

With trembling hands, he started the car and they disappeared into the night. He knew where they were going. It was a small apartment of his that nobody knew about, not even his father. They reached it quickly and went inside. Franco didn't turn on the light. He picked his precious cargo up in his arms and headed for the bedroom. Their breath, hurried and short, was the only sound to be heard in the utter silence.

With adoration bordering on awe, he bent to kiss her. Now that his erotic dream had reached the point of becoming reality, he felt himself shaking with anticipation. His lips traveled to her pure white throat whose softness he'd dreamed of a dozen times. Her dress ended up on the floor, and her body seemed to be wrapped in its own light, which tore the darkness of the room in two. His hands moved lightly along her skin on an intoxicating voyage. Lost in a vortex he didn't know existed, he couldn't breathe and he felt like he didn't even have a body. He was a shadow, a transparent cloak that covered her, unable to move away from her velvety softness.

He took her face in his hands and his eyes met hers in adoration. "I love you," he told her as if he were swearing an oath.

"I love you too," she answered in a voice that sounded like music.

He went to free her from his weight but she held him.

"Don't leave," she whispered. "This is your place. And mine is in your arms."

◆ ◆ ◆

Anna had reached a state of hysteria. She had waited all night for Magdalini to return. Peter tried to comfort her and bring her back to reason.

"Calm down, my sweet. I'm sure that nothing bad has happened. Unless you mean it's bad that finally . . ."

"What do you mean?"

"Well, just think a little, my dear. They're young and very much in love. They probably spent the night together. You shouldn't put Lyn in a difficult position by letting her know we were aware of her absence."

"So you don't want me to say anything?"

"Exactly. If Lyn wants to tell you, let her do it herself."

"Do you know what I've been thinking more and more recently? If I hadn't brought Magdalini here, right now she'd probably be married to one of the village lads. She'd have children and they'd be living a peaceful life."

"And an unbearably boring one for her," Peter added. "If Lyn wanted something like that she wouldn't have agreed to follow you! But she wanted something else."

"She came here to study, not fall in love with some man we hardly know."

"In God's name, Anna, I don't know why you're objecting like this! Franco loves her. Or maybe you even doubt that?"

"No," she admitted. "I'd be blind if I didn't see the adoration in his eyes when he looks at her. But we don't know anything about him. If only he was one of the young people we knew . . ."

"The heart doesn't like to be directed, my dear, and you know that. Your niece loves Franco and it's up to you to show some understanding."

"I'm afraid I don't have a choice," his wife muttered sadly.

◆ ◆ ◆

Magdalini stirred lightly in Franco's arms and he woke immediately. Light sleep was necessary in the work he did.

"Did you wake up, my love?" he asked.

"Mmm . . . what time is it?"

"Nearly five."

Magdalini jumped up as if an electric shock had passed through her. "Good Lord! I must leave. My aunt and uncle will have gone crazy with worry."

"We'll be at your house in twenty minutes, don't worry. Your aunt doesn't seem to particularly like me."

"Don't blame her. She loves me very much and she's even more afraid for me."

"I don't blame her. I respect her and I'd like her to trust me. You know, I lost my mother when I was very young."

Magdalini sat up and looked at him with interest. They'd been together a month now, and she hadn't managed to persuade Franco to tell her about himself. When she asked him about his life, he would immediately change the subject, and Magdalini never persisted. Her mother had always told her that every soul is like a box with a heavy lock. There are hundreds of keys but only one opens it, and that happens when the moment is right. If you hurry, if you insist, it's as if you're holding an axe, and the box will break, come to pieces, disappear before you, and you'll never learn its secrets. If you wait for it to open by itself, it will reveal its treasures to you.

"Do you remember her at all?" she dared to ask him.

"Hardly at all. She was beautiful and tender. I remember her hands holding me. I remember how safe I felt in her arms."

"And your father? He must have suffered very much when he lost her, and so young."

"My father, Lyn, is a hard person. He never felt anything except for the pleasure he got from bullying people around him."

Magdalini smiled. "We have more in common than I knew. The way you describe your father—my grandfather was like that. My mother told me that she never saw him smile. He was always grim—demanding and complaining. All of us were afraid of him except my sister Julia. Only she could do what she wanted around him. To the point where the difficult old man would let her sit on his knee."

Franco was sure that Magdalini's grandfather was nothing like hard Charley Giotto. At worst, the old man in Greece might have killed a wild pig. Charley, on the other hand, didn't hesitate to shoot someone who was useless to him, or even just annoying. *Just like you.* Franco hardly heard the little voice that whispered that last phrase to him. Since he'd fallen in love, he'd concluded that he could be two people. One would always be the Franco Lyn adored. He would do anything to make her happy. He'd give her the world if she asked for it. But the other was the opposite of the first, the dark side of Franco Giotto. Like his father, he could manage "family business" well; he could be tough and scatter death around without regrets.

Before he left her house, Franco waited to see her disappear behind the front door. Then he set off whistling. It had been the best night of his life. This creature was the best thing he could ask for in his prayers. After the magical moments she had given him, he was forever her slave. When he got home, he went into his room still whistling, and was startled to find his father waiting for him, sitting in an armchair. The smell of his cigar had filled the room, a sign that he'd been waiting a rather long time.

"What's going on, Charley?" Franco asked. For years now, he'd been calling his father by his first name. After all, he was no longer a father, really; he was more like a colleague.

"I was waiting for you," Charley answered drily.

"I can see that. I want to know why. You don't usually wait for me like an anxious mother."

"I wanted to speak to you."

"And this conversation couldn't wait till the morning?"

"It's morning already. Sit down, Franco! It's a very serious subject."

Franco first poured himself a drink, then sat down opposite his father.

"I know that you've been going out with a girl for some time now. I also know she's not one of ours."

"Have you been following me?"

"You could call it that."

"And since when have you cared what I do and who I do it with? Is this a delayed feeling of responsibility or paternal anxiety?"

"Neither one nor the other. I brought you up in a way that would make you capable of running the sort of business we're in. I brought you up to take over some day. But, from what I understand, I wasn't smart enough."

"Charley, if you have something to say to me, say it and let's be done with it. I want to sleep."

"Do you know someone called Peter Carver?"

"Yes, that is . . ."

"He's of Greek origin, a third- or fourth-generation immigrant. He married a Greek woman from his family's village and brought her here."

"Why are you telling me all this now? What do I care about the origins of Lyn's aunt and uncle?"

"I'm coming to that."

"Don't even think about saying a word about her."

"Well, well! What's this I'm hearing? My son's in love?"

"And what am I hearing from you? Do you even remember what our relationship is like? Anyway, father or not, I won't let you interfere in my personal life."

Franco's eyes flashed fire, but Charley stopped him with a movement of his hand. "Calm down. The Carver family never managed to make any money. They were workers when they came to America and they stayed workers. But Peter was cleverer. When he realized that he wouldn't get anywhere just by working, he began moving in other circles. He began with smuggling, and I must confess I underestimated him. I should have confronted him as a real rival and cleared him off the scene years ago. A year ago Peter met Matthew Bowden, and they became inseparable. They did a lot of business together and Bowden introduced him to quite a few of our boys, who backed him because he's bringing in a big shipment of cocaine. They're expecting it any day now."

Franco froze like a statue, unable to believe what he was hearing. "Are you saying that Peter has joined the Mafia?"

"And without my approval, of course. What do you say to that?"

"Unbelievable!"

"But there's more to it. That fox Bowden realized that I wouldn't just be sitting there with my arms crossed. Peter had already noticed that my people were following him so he got himself some hired guns to protect him, his wife, and your precious beloved. But his friend thought, and correctly, that if I wanted to get rid of Peter, a few heavy-weight idiots wouldn't stop me. So he decided to do something that would relieve him forever of the danger I represented: he arranged for you to be at his house on New Year's Eve."

"Wait! Where are you going with this? Do you mean to tell me that Lyn—"

"The girl, unwittingly, was the bait he threw to you, and you were hooked like a trout! Do you finally get it? With you in love with your Greek beauty, I wouldn't do anything, in case I fell out with you."

Franco emptied his glass in one gulp, then refilled it. His head was ready to burst. "Does she know?" was all he asked, holding his breath until the answer came.

"From what I know, no. They took her like a lamb to the slaughter. They bet on her like a racehorse. As you can understand, nothing was certain. She might have made no impression on you, then their plan would have failed. The word's going around that they planned to finish me off if the seduction hadn't worked. Now do you finally get it?"

"Very well. And what do you want now?"

"I want you to act smartly. Try to find out as much as you can about the shipment, and the day it arrives we'll be there. Once again the newspapers will write about the settling of scores in the Mafia, and Peter will be history, while we'll have the whole shipment of goods at our disposal. Besides that, we'll send a clear message to anyone else who has their sights on expanding into our territory. As for the girl, enjoy her as much as you like, but fast, because afterward she'll be . . . used up. Unless you think she'd could be useful for some job, in which case, bring her to me. Linda's disappeared—we need a new one."

Franco looked at his father, and for the first time, Charley felt uncomfortable under his son's gaze. The younger man sat down again in his chair. The silence that reigned in the room now went through him like an electric current. Without hurrying, he emptied his glass, then stood up to fill it one more time. "So," he said finally, but his voice had changed. "So the story goes like this, and it doesn't even occur to you that it could happen differently. For example, perhaps for the first time in Mafia history, the son gets rid of the father."

Charley went to stand up but his son's look stopped him.

"I listened to you," Franco went on, his voice ominously low. "Now you'll listen to me, and very carefully! Your life depends on what I'm going to tell you."

"Do you dare to threaten me?" Charlie objected, red in the face.

"I'll dare a lot more . . . my dear father. I love Lyn very much."

"Even after what I've told you?"

"Especially after what you've told me. She has no idea what's going on around her. She's only a victim in this story, like her aunt. She's a rare creature, and I'm very lucky that she loves me. I'm going to marry Lyn, and very soon. And you won't lift a finger to stop it, Charley. We'll be a loving family, and you'll accept Peter with open arms. You'll introduce yourself to him, and officially at that. And to show you I'm not a fool, I'll speak to Peter. One third of his shipment will belong to us as punishment for what he plotted under our noses, unless he wants to wind up with a bullet through his head. Work is one thing; Lyn is another. Neither she nor Anna will ever find out anything, like most of the women in our circle."

"I can't believe what I'm hearing."

"A pity! Because that's exactly how things are going to happen."

"And if I refuse?"

"Then the newspapers will have a lot of work to do in the next few days, dealing with the Mafia settling its scores. We can start now if you wish."

Charley didn't manage to see any of his son's rapid movements. The only thing he saw was the barrel of a gun pointing at him. The shock was intense. "You dare . . ." he began, out of breath, but he couldn't continue. The cold steel was resting now on his temple.

"After your dirty schemes involving Lyn, you're lucky to be alive. And I may still decide to open the gates of Hell!"

"What do you mean?"

"That I'm not an idiot! I know very well that Nero—do you remember him?—was the boss of this area before you, and you were one of his boys, right? So, I know that it wasn't Bik who finished him off, although he paid for it, but you. You killed Bik too, because he was next in succession, and everyone worshipped you for avenging an unjust death—and they celebrated by announcing that you were their new boss."

"How could you know all that? You were a baby when those things happened."

"You always told me I had to know everything about my enemies."

"And you regard me as an enemy?"

"You don't want to have this conversation, believe me. So, tonight I'm going to propose to Lyn. But first I have to have a few words with my future . . . uncle. You put on your best manners to receive my bride's family! And something else. I want my mother's ring."

"Franco, think again about what you're doing. You're letting them celebrate at our expense!"

Franco ridiculed him. "You're getting old, Charley. You're getting old and you don't see what's happening under your nose. It's been years since you had the monopoly, and sooner or later, someone like this was bound to spring up. It could have been someone from the west. At least these guys are amateurs and we can control them. But now the market will be saturated. That's why I told you to introduce yourself to him, and officially. You, Peter, and Bowden will start to go out regularly, and the newspapers will write about the three large enterprises that decided to join forces. The message will reach where it needs to and yet again you'll get credit you don't deserve, this time for your foresight. Once we've got those two crooks tied to you, we'll stop losing the small percentages from their smuggling, and we'll be able to expand to the east. I've heard that Nick's not doing well. He keeps losing ground to some newcomer, someone called Harley, or something like that. We'll get rid of him and we'll expand ourselves. You see—while you waste your time on small, unimportant things, I've been working."

"Could you please lower your weapon?" Charley was now speaking calmly. "I don't know what annoys me more, the gun pointed at me or the fact that you're holding it."

Franco obeyed. "You didn't leave me much choice," he said without any remorse. "It's really up to you whether this scene will be repeated. Maybe next time I'll be more upset and my finger will slip on the trigger."

"Are you threatening me again?"

"You haven't given me your word that things will go as I said."

"You have it," said Charley and got up. Before he left the room he turned and looked at his son. "In the end you may be right. I'm getting old, and I underestimate people I shouldn't. I underestimated you."

Charley left the room, closing the door behind him, and Franco collapsed on his bed like an empty sack. He'd said and done things he never thought he would ever do. He looked at the weapon in his hands. A short time ago he had rested it against his father's head without feeling any shame, nor did he feel any now. He loved Lyn. She was his and in a little while she'd be his wife. Only that had any meaning.

◆ ◆ ◆

Dressed as a bride, Magdalini was the most beautiful thing Franco had ever seen. She was a vision in her white gown, her pale face shining with love for him. Peter was proud and smiling, while Anna couldn't hide her complex emotions. Despite all her objections, when Franco asked formally for her niece's hand, she gave her approval because the young man was so obviously in love with Magdalini and moreover he had managed to earn her trust. When the bride left her uncle's arm to take the hand of her fiancé, the two men exchanged a glance that only they understood.

After Franco's visit to Peter's office on that morning a short time ago, they both understood the path they were walking on. It was a lovely spring day and Peter had begun it in a good mood. In three days the shipment would be in their hands, the dealers were waiting, and his bank account would fill with new zeros. It was the biggest haul he'd made in recent years, and he was grateful to Bowden, who had opened his eyes. Not that his smuggling hadn't been profitable, but now they'd see him differently. The Mafia had begun to accept him; they'd make Charley accept him too. Franco's arrival made him uneasy, however. The secretary announced him, and by the time they met, Peter had barely managed to drive away his frowning expression and replace it with a warm smile.

"Welcome," he called, as soon as Franco entered his office, but he couldn't make anything out from the young man's expression.

They shook hands and Franco sat down comfortably. He looked around inquiringly before turning to Peter, who hadn't yet sat down.

"What time does your secretary take a break?" the young man asked calmly.

"But . . . whatever time I tell her. Why?"

"Tell her to leave now. I don't want her secretly listening to our conversation."

Peter didn't consider disobeying for a moment. He sent his secretary away and sat down opposite Franco, worried.

"What's going on, son?" he asked.

"I like you calling me son. Soon we'll be related. I plan to ask Lyn to marry me," Franco announced drily, without smiling.

Peter went to stand up and offer his hand, but Franco stopped him with a movement.

"Don't be in too much of a hurry . . . Uncle! First, we two have to have a little chat."

"Really, I don't understand," Peter stammered, now full of unpleasant foreboding.

"You *will* understand soon. You're a smart man, from what I've learned, and your trick with Bowden—"

Peter abruptly cut him off. "What are you talking about?"

"If you interrupt me again, I'll make sure you won't even be able to say your own name from now on."

Peter nodded, frightened now, and Franco continued.

"As I was saying, it was a clever trick, and it worked. Lyn and I fell in love, just as you wanted us to. I'll disregard the fact that it was the most immoral and disgusting thing an uncle could do to his niece. What you didn't take into account, neither you nor your buddy Bowden, was that I'm not an idiot. I know very well how to separate my work from my personal life. I'd have killed you on the spot if that wouldn't bring unbearable sadness to Lyn and Anna, who I respect very much because she has real class, unlike you, who's just another bastard. So listen carefully to how things are going to happen. Tonight I'm going to ask for Lyn's hand, and of course you're going to agree. The wedding will take place in two months. The shipment is due on Tuesday, and you're going to give me a third of it."

"But—"

"That's the third time you've interrupted me and each time you do it, you're risking your life. Right after my engagement to Lyn, my dear uncle, you'll start to make public appearances with my father, and the Mafia will get the message. From now on you won't do anything without informing me and the profits will always be split three ways. I don't know if you and Bowden imagine yourselves as bosses, but you'll only be the operatives of me and my father, and you'll take your orders from us. Do I make myself understood? If you or Bowden, or the two of you together, have any objection, you'll be found with a bullet through the head and I'll be rid of you. The same thing will happen if you try to mess with me again!"

Peter listened without speaking, while beads of sweat began appearing on his forehead.

Franco continued, "I gather I've made myself more than understood. Naturally the women won't find out anything; we'll be a loving family, but apart from family ties, we'll also be bound by the vow of silence. *Omertà*, Uncle Peter!"

He left without saying anything else, certain that behind him, Peter had collapsed. Caught at his own game, Peter hadn't expected that the tender Franco would behave like a true Giotto. He had to call Bowden, but he didn't have the courage to pick up the telephone.

Everything happened as Franco said it would. The shipment was divided, and in the two months leading up to the wedding, Peter went out quite often with Charley and Franco, while the newspapers began to write that some big business deal was in the pipeline. Following his meeting with Franco, Peter received a pair of diamond cufflinks and on the card was written one word: *omertà*. Bowden received the same gift.

On the day he'd met with Peter, Franco had dropped by Magdalini's house in the evening as if nothing had happened, and her uncle's coolness and impeccable behavior had impressed him. Peter behaved as warmly toward his niece's suitor as usual, and only Franco could detect the fear in his eyes. He'd seen it so many times in his other victims that it was easy for him to recognize. He didn't know for sure, but he suspected that Peter and Bowden had had an intense discussion after he'd left the office and Peter must have scared Bowden as much as he'd been scared himself. Franco knew he didn't need to worry about those two anymore.

He had left the house with Magdalini and headed directly for his little apartment, where, as soon as the door closed behind him, she fell into his arms with longing.

"I missed you," she said, and her voice had a childish tone that moved him.

"Me too," he whispered. "We'd only been separated for a few hours, but the only thing I wanted was to have you in my arms forever. I love you, Lyn. I worship you!"

His lips found hers eager to respond. Her body was more ready than his, and her hunger for him was even greater than his own. She gave herself to him with an intensity that shook him, leaving him breathless in her naked embrace, while at the same time he still felt thirsty for her. Only a few moments passed before an unexpected movement of her body made him lose control again. He wanted to propose to her. His mother's ring was waiting in a box hidden in his jacket, but the shapely legs of his beloved had already wrapped themselves around him. Her lips were exploring his face, and her hands spread a shudder of delight across his back. He couldn't hold back. This woman drove him crazy. All other thoughts evaporated. Her body was the paradise that made him feel complete happiness.

The diamond ring found its place on her finger some hours later, but even its myriad of iridescent glints couldn't compare with the light that shone from her eyes and the alabaster beauty of her body. Magdalini looked uncertainly at the huge stone and her expression filled with wonder.

"What's that?" she asked him softly.

"That is my mother's ring. She always wore it on her hand. I remember how it shone."

"And why are you giving it to me?"

"Because it's my way of saying that I love you and I'll honor you all my life. Be my wife, Lyn. That's the only way I can go on living! From the first moment I met you I understood that if I didn't make you mine, I'd go crazy."

Magdalini fixed her eyes, full of tears, on his. She tried to find the truth in their depths. She found the love that burned in his heart and hid herself in his arms. As soon as her naked body touched his, Franco felt the intoxication of her perfume again. He laid her down and, despite her slight objections, began to explore her hidden hollows. Like a thirsty bee he began to drink the nectar of the flower he was holding, and he stayed there until he felt her body shudder uncontrollably, abandoned to a pleasure she had never known. But Franco experienced an even greater surprise. For the first time in his life, a woman's climax brought him to the same dizzying height, the same emotional peak. For the first time the satisfaction of another being was more meaningful than his own. Afterward he embraced Magdalini, who hadn't yet got her breath back, like a precious piece of porcelain.

On the day of their wedding, the young couple didn't stay long at the reception that followed the ceremony. They were in a hurry and they didn't bother to hide it. Most of the guests smiled understandingly. The two newlyweds were so lovely. Anna said good-bye to her niece with tears in her eyes. Franco had arranged a monthlong honeymoon in Europe, but it would last longer than that.

Before Franco left he gave strict instructions to his people as well as to his father. He didn't want any trouble while he was away; he didn't want anything to go wrong that would require them to bother him. It was obvious to everyone that Franco had taken the reins of control in his hands. He did it in such a complete, strong way that Charley didn't know whether he should feel sorry that he'd unwittingly lost the role of boss so soon, or be proud of his son who was carrying on what he'd begun in a way worthy of the Giotto name. He preferred the latter. His son seemed ready for everything, and Charley didn't want a confrontation with him. Besides, he had to admit that Franco had brought a new impetus to their work. Their control over their territory was now undisputed and the marriage to Lyn was regarded as a smart move. Peter's rise had made the other big bosses uneasy, but Franco's new role pleased them. There was always a need for new blood and the young man had guts and brains; he'd demonstrated that on many occasions.

In addition, Lyn's wholesomeness and virginal beauty completed the image of the good family that the Mafia demanded. Franco would go far, they all said.

◆ ◆ ◆

The honeymoon, which lasted two months, was an endless fairy tale for them both. When they finally had to go back, they reluctantly said good-bye to their carefree life. Back in Chicago, everyday reality was waiting for them and they couldn't live forever as tourists. When they arrived at the Giotto family's enormous house, the staff was lined up waiting to wish them well, and Magdalini greeted, one by one, the army of people who would be working for her from now on.

Charley was waiting for them in his office. He stood up to greet them and kissed his son and his bride, then placed a small box in the young woman's hands. "It's my wife's jewelry," he explained. "I think from now on you should be wearing it," he added, without a trace of emotion.

Magdalini hugged the box to her chest before raising her tear-filled eyes to her father-in-law. "Thank you very much," she said, as a lump rose in her throat.

Immediately afterward Franco showed his wife their bedroom, where Magdalini looked around her, enchanted.

"And to think, when I came to America, I thought the room in my aunt's house was enormous. This is a whole house!" she cried out happily.

"Whatever you don't like you can change. Not only here, but every-where. Except, of course, for my father's room and office."

"I wouldn't even think of changing his rooms. By the way, Franco, what should I call him? Do you think he would like it if I called him 'father'?"

"It's better if you call him by his name."

"But . . ." Magdalini seemed embarrassed. "Should I call him just Charley, as if he were my friend?"

"Believe me, it won't annoy him at all. Besides, that's what I call him."

"That's not right. He's your father, and you owe him respect. Didn't you see how he welcomed us into his house?"

"This was my mother's house, and it will pass to me. Basically we're showing Charley hospitality."

Magdalini scolded him. "Franco, that's no way to talk, after his kind gesture, giving me his wife's jewelry."

Franco didn't know whether to destroy the delusions of the innocent girl, who was looking at him admonishingly, or to let her go on believing that Charley had made the ultimate sacrifice, parting with his wife's jewels. He may have been young when his mother died, but from the careless gossip of the staff, he'd learned that their marriage wasn't happy, except for during a very short time. Charley's hard character on the one hand, and his mother's sensitive soul on the other, didn't help create harmony in the relationship. He knew that his father had begun to neglect his wife from early on, to the point where he completely ignored her, while she grew more and more unhappy. Franco decided to say nothing to his wife. It was too soon to poison her mind and her spirit. Perhaps it was unnecessary. For now, Charley obeyed his orders to the letter. Franco had managed to warn him about their return and had told him exactly what to do to welcome Magdalini. He looked at his new bride now, as she held open the box of jewels and admired them like a child with her toys. Her eyes were full of tenderness as she devoutly touched the pearls and diamonds that adorned the exquisite pieces.

"They're so beautiful," the girl commented in admiration. "She must have glowed when she wore them. How I wish I'd seen her."

"There's a portrait of her in the sitting room," Franco responded.

Magdalini's reaction caught him by surprise. With the box still in her hands, she dashed out of the room. Franco followed her as she ran through the great house like a child until she stopped suddenly in front of the painting. The young woman fixed her eyes on the image of her husband's mother.

"You look like her," she said to him in a low voice.

"Everyone says I look just like Charley," Franco replied wryly.

"The people who say that don't have any perception. You have your father's eyes, of course, but the look in them is your mother's. Your lips are like hers too. And look! In the portrait she's wearing that pearl necklace. How beautiful she is."

Franco felt a tug at his heart; his wife's reaction had moved him. He coughed to clear his throat, and Magdalini turned toward him.

"I'm sorry if I made you feel sad," she murmured, embarrassed.

"No. But it's been a long time since anyone in this house thought about my mother. Perhaps nobody ever did, not even her husband."

"Franco," she scolded him again. "Now you're not being nice. And even you don't know what went on between the two of them."

"What I know is that you have a heart of gold," he said and hugged her.

Life in the Giotto house soon began to resume its everyday ways, ways that Magdalini had to learn. In the beginning Franco was worried that his wife would be bored in the big house, that she would perhaps experience the loneliness his mother once felt. But he soon realized his mistake. She might have the airs and the ways of a true American, but inside Magdalini was and would always remain a dynamic and very clever Greek girl, ready to meet every challenge. Franco received a report each evening from his people, who stayed at the house to provide security. He learned what had happened throughout each day and it was as entertaining as it was admirable.

When the father and son left after breakfast that first morning, Magdalini went straight to the kitchen. The staff, who were having their own breakfast at that hour, didn't know what to do. They all jumped up and stood in line, but his wife poured herself a coffee and sat down with them at the table.

"I refuse to drink coffee by myself, and anyway, there's so much I have to learn that this way I can save time," she explained to them.

At first the staff was very formal and stiff around her, but she soon won them all over and easily crossed the lines that separated them. After that first intrusion into the kitchen, she wandered through the whole house, examining the rooms one by one, except for those that belonged to her father-in-law, and making notes on a pad. At the evening meal, Magdalini was very cheerful. Franco noticed that there were flowers in all the vases, the place settings were different from the usual ones, and the food wasn't like anything he'd eaten at this table before. He looked at his father, who had also observed the changes.

"What sort of service set is this? Where did you find it?" he asked his daughter-in-law, trying to make his voice sound strict.

"It's not the only one," Magdalini answered cheerfully. "The house has twelve everyday sets and sixteen formal ones. Do you believe it? I couldn't count the tablecloths, although I can't understand why we have so many because they're all the same. There's not a single colored one. They're all white," she concluded sadly.

"You can buy new ones, my love," Franco suggested affectionately.

She smiled at him. "That's what I plan to do. I don't see any reason for us to eat as if we're expecting some ambassador, especially when it's just the three of us. Besides, it's boring."

Charley stopped himself from saying what he wanted to in reply; instead, he stayed silent. He was irritated by this creature who seemed to have inexhaustible reserves of stamina and enthusiasm, nor did he like seeing his son behaving like a lovestruck schoolboy.

"They told me that you went to the kitchen today," Franco said.

They had finished eating and were drinking coffee in the sitting room, while Charley had withdrawn to his office.

"Yes, I had to get to know the staff and learn some things. Why do you ask?"

"You must have surprised them."

Magdalini sat up straight in her chair. "Ah, Franco, we have to discuss a few things, while we're still at the beginning," she said seriously. "In my aunt's house, they didn't let me do anything. I was bored to death, but it wasn't my house and I didn't want to upset the order of things, so I went along with it. But I refuse to spend my time like a woman of leisure here. I refuse to have areas of my house that are 'forbidden zones,' except, of course, for Charley's spaces. If I want to dig in the garden, I won't ask Joshua, the gardener. If I feel like drinking my coffee in the kitchen with Mary, the cook, I'll do it without a second thought. And if I'm dying for some sort of food, I'll cook it myself. Do you know that the menu that's hanging up in the kitchen has just ten dishes, to be served in rotation? How can we eat the exact same thing every ten days?"

"I always said there was something that annoyed me about the food here," Franco said cheerfully.

"It's as if we're in jail with a strict routine! I've made up my mind to oversee this household, not just be a guest in some hotel. Unless you prefer us to rent a small, convenient apartment where I'll do all the work myself."

"I don't think it's necessary for us to do something so drastic."

"Then don't interfere again in my work!" she declared abruptly, although her eyes were smiling.

"OK—I only hope we won't have a mass exodus of the staff because you've disturbed their routine."

"There's no way that will happen. They've already accepted everything I've told them, and they're happy. Don't forget you married a

Greek, and now you'll have to put up with the consequences. In my country, a woman who gets married busies herself with her household."

"In fact, my little Greek woman, I underestimated you, and I never do that. I'm surprised I did it with you. I didn't expect you to fit in so well here. Tell me, though, will your . . . housekeeping allow you time to see Anna?"

The next day she left for her aunt's house, having given clear instructions to the staff about what tasks they should do in her absence. The cook was happily surprised when she told her not to prepare anything because she would cook herself when she got back. She had been dying to finally eat some Greek food and she'd made up her mind to put some Greek dishes on the table.

"So, bravo!" the cook announced as soon as the kitchen door had closed behind Magdalini. "It's been a long time since a woman set foot in here, and she's a woman with guts, this little one!"

The whole staff was pleasantly surprised by Magdalini. Some, like Mary, had spent their whole lives in the big house. They'd known Charley's wife, the beautiful but passive housewife. They'd tested their endurance under the harshness of Charley. They were tired of cleaning and taking care of a virtually empty house and now that they saw it coming to life, they liked it.

Anna stood in her living room, impatiently waiting for her niece to arrive. When Magdalini finally got there, her aunt saw her looking beautiful and smiling, and a weight was lifted from her shoulders. She hugged her niece eagerly and listened carefully to her news. She laughed when Magdalini described her energetic involvement in the everyday management of her new house. Anna mentally congratulated her sister on the way she'd brought up her daughter, on how she'd allowed her spirit to grow strong and her sharp mind to develop. When Magdalini was staying with her aunt and uncle, she'd behaved differently, more shyly, but now Anna saw a changed woman. Franco's love had filled Magdalini with self-confidence. The girl knew both her strength and her limits perfectly, and Anna admired her for that. She was delighted when Magdalini invited her to the Giotto house for traditional Greek food.

On the night that Anna and Peter joined them for dinner, Charley sat at the table and groaned with displeasure. He didn't recognize any of the dishes he saw on the cheerful tablecloth embroidered with daisies. When he raised his eyes to his son and saw the adoration with which he looked at his wife, it took all his self-control not to throw down his napkin and leave the table. He had put up with a great deal during the past week, as his daughter-in-law had taken over the household, and he hardly recognized where he was anymore. Even the arrangement of the furniture had changed under this wretched woman. The dissatisfaction he felt didn't allow him to admit how tasty the meal was. His intense dislike of her didn't let him see how much warmer the house, which used to look like a hotel, had become.

As Charley saw it, the worst thing was Magdalini's own demeanor. She appeared not to notice how coldly he behaved to her. Instead, she was always polite and affectionate toward him. She greeted him happily at the table each night, and when she bought him a really beautiful silk robe as a gift, she presented it to him with a kiss for which he'd been quite unprepared. In Charley's eyes, all this seemed hypocritical, and often he reached his limit. But he didn't dare say anything. His son's eyes were always on him. And it wasn't the right time to clash with him. In the eastern region, Franco had taken over completely now, while the annoyances from the west had disappeared. Everyone was subservient to his strength. Charley was choking but he was hemmed in. He missed his old days of glory very much. He couldn't get it into his head that the game had passed out of his hands, but he had to admit that things were getting better and better. So he kept his mouth shut.

The party that Franco wanted to give on New Year's Eve forced Magdalini into overdrive. She wanted to make the evening unforgettable for all the guests. In the few months that she'd been married, she had entertained some of her husband's colleagues, but now she would have to receive at least a hundred guests, among them a politician. She worked with Mary on the menu. She hired special artists to enliven the evening and found, by herself, the best orchestra in Chicago. Franco watched her erasing and writing continuously in her now-famous notebook, and he smiled contentedly. His happiness filled him in a way he had never experienced before. His wife was the ornament of his life. Whoever met her hastened to congratulate him warmly on his choice and bless him for his good fortune. What they didn't know and couldn't imagine was that his greatest joys were lived in her arms. Her body was an ark in which he traveled to harbors filled with magical experiences and intoxicating smells. Her embrace was like a hospitable city, brightly lit, but with a thousand secrets he never tired of exploring.

That New Year's Eve, Magdalini had managed to make everything magical. Even Charley had to admit it and congratulate her. Magdalini herself was in a panic at first. The faces and names of the guests seemed to form a crazy dance in her head, but fortunately Franco was beside her most of the time and reminded her whenever she forgot. The politician made an impression on her; his appearance was pleasant and his smile was sweet, although his wife acted like she'd been obliged to come and couldn't wait to leave. In fact, both the politician and his wife had been obligated to attend. His candidacy had been supported and financed by the Mafia, naturally not without certain promises in exchange.

When Franco introduced Alan as his right-hand man, Magdalini had trouble smiling. The very tall man standing in front of her provoked such distaste that she nearly wiped the back of her hand where he had left a polite kiss. This man frightened her. His eyes were strangely small for the size of his face, he had a nasty look, and his smile was completely false. The emotions he provoked were entirely in contrast to what Franco had told her about him. Her husband seemed to have complete confidence in this man, and sang his praises as they moved on to another group, lawyers this time.

Shortly after midnight, when the spectacular fireworks were over and the couples were dancing in the huge main room, Magdalini saw Mary half open the door leading to the kitchen and look intently at her. She excused herself from the group she was talking to and disappeared behind the same door, where Mary took her by the hand and led her to the room the staff used as a lounge. It was completely dark inside, with only the moon providing a dim light. Magdalini turned inquiringly to the cook, but Mary put her finger to her lips. She moved easily through the dark room, and Magdalini followed her, feeling her curiosity growing by the minute. Mary opened a door to the outside and went out into the garden. They walked carefully toward a small gazebo and hid themselves in the nearby foliage. Magdalini held her breath when she saw Alan talking to another man who Franco had introduced to her as Mr. McLondon. She pricked up her ears to listen to them. They couldn't go any nearer or they'd be discovered.

"You're hurrying," Alan said now and his voice sounded irritated. "We shouldn't have come here. Someone might see us and then the whole game will be over."

"We're late, though," McLondon answered. "And down there, they're in a hurry for results. I worked hard to get into Giotto's circle and time's precious."

"Yes, but for a job like this, you need patience. The Giottos are tough nuts to crack, and they won't break easily. Nor will we get rid of them fast. When the old man was in charge it was easier. But Franco's as cunning as a fox."

"He trusts you, though."

"Yes, but I had to take a bullet in the leg while pretending to save his life. That's why I'm saying, be patient! We've been through a lot to get where we are—let's not spoil everything."

"You're right, but they're putting pressure on me from the west. You understand?"

"Tell them that in a month, Franco will be wondering where his control went. Tell them to trust me. Let's go inside before anyone notices we're missing, especially together, seeing as we're not supposed to know each other."

The two men left, but Magdalini couldn't move. She was paralyzed with shock. Suddenly she began to shake, so Mary took off her own jacket and put it around her mistress's shoulders, then held her gently for a moment before leading her back to the staff lounge. She turned on a small lamp and poured a glass of brandy for Magdalini, who was as white as a sheet. The young woman swallowed the drink in one gulp and felt it go down like a fiery tongue into her stomach, but she stopped shaking.

"How did you know?" was all she asked.

"I didn't know, madam. When I called you, I had no idea what we would stumble on. When there are people at the house, I like to look at the guests in their nice clothes. When I was taking a peek, I saw the man signal to Alan, and him nodding before they both disappeared. I didn't know what I didn't like about it, or what made me call you. But something inside me told me to let you know."

Magdalini had recovered now. She looked at Mary with a smile. "You may have saved my husband's life, Mary. You and your peeking! You're priceless!" She got up in a hurry to leave, but she turned back and stroked the older woman's cheek affectionately. "Thank you," she said softly, and Mary wiped the tears from her eyes.

Magdalini returned to the party, completely in control of herself. She looked for Alan and saw him talking to her husband. She wasn't wrong, then. Now that she knew and observed him again, he looked very dangerous indeed. His expression was dark, while Franco looked relaxed and was laughing. She went up to them with a cheerful expression on her face.

"If I suspect that on such a night you two are talking about work, I'll make trouble," she said brightly, and she noticed that Alan hurried to put a happy mask over his impassive face. "I hope my husband isn't making use of your spare time. Even a 'right hand' has to relax!"

"It's a pleasure to work for Franco," Alan answered in a servile tone.

Magdalini felt the blood rush to her head. His hypocrisy made her furious, but she hid her anger. "My husband is happy to have you beside him too. It's so rare to find devoted people whom you can trust."

Alan fixed his eyes on her, looking to see if there was any irony in what she'd just said, or even suspicion, but her innocent expression put his doubts to rest. Inwardly, he was annoyed with himself. She was just a stupid nobody.

Excusing herself, Magdalini dragged her husband onto the floor for a dance. She felt the need to distance him from the nasty snake that he was unknowingly nurturing at his breast. Dozens of questions hammered at her brain. What she had heard made her very anxious. And she felt that something had escaped her, certainly, but she didn't yet know what—her reasoning was blocked by anxiety.

The last guests left a little before dawn, and everyone assured their hosts that it was the best New Year's Eve they'd ever spent. As soon as the doors closed, Magdalini took off her shoes with a grimace of pain and turned to her father-in-law.

"Charley, are you tired?" she asked curtly.

He was surprised by her tone. "Not very . . ."

"Good, because I want us to talk."

"My dear, do you know what time it is?" Franco asked. "It's late."

"On the contrary. It's early. And enough time has been lost!"

"And what do you want with me?" Charley asked roughly.

"What we're talking about concerns you, unless you've completely retired from the work."

"What work?" Franco was anxious now.

"Your work, Franco. You do business, don't you?"

"Yes—of course."

Magdalini went ahead of them and for the first time ever entered her father-in-law's office. Father and son looked at each other. Charley's expression was angry, but Franco's was uneasy. They followed the girl, unable to do anything else. She waited for them, standing with her arms crossed on her chest.

"What's going on, my love?" asked Franco, closing the door behind them.

"You must get Alan away from you at once. And when I say at once, I mean today! I'm surprised you call such a man your right hand and put all your trust in him."

Silence followed her words, until Charley broke out into loud laughter. When he'd stopped laughing, though, he looked at his daughter-in-law with the familiar daggers shooting out from his eyes. "That's all we needed! After her flowery tablecloths and her Greek specialties, the little village girl has decided to stick her nose in our work. Stay with your saucepans, silly girl, and let men look after their work like they know how to. I've put up with enough from you and your village ways. I'm not about to make you the boss. My son may be fixated on your wide-open beautiful legs, but I can still think logically!"

"Charley!" Franco's voice sounded like a gunshot. "Ask my wife for forgiveness right now, because otherwise—"

"One moment, Franco!" Magdalini was now deathly pale, but calm. "Your father spoke to me, so I will answer him." She went up to Charley, who was breathing heavily and looked directly at him. "I'm sorry I made you angry," she said. "I really should be angry with you, because you spoke rudely, if not disgustingly, but you are my husband's father, and so mine too. You see, this village girl was brought up in a place where they teach us to respect our parents. So I don't hold anything against you, nor does your way of speaking upset me. I'm not stupid—I know you didn't want me as Franco's wife. However I'm used to it. My grandfather didn't want my mother as his daughter-in-law, but at the end of his life they became friends. I hope it won't take us that long.

As for Alan . . ." She turned to Franco. "I would never interfere in your business and you know it. But tonight something terrible happened."

Without any more delay, she told her husband every detail of what she'd learned after Mary had alerted her. She repeated, word for word, what she'd heard in the garden. With everything she said, Franco looked more surprised but at the end his expression was hellish.

"I'll kill him with my own hands!" Charley yelled.

Magdalini smiled. "All right, let's not go too far. You're business-men, not gangsters."

Her words threw the room into complete silence.

"Always the same Charley," Franco hurried to comment. "He threatens gods and demons!"

They both looked at the elder Giotto. Magdalini seemed to be scolding him gently for his exaggerated reaction, but Franco's look exuded a warning.

Later, when they were alone in their room Magdalini turned to her husband. "Anyway, you have to admit that what I overheard didn't sound like regular business," she observed calmly.

"What do you mean?" Franco hastened to ask.

"That I felt as if I was hearing a conversation from the underworld. Who are these people from the west who are plotting against you?"

"Competitors in the market."

"And why did they shoot at you, when that man got in the way? That sort of thing reminds me of the Mafia."

Franco pretended to be amused. "My dear, nothing shady is going on. That day they shot at me I was with the politician and I naturally assumed that the bullet was meant for him. Now that I've found out the whole thing was rigged so that bastard could win my trust, I can't forgive myself for being so naive about him."

"To be honest, I was surprised when you introduced him to me. From that first moment, my instincts told me to warn you. The instant we met, I disliked him."

"Then perhaps I'd better introduce you to all my colleagues, darling. Your instinct is real and precious, just as you are. The way you spoke to my father—"

But Magdalini interrupted him. "Do you know something, Franco? You talk too much." And in one movement she was naked in front of him.

◆ ◆ ◆

The first light of the sun, peeking in through the window, lit her body in such a way that it looked like a marble statue. Franco felt a strange jealousy as its rays played over her and caressed her. Alan was far away now. No one would hear anything from him again.

When Magdalini asked what had happened, Franco answered almost indifferently: He'd found out from Alan everything he wanted to know, then he'd gotten rid of him without compensating him, naturally. He never let his wife find out that Alan's body lay at the bottom of the lake, somewhere far away, buried in a block of concrete.

Yet again the message had reached the people it was intended for.

◆ ◆ ◆

Magdalini's pregnancy made Franco so happy it nearly brought him to the point of madness. Even Charley managed a smile. His relationship with his daughter-in-law hadn't changed since the night of the party, but now he treated her with more respect. However much he didn't want to admit it, the girl had guts, and unfortunately, a brain in her head. This last fact really troubled him. After a lifetime of seeing women only as decorative objects whose only useful purpose was to satisfy men's desires, it was difficult for him to accept that his daughter-in-law was different. She ruled the household with a hand as soft as velvet but as strong as iron and the entire staff respected and admired her for it. She was a wonderful housewife, with a calmness that wasn't a sign of obedience; rather it was an indication of her self-control. In the old man's eyes, she was a strange creature.

From the first moment that she announced her pregnancy, Magdalini regretted it. Franco had gone crazy, her aunt transformed herself into her guardian angel, and she had had to let Mary take over certain tasks.

Magdalini sighed helplessly one day as she shared her frustrations with her aunt. "I feel as if I have a collar on," she complained. "I don't dare do anything in the house. If I lift a vase, a maid appears from somewhere and runs to take it out of my hands. I'm pregnant, not about to die!"

"What sort of talk is that, Magdalini?" Anna scolded her. "Is it bad that they all love you so much they try to stop you from tiring yourself? And if you absolutely must do something, why don't you start preparing the baby's room?"

"Mercy, Aunt! I'm not even at five months yet."

"And must you wait till the last minute?"

"The worst thing is that I have no friends, since Judy got married and moved to the other side of the world."

It was true. After her marriage to Alex, Magdalini's only friend had followed him to Canada. Alex was a lawyer and a big Canadian company had hired him. The two friends had said an emotional goodbye to each other, and they would have stayed in touch through letters if they hadn't both been so distracted. Occasionally they exchanged a short letter or card, and sometimes they spoke on the phone. After Judy, Magdalini hadn't become close with any other girl. The wives of Franco's colleagues were much older than she was and her relationships with them were formal.

Her aunt was right again, and Magdalini realized it when she followed her advice and began decorating the baby's room. She hired a decorator, of course, and after endless consultations with him the work began. She followed everything closely, despite the objections of Franco and of the decorator himself, who felt the eye of his customer always on him. When it was finished, everyone agreed that whether the baby was a boy or a girl, it would feel happy in the space she had created. It was a large, bright room, full of butterflies, horses, and mermaids, and the colors were soft and neutral so as to suit whichever gender the child happened to be. The prints on the walls were figures from movies and there was an endless number of toys.

Franco laughed happily when he saw it finished, but Charley growled with distaste.

"What exactly don't you like, Charley?" his daughter-in-law asked him patiently.

"Is it for me to like?" he shot roughly at her. "If it's a boy, how are you going to make him a man in here?"

"I promise you that if it's a boy, by the time he grows up I'll make it more . . . severe," Magdalini answered, but Charley left with a final disapproving glance.

The last month of her pregnancy was miserable for the expectant mother. Her belly was enormous, her feet had swollen, and she had stopped complaining that they wouldn't let her do anything because it was so hard for her to move. Her nights were the worst, as the baby kicked all the time, keeping her awake. As her due date approached, Magdalini grew more and more anxious, especially after the doctor informed her that the baby was very large. Franco restricted his hours outside the house so he could be near her. He preferred working in his father's office.

That night Magdalini was worse than ever. At dinner, she forced herself to eat two mouthfuls of food, but her belly seemed ready to burst. Even Charley was worried and didn't take his eyes off her. He was, in fact, the first to see an unexpected spasm on her face when the dessert arrived.

"Lyn," he said softly.

It was one of the few times he had said her name and the girl looked at him with a pained smile.

"What's happening, Charley?" she asked him with difficulty through her contraction. "Now that I'm giving birth, is it time for a truce?"

"You're giving birth!" It was Franco who shouted and jumped up to race to her side.

"Don't shout, my dear," she said in a calm voice. "It was a pain and it's passed. But it's probably time."

"What are you sitting there for, you idiot! The girl's giving birth! Tell Jack to bring the car! Call the doctor! Tell the midwife!" Charley was on his feet, giving orders like the captain of a ship in a storm, and Magdalini couldn't hold back a little laugh.

With difficulty she got up and moved toward him. "I'm happy to have two such coolheaded men beside me."

Charley turned to glare at her, but another sharp pain made Magdalini crumple, and he had to support her so she wouldn't fall down.

The next few hours were a whirlwind for all of them. The only thing that Magdalini remembered afterward was Franco's pale face and Charley's bright-red one. Every time poor Jack, who was driving the car, got into traffic, he became the target of threats from the father and son. Through her pain she heard them threatening him dozens of times; now they'd skin him alive, now they'd feed his brains to the dogs, until she was forced to intervene. "Stop it, both of you!" she gasped. "You're driving the man mad. He's doing what he can, but he's driving a car. Not to mention that you've made my hair stand on end with your threats. Whoever threatens Jack again can get out of the car right now!" She stopped, breathing heavily, but she managed to see Jack looking gratefully at her in the mirror.

However optimistic she wanted to be, Magdalini knew that something wasn't going right; she could feel it. It had been an hour since her water had broken, and when it had, it was full of blood. When they took her in for surgery, the anxious expression on her doctor's face confirmed her suspicions.

Anna and Peter found Franco and Charley in the waiting room. When Anna saw the two men on the point of collapse, she took charge of the situation, and Franco realized that calmness and coolheadedness were inherited virtues. Anna sent Peter to bring coffee for everyone, and then, in her calm voice, began to speak to them and tell them everything they needed to hear. She sat next to Franco, holding his hand gently, and every now and then stroking his hair. When she began to pray in Greek, although he didn't understand a word, Franco felt himself calming down. He too raised his eyes toward heaven, asking for everything to go well. But the doctor, who came out after an hour, had nothing good to say to them. The birth wasn't proceeding normally. The child didn't seem ready to come out and its size made things even more difficult. Magdalini was completely exhausted. She had lost a lot of blood and she couldn't endure any more effort.

Franco, white and tight lipped, grasped the doctor by the lapel. "It doesn't matter what you do. But I need to take my wife away from here healthy!" he managed to say, his words somewhat muddled by the effort it took him to speak. "The child doesn't matter to me. Nothing matters except Lyn herself!"

The doctor nodded understandingly. "Calm down, Franco. I'll proceed with a Cesarean section, which means I won't face the dilemma of deciding which of the two to save. I simply came out to tell you . . ."

"Why didn't you do the Cesarean before now?"

"Because in the beginning everything seemed to indicate that the birth would be difficult but smooth. We prefer, you know, for women to give birth naturally."

Franco was shouting now. "You're saying a lot, Doctor! Stop talking and go do your work! When you come out again, I want you to tell me that everything is all right, otherwise leave by the other door to save yourself. If something happens to my wife, it'll be the end of you!"

The doctor left, frowning. He'd heard rumors before about the Giotto family, but he hadn't believed them until now. Suddenly he asked himself how he'd gotten mixed up with this man. His threats didn't sound like empty words.

After the doctor had left, Franco collapsed in Anna's embrace. She took him in her arms like a baby and continued praying, her lips white as paper. Charley was bright red and agitated—now sitting down, now pacing nervously up and down—while Peter, sitting in a chair, looked pale as a lifeless doll.

This time the doctor's appearance was different. He greeted them with a broad smile and they all hurried up to him.

"We're all done!" he said. "Everything went well."

"My wife?" was all Franco asked.

"Lyn was a heroine. She's sleeping now, but in a little while you can see her. Aren't you going to ask me about your child?"

"Now that my wife is all right, tell me."

"You have a great big son, full of health and with terrific lungs."

Franco and Magdalini's son was truly beautiful. Nature had contrived to combine the best of father and mother. He looked like a giant compared to the other children, and his cries were certainly loud.

Franco could hardly wait to see his wife. He went into her room and was at first frightened by her pale face, but the doctor reassured him. She was young and healthy, the ordeal of the birth would pass, and she would be just as she was before.

When the family returned home with its new member, the entire household celebrated. Again the staff lined up to greet them and everyone's eyes filled with emotion. Mary didn't restrain her tears and began to cry. Magdalini was moved and hugged her despite the fact that she hadn't quite recovered. Her incision hurt a great deal and she felt weak.

Despite her protests, Franco put his wife to bed and stayed beside her, holding her hand until he saw her eyelids begin to droop. Then he went straight to his son's room where he too was asleep, with his nanny watching him. Over Magdalini's objections, Franco had hired an experienced woman to care for his son. Yes, Magdalini would have the responsibility of bringing up her child, but she must have some help, and for the first time he was adamant.

Magdalini's recovery after her return was impressive. The color in her cheeks came back first, followed by her strength and her energy. Every day she spent hours with her son beside her in the bed and talked to him.

Franco and Magdalini had decided to name the child Charles Giotto, and when they told his namesake, Charley gave his daughter-in-law a ring with a diamond so enormous that Magdalini was moved to complain, "It's so big that I'll have to hire someone to hold my hand!"

"In the end, we two didn't have to wait as long as your grandfather and your mother," he said and winked at her conspiratorially.

A month later it was as if Magdalini had never passed through such a difficult trial. She reassumed all her duties, and was so full of energy that the governess asked if she still needed her services. Mary explained to the new member of staff the peculiarities of her mistress.

Charley had become Magdalini's warmest supporter, a marvel that Franco couldn't believe. Every day that passed was better than the one before, and little Charles became the center of everyone's world, his room the most visited in the house. He didn't seem to mind his admirers. When it was time to sleep he didn't bother to concern himself with anyone. His huge eyes, so like his father's, closed gently and he abandoned himself to Morpheus even if all hell was breaking out around him. The only things that made him cry were if he was hungry or dirty. Then his eyes would grow wild, which made Charley boast that his grandson was just like him. The baby's wails were like the trumpets of

Jericho. They echoed through the whole house and everyone ran in a panic to satisfy the child's needs.

Nobody understood how the first year of Charles's life had passed so quickly. It was as if some otherworldly being had bewitched time, making the months run by in a hurry. The boy's first birthday was celebrated in style. The cake that Mary made was so large that it would have fit the whole child inside. His grandfather made the night sky look like day with all the fireworks he bought. Any objections from Magdalini about the excessive nature of the celebrations fell on deaf ears.

Franco was utterly happy but he made it clear to Magdalini that there wouldn't be any more children. However much she complained, however she pleaded, her husband was adamant. He had nearly lost her once; he wasn't going to risk a second time. He listened to none of his wife's logical arguments. But he hadn't reckoned on the determination of the Greek woman he had married, or her womanly cunning.

Magdalini carefully calculated her fertile days with the help of her doctor. She booked herself and her husband a room at a hotel, where she welcomed him nearly naked with a glass of champagne in her hand. She explored his whole body slowly, pleasurably, almost painfully, to a point where for the first time for a long while she was overwhelmed herself by the force of his lovemaking. Franco, who was always careful after the birth of his son, forgot all precautions and tasted her body again and again as he had never done before. He stopped only when he felt his legs trembling from sated desire.

She knew she was pregnant before the doctor confirmed it, but now that her plan had succeeded, she was afraid to tell Franco—she feared his objections and she wasn't wrong. As soon as he heard the news, his face darkened, and Magdalini suddenly remembered how threatening clouds used to gather over Mount Olympus, when Zeus would hide in its peaks ready to hurl his thunderbolts. The room was filled with the same unearthly silence that fell before the storm broke. But just as she had learned to cope with the anger of nature, she kept calm in the face of Franco's outburst. However much he yelled and howled that she had tricked him, however many times he kicked the furniture and threatened gods and demons, she sat calmly watching his reactions. She knew that they were provoked by his fears for her, by the absolute devotion that had always fortified her. Besides, a storm of such intensity would die down quickly.

When Franco collapsed on the bed, sweating and out of breath, she knelt in front of him.

"I know you love me," she said. "I know you're afraid for me, but the doctor assures me that I'm fine and quite capable of getting through another pregnancy without any problems. This time I won't go through any pain. I'll make an appointment and have another Cesarean section. And what's more"—and this time her voice was severe—"children are a joy and a blessing. We won't go without them because you're a coward."

Her last words shot him out of his chair, almost dragging her with him. "Me, a coward? How dare you say that to me!"

"How else can I describe you when you've been behaving like a badly brought-up child? The whole household heard you, as if I'd brought you some bad news! We're having a child, Franco. I didn't tell you some disaster had happened."

"But don't you understand that I'm afraid for you! After all you went through, why should we have another child?"

"Because our son should have a little brother. We're young and healthy and why not? And anyway I'm pregnant already and you can't change that. So, my dear loudmouth, you must accept it!"

She had won and he knew it. When Franco left the room and saw his father in the hall, he met his look with a scowl. Charley must have heard everything, the way Franco had been shouting.

With every day that passed Franco felt his soul contracting with fear. As his wife's due date grew closer, every minor change in Magdalini made him lose his color. On the day they went to the maternity ward, he was so pale that Magdalini pitied him. Her aunt tried everything to calm him down but this time she didn't have to try for long. By the time they'd realized that Magdalini had gone into the surgery, the nurse had come out announcing the birth of a daughter.

A new sun was added to their galaxy. The little one was just like her mother, to the point where everyone teased Franco that Magdalini had managed it by herself without his participation. They gave her the name of her grandmother in Greece, but since Theodora was difficult for Americans to pronounce, they turned it into Doris. Magdalini, however, always called her Theodora.

New photographs were added to the elder Theodora's box of icons, and both she and Great-Grandmother Julia prayed for the happiness of the grandchildren and great-grandchildren they would probably never see.

◆ ◆ ◆

Five more years disappeared before they were really aware of it. Charles and Doris—both exact replicas of their parents—turned seven and five respectively. Charley had been transformed into a grandfather whom all the grandchildren in the world would envy. He hardly bothered with his work anymore. Anyone who saw him now would have trouble believing he was once the famous Giotto, the terror of Chicago. The sharp and wounding look in his eyes was a thing of the past, especially when they rested on his grandchildren. Both Charles and Doris adored him and he played with them for hours. Magdalini laughed till she cried when she saw him trying to drink coffee from one of his granddaughter's microscopic porcelain cups. She still had no idea—nor could she ever have imagined—that his hands, which had trouble holding the tiny toys steady, were the same hands that handled a gun with ease and mercilessly planted bullets in his enemies' heads. Nor did she have any idea that the dear old man who allowed his grandchildren to disturb him mercilessly had once tortured terrified women to satisfy his unhealthy desires. Two small typhoons had swept the past away; they had made one of the most dangerous criminals disappear, and left in his place a precious grandfather.

"Where was all this tenderness hiding for so long?" his son asked his wife.

But Magdalini just laughed.

◆　◆　◆

Bad things always happen unexpectedly. They find their victims unprepared and so unable to oppose them. Nobody expected what happened; no sign had appeared to put Franco on his guard. Everything was calm, so calm that it should have made him anxious, he thought later, but there was no way to turn back time.

Franco's domination and supremacy were now undisputed. Peter had stood by him, he had to respectfully admit that. Even Bowden hadn't created any problems. The endless provocations from the west had stopped. It appeared that the new leader there, someone called Mike, had decided to look after his own territory and leave him in peace. Naturally he couldn't know that this Mike was just like his father had once been in his glory days. He couldn't know that Mike had made up his mind to put an end to the Giottos' control and that the methods he would use to get rid of his enemies were like those of a madman. The competitor ignored the fact that after so many decades, every attempt to overthrow the Giottos had failed. Three attempts had been made at murdering them, and each time the culprits ended up at the bottom of the lake. Mike had seen the Giottos take over the east; he knew it was a matter of time before they would develop an appetite for his own territory. He decided that the blow must be impressive and exemplary.

That afternoon, Magdalini took the children and went out. Her aunt and Peter were celebrating their wedding anniversary and they had invited a lot of friends to join them, among them, naturally, herself and

Franco, but since he had work to do, he would join them later. However much she begged Charley to join them, he refused. He had a slight cold, so he would go to bed early.

Sitting in his car, Franco whistled, and Jack smiled, watching him in the rearview mirror. Many things had changed since Franco had gotten married. The very fact that Charley had calmed down seemed a miracle. The big boss had pulled back, but Franco didn't let that information travel too far. Everyone on the outside thought Charley was still in charge. Jack turned the wheel. They'd be home soon. Franco would collect some papers and then go to meet his wife at Peter's house. Then Jack would be free for the night. That's what his boss had told him.

Something that felt like an earthquake made Jack lose control of the car, and it took all his strength to right it before they hit some tree. But the deafening noise that accompanied the tremor couldn't have come from an earthquake.

Jack turned toward Franco. "Are you OK?" he asked anxiously.

He saw Franco sitting perfectly still, his eyes fixed straight ahead, looking at something in horror. Jack turned to see what it was and froze like a statue himself. From the direction where the house had to be, flames were shooting up and other small explosions could be heard. Without waiting for an order, Jack drove fast toward the house.

In the place where the beautiful house had once stood, giant tongues of flame shot up, while windows shattered noisily. The road had already filled with people who had fled the surrounding houses in fear and were staring with awe at the terrible sight. Franco jumped out of the car and began running toward the house, but Jack, who had moved more quickly, grabbed him hard and threw him on the grass.

"Don't, boss! There's nothing left! You'll be in danger if you go in."

"My father's inside, idiot!" Franco yelled, and tried to free himself.

But the faithful man squeezed him tighter. "He's finished, boss . . . don't you understand? If you go in you'll risk your own life. Think of your wife, your kids!"

At the thought of his loved ones Franco stayed still, lowering his head in defeat. Sirens could be heard coming from all directions. Police and fire engines arrived together. Jack finally let out his breath. With the police beside them, he didn't need to worry about Franco's life anymore. He had no doubt that the house didn't blow itself up. Somebody had his eye on the Giottos and wanted them out of the way. It seemed as if their information was incomplete and whoever dared to mess with his boss didn't know that Charley was the only one at home.

◆　◆　◆

Magdalini looked at her watch uneasily for the tenth time. Franco was really late and he hadn't called, something she wasn't used to. They had finished their dinner, the coffee and dessert had been served, and people had begun to leave. Still, they hadn't heard a word.

Anna's cook came out of the kitchen, looking very pale. She looked helplessly at Magdalini and then turned to Anna. "Madam . . ." she whispered, and Magdalini felt her breath stop.

"What's going on?" asked Anna unsuspectingly. "What's wrong with you?"

"Madam . . . in the kitchen . . . on the television . . ."

Like lightning, Magdalini ran past them into the kitchen, where there was a television set up so that Juanita wouldn't miss her beloved soap operas. Her feet fixed to the floor, she saw a reporter on the screen talking about a bomb. Without a trace of color on her face she watched her house burning and recognized among the crowd gathered nearby some of her neighbors. Anna had run in and the two women looked tensely at each other.

"Oh, Franco!" whispered Magdalini. "He was going by the house to collect some papers for Peter."

Anna raised her hand to her mouth to smother the cry of fear that came from the depths of her being, but Magdalini had already left the room. She ran right into Peter, who had no idea what was happening.

"What's going on, Lyn?" he asked cheerfully. "Are you leaving already?"

"They've bombed my house," she answered calmly. "Franco was probably there. I'm going to see what's happening. Keep an eye on the children!"

"Your aunt can look after the children. I'm going with you."

It took Peter a few seconds to get over his shock at his niece's decisiveness. With steady hands he drove the car while Magdalini sat quietly beside him. Her features were drawn, but she maintained her composure. Shortly before they reached the house the police stopped them. Nobody could pass, they told them. A bomb had gone off in some house.

"I'm Lyn Giotto," said Magdalini abruptly. "It's my house, and my husband may be inside. The only way you can stop me getting through is if you arrest me."

The policeman stood aside in awe and Peter drove ahead. When they got there, the fire had gone out. The house was just a smoking ruin while the spotlights on the patrol cars spun around silently, lighting up the faces in the crowd and lending them a diabolical look that matched the hellish spectacle.

With a steady walk, Magdalini approached a policeman. "I'm Lyn Giotto," she said again. "Where is the officer in charge so that I can find some information?"

The policeman led her to a very tall man in civilian clothes who turned to face her.

"Mrs. Giotto, I'm Jim McLeod. I'm really sorry for what's happened," he said.

"First, I need to know exactly what happened, officer. I was out, at my relatives' house, and I found out from the television."

"It looks like a bomb was planted in your house. Based on the information I have, there were probably no survivors. I'm sorry."

Magdalini fixed her eyes on his face, which was full of embarrassment. Behind her, Peter had put his arms around her shoulders. He squeezed them to remind her that she was not alone.

"Who did it?" she asked in an expressionless voice.

"It's too early for us to know. Mrs. Giotto, do you know who was inside? It would help us to know how many . . . we were looking for, at least."

"There were a total of sixteen staff . . ." Her voice broke as the faces she'd lived with for so long passed in front of her eyes. But she took a deep breath and continued. "There was also my father-in-law, Charley Giotto, and perhaps my husband."

"Your husband? No, he wasn't!" the office exclaimed. "I only just spoke to him."

"Where is he?" Magdalini's voice was distorted by tension.

"They're taking his statement. Look! There he is."

Slowly, like someone for whom time has stopped, Magdalini turned and saw her husband talking to a policeman who was taking notes. As if her eyes had magnets, they attracted Franco's gaze and it met hers. For a moment she seemed not to believe what she saw and then they both started running. They clutched each other. Magdalini was crying loudly like a madwoman. She kissed her husband's face. He pulled back and stroked her hair, then drew her close again.

"I thought I'd lost you!" Magdalini stammered breathlessly. "I thought you were inside."

"I was on my way at that time. I saw the explosion, the fire . . . it was terrible, Lyn. Charley . . ."

"Yes, I know." Magdalini looked at her husband's eyes. They were full of tears.

"They'll pay, whoever did it. Very dearly. My father's death—like this, can't not be avenged."

"That's the police's job, Franco."

Franco shook his head and turned to look again at what remained of the house where he'd spent all his life.

"So many lives," Magdalini said softly. "What did they do wrong? Who could have wanted to kill all of us?"

Franco turned to look at her and his face brightened. "What did you say, Lyn?"

"What did I say? That somebody wanted to get rid of the whole family. Whoever did it probably didn't know that my aunt would be celebrating her anniversary today and imagined that they'd send us all to the next world. At the time it happened we're usually all at home."

"You're right!" He nodded as if he'd woken from some lethargy. "That way they'd have gotten rid of the Giotto family once and for all! Now I understand . . ."

"What? Do you know who did this?"

"No, but I know why they did it and it won't take me long to find out the rest."

"You? You must speak to the police."

"I'll do that. Don't worry!"

Slowly the crowd began to disperse. The first witnesses had been questioned, but they didn't have anything important to say. Nothing suspicious had been seen in the neighborhood. Besides, everyone minded their own business. The houses were large and set well apart from each other so it would have been difficult to see anything. And if Charley had become aware of anything a second before the explosion, he had taken that information with him.

The days that followed were full of tension, tiredness, and sadness. Franco identified all the bodies, first of all his father's. He arranged all the funerals, and there were times when Magdalini wondered how he managed to stand up with so little sleep. For the time being they remained in the hospitable house of her aunt. She had taken over everything, including the children, who were at a loss to understand how their lives had been turned upside down in a single day. They asked for their grandfather and both of them cried when they found out that he was now in heaven and wouldn't be playing with them anymore.

Charley's funeral was like an awakening for Magdalini. Huge limousines arrived, and the guests who got out of them looked as if they had sprung from a gangster movie. In spite of her grief, Magdalini finally began to understand. Each arrival had three bodyguards, all of them armed, and yet everyone looked around them as if they were uneasy about something. Even Franco had a look about him that she didn't like. Something had changed in him. Instead of sadness in his eyes, she saw a slow-burning flame she had never seen before.

When they got back to Anna's house, Franco immediately closed himself in the study with Peter, Bowden, and several other men. For the first time in her life, Magdalini wanted to know what they were talking about, but she was surrounded by people and trapped in polite conversation and condolences.

As soon as the door closed behind them, Franco turned to the others. "So," he said ironically. "I'm listening." At that moment he looked exactly like Charley, with his eyes flashing lightning and his expression dark and full of death.

Peter coughed nervously and took a step forward. The man standing opposite him was no longer his nephew, but the big boss, full of rage, and he knew it. "I think we have something," he said decisively. "No one's slept for three days now, and we've found out some things. The job was set up by Mike, from the west—that much is confirmed. From what our people learned, he wanted to get rid of you all and spread out in this direction. After the way he'd taken care of the Giotto family, who would dare to challenge him?"

"Yes, I see, and what do we know about Mike?"

It was Bowden's turn to speak. "He's around forty, has no family, and only recently took over the district. It's an open secret that he did away with the previous boss in a terrible way. He's paranoid, Franco.

Everyone says so. He's sick. He doesn't operate in the usual way. The way he acts is like a terrorist."

Silence fell. Nobody dared to interrupt Franco, who seemed to be thinking. When he raised his head a few minutes later, everyone knew that a new era was beginning and that Franco's plans would ensure it was bathed in blood.

◆ ◆ ◆

The police couldn't understand what had happened. Chicago, which always teetered dangerously between good and evil, had become a war zone under their noses, and they couldn't keep up with all the bodies. Franco's orders were clear: a war was beginning. He didn't have his eye on the west, but after these developments he didn't have a choice. If he didn't respond to Mike's cowardly attack, the next victims would be himself, his wife, and his children.

Magdalini observed everything that was going on. Her ears and eyes were constantly alert and what she saw and understood, she didn't like at all. Her aunt's house had been transformed into a fortress. Armed men moved around them and searched every visitor. Nobody dared to leave without company. Franco came home very late each night, bathed without eating, and slid into bed beside her, taking her in his arms. His lovemaking was as tender as always, but the message was different. He needed it. Her body was like a purge for his soul. In her arms the man she had married was baptized again.

Neither she nor Anna dared to speak openly about what was happening, even between themselves. The silent agreement between them was like an illusion that warded off evil. Since they didn't talk about it, it didn't exist.

Franco rented an enormous apartment in a skyscraper for his family to stay in. Even though she didn't like the idea of the children living in an apartment, Magdalini obeyed Franco's wishes. "I have to be near my work," her husband had explained, and she wondered how much longer they would go on playing this game. She wasn't stupid; her suspicions had been confirmed. The wave of violence in the city had to be connected with the destruction of their house and Charley's death.

"How long have you been mixed up with the Mafia?" she finally asked her husband one day.

Her question fell like thunder and spread like a threat around the large room. They had moved into their new home a month ago, the children had gone to bed, and for the first time in a long while, Franco seemed at peace. That morning Magdalini had read that someone called Mike, who was probably the biggest Mafia boss in the west, had been found dead with two bullets in his head. A note beside the body indicated that it was suicide. But the police weren't laughing at the killer's joke. Mike was dead as soon as the first bullet entered his brain; he couldn't have fired at himself again.

When he heard his wife's question, Franco stood still, the glass in his hand held in midair. He knew there was no point in trying to fool her.

"Since I was born," he answered.

"Yes. So Charley . . ."

"Charley was the boss of the area before me."

"And why did they get rid of him?"

"To take over his turf."

"That is, for the same reason they wanted to kill you and our children."

"That's about it."

"And why did you lie to me for so long?"

"Lyn, try to understand. It's not so simple. You don't tell your wife such things!"

"Right! It's better to let her live under the delusion that you are a respectable citizen and decent businessman, without knowing that at any moment she might find herself murdered along with her children, victims of some paranoid creature who wants to take over her husband's leadership. Wasn't this Mike who 'committed suicide' a boss? Was he involved in the explosion at our house?"

"Yes. You're very clever, Lyn."

"But yet again you underestimated me. You left me to lead a false life."

"And if I'd told you the truth, what would you have done, Lyn?"

"What I'm about to do right now!"

Franco looked at her with a pleading expression.

"Ah, no," Magdalini said. "You don't know me very well, my love. I'm not about to leave you. Murderer or not, in the Mafia or not, I love you. It may sound crazy to love a man who can kill so easily like you, who sells drugs and deals in women, but I didn't ever say that I was rational."

"What are you asking, Lyn?"

"You have three months' grace. You'll get out of all your . . . work, and then we'll leave Chicago forever, if necessary we'll leave America. Now that I know, I refuse to live moment to moment with the fear that they may kill us."

"But Lyn, what you're asking can't be done. What do you think the Mafia is? An organization you can leave whenever you like? If I leave, then we'll all be in danger of being killed."

"Why?"

"Haven't you heard of the oath of silence? Nobody leaves the Mafia alive."

"Yes, but nobody who stays is left alive either. From what I understand, none of you are satisfied with what you have. You'll attack someone like jackals to get rid of him so you can expand. You're completely crazy, sick with power and control. I can't live with a man who's like that."

"But you've lived with him for this long! I'm the same man, Lyn, the man who worships you, the man who loves you."

"Then it appears that I loved a lie. And if it was just the two of us, I could accept that, because, like I said, I still love you. But I have to think of the children. I refuse to raise my son to follow in your footsteps. I don't want my daughter to get mixed up with any of you like I did." Magdalini was suddenly silent. She looked wide eyed at her husband. "Franco," she said, then stopped.

"Lyn, don't go any further . . . please!"

"What business does Peter have with all this? He's mixed up in it too, isn't he?"

"Yes."

The answer struck her like a lightning bolt.

"He knew about you, then. Even when Bowden introduced us." Magdalini laughed bitterly. "So he was in on the plot too?"

Franco's silence told her that there was something more.

"If you don't tell me the whole truth right this moment, I'll take the children and leave," she said, her eyes flashing with anger.

Very slowly, as if he had lost all his energy, Franco told her the whole story from the beginning. When he'd finished, he felt her eyes piercing him like red-hot needles. He didn't dare look at her.

"Lyn, you must understand," he whispered.

"No! Now it's time for you to understand. Three months, Franco. Then you'll lose all trace of us."

Magdalini didn't know then that she'd opened the door to her own personal hell. She didn't realize just how true her husband's words would prove to be. The developments that followed came like a storm. Franco's announcement that he was pulling out rallied another front against him. Mike's remaining followers were already out for blood, although Franco wasn't aware of it. Now, the angry and uneasy big shots rattled by Franco's disloyalty would join the attack. The two forces moved in parallel and at the same time.

Magdalini kissed her son as she did every afternoon then handed him over to Jack to take him to baseball practice. Franco was out at a lunch meeting with Peter and Bowden to discuss another detail of the big exodus, so Magdalini sat alone with her daughter, helping her with her arithmetic. From the family's apartment on the fifteenth floor, she was completely unaware of what happened next.

Two black cars appeared from nowhere at the same moment. The first braked suddenly at the entrance to the apartment building at the exact moment when Jack was holding the door open for little Charles. One window was lowered, a submachine gun emerged from the opening and the bullets raked Jack and Charles, who both collapsed, dead, on the sidewalk. Then the car disappeared, its tires screeching demonically. At that same moment, a second car was doing exactly the same thing as Franco, Peter, and Bowden were coming out of the restaurant.

Complete success in a double hit.

◆　◆　◆

Anna seemed to have aged suddenly in a single year. Twelve months had passed since that black day and still there were moments when she wondered how she had managed to keep her sanity, how she hadn't lost herself in a world of silence like Magdalini. The light had been extinguished from the younger woman's eyes and she hadn't spoken a word since the shootings. The doctors said she would eventually recover from the shock, but they couldn't say when that would happen.

As soon as Magdalini had heard the news, she fell to the floor, as little Doris screamed in fear. When she recovered she was a body without a soul, totally catatonic. She was kept in the hospital for nearly two weeks, but all the tests they did failed to detect any physical problem.

Anna was left alone with a child who needed her, dozens of responsibilities, and thousands of questions. Charlene and her husband stayed beside her like sleepless guards, while Judy and her husband, who'd been offered a job in Chicago, moved back home to help, as much as they could, the family that had been blown to pieces without any obvious cause. As the newspapers began to report the details behind the tragedies, Anna finally understood how deeply she had been sleeping all these years. She almost wished that she'd become like her niece, so she wouldn't understand and hurt so much.

Judy visited Magdalini for hours every day. Sitting beside her, she read to her and talked to her about the old days, about the parties they used to go to, and the crazy things they did. When Anna would take over, Charlene would look after little Doris, who was finally recovering with the help of an experienced psychologist. The specialist tried to heal the wounds of the little girl who wanted her family back as she had known it, a family she had lost so suddenly that her child's brain couldn't comprehend it.

The vision of the beautiful statue that had been her mother frightened the little girl at first, but she got used to it. When she visited her bedside, she spoke to her mother as if she could answer her, and before she left she always kissed her tenderly. The last time, a tear rolled down Magdalini's face, a very good sign of improvement, the doctor said. Anna began to weep and pray to God that a miracle might happen.

"Aunt?"

Anna jumped up in fright and looked around her to see where the voice was coming from. Magdalini was looking at her for the first time in fourteen whole months, and Anna's breath stopped for a moment from the shock and joy. Her prayers had been answered.

"My girl!" she exclaimed.

"Where am I?" Magdalini spoke slowly as if she was searching for the words.

"At my house, darling, with me. Thank God! You're back with me again."

Magdalini's recovery progressed quickly from that point on. With every day that passed, she took another leap forward, thanks to the help of her daughter. Overwhelmed with joy, Doris couldn't be pried away from her mother's room. The child made her read her favorite stories to her and her dolls put on performances for her mother's entertainment.

Nobody spoke about what had happened. They were waiting for Magdalini herself to talk about it. They knew she would when she was ready to face it. That's what the doctors said and everyone believed them.

Judy's husband, Alex, had managed to clean up Franco and Peter's affairs on behalf of the two women. Very discreetly, so as not to stir up more trouble, he had secured their finances for them. He had managed to save the largest part of the fortune the two men had made. Naturally, he didn't touch any accounts that directly concerned the activities of the Mafia. He also put out the word that Franco's widow was seriously ill and had left for Greece. And he posted a "For Sale" sign outside Anna's house, which he took down after two weeks, when he and Judy moved in. Anyone watching would think Judy and Alex had bought the house and Peter's widow had moved away. The plan was safe enough, as Anna never went out, not even into the garden. A year and a half later, nobody remembered the two women.

One Sunday afternoon, Magdalini looked around at her dear friends, as they sat together after their meal. It had become a custom for all of them to eat together on Sundays. Judy was admiring her round belly. After many miscarriages she and Alex were finally about to have their first child. Charlene was talking to Anna. Little Doris was dressing and undressing a doll, and Charlene's husband was talking to his son-in-law about the country's economic situation. Everything was so peaceful. Magdalini knew that, had it not been for these loved ones, she would have never survived the last few years. She'd crossed a stormy ocean. The waves were mountainous, her ship had broken, and if the people before her now hadn't been holding life jackets, she and her daughter would have drowned. Since the day she woke up, she hadn't stopped thinking about the future, even though she said nothing about it to anyone. Two angels in her life had flown far away, but there was one angel left that she must protect. And as long as she stayed in Chicago, she would never feel safe again.

"I want to tell you something," she began and everyone turned to her with interest. "I've never told you how grateful I am to you all for what you did after Franco and Charles died. Of course however many thank-yous I say, they won't be enough, compared to the effort you've made for us. I know that at times it was probably dangerous, particularly for you, Alex."

Alex looked embarrassed. "Lyn, you don't need to say that."

"It's the truth, though. You're good people. To me, the best in the world. A strong, loving family. That's why I want you to know about my decision."

The room grew perfectly silent.

"It's impossible for me to go on living here," Magdalini said. "Every step I take frightens me, I think every car is following me, I shake with fear for my daughter. I don't like living in fear. So I'm going home to my country, and I'm hoping that my aunt will follow me."

Anna was beside her before she could speak the last word. "Of course I'll come with you!" she said. "To be very honest, I was hoping you'd make a decision like this." Then she turned to face the others. "However much I love you all, and despite the fact that I've lived here nearly my whole life, there are things that are driving me away. Memories that I'd prefer to forget." Turning back to her niece, she asked, "When shall we go?"

"Tomorrow."

"But the house?"

Magdalini looked at Alex. "This will be the last favor I ask of you, Alex. To sell the house and send the money to us in Greece."

Charlene wiped her eyes, which were streaming with tears. "However much my heart aches because I'll lose you, I know you're doing the right thing. In your own country you can start a new life.

Far away from the pain. But where will you go? Do you have a place to stay?"

The younger woman looked off into space for a moment with dreamy eyes, then cast her gaze back to her aunt, still standing at her side. Anna understood and nodded her head in agreement.

Magdalini suddenly remembered the forgotten sounds the trees make when they dance in the wind, their leaves singing happily. She recalled the smell of the earth after rain, the scent of wood fires burning, and the steamy fragrance of her mother's freshly baked bread. She saw a house embraced by two huge chestnut trees and the river that always flowed lazily beside it.

That was where she wanted to go. She wanted to drown her pain in that river. She wanted to be held in her mother's arms and let her tears finally flow. She wanted her daughter to grow up under Mount Olympus, free and happy, without being afraid of anything.

Back, then. Back home . . .

To the house by the river.

THE RETURN

Theodora put the lit candle carefully back in its place among the icons, and crossed herself devoutly as she did every morning. The soft light spread around the half-dark room. Despite the fact that April had arrived a week ago, it was still quite cold. Spring was still only a promise. Without switching on the light she went to the kitchen, and when she heard the crackle of the fire in the hearth she knew she hadn't been the first one up.

Her mother, sitting on a chair in front of the fire, was already drinking her coffee. "Good morning!" Julia said, as soon as she saw her daughter come in.

Theodora smiled affectionately. Julia was nearly eighty, but she was as energetic as she had been at sixty. Her hair had turned completely white and her fingers were bent, but she herself was not. Erect as ever, she walked slowly but was still strong. No illness had bothered her and the doctor said she was in great physical condition for her age, which Theodora was grateful for. She didn't know what she would have done all these lonely years without her mother.

Theodora went to the fireplace and sat down beside Julia.

"Will you have some coffee? Shall I make it for you?" Julia asked.

"Yes, Mother, I'll have some."

Every morning for years now, her mother had asked the same thing and she had given the same answer. For a little while they enjoyed the company of the fire without speaking. In the summer they drank their first coffee on the verandah, watching the river reflect the first rays of the sun. They'd both passed through difficult years, but they had managed to cope. When they were completely alone—after Magdalini had left and when Polyxeni had secretly run off—Theodora thought the sun had lost its luster, the colors had faded, and life itself was a heavy burden she couldn't bear. There was no point in going on. The thought was fixed in her mind.

But Julia refused to let her daughter give up. She let her cry and rant for weeks. She watched with sleepless eyes as Theodora neglected her everyday work in favor of sitting on the riverbank and letting her thoughts travel like the water to her children, who now lived so far away. Julia pretended not to notice that her daughter ate very little, although it worried her. She pretended not to see that the lines around her eyes were deepening, and that her expression was empty. Instead, she waited patiently until she thought her daughter had mourned long enough. Then she decided to take the situation into her own hands. She went and found Theodora, who was sitting on the riverbank again.

"How long is this going to go on?" she asked.

"What do you want, Mother?" Theodora responded in a tired voice.

"I want you to recover. You've wept, you've beaten your breast, you've exhausted yourself—enough! You've tried to kill yourself in the prime of your life."

"Do you know how old I am?" Theodora sadly reminded her.

"What do you think? I'm your mother, I know when I gave birth to you. You're still young."

"So what do you want me to do? Get married again?"

"That wouldn't be a bad idea. What's eating you, my girl? Why have you given up like this?"

"Because there's no reason to go on living. I raised five children and look at me—alone, without anything to wait for."

"And I thought you were smart! This was their home, Theodora, and it will be their refuge if they ever need it. If something ever goes wrong in their lives, they'll need comfort and support. They'll need their mother. So get back on your feet and stay strong!"

"Mother, you're dreaming. They won't come back. They've left for good. Melissanthi only sends a postcard once a year; Julia does the same. I don't even know what Aspasia's doing, and Polyxeni—I still can't believe she left like that. Magdalini is the only one who sends me letters, which is how I know she's doing very well and is happy where she is. So why should they come back?"

"Don't wear yourself out with grief, my girl. You never know what life will bring. Time has its returns . . ."

"If they ever come back it will be because there, where they went, they didn't find their dreams. And I don't want that either. Let them be well, let them be happy."

"There, you see? That's a good attitude to have. You can get through this."

"The only thing I see is my loneliness, and I can't bear it."

"You'll get used to it. You'll stand on your own two feet again and you'll go on living, and you'll wait for them to come back if they need you. And if you can't bear the loneliness, as you say, there are still men for you in the village."

"Mother, please! Don't start with the matchmaking again."

"Fine. Then learn to take life as it comes, and don't let it bring you down."

Julia was right. Theodora didn't want to go on, but she had to. She didn't think she could manage it, but in the end she stood on her own two feet again. Everyday routine returned to the two women's lives. The kitchen smelled of Theodora's hot bread again, and the garden filled up with the vegetables she sowed in orderly rows and tended with love.

The wait for mail was agonizing for them both, but neither of them showed it. When there was news from the children, Theodora read it again and again before the letter or card was placed among the icons. The few photographs that reached her hands would be worn out from her kisses before they too took their place on the mantel.

With every year that passed, however, the postman stopped by less and less often. One spring, after the trees and flowers bloomed and the days had grown noticeably longer, Theodora decided to pass the time by fixing up her mother's old house. Even she didn't know what had inspired her to restore the forgotten little house that was falling to ruins a little distance from her own. She brought in workmen to repaint, build a completely new indoor bathroom, and replace the roof tiles.

"Will you sell it?" her mother asked, when she saw the house looking once again as if it had just been built.

"Of course not! Where did you get that idea?"

"So why did you spend so much on it? What will you do with it? Perhaps we should rent it?"

"I'll think about that. Let's wait and see. For now, I think I'll fix up the house we're living in too. It's been years since the girls left and we haven't really looked after it. And it's time we had a few comforts. Besides, what else can I do with the money I've saved from the crops?"

The two women moved into Julia's house while the renovation took place. Theodora didn't have to scrimp at all. She even built new kitchen cupboards from scratch. She painted the house, built a new, large bathroom, and ordered a television. Julia was angry when she first saw the big box that had a voice like the radio but pictures as well. Theodora laughed at her mother when she would only watch from a hiding place behind a door like a little child. But after a while, curiosity drew the old woman to the "magic box" and she sat next to her daughter to watch the news. She said nothing, but her eyes were open wide.

"Do you like it, Mother?" Theodora asked.

Julia put her finger to her lips to shush her daughter. "Shhh!"

"What on earth's the matter with you?"

"Speak more softly, my child," the old woman scolded. "Can't you see? The man's speaking. It's not polite to interrupt him."

Theodora started to laugh. She then turned off the television and explained as simply as she could to her mother the technology she was experiencing for the first time.

In time, Julia became fanatical about television, to the point where Theodora was uneasy. As soon as she switched it on, her mother sat motionless, watching everything with fascination. Even the foreign serials interested her, despite the fact that she couldn't read the subtitles. When she didn't have any work to do, Theodora would patiently explain to her what was going on.

Theodora seldom read newspapers and magazines, so during the years when they were full of stories about Leonidas and Polyxeni, she was totally unaware. That is, until the village grocer filled her in. When she came down to the village to shop one day, the expression on Mr. Karavassilis's face made an impression on her. The old man looked at her as if he wanted to tell her something but was hesitant.

"What's new, Kyria Theodora?" he finally asked. "Do you hear any news from your daughters? How are they getting along?"

"They're fine," she answered as she filled her basket.

"And Polyxeni? Have you heard any news from her?"

Theodora looked him in the eye and his expression made her chest feel tight. "There's something you want to tell me," she said uneasily. "Has something happened to my child?"

"No . . . don't be afraid. But down there, where she went, she became famous, Kyria Theodora. They say she's an actress."

"Where does it say all that?"

The grocer spread the newspaper out in front of her. It was hard to make out her daughter's face in the badly printed photograph, but it was definitely Polyxeni, even though another name was written in the caption. This "Xenia Olympiou" was certainly her child. Theodora's eyes opened wide when she read further down about the man who had died outside her daughter's home. *Miss Olympiou collapsed when she heard the tragic news.* Theodora looked in bewilderment at Mr. Karavassilis. She was as white as a sheet so he hurried to offer her a chair so she could sit down.

"Don't be upset, madam," he said soothingly. "At least Polyxeni is well."

"Well? How could she be well after what happened to her?"

"Maybe you should go to her?"

The simple question struck Theodora square in her chest. Since Polyxeni had left home, she'd only sent them two cards and they had said coolly and simply that she was well. Theodora knew her daughter didn't need her—and perhaps she didn't even want her around. She got up slowly from Mr. Karavassilis's chair and straightened herself up.

"Polyxeni chose her own road. If she wanted peace and quiet she could have stayed here. I don't need to go anywhere."

Theodora left, unbending and dry eyed, which surprised the old grocer. She was a very hard woman indeed, he thought. Of course, news of Polyxeni spread across the village again and again. From that day on, whenever the newspapers wrote about the young starlet, Theodora drank in every word. At least that way she knew what was going on in her daughter's life, even if she didn't like what she read. At first she tried to hide all news of Polyxeni from her mother, but Julia caught her one day with a newspaper and when her eyes fell on the photograph of her granddaughter, the game was over.

"What business does our daughter have in the newspapers?" the old woman asked. Theodora had no choice but to tell the truth. Julia listened carefully and then shook her head sadly. "Who do you think she takes after?" she asked.

"Did she have to take after someone? That one, Mother, was different from the time she was a very young child."

"At least she succeeded," Julia noted and a glint of pride shone in her eyes.

"What are you saying? What did she succeed at? At making fools of us?"

"Why is she making fools of us? She's doing her job—the papers don't say that she's doing cheap and scandalous things. If you think about the fact that she left here a few years ago with nothing but a bag of bread, and today she's acting on the stage and in the movies . . . I'd say she takes after you."

"Me?"

"Hmm . . . who else had so much stubbornness in them except you? And anyway, instead of being happy that our daughter was so successful, are we supposed to be ashamed?"

"Do you know what the village is saying, though?"

"The village can mind its own business! Are we going to have them judging us? Let them look at their own daughters—all they did was get married, have three kids each, get fat as cows, and spend their time fetching their men from the café where they get drunk. No. Our girl was clever not to end up like that."

Theodora finally gave in. She had to admit, against all the odds, Polyxeni had made an enviable life for herself. She hugged her mother with her eyes full of tears. "Oh Mother, what would I have done without you all these years?"

"You'd have cried over your bad luck. That's what you'd have done."

The next summer, a traveling cinema company brought the first film Polyxeni had made to the village. Julia was adamant about attending. She wasn't about to miss her chance to see a film in which her granddaughter was acting. When she and Theodora turned up just before it began, a mutter spread through the crowd. But in spite of the reaction of the gossip-hungry villagers, Julia made her way to the front row with her back straight and her head high. When the film ended, everyone came up to the two women to congratulate them. At first

Theodora thought she would faint from embarrassment—she wasn't used to so much attention and she still wasn't entirely sure about her daughter's chosen profession—but she finally accepted their congratulations with dignity, just as her mother did.

"I wonder how I did that," she said later, when they returned home.

"If you hadn't done it today, you wouldn't have been able to face going out tomorrow. That's why I forced you to go—besides the fact that I wanted to see the child. This is how we shut those small-minded gossipers up. Why should a mother be ashamed of a daughter who makes money and is so successful in her career that the newspapers write about her all the time? It should be your pride and joy that your child is a success."

Yet again, Julia was right. The village not only accepted the fact that it had birthed an actress, but the locals began to boast about Polyxeni's success as if she was their own daughter. A crowd of people went to see every film, including some from neighboring villages, and every achievement of Polyxeni's in Athens was discussed with unbelievable pride. When they read that their girl, their Polyxeni, would be playing in a film in Italy, it became the sole topic of conversation. Some of the villagers even brought gifts to Theodora.

Still, in spite of what her mother had said, Theodora worried about her daughter. Polyxeni might have money and success, but was she happy? Years later, when Polyxeni began to act on television, Theodora would look intently at the lifeless box and try to decipher from her daughter's expression if she was all right, but her efforts were always in vain. She began to escape more and more frequently to her icons, reading again the letters she had already read a thousand times, looking at the photographs and crying. She hid all this from her mother, of course. She only shared her sorrow and distress with her husband. Theodora often went to his grave, lit a candle, and sat beside him.

"I don't know if you're so high up that you can't hear my voice, but I'm telling you again that you made a mistake, choosing to leave like that. You left me alone, Gerasimos, and you did the wrong thing by me! I needed you and you abandoned me. If you were here, maybe things would have been different. Maybe the children wouldn't have left. And even if they had still left, we would have at least had each other."

More than twenty years had passed. More than twenty years since the wedding of Julia and Fokas. It was as if that ceremony had opened the gates for all of her children to leave, one by one. Where were her daughters now, she wondered. Had fate been kind to them? Had they known happiness, there where they'd chosen to go? Would she die without seeing them again?

◆ ◆ ◆

Melissanthi got off the bus and looked around the familiar village square of her childhood. She had sold the car before she left, and Christos had undertaken to sell the factory and the house as well. She'd made it clear to him that her return home was final. Athens would never see her again.

The plane tree welcomed her with a gentle rustling of its leaves and she smiled. Countless times she'd sat in its shade. It was there, on the bench under its branches, that she had noticed Apostolos for the first time. Everything had started from there. She picked up her suitcase and moved on before anyone recognized her; she wasn't ready to meet anyone she knew. Her feet seemed to carry her by themselves to the only place where she hoped to find peace: her home.

A few minutes before she reached the last bend, her courage deserted her. She sat on a large rock and hid her head in her hands. What if her mother wasn't alive? What if the house had been abandoned and was now in ruins? She had been gone for more than twenty years. A lot could have happened. And Grandmother? Grandfather? What could have happened to them, she wondered. How could she have been so hardhearted toward her own family? How could she have turned her back on the people who raised her? What would it have cost her to visit, even for a day, the place where she'd grown up?

"In the end you were right, Mother," she said to herself. "The river carried me away like a little branch. It took me away and now I see that it was a journey without a destination. But everything is finished. It's enough if you're still alive to forgive me."

She got up determinedly. Whatever was waiting for her around the bend, the hour had come for her to face it. She leaned against a tree and the view took her breath away. The river was shining in the rays of the sun, the house looked bright and new, and smoke was coming from the chimney. Tears blurred her vision, and she closed her eyes for a moment, thinking that she might be dreaming, that the longing in her heart might be creating what she wanted to see rather than letting her see what was really there. When she opened her eyes again the picture was clearer. Her house was in its place. She began to run toward it, not feeling the weight of her suitcase, then she stopped and stared at the river.

"In the end you didn't manage it," she said to the flowing water. "You took me away as you promised, but I managed to go against your current. I managed to come back."

Melissanthi managed to drag her eyes away from the green reflections and fix them again on the house. The garden was planted as it always was. Now she was certain that her mother was fine; only she could keep the garden like that. She pushed open the garden gate, and walked on, looking straight ahead. The old chestnut trees seemed to be waiting for her. *Maybe the plane tree in the square told them*, she thought, and smiled. Everything was full of life around her. Everything looked like people welcoming her. She pushed open the front door, which was unlocked as usual, and went inside, where she took in all the changes that had taken place. She smiled when she saw the television. So civilization had reached here at last. It must have passed under Mount Olympus's nose secretly. Perhaps Prometheus had defied Zeus again, as he did when he gave people fire.

She put down her suitcase, which contained only the bare necessities; she didn't want to return with baggage from a past she wanted to forget. Apart from her simplest clothes, in a box in a corner of her suitcase she had placed photographs of Apostolos, of her son, and of Angelos. She didn't have the courage to leave those behind. Lovingly she stroked the furniture of the large living room where her parents had once received their visitors, then she went on to the other rooms that had once been the jumping-off place for the five girls of the family. It was almost as if not a day had passed. The house had been updated, but almost everything had been put back in its place, even some of her sisters' broken toys. In the room where she had slept with Julia, carefully folded in a drawer, were the ribbons their mother had used to tie their hair into braids. Moved, she sat down on her bed and from there she heard the voices of her mother and . . . yes! That was her grandmother. So she was alive. Melissanthi was overcome with so much joy that she wanted to run and embrace the two of them but she was afraid.

Just then, she heard Theodora's voice. "Oh, Mother! What do you want with the wool? Who are you knitting for?"

"For you," Julia answered. "A jacket for the winter. And anyway, what would I do with my hands otherwise? What would I busy myself with? Perhaps I should start smoking?"

"So for you it's either knitting or smoking. There's no other option . . ." Theodora suddenly stopped speaking when she noticed the suitcase. "What's this suitcase?" she asked. "How did it get here?"

Melissanthi finally found the courage to stand up. She went toward the living room and stood like a statue in the doorway. Theodora noticed her immediately and just stared at her for a while as if she couldn't believe her eyes. She brought her hand to her mouth to hold back a cry of joy and surprise, while Julia crossed herself as her lips formed a prayer of thanksgiving. Melissanthi couldn't hold back any longer. Her mother's arms were open now, waiting to hug her, and she had a great need to be wrapped in their tender embrace. Theodora held her daughter joyfully and began kissing her face, her tears merging with Melissanthi's. The younger woman then found herself going from her mother to her grandmother and back, as the two older women stroked her, as if they were trying to make sure that their minds hadn't deceived them, that the firstborn of the family had returned.

None of them slept that night. Instead, they sat in front of the fire while Melissanthi talked nonstop until the dawn broke and her voice was hoarse. She hid nothing from her mother and her grandmother. Her whole life, from the day she left, became like a confession. She had to get out all the bad things that life had burdened her with. She wanted to cry again for her loved ones who had died, for the joy that life had denied her, for the mistakes that had left her alone with only photographs in her hands.

With the first shy rays of the sun, Theodora took her daughter's hand and led her to bed. She undressed her as if she was a little girl and made her lie down under the covers. Then she sat beside her and stroked her hair. Their eyes met.

"You were right, Mother," Melissanthi said softly. "The river carried me a long way away."

"I was wrong, then," Theodora answered, and when she saw her daughter's confused expression, she went on: "I told you that life was like the river. If it carries you away, you never return. But you returned."

"I've come back forever, Mother. This is my place. I want to end my life here."

"Life doesn't end, my daughter. It flows forever, like the river. Except that you're in a boat now, and you're the one holding the oars. Sleep. The past is over. You have three men in heaven looking after you, and two women on earth who love you. Sleep!"

Melissanthi closed her eyes. Her mother's soft hand, the night-long confession of her painful past, and the stress of the recent weeks had all exhausted her.

As soon as Theodora realized her daughter was sleeping heavily, she returned to the kitchen. Julia had thrown more wood on the fire and was waiting with the coffee in her hand.

"Come," she said. "I've made you coffee."

Theodora collapsed into a chair. Her mother gave her the cup and then stood beside her, stroking her hair.

"Courage, my dear," she said softly. "Our girl has come back, but she's covered in wounds. We'll have to heal them."

"My God! What my child has gone through!" Theodora's tears began to flow.

"The child paid dearly for her mistakes—and she did make mistakes. But now she's here, and what happened can't be undone."

"How can I comfort her for all that? For her child . . . my grandchild?"

"Time will be the doctor, and we two will be the nurses. Drink your coffee now, then let's go and light a candle for the poor souls that were lost."

◆ ◆ ◆

Melissanthi slept for a whole twenty-four hours, to the point where Theodora became anxious and kept going to her room to check on her. When she finally woke up, she was much better. Her grandmother sat her down with some milk and bread and honey in front of her, then stood over her until she had consumed every last bit of it.

It was almost strange how fast Melissanthi took up the rhythms of the village again, as if she hadn't been gone for a single day. Every morning, she drank her coffee with her mother and grandmother, went shopping, and helped with all the household jobs as she had once upon a time. In the afternoons she sat with them on the verandah as they talked about the news of the village, the weddings, the funerals, and the gossip that Mr. Karavassilis was the first to learn and spread around. The only subject they didn't mention was Polyxeni. Theodora had, of course, explained to her eldest daughter the manner in which her sister had left, then the two of them quickly changed the subject as if by prearrangement. But Julia wasn't the sort of person who buried her head in the sand, so one afternoon as they were drinking their usual coffee on the verandah, she brought up the subject again.

"Tell me, granddaughter," she began cheerfully. "When you were living in Athens, didn't you hear anything about our Polyxeni?"

Mother and daughter exchanged a quick glance, then Melissanthi looked down at her cup.

But her grandmother persisted. "What? Didn't you hear?" she continued. "The news reached us here, and you, who were living in Athens, didn't know?"

"The truth is that I knew about her," Melissanthi finally answered. "Our Polyxeni became very well known."

"Did you ever see her?" Theodora wanted to know.

"Yes. A few years ago, Apostolos took me to the theater. We didn't know that this Xenia Olympiou, whose performances everyone was talking about, was Polyxeni. But we realized it when we saw her on the stage."

"How was she?" Theodora asked.

"Beautiful . . . very beautiful, Mother. Everyone was enchanted, watching her."

"Did you speak to her?" Julia inquired longingly.

"No, Grandmother. After the performance a lot of people from the audience rushed to the dressing room to get her autograph, but I took my husband and we left."

"Why, my girl?" Theodora asked. "Why didn't you go and find her and speak to her, so that you two, at least, could be together?"

"I don't know. Truly, I don't know. The way I saw her on the stage—beautiful, radiant—it was as if she were someone else. It wasn't the Polyxeni who scraped her knees with me when we played, my sister who I struggled with so she would learn her multiplication. She was a famous actress, not the girl I left behind when I went away."

"I understand," Theodora murmured. "When I see her on the screen in the films that show here sometimes, I don't recognize the daughter whose hair I braided so tightly."

"Anyway, I learned all about her from the newspapers. Later her life was turned upside down too." Melissanthi was silent. She turned her eyes again to the river. It had been nearly a month since she'd returned and she hadn't approached it. She still avoided even looking at it until now.

"What's going on, Melissanthi?" her mother asked. "Why are you looking at the river? Why don't you go near it anymore? The river's not responsible for what happened to you. It was always here, but you left. You let life take you from your path."

"The same as Polyxeni," the young woman whispered and looked sadly at Theodora. "Something tells me that she'll come back here too—with open wounds."

Theodora's heart contracted. She prayed with all her strength that this premonition of Melissanthi's wasn't true.

◆ ◆ ◆

Theodora swept the wooden verandah with all her strength, more because she wanted something to do than because it was dirty. Her mother had lain down for a rest, as had Melissanthi, but Theodora herself never slept during the day. As the years passed, she seemed to need less and less sleep, and besides she considered naps a waste of time.

Spring had worked its miracle again, adorning the garden with flowers of every color and filling the air with their scent. Theodora had loved spring since she was a child. In a few days they would be celebrating the first of May, and she was sad that she didn't have a single grandchild near her to teach how to weave a wreath.

She looked down at the river, out of habit more than anything, and the broom fell from her hands. The head that emerged from the water was her daughter's.

◆ ◆ ◆

Aspasia had arrived at midday that day holding little Theodora's hand tightly. The bus had made the child a little dizzy, but as soon as she set foot in the square she recovered and looked around her with interest.

"Is this your village, Mama?" she asked.

"Yes, this is the square. In the summer it's full of children playing, old men drinking coffee, and girls sharing their first secrets under the plane tree."

"Did you do that too?"

"Yes, but that was a lifetime ago! My sisters and I used to sit here and watch the village boys, and we'd laugh when we saw them trying to impress us."

Theodora looked at her mother and smiled. She'd never seen her like this. This calmness and that sweet smile, which gently raised the corners of her lips, was something she liked very much. A slight wind lifted their hair. Aspasia raised her eyes and saw the plane tree shaking its leaves, making a soft noise like a whisper, and only she knew what it was saying to her: "Welcome!"

"And where's your house, Mama? Where's the river?" her daughter asked, interrupting her reverie.

"We'll have to walk. Are you tired? Do you want us to sit and drink an orange soda first?"

"No! No, Mama! I want to see where you grew up so much."

Picking up her suitcase, Aspasia showed Theodora the way. At the clearing where she'd first met Stavros, she stood still and her daughter looked at her anxiously.

"What's the matter, Mama? Don't you feel well?"

"I'm fine. But this is where I first met your father."

"Really?" Theodora's eyes widened and she looked around her with interest.

"Yes, he used to bring supplies for Mr. Karavassilis's grocery store—the one you saw when we got off the bus—and he was lost. I was looking for a quiet place where I could practice the latest popular song." Aspasia stopped and her bitter smile made Theodora squeeze her hand encouragingly so she would continue. "I showed him the way, and afterward, because it was late and he couldn't go back, I took him to your grandmother and asked her to let him stay."

"And Grandmother? Did she agree?"

"Yes. She let him sleep in the kitchen and I'm sure that she didn't close her eyes all night because she was so anxious with a strange man in our house. I remember she locked us in our rooms."

"And then . . ."

"Then your father began to come more and more often . . . and I waited for him, each time looking forward to it more and more."

"Did you love him, Mama?"

"I think I loved him from the first moment I saw him. Don't ask me anything else, though. I don't know what happened to us afterward; somehow we lost what we had."

They went on walking in silence. Aspasia was almost holding her breath. What sort of state would the house be in, she wondered. Was her mother well? And Grandmother? And Grandfather? She had never been interested in finding out how they were doing in all these years and now . . . She had trouble holding back a cry that rose to her lips when she saw the house looking like new and when her eyes rested on the lazy river. It was as if a day hadn't passed since she'd left. She walked toward the riverbank as if she was hypnotized, remembering her mother's words: *And if the trials are very strong, remember that here, in this corner of the earth, is the river. Dive into it to purify yourself again!*

When she reached the river's edge, Aspasia didn't hesitate for a moment. The freezing water first touched her feet, then reached her knees. She went ahead and submerged herself until she felt it enveloping her entire body. A thousand freezing needles pierced her skin and she abandoned herself to them. She didn't know whether her encounter with the frigid water would be enough to wash away all the mistakes she'd made. She didn't know if one immersion would be enough to dissolve the shame she felt.

"Come out, Aspasia!"

She turned and saw her mother standing on the bank with a blanket in her hand, looking at her with tear-filled eyes.

"Whatever it is you want the river to wash off you, it's gone now," Theodora continued. "You don't have to catch pneumonia!"

Aspasia came out and stood in front of her mother, shivering from cold and emotion. Theodora wrapped the blanket around her and held her. The younger woman felt like a boat that had been smashed by a storm and had finally entered a calm harbor. Her mother stroked her tenderly and rested her lips on her wet hair, leaving hungry kisses there. Aspasia felt burning tears well up in her eyes, scorching her like molten metal, and sobs shook her body.

"Shhh!" her mother quieted her. "Enough. You came back; everything will be fine. Everything will be mended."

Aspasia pulled back from her mother's arms and fixed her eyes on hers. "Mama, I'm sorry," she managed to say, her chin trembling uncontrollably.

"Only God forgives, my child. People give understanding and love. Welcome home."

Little Theodora had stood back watching her mother and grandmother's reunion, but now she thought she'd waited long enough. She also wanted to know her grandmother's embrace and came closer. Sensing the girl's presence, Theodora turned toward her. She looked so much like Aspasia at that age that Theodora was overwhelmed.

"Mother, this is your granddaughter and she's named after you," Aspasia said quietly.

"Hello, Grandma."

With tears of joy, the elder Theodora folded the child in her arms. She let her hands pass over her, as if she wanted an imprint of every inch of her on her palms. Then she turned her gaze toward the blue sky and whispered her thanks to God. "Praised be your name who made me worthy of holding at least one grandchild in my arms!" As if she'd suddenly remembered, the elder Theodora turned to Aspasia and asked, "And the other one? You had another daughter, didn't you?" Aspasia's look froze her soul. "What happened to Stella, Aspasia? Why isn't she with you?"

Aspasia lowered her head and Theodora turned to her grandchild.

"She might be watching us now," the girl answered.

Theodora brought her hand to her lips. Pain distorted her features for a moment, but her granddaughter's eyes, which were looking at her pleadingly, brought her back to herself. "Let's go!" she said decisively. "Your mother must change out of those wet clothes and then the others have to see you."

"What others?" Aspasia wanted to know.

"First, your grandmother!"

"Has Mama got a grandmother?" Little Theodora seemed excited by the news.

"Of course she has! And you have a great-grandmother!"

"Is Grandmother well?" Aspasia asked.

"Better than all of us. Come, let's go! And it's not only Julia in the house; Melissanthi has come back too."

Aspasia's eyes opened wide. "Is my sister really here?" she asked, and when her mother nodded, she threw off the blanket and started running toward the house.

Melissanthi had gotten up from the bed with a strange feeling. She had enjoyed the book she was reading until yesterday, but now she felt she didn't understand it. She gave up the effort and went to look for her mother with the intention of taking her to the village for an afternoon dessert at Mr. Karavassilis's shop. When she didn't find her in the house, she went out onto the verandah to look for her. It was at that very moment that Aspasia came out of the river.

The shock was so strong it left Melissanthi stunned. She couldn't believe her eyes—the scene in front of her seemed crazy. As if of their own volition, her legs began to take her down the steps, but her strength abandoned her and she found herself sitting on the fifth step watching the two women embrace. When her eyes rested on the young girl that her mother was holding in her arms, she stopped breathing. It must be her sister's daughter, her niece.

She jumped up like a spring and began to run at the same moment that Aspasia came running to meet her. Their hearts met before they did, and when their bodies caught up, each hugged the other with the hunger of two decades. Theodora walked toward them, holding her granddaughter around the shoulders, her heart singing with joy.

"It's a lovely picture, isn't it, Grandma?" little Theodora asked.

"The most beautiful! My sweet child, I'm so happy. I think I must be dreaming!"

Melissanthi managed to let go of her sister long enough to turn toward her niece. "This is your daughter, isn't it?" she asked Aspasia.

"Yes . . . Theodora."

Melissanthi approached the girl and hugged her. "You're exactly like your mother!" she said after she'd planted many kisses on her cheeks.

That night the moon came out to shine on their happy home. The two chestnut trees were still—not a rustle, not a stir—so as not to disturb the women sitting in the kitchen, trying to fill the gap of twenty years, however painful that was. Julia held her great-granddaughter's hand as if she was afraid that this miracle that life had granted her might disappear. The elder Theodora kept wiping her eyes as Aspasia told her about Stella's death. She didn't have the courage to tell her mother the rest of the story, at least not in front of the child.

When the little one's eyes grew heavy and she'd been put to bed, mother and grandmother tactfully withdrew, leaving the two sisters alone. Only then did Aspasia release what she had carried inside her with so much pain. Melissanthi listened to the confession carefully. Aspasia stopped talking when she'd finished the story and looked at her sister, who was sitting in silence.

"Don't you have anything to say?" she asked.

"What should I say?"

"I don't know . . . I imagine you didn't expect that your sister could fall so low. Maybe you despise me. I wouldn't blame you, of course."

"You're very far from the truth," Melissanthi said. "I'm not one to cast stones."

It was now her turn to talk, to bare her soul and tell the story of the journey that had led her to take the road of return.

"Do you understand now why I don't judge you?" Melissanthi asked when she had finished. "The worst thing is that I returned with empty arms. What I wouldn't give to have my child with me."

"Yes, I understand. I lost a child too, and I lost my husband. And if little Theodora had followed her father and I'd lost her, as well, I would have made up my mind to . . . leave."

"You mean to commit suicide?"

"That was one thought I had. I had lost everything."

"Like me. I don't know what kept me alive after the death of my child. I think I kept myself going so I could accept the punishment that I received. I didn't want to run away and save myself from it. I bent my head as if God had slapped me. After my husband's death, I had no doubt that God had condemned me to loneliness and I accepted it. Apostolos himself showed me the way to come back. He loved me so much that he didn't want to leave me without help, even after his death."

"I didn't leave either love or respect in my husband's heart," Aspasia admitted, and her eyes filled with tears again. "I destroyed everything!"

"Do you still love him?"

"Yes, but I accept the fact that he found what he deserved in another woman. I wasn't worthy. I don't know what got into me all those years when I was indifferent, and I don't know what I was looking for in the arms of all those other men. Nor do I know now why my daughter came with me instead of turning her back on me. She would have been within her rights to pay me back with the same indifference I'd shown to her all those years. I was an unworthy mother and yet my daughter forgave me."

"Then maybe you'd better forgive yourself too, Aspasia. And perhaps I should forgive myself as well. We came back, and that says something."

"I don't know if it's enough. I don't know how much power the present has to erase the past, or at least to correct the mistakes."

In spite of Aspasia's doubts, the magical influence of return became quite clear the very next day. Little Theodora had become attached to her grandmother and followed her every step. Aspasia, like Melissanthi, had the feeling that she had only been away from home for a day. Without even having to think about it, she went to the pantry and took out the flour for her mother to make the bread, just as she'd done as a child. Then she prepared the big trough to knead the dough. Melissanthi had already put the pan of water on to heat. As Grandmother was in the yard plucking a chicken for their dinner, Aspasia began to peel the potatoes. The house suddenly felt like a working beehive. This spring promised to be the best in many years for all of them.

On the first of May, the two Theodoras made a large, multicolored wreath. Aspasia pinned it to the door and they all sat on the verandah to admire it. In the afternoon they went for a walk to the square and Mr. Karavassilis was so pleased to see the family together that he refused to accept any money for the sweet treats they had eaten.

In time, a few of Aspasia's old schoolmates dropped by the house and she found herself laughing aloud at some of their memories, while her daughter looked on, happily admiring her. It was the first time Aspasia saw such pride in her daughter's eyes. And if she hadn't been with so many people at the time, she would certainly have cried.

Melissanthi still hadn't gone near the river. One day, when Aspasia insisted, she tried to approach it. But when she got close, she stopped.

Aspasia turned toward her. "It can't carry us away anymore, Melissanthi. In any case it's not responsible for the way our lives ended up."

"Mother said the same thing. But I know I have a debt to pay for everything I did."

"Do you remember when we were kids? This is where we played, and later as young girls, this is where we dreamed."

"And what did we achieve of those dreams? We came back defeated, carrying a need for the peace of the river."

"But we became wiser. Grandmother says, if you don't suffer, you don't learn."

Melissanthi came closer and sat on the bank beside Aspasia.

"I wonder what happened to the others," she said after a few minutes of silence. "Do you think they'll come back too?"

"What for?" Aspasia answered. "Julia, from what Mother says, is in Africa with her husband and has three children! Imagine! As for Magdalini, since her husband has a business in America, why would she come here? Then there's Polyxeni, who's famous and rich. Why would she return? She was the one who wanted to leave more than any of us, remember?"

"She didn't marry," Melissanthi said thoughtfully. "At least that's what the newspapers say."

"She never spoke about marriage or children. She was strange . . ."

"In the village, they said she had her nose stuck up in the air."

"And were they wrong? Do you remember how she used to raise one eyebrow and look at people in such a superior way? Stavros told me that when she looked at him, he never knew what to say. He thought whatever he said would be wrong!"

Both sisters laughed at the memory.

◆ ◆ ◆

That year, the summer was in a hurry. So much so that it pushed spring aside long before the end of May. The woolen carpets were washed and put in storage with mothballs, as were the blankets. Little Theodora was thrilled with all these jobs.

That afternoon the two grandmothers set out for the cemetery to light candles for their husbands and the child accompanied them. Melissanthi and Aspasia sat down on the verandah, ready to enjoy their afternoon coffee in the peace and fresh air.

"I adore them," Melissanthi said as soon as they left. "But the truth is, they make a lot of noise."

Aspasia nodded and smiled before she answered. "The little one is happier than I've seen her for years. She's become a child of her own age again."

"Your daughter is lovable."

"She loves you; she told me last night. She also told me that your eyes, even when you laugh, are sad," Aspasia added.

"She's very clever and observant. You must be proud."

Aspasia nodded her head again and her eyes turned toward the horizon, where, the very next moment, something drew her attention. Melissanthi noticed and followed her sister's gaze. Two figures who were coming down the hill.

"Polyxeni?" Melissanthi said in a whisper.

"We can't both be seeing this and both be wrong!" Aspasia exclaimed.

The two sisters stood up at the same time.

Polyxeni had arrived in the village a little while earlier with Vassiliki. It had been a difficult journey for her. The familiar landscape outside the window of the bus had plunged her into a melancholy silence. Vassiliki was sensitive to her mother's moods and stayed silent too. When they got off in the village square, Polyxeni surveyed her surroundings and caught sight of the old plane tree. It moved its branches to welcome her as it had done to her sisters, but Polyxeni didn't know that. At first it seemed to her that the old tree was making fun of her. Still, she smiled.

"Is this the village you told me about, Mama?" Vassiliki asked, finally breaking the silence of the last hours.

"Yes, my darling. This is where I grew up, where I played, where I dreamed," Polyxeni answered, planting a kiss on the child's forehead.

"It's very beautiful. Look at that big tree. It's really enormous!"

"It's a plane tree. In the afternoon the square fills with people and lots of children run around and shout. Before my father died he would bring us here on Sundays and we'd each get a treat at Mr. Karavassilis's. He's famous for his cakes and pies."

"And your house? Where's your house, Mama? Where's the house by the river that you told me about?"

Vassiliki seemed impatient and Polyxeni smiled.

"We'll have to walk a little, my little miss!"

"Let's go then! What are we waiting for?" The child pulled her by the hand.

They started walking away from the square just as Mr. Karavassilis came outside his shop to drink his coffee. He immediately recognized the actress.

"Ah, that," he said to himself, "that seems like a miracle!"

He wondered who the girl was who was holding Polyxeni's hand. Thanks to Stathis's lawyer friend, no information had come out in the press about Vassiliki so that the child would be protected.

Polyxeni quickened her step as she drew closer to the house. She was in a hurry to see the nest she had flown from so many years ago. Just before the final bend, she stopped, frozen. What if her mother was no longer alive? What if something had happened? What if the house didn't belong to the family anymore? What would she do then? Where would she go?

She continued walking with her mind made up. Whatever had happened, she wouldn't go back.

The sun shone blindingly on the river's surface. The reflection was so bright it made Polyxeni turn her eyes toward the house instead. A smile broke out on her face when she saw it looking so strong and new.

"How beautiful it is here!" Vassiliki declared.

Polyxeni turned to her daughter. "Do you like it, my dear?" she asked.

"It's wonderful, Mama! Did you really grow up here?"

"Yes. Here."

"How could you leave such a paradise?" Vassiliki wondered.

Polyxeni smiled somewhat bitterly now. "I was looking for another paradise, my dear, but I was wrong. After so many years, I've learned that every person has the right to just one paradise, and when he has it before him, he must respect it."

"But for me, anyway, it's better that you left."

"Why do you say that?"

"Because if you hadn't left here you wouldn't have met my mother, and I wouldn't have you, now that she is dead."

Polyxeni took the child in her arms and held her for a few moments, long enough for Vassiliki to look toward the house and ask, "Mama, who are those two ladies standing and looking at us?"

Polyxeni let her daughter go and turned to see what she was talking about. Her breath came out noisily when she recognized them. "My Lord!" she called out. "Melissanthi! Aspasia! My sisters!"

Almost at the exact same moment, the three started forward to meet each other. Melissanthi and Aspasia had already come out of the garden gate and Polyxeni ran toward them as Vassiliki followed without any hurry. She knew everything about her mother's sisters. Her mother had told her about them and she knew she should be tactful at this first meeting after so many years. She stopped a little way off and watched her mother disappear in the arms of the other two women. She could see their tear-filled eyes and hear their laughter and every word clearly.

"I can't believe it!" Polyxeni said over and over. "How come you're here? What are you doing at home?"

"You've come back! You've come back too!" Aspasia said as she held her sister's face in her hands, as if she wanted to make sure it was really her and not someone who just looked like her.

Melissanthi didn't say anything. The lump that had formed in her throat wouldn't let her say a word. She held Polyxeni's hand and kissed it. Vassiliki moved forward and caught up with them.

Polyxeni pulled herself away from her sisters' arms and placed her hands on her daughter's shoulders before turning to them again. "This is Vassiliki," she announced. "She's my daughter. I adopted her when her parents were killed. They were my dear friends. And their child is my child, my blood."

It was Vassiliki's turn to disappear into the arms of the two women, and strangely, the child felt as if she had found her aunts, that she had suddenly acquired a family.

They all went into the house together. Polyxeni looked around her with tears in her eyes. Everything was new, and yet nothing had changed. It was obvious that things had been updated, but without spoiling the character of the house. Even her mother's beloved armchair in front of the fireplace was the same, but the varnish on the arms now shone; it had clearly been preserved with care.

She turned to her sisters, who were observing her with love. "Mother?" she dared to ask.

"She's fine," answered Melissanthi, who was able to speak now. "And so is Grandmother!"

"Grandmother is still alive?" Polyxeni's voice was full of emotion.

"Of course she's alive!" Aspasia said. "A little older, of course, but strong."

"Where is she?"

"They've gone to the cemetery to light candles for Father and Grandfather," Melissanthi answered. Then she added, "Aspasia's daughter Theodora is with them."

Polyxeni looked at both her sisters in amazement. "I don't believe it! We're together, along with our children too!" Then she thought to ask, "And you, Melissanthi? Do you have children as well?"

Melissanthi gave her a sad look. "I had a son, but I lost him."

Polyxeni approached her sister and embraced her. "I'm sorry. I'm guessing that all three of our ships were wrecked. That's why you came back, like I did, isn't it?"

But Aspasia interrupted them. "It's not the time for that. We have the child here," she said and nodded toward Vassiliki. The girl approached her then, ready to cry herself. "Not you too, my dear," Aspasia said and hugged her. "You mustn't cry. You're with us now, and in a little while, when the others come back, you'll meet my daughter. You'll have your cousin to play with, just like we three had each other back then."

Little Theodora's voice could be heard from the road, singing with her grandmothers.

"They're coming!" Aspasia said, running to the window. "Hide! Let's surprise them!"

As if they'd gone back to their childhood, when the five of them invented tricks to play on their parents, Polyxeni scrambled to find a place to hide. She took Vassiliki, who was laughing at the game, and the two hid in the kitchen. The elder Theodora came in first and found her daughters sitting on the sofa, smiling for no reason.

"Why are you two looking so excited?" she asked.

"Us? There's nothing wrong with us," Aspasia hurried to answer.

"I don't believe a word of it! It's written all over your faces that you've cooked something up!" she said, pretending to be annoyed.

Now Grandmother Julia and little Theodora came into the room.

"What makes you say something like that?" Melissanthi chimed in. "We're just sitting here nice and quiet."

"Ah, so now you're helping your sister," Theodora teased. "Now I'm sure you two are up to something. You've done the same thing since you were children. One would tell a lie and the other one would back her up. I'm sure that if Polyxeni were here she'd have poured some sauce on the top to make me believe you! She had plenty of imagination when it came to lies!"

"I'm here, Mother . . . but this time there's no need for lies."

Theodora turned toward her daughter, who was looking at her with a guilty expression from the doorway of the living room. She opened and closed her eyes as if she wanted to clear them, to drive away the false image she was seeing. It couldn't be . . . but it was so beautiful and real looking!

Polyxeni didn't leave her mother in doubt any longer. She ran to her, held her tightly, and whispered a single phrase in her ear: "I'm sorry!"

As if she had woken up from some lethargy, Theodora folded her child in her arms, unable to speak or do anything but kiss Polyxeni again and again. The house filled with even more voices, just like the old days, with everyone talking at once. Theodora hugged Vassiliki, her second granddaughter. When Polyxeni explained that she had adopted her, her mother cut her off immediately. "Why are you telling me that?" she said. "What difference does it make? To me, it's as if this child came from you. She's my flesh and blood from now on, just like Theodora!"

As for little Theodora, having lost her sister so tragically, she felt an immediate attachment to Vassiliki and didn't let her out of her sight. They even slept in the same bed, and often their mothers would see the two of them sitting together by the river, talking for hours.

"Do they remind you of anything?" Polyxeni asked her sisters two weeks later, when it had become obvious to everyone that the two girls were like conjoined twins.

Melissanthi nodded. Evening had fallen and the three women were sitting beside the river.

"It's as strange as it is moving. They're our future and they're behaving just like us! I just hope they don't make the same mistakes we did," Aspasia answered.

They were all silent for a while. Suddenly, Polyxeni began talking about her life. She hadn't revealed anything to anyone since the day she'd returned. That night, though, she began to unwind the ball of her life. Only when she reached the death of Leonidas did she stop for a moment and turn to Melissanthi. "As you see, you're not the only one who caused the death of a young man," she said. "Except that I didn't love Leonidas as you loved Angelos. I used him. And even if I didn't understand what I was doing then, I still can't forgive myself now."

"None of us can forgive ourselves for what we've done," Aspasia said quietly, as if she were afraid the river itself might hear her words.

Polyxeni went on until she reached the accident that took Stathis and Martha from her. Sobs interrupted her story. The two sisters hurried to embrace her and let her mourn again for the beloved friends she had lost, while they wept with her for their own losses.

When they'd recovered Melissanthi mused, "In the end we were so ungrateful for everything life gave us that I doubt we could atone for it, even if we had another whole lifetime to do it."

"I'll always ask myself why I left here," Polyxeni went on. "And it wasn't enough that I left the way I did, knowing how much I'd hurt my mother; during all those years I wasn't even interested in knowing how she was! As least with you it was different. You fell in love, you got married, and you followed your men. But me?"

"You were the most honest!" Melissanthi protested. "You followed your dream. Me, though? I married Apostolos for his money. At least in the beginning, that's all I saw. And even though I had all the time in the world, I didn't visit our mother either. What was a little trip up here to me? And yet I never did it! I was away for twenty years and in the end I stopped even writing. I never wondered if she was alive, or how she was living until I came back, and that was because I needed her!"

"It's the same with me!" Aspasia began. "I was supposed to be in love with Stavros, and yet as soon as I left I began to feel bored. The desire to sing professionally rose up in me, and along with it came another side of my character that I didn't even know existed. As for our mother, I wasn't interested in finding out how she was either, and I never thought of coming for a visit. She lived alone with Grandmother. Who knows how difficult it was for her all those years, and yet she welcomed us without ever saying a word about our having ignored her, without complaining. I'm ashamed to look her in the eye. At least you, Polyxeni, never betrayed anyone!"

"I'm not so sure about that. The very fact that I put our mother in such a difficult position, leaving like a thief—I'd say that was a betrayal. Do you know that I only sent her two postcards during all the years I was away? Never mind the life I've led since the day I left! You'd think this house had turned us into something evil. We abandoned it without a second thought and remembered it only when we'd ruined our lives."

The three of them hung their heads, feeling ashamed, until the sound of a car approaching attracted their attention. *A car at this hour?* each one thought.

"Somebody's lost again," Aspasia suggested.

They got up and walked toward the road. The moon was full and lit up the countryside like an enormous lamp. By its light they saw two women and a girl getting out of the car. The driver unloaded a few things, then got back into the car and drove away.

All three of them put their hands to their mouths to hold back their cries at the sight of Magdalini, Anna, and a child they didn't recognize.

"Magdalini?" It was Melissanthi who dared to speak first.

Magdalini looked up to see her three sisters looking at her, frozen like statues in the moonlight. "Melissanthi? Aspasia? Polyxeni?" She said their names in disbelief, certain that the three visions in front of her would vanish at any moment.

But they didn't. Instead, she saw the heads of her sisters nodding as they approached her. She touched their faces with awe, still unable to believe what she was seeing. She had covered endless miles without stopping. She'd paid a fortune to the driver to persuade him to bring her all the way to the foothills of Olympus, and she never expected that the first people she'd see would be her sisters. She lost herself in their arms, her heart swelling with unspoken joy. For a moment she was afraid she would faint from emotion, but their kisses, hugs, and laughter brought her to herself again. Magdalini managed to disentangle herself from their hands and to give her aunt a chance to meet them since Anna had never met either Melissanthi or Aspasia. Finally, it was Magdalini's daughter who found herself in the foreground. "And this is little Theodora, though we call her Doris!" Magdalini introduced her proudly.

Polyxeni burst out laughing. "Now there are three Theodoras in the house! This could get complicated!"

Aspasia, who was now laughing as well, undertook to explain. "I have a daughter called Theodora too."

"Speaking of Theodoras," added Melissanthi, "the senior one will be thunderstruck by the return of her fourth daughter!"

They all ran toward the house. Melissanthi, Aspasia, and Polyxeni entered first. When they walked into the kitchen, still laughing, the eldest Theodora, who was serving plates of food to little Theodora and Vassiliki, looked at them in surprise.

"What's wrong with you that you're behaving like babies?" she asked. The three sisters stood in a row with their hands crossed behind their backs, just as they had done as children.

Theodora now looked a little uneasy. "Ah, you'll upset me!" she sighed, half serious, half joking. "What have you done this time?"

"Mama, I swear, we haven't done anything!" Polyxeni hurried to answer.

But her expression made her daughter giggle happily.

"Grandma, don't believe her!" said Vassiliki. "All the time we were away, they were cooking something up."

"Shhh, you!" Polyxeni scolded her affectionately.

"It's true, Mother," Melissanthi began seriously. "Your daughters have been returning one by one—aren't you jealous?"

"What should I be jealous of, daughter? Are you crazy?"

Aspasia jumped in next. "Because we sisters have all been reunited with one another. Wouldn't you like to be with your sister too?"

Theodora was confused for a moment, but suddenly her face brightened. She turned toward the door and Anna, who came in first, took her breath away. She stood still, as if she'd turned into stone, while her sister smiled at her. Grandmother Julia, with the agility of a girl, ran to embrace her daughter, weeping. Before the hugs had ended, Magdalini's Theodora ran into the house and the tears turned to laughter, then back to tears again, when Magdalini finally came in.

Whoever passed by the house that evening would have thought there was a celebration going on, one that was interrupted, now and then, by a sob. Magdalini told her family about the terror she had lived through in Chicago. She also described what she had loved about America in general and what she hadn't. The three youngest members of the family had their arms around each other, their faces now shining, now darkening at what they heard. At the end they fell asleep, tired, and their mothers put all three of them in the double bed.

Anna and Theodora had gone out into the fresh night air and no one thought of disturbing them. Seated side by side on the steps, they looked at the dark horizon in silence.

Anna's voice was the first to break the silence. "Will you ever be able to forgive me?"

"What are you asking me to forgive you for?"

"For everything I was responsible for in your child's life. Of course I didn't want any of it to happen, and I couldn't know that it would, but the result remains the same. I took her with me to have a better future and ruined her life."

"You said it yourself, Anna. You couldn't know."

"Yes, but who was I to believe that I could do something better for her than her own mother could? How could I, with so much pride, argue that she would be better off in America?"

"There's no point in your saying all that," Theodora said, trying to calm her. "In the end, Magdalini herself wanted to go—you didn't force her to. Nor did anyone put pressure on the other girls to leave. They wanted it themselves, and look what happened. One by one they turned their lives upside down, their souls destroyed by endless mistakes. Each one is carrying a cross; even now that they've returned to the security of the familiar, I don't think they've managed to put that cross down for a moment and rest, to find peace."

"They seem fine, but . . . Melissanthi, even when she smiles, you see from her expression that her soul is crying."

"She's the only one who lost everything. The others chased the same sun, and when they touched it, they got burned by its flame too. But they managed to hold on to something—a ray. They lost husbands and children, but each one returned with a daughter. That's something! But Melissanthi is alone."

"And you? How do you feel with your children around you again?"

"I don't know, Anna. At first I was glad. The loneliness was painful all those years, and if I hadn't had our mother, I don't know if I could have managed. I might have drowned myself in the river. But now that I see them, now that I know what they've been through . . . It would have been better if I'd died lonely rather than see my children suffering so much."

"I understand. But now they'll make a new beginning. They're still young. They can fix up their lives again."

"Do you know something? Our mother said the same thing to me when I lost Gerasimos. She tried to persuade me to remarry many times, but like my daughters, I'd experienced the real thing. I couldn't compromise with something less. At least they'll always have one another, but I didn't have you."

Hesitantly, Anna reached out her hand and stroked Theodora's hair. She was relieved to feel her sister's body lean toward her and hurried to embrace her. "I lived a life far away from you," she said to her in a low voice. "I'm afraid we two will have to get to know each other again from the beginning."

"We've got plenty of time ahead of us!" Theodora said, and a look of peace spread across her face at last.

That summer was like a fairy tale. The house overflowed with life and children's voices. Theodora seemed to have shed decades, as did Grandmother Julia. Three great-grandchildren surrounded her every day and she shared her attention with them equally, while at the same time her hands never stopped working. In a little while winter would be coming and she wanted to make jackets for all of them. The housework was finished early each day with so many hands ready to work. At lunchtime, the big kitchen table—the same one that had hidden the secret trapdoor during the war—was only just big enough for them all. Theodora got out the large saucepans again and the baking dishes she had used back then, and the smell of the enormous loaves and pies she baked with her grandchildren's help filled the house.

On Sundays they all put on their best clothes and went to Mr. Karavassilis's shop, where they settled in at a table to order sweets and orange sodas. Everyone in the village was happy about the reunion of Theodora's family. The whole village had watched her walk along her lonely path all those years and their respect for her was quite clear.

That Sunday, at the end of August, they were all together again, looking for a little shade under the big plane tree. A lot of people came to their table to chat—the news of the village was always full of interest—while the children in the square made a terrible noise with their shouting and their games. Doris, the youngest Theodora, had completely found herself; she'd already made friends with the children she would go to school with in the autumn. The two older girls, having quickly eaten their treats, sat with the other children their age under the plane tree and chatted, while keeping a watchful eye on the little one.

The big bus arrived spluttering at the square. When its doors opened, everyone looked to see who was getting off—on Sundays, few people came to the village. A short woman stepped down first and helped an old lady who followed her. Behind her were three girls and a black woman. This last arrival, in particular, attracted everyone's attention. They'd never seen a person with different-colored skin before. Perhaps it was this distraction that kept them from realizing that the woman leading this little band of travelers was Julia.

Theodora felt her heart thumping before she even recognized her daughter. When she finally realized who this new arrival was, she raised her hand to her chest, while tears started streaming from her eyes.

Melissanthi was the first to notice. "Mama!" she shouted. "What's the matter? What's wrong with you?"

They all turned to her. Unable to speak, Theodora stood up and walked toward Julia, who was examining her bags to make sure they'd all been unloaded from the bus. She raised her eyes instinctively and saw her mother's tears and her trembling lips.

For years in the village they talked about that meeting. No one remembered who first embraced who, but they recalled that their voices were full of joy and their scattered laughter reached the old plane tree. Lefteris's son happened to be there. In the large back of his new truck, he loaded Julia and her mother-in-law, Evanthia, her daughters Hara, Theodora, and Evanthia, and her friend Faida, and all of their baggage. Grandmother Julia sat in the front seat beside him, and he took them to the house, which overflowed with grown-ups and children. There wasn't enough room for them to all stay together, but it didn't matter; that night, apart from the children, no one slept.

"I still can't believe it," Julia said for about the tenth time. "We're all here, after so many years, and all determined to stay forever!"

"Who could have predicted it?" Grandmother Julia joined in. "Now I'll be able to close my eyes peacefully," she quietly added.

"It's now, Mother, that you need to stay with us," Theodora answered her. "We spent all those years by ourselves. Now that the children and grandchildren have arrived, it's time for us to laugh, despite everything that's happened."

Grandmother Julia's renovated house was perfect for the younger Julia and her family. With Faida's help, they cleaned it and set themselves up there, but every day they went back to Theodora's so they could all be together. The six youngest members of the family, from Julia's daughter Hara down to Magdalini's daughter Doris, were inseparable. The subjects of their conversations were inexhaustible and their excuses for laughter endless.

One evening Hara pointed out, "If you really think about it, we have a problem. There are not one, not two, not ten, but sixteen women living together here. Maybe a man had better come here soon to break up the monotony? But who would dare come into this women's lair?"

"It reminds me of the Amazons!" Vassiliki shot out.

"That means there can't be a male, even as an example!" said the older Theodora.

They all burst out laughing and only Grandmother Theodora had a little sadness in her expression. Neither her mother, nor herself, nor her daughters had managed to see the male children they'd given birth to grow into men. God had delivered his verdict. At least she had the comfort of knowing that her six granddaughters had made up their minds to stay in their mother's village and make their home in the shadow of Olympus.

Every afternoon Grandmother Julia, the elder Theodora, Anna, and the elder Evanthia drank their coffee on the verandah and talked. One afternoon, Evanthia turned to Theodora and declared, "I want to ask your forgiveness."

Theodora looked at her in surprise. "What do you want my forgiveness for?" she asked.

"Because really I don't have the right to be here. I don't deserve so much kindness, not from you, and not from your daughter after—"

Theodora cut her off. "I know what you're going to say, but please don't say it. All my children were destroyed and came back here to their roots to make a new beginning. You make sure you do the same and leave the past in peace!"

"You speak like that because you don't know. It wouldn't even cross your mind, what I did when . . ."

"No. The truth is that it wouldn't have crossed my mind, but my daughter told me."

"She did?"

"Yes."

"And you accepted me in your home?" Evanthia was moved.

"Evanthia, we all make mistakes, but the moment comes when we pay for them. And you paid for yours, and very dearly. So I have nothing to forgive you for. Look at our children and grandchildren, and pray to God that they'll finally find peace."

Theodora touched Evanthia's hand and the two of them turned to look at the river. The grandchildren were playing happily there, while their mothers watched them, sitting together on the bank.

"It's like a dream, isn't it?" Melissanthi said to her sisters. "We're all gathered together again under the same roof, looking at the same river, and none of us can imagine our lives far from this corner of the earth. And yet this place used to suffocate us; we couldn't wait to leave it."

"The strangest thing," said Julia, "is that, for some of us, our own children wanted us to return. What drove us out of the village drew them here like a magnet!"

"For me, it was as if God himself planted the idea of returning in my mind," Magdalini said. "In this quiet place I feel I'm near Him. I feel as if He's protecting me and remembering me."

"You're right," Aspasia agreed. "We're back here and all together after years, and I catch myself looking at the future with optimism. For the first time I hope my sins will be forgiven. It's as if I've come into a large, peaceful church. What does it matter who or what made me come back?"

Polyxeni didn't speak. Instead, she jumped up like a spring.

"What's the matter?" Julia asked her.

"I'm going to get something," she shouted and ran toward the house. When she came back she was holding an old, dog-eared book.

"What's that?" Aspasia asked.

"Don't you remember it? It was Father's Bible. He used to read to us from it."

"You're right," Melissanthi said. "We didn't understand much, but we liked to listen."

"So, I found it last night and as I was leafing through it, my eye fell on a passage that he himself probably underlined. Listen. I'm sure we'll all understand it now."

Polyxeni opened the book to the page she had found and stood facing her sisters with the river flowing behind her. The four older women had left the verandah and were coming closer to listen and the children had abandoned their games to sit beside their mothers.

With a strong, clear voice and a peaceful expression, Polyxeni began to read:

> Brethren, if any of you do err from the truth, and
>   one convert him;
> Let him know, that he which converteth the sinner
>   from the error of his way shall save a soul from
>   death, and shall hide a multitude of sins.

James 5:19–20

ABOUT THE AUTHOR

Photo © 2016

Lena Manta was born in Istanbul, Turkey, to Greek parents. She moved to Greece at a very young age and now lives with her husband and two children on the outskirts of Athens. Although she studied to be a nursery school teacher, Lena instead directed her own puppet theater before writing articles for local newspapers and working as a director for a local radio station. Manta was proclaimed Author of the Year in both 2009 and 2011 by *Greek Life & Style* magazine. She has written thirteen books, all of them published by Psichogios Publications, including the bestselling *The House by the River*, which has sold almost 250,000 copies and is the first of her books to be translated into English. Hers is a voice to be reckoned with, and each new book is a tour de force in the Greek publishing world.

ABOUT THE TRANSLATOR

Photo © 2016 Cornell Publicity

Gail Holst-Warhaft is a poet and translator and has worked as a journalist, broadcaster, prose writer, academic, and musician. Among her many publications are *Road to Rembetika, Theodorakis: Myth and Politics in Modern Greek Music, The Collected Poems of Nikos Kavadias, Dangerous Voices: Women's Laments and Greek Literature, The Cue for Passion: Grief and Its Political Uses, I Had Three Lives: Selected Poems of Mikis Theodorakis,* and *Penelope's Confession.* She has published translations of Aeschylus and several of Greece's leading novelists and poets. Her poems and translations have appeared in journals in the United States, the United Kingdom, and Australia. Her Kavadias translations won the Van der Bovenkamp award from Columbia University's Translation Center, and her poem "Three Landscapes" won the Poetry Greece Award in 2001. *The Fall of Athens,* her most recent collection of poetry, essays, and stories about Greece, was published by Fomite Press (Vermont) in 2016.